CW01583214

BBC

DOCTOR WHO

PRAISE FOR DAVE RUDDEN

'Scary and funny – my two favourites. Dave Rudden is more than a rising star, he is a shooting star'

Eoin Colfer

'[*Knights of the Borrowed Dark*] is action-packed, atmospheric and powerfully imagined. But it is most notable for writerly wit and unexpected turns of phrase . . . this is engaging storytelling for any age'

Sunday Times

'Dave Rudden writes brilliantly: his sentences are full of surprises, his ideas are shiny and fluid or sharp and shocking'

Times Educational Supplement

'Rudden is an author to watch. *Knights of the Borrowed Dark* is a pacy, entertaining read, but it has heart too'

Guardian

'Wonderful style. Reminded me of Douglas Adams'

R. L. Stine, author of the *Goosebumps* series

This book is dedicated to anybody who has ever been told that writing fan fiction is a waste of time.

BBC CHILDREN'S BOOKS

UK | USA | Canada | Ireland | Australia
India | New Zealand | South Africa

BBC Children's Books are published by Puffin Books,
part of the Penguin Random House group of companies
whose addresses can be found at global.penguinrandomhouse.com.

www.penguin.co.uk www.puffin.co.uk www.ladybird.co.uk

Penguin Random House UK

First published 2020
Published in this edition 2021
002

Written by Dave Rudden
Illustrated by Alexis Snell

Set in 12/19pt Baskerville MT Std
Typeset by Jouve (UK), Milton Keynes
Printed and bound in Great Britain by Clays Ltd, Elcograf S.p.A.

The authorized representative in the EEA in Penguin Random House Ireland,
Morrison Chambers, 32 Nassau Street, Dublin D02 YH68

A CIP catalogue record for this book is available from the British Library

ISBN: 978-1-405-95015-2

All correspondence to:
BBC Children's Books
Penguin Random House Children's UK
One Embassy Gardens, 8 Viaduct Gardens, London SW11 7BW

FSC www.fsc.org MIX Paper from responsible sources FSC® C018179

Penguin Random House is committed to a sustainable future for our business, our readers and our planet. This book is made from Forest Stewardship Council® certified paper.

BBC

DOCTOR WHO

THE WINTERTIME PARADOX

DAVE RUDDEN

Illustrated by Alexis Snell

PUFFIN

CONTENTS

FOREWORD

UNIT scientist Petronella Osgood is one of my very favourite characters in *Doctor Who*, so it is a lucky thing indeed that I have the good fortune of being the actress who gets to play her. From the very first moment I put on her lab coat (complete with ink stain on the breast pocket) and donned her large black-rimmed glasses, I felt I had found a friend. A friend that I have been lucky enough to meet several times now on the television screen, in audio plays and, more recently, in video games. And now, I get to read about her adventures in this book!

I am so delighted that Dave Rudden has chosen to include Osgood in this beautiful collection of *Doctor Who* Christmas stories and I hope that you, dear reader, will enjoy her festive escapades as much as I did.

'For The Girl Who Has Everything' is a wonderful insight into Osgood's first month at UNIT – her 'origin story', if you will. In these pages we see the first sparks of the brave and intelligent woman that is destined to become a friend and ally of the Doctor. And, perhaps even more importantly, we see the moment that Kate Lethbridge-Stewart, UNIT's Commander in Chief, spots something in this young scientific officer and decides to take her under her wing – a moment that will change Osgood's life forever.

And yes (of course) there are monsters, and yes (naturally) there is sciencey stuff, but there is also a touching glimpse into Osgood's home life and her complicated relationship with her sister. Because, let's be honest, who hasn't been exasperated by their families at Christmas?

When I'd finished 'For The Girl Who Has Everything', it left me feeling that I knew Osgood a little better. And isn't that after all, what a good story is supposed to do?

I will say this though – the story left me wanting to know the answer to one particularly burning question: Is the scarf that she finds THE scarf? I know what I think.

All that's left for me to say is I hope that you enjoy reading about Petronella Osgood as much as I enjoy playing her. Oh, and look out for the best Christmas jumper joke you'll ever read.

All my love,

Ingrid Oliver

INTRODUCTION

THE WINTERTIME PARADOX

Doctor Who is a show about . . .

Well. That's kind of a moving target. Oh, generalities are easy. It's a show about a time traveller. That's certainly true. But there are lots of shows about time travellers. We'll need to be more specific.

What about genre? OK, that's easier. It's science fiction. Isn't it? Well, yes. Except for when it's horror, obviously. Or comedy. Or drama. Or fantasy. Or all the above at the same time. *Doctor Who* changes genre with all the wit and charisma and sleight of hand of a magician changing cards, until you can't help but be swept along with the trick.

And, speaking of magicians, we can at least be certain of the main character, right? *Doctor Who* is a show about the Doctor, of course. Except for when it's not. And even when it *is* you've got thirteen to choose from – except for when there's fourteen, or fifteen, and maybe a whole lot more.

There's a reason why the show keeps advising you to run. It's not because of the monsters. It's so you can keep up.

It's a little easier, therefore, if we get specific. If we talk about what *Doctor Who* is about to *you*. People light up when you ask them that, which is funny because usually the very next thing they'll tell you is about how *Doctor Who* scared them so badly they had to hide behind the couch, or about how sad they were to see a Doctor leave. Sometimes, they'll tell you what they *don't* like about *Doctor Who*, and even then they complain with the peculiar, granular delight of someone complaining about a friend they dearly love.

And, if you've never heard of *Doctor Who* and are simply picking up this book because you are a fan of paradoxes, or of Christmas, or because you liked Alexis's stunning cover, then there's something lovely about that too, because *Doctor Who* is a show built on new beginnings. Every episode is the beginning of someone's story – a companion's, a civilian's, a monster's – and any Doctor can be your first. Don't worry, confusion is normal. You're travelling with the Doctor now. They don't really know where they're going, and neither should you. If you experience things out of order, that's OK. In fact, it's kind of on-brand.

My favourite thing about *Doctor Who* is the occasional allusion to other adventures. Sometimes, a reference will be to an actual story. Other times, it's just a joke (I'm looking at you, Zodin). Every now and then, an allusion will end up inspiring a new storyline, which means that it *was* a reference, but just appeared before the story it was referencing. Again, very on-brand.

Interacting with *Doctor Who* on any level feels like stepping into a house – a huge, sprawling, beautiful, contradictory mansion built and maintained and added to by thousands upon thousands of hands. You can't have time travel without paradoxes, and one of the biggest nestled at the heart of *Who* is this: the more you explore, the more you realise there are always more rooms you have yet to reach.

Paradoxes crop up a lot in this book. Not just in the narrative tying the stories together, but in the stories themselves. In Stormcage, a father and his daughter will find normality in shared strangeness. In Edinburgh, a series of murders will remind a Time Lord that only her worst enemy can be her best friend. At the end of five Christmases, the Doctor will learn that the only way to move forward is to finally go home.

Here are twelve short stories – twelve glimpses into twelve different rooms in that weird, glorious, sprawling mansion, which is still being added to, even as we speak. I hope you like them.

Dave Rudden, May 2020

1

HE'S BEHIND YOU

It was said, in the dark corners of the universe, that the fury of a Time Lord could burn worlds.

It was whispered, in rad-lairs and necro-domes and other shadowy refuges too dangerous to name aloud, that the Time Lords had meddled so long and so deeply with the fabric of the cosmos that their will had become a law unto itself.

The rage of Gallifrey was a celestial event. No being could stand against it, no more than one could weather a black hole's hunger or the fury of a newborn star.

And, of all those wayward, volatile children of Time, none was more feared than the Doctor, for his fury had burned the Time Lords themselves.

'What do you mean,' he whispered, 'you "don't like panto"?'

Rose Tyler shrugged. 'Just think it's a bit silly, that's all.'

Cyan lights chased each other around the walls. Honey-hued pillars curled from floor to ceiling, like nerve endings or candy floss under a microscope. But what the inside of the TARDIS *really* reminded Rose of was the ferry she and her mum had taken to France when she was eight, and they'd sat there in what could have been a shopping centre, except for the hidden engines vibrating everything from the tea in their flasks to little Rose's little bones.

That was what it was like being in the TARDIS. She'd had chips here. They'd hooked her MP3 player up to the console and blasted Destiny's Child across the cold vacuum of space. But you never stopped feeling that vibration. You never forgot you were crossing a deep and dangerous sea.

'*Silly?*' the Doctor repeated, his new face scrunching around the word as if someone had soaked it in lemon juice. 'Silly? No, no, no. It's not silly. It's *theatre.* You can be anything you want with theatre.' He grinned suddenly. 'Buy a ticket to hear someone lie. It's glorious.'

Rose wasn't quite used to that smile. Her Doctor – her *first* Doctor – had worry etched so deep in his face that it seemed to eclipse anything else he might be feeling. Part of that was just his face – that wonderful, ridiculous face, like one of those eternally surprised birds of prey you saw on nature shows. And part of it had just been *him.* Him and his memories. The memories he couldn't run from, no matter how far he fled.

This Doctor, however, was different. Far more at ease, like he'd changed those memories the way he'd changed his clothes. And they'd been on such a breathless whirl of adventure these last few weeks that there were moments, amid the running and the peril and the excitement, when Rose was troubled to find herself forgetting too. Forgetting that the reason the Doctor had a new face at all was because he had sacrificed his old one for her.

'Come on, Doctor,' she said, shoving the thought to the back of her head. 'All that running around, "Oh, yes he is!", "Oh, no he isn't!" stuff?'

The Doctor raised an eyebrow. She arched hers.

'*He's behind yooooooouuuuu!*' they warbled in unison, then fell about laughing.

'Well, they usually *are* behind you,' the Doctor added, when their cackling had died down. 'That's just sound life advice. But, come on. How can anyone *hate* panto?'

Rose sighed. 'Jericho Street Junior School,' she said. 'We were the only school around with a proper auditorium, so we did all the Christmas plays. I was playing the Angel

Gabriel – the narrator, basically – and . . .' She blushed. 'I was eight, OK? And I panicked. All those faces looking at me, expecting me to know what to say, and I . . . just choked. I think, if the teacher hadn't come to take me off the stage, I'd still be standing there frozen. Haven't been in a theatre since.'

'Oh, Rose,' the Doctor said. 'I'm so sorry.'

She shrugged. 'It's fine. Of course *you* love panto. You're basically living in one – Doctor, why are you looking at me like that?'

'I've just had an idea.'

He spun away from her, fingers dancing across the controls, and Rose grabbed a railing as the TARDIS began to heave and growl, a ship turning into the storm.

'There's a Christmas I've been meaning to visit. A play I've been meaning to see.'

Course set, he bounded past her as the deck of the timeship rolled and shook.

'Mind her for me for a second, will you?'

'Um . . .' Rose gave the console a wary look.

It had only been a couple of weeks since they'd faced the Dalek Emperor. Since Rose had stared into the TARDIS's heart and absorbed a power no human could survive, until the Doctor had taken it from her. *Have you forgiven me yet?* she asked it silently. *I wouldn't blame you if you –*

'Rose?'

She turned.

It had helped her, in the weeks since the Doctor's regeneration, to focus on the similarities between one incarnation and the next. The differences were obvious. Her first Doctor had been all angles and scruffy grace. He was quick to laugh, and even quicker to frown. He was very kind, and he was very angry, and he never seemed sure which he was going to be from one moment to the next.

This Doctor was a little more . . . settled. Not *older.* Not his face anyway – he had the face of someone who might have spent the early 2000s in a boy band. The one who did all the earnest singing while everyone else in the music video got to laugh or ride mopeds. So, not settled, then. Maybe more *set.* Less fragile. Those deep-lined worries smoothed away.

Also, she saw, he was now wearing a tuxedo.

'How did you change into that so fast?' she said, finding to her shock that she was blushing again.

'Time Lord,' he offered airily. 'Would you like one too?'

He held out his hand. She hesitated, then took it. Even his hands felt different.

'OK,' she said. Above them, the electric-blue pistons rose and fell. 'What are we going to see?'

*

THE SAGA OF THE TIME LORDS

THIS CHRISTMAS, AN ANCIENT SPECIES
RISES, THRIVES AND PASSES INTO
LEGEND BEFORE YOUR VERY EYES
(OR EQUIVALENT SENSORY ORGAN).
NO INTERVAL

Imagine a Christmas ornament the size of the moon. A scarlet sphere, dusted with sparkles – each one a spotlight the size of a swimming pool – that send spears of light out into the dark, flashing and spinning and flashing again as if signalling the stars to land. And, atop the great, glittering orb, a palace glowing in crimson and shining gold.

'Welcome,' the Doctor said grandly, 'to the Masque Magestrix.'

They set the TARDIS down between a blocky Judoon patrol ship and a sleek Draconian cruiser, then made their way up the curving plain to the palace. Its gleaming gates were alive with flashing scarlet words.

WITNESS THEIR MARVELS
EXCLAIM AT THEIR TRIUMPHS

SPECULATE ON THEIR MYSTERIOUS DISAPPEARANCE

Around them, other patrons milled about and chatted in a riot of shapes and species. Hulking reptiles in plate armour waved great two-handed blades, arguing for exemption from the Masque's anti-weapon laws. A group of thirty-foot tall tripods patiently waited in line at one of a hundred floating concession stands.

And yet – for all the strange and wonderful creatures on display, and despite the glowing starfield above them and the crimson alien landscape – it all felt oddly *familiar.*

A cluster of chittering larvae squeaked to each other like excited children on a school trip. A girl in a gleaming mask made delicate notes in the corner of her programme. Two huge dragons dipped their leathery snouts in fizzing, smoking glasses, clinging to each other with the fragile delight of newlyweds. It felt just like waiting for a show to begin on Earth. Admittedly, Jericho Street Junior School had fewer spaceships in orbit and smelled a lot more like school dinners, but it never failed to impress Rose how, no matter how far they travelled, certain things turned out to be the same.

Similarities, she thought, as the Time Lord beside her patted his pockets, muttering to himself about jelly babies. *That's how you hold on all the way out here.*

'*The Saga of the Time Lords*,' Rose repeated, as the play's title flashed up once again. 'Isn't this a bit like watching a home movie for you?' She looked around. 'With really high production values?'

'From what I've heard, it's more like fan fiction,' the Doctor said. 'And don't get me wrong. I *love* fan fiction. You should read some of mine. But I sincerely doubt anybody here has ever actually met a Time Lord, let alone been to Gallifrey.'

'So, it's not going to be accurate?' Rose said.

'Accurate?' The Doctor snorted. 'I hope not. I came here to be lied to, Rose Tyler. I mean, look at that.'

He pointed up at the glowing scarlet words, now announcing cast members and the Time Lords they were playing:

REMIERE DUPONT AS RASSILON
THE DASHING
CAMBO RAIMI AS BROTHER BRAXIATEL
AND SHARA BETOMAX AS
THE HAND OF MEG

Next were some safety warnings:

DO NOT ATTEND IF SUFFERING FROM
THE FOLLOWING:
CHRONAL DISPLACEMENT
ELECTROMAGNETIC ANGST
SCURVY

And, beneath it all, two simple words:

FAMOUSLY UNFINISHED

'Theatre in a nutshell, that is,' the Doctor said with a grin. 'It's only in show business that "famously unfinished" becomes a selling point. Like proudly announcing you haven't done your homework.' Something like sadness flickered across his face. 'Even if it's not true.'

'Doctor?'

'Well.' For a moment he looked like her old Doctor – tired and lonely and a little angry at it all. 'The saga *is* over. Isn't it?'

'Greetings, entities! May I scan your purchase confirmation and provide your tickets?'

A primly smiling holographic attendant fizzed into view in front of them, flickering like a fluorescent ghost.

His features were human – or Time Lord, Rose supposed – and he wore an ornate robe with a collar so high and curved he looked like a very dignified dessert spoon.

'God, you were right about the accuracy,' Rose said behind her hand, trying to lighten the mood. 'Is that what they think Time Lords *wore*?'

The Doctor cleared his throat. 'Here you are.'

He held up his psychic paper, and the ghostly attendant looked at it closely, before clapping both hands together in a soundless drizzle of sparks.

'Forgive me, Doctor. I was not informed you would be attending!'

Rose and the Doctor exchanged glances.

'What're you betting?' she murmured under her breath. Psychic paper was supposed to display whatever credentials its bearer required; the Doctor's, however, tended to be a little more . . . creative in the roles it assigned. 'Private investigators here for a murder?'

'Oh, I'd say it's much worse than that,' the Doctor responded. 'Probably diplomats here to prevent an interstellar war.'

The holographic attendant beamed, executing a perfect bow. 'To have the galaxy's pre-eminent expert on Gallifreyan culture attend our little show is such an honour –'

The Doctor beamed back. 'Well, I –'

'Doctor Tyler,' the attendant finished.

The Doctor's smile disappeared.

'Don't mention it,' Rose said, grinning. 'Really.'

'Oh, but it is!' the attendant continued. He squinted at the psychic paper still in the Doctor's outstretched hand. 'Doctor Rose Tyler, expert in time vortexes and –' he frowned – 'lupine morality?'

The Doctor gave the psychic paper an experimental shake. 'Rose, I think you might be confusing the paper. Side effect of the vortex, maybe. It thinks you're a little bit Time Lord.'

The attendant's brow furrowed in confusion, but before he could speak a great chime rang through the air. More and more holographic attendants were shimmering into view. The glowing words were flashing faster now, almost strobing. It seemed the show was about to begin.

'Doctor Tyler?' The attendant's expression had gone from welcoming to shrewd, his fingers dancing over a console on his wrist. 'I have just consulted with my superiors, and they have conveyed to me a very generous offer. How would you like a backstage tour?'

The Doctor held up his hands. 'We wouldn't like to get in the way –'

'Oh, not at all! And I don't mind telling you that a recommendation from such a respected expert of Gallifreyan culture would do wonders for our reviews.' He looked at his console again. 'Perhaps I could even introduce you to Ms Betomax herself?'

Even as he spoke, the name SHARA BETOMAX appeared again in type so large it barely fitted on the screen. Even Rose knew that, in panto-speak, that meant the actor named was a big deal.

Rose pretended to think for a moment. 'Can I wear one of the silly collars?'

A pained look crossed the Doctor's face.

'I am sure that can be arranged,' the attendant said. He snapped his fingers, and two thin plastic rectangles materialised before them. 'Please take your tickets. Do not misplace them, as they are used for the teleportation lock.'

'Teleportation lock?' Rose asked.

'Oh yes,' the Doctor said, as the other patrons around them began to vanish. 'Everyone knows the worst part of going to the theatre is having to climb over people to your seat. That's why now it's all done by –'

All of a sudden, both Rose and the Doctor turned sideways and disappeared.

*

There was a dark and weightless moment, a feeling that was a little like being in an elevator and a little like being in love, and then Rose was abruptly un-sidewayed like a paper hat from a Christmas cracker.

The golden palace and crowds of theatregoers were gone. So, Rose realised, was the Doctor.

She was alone.

Alone in a rather ordinary-looking storeroom, which was, by itself, not a reason to panic. Rose had spent enough time backstage (before what her mum called her 'little acting hiccup') to know that the gilt and sparkles always faced out. The inside of a theatre – the *real* inside, the bit the audience never saw – tended to be mostly peeling floor tiles and cardboard boxes.

No, that wasn't the problem.

The problem, she decided, was all the Daleks staring at her.

'Hello,' came a voice in clipped, arch tones. 'You must be the *expert*.'

In theatres across the universe, it is common to have a code for when an important person is in the audience. This important person might be a critic, or a famous actor, or a casting agent looking for the next great star.

Throughout the Masque Magestrix, the message was conveyed. Flesh melted and ran. New faces were prepared.

The correct audience had been detected.

After so long, the show could begin.

'More tea, my darling?'

Rose nodded raptly.

She was dimly aware that this probably wasn't the time for conversation. Someone or something had neatly separated her from the Doctor. She had been teleported into the middle of a hundred Daleks. Admittedly, they were *prop* Daleks, but this was not Rose's first outing. Something was definitely afoot.

Unfortunately, it was rather hard to focus on this while Shara Betomax was in the room.

Shara Betomax, whose performance in *The Empress Magdalene* had spawned a new religion overnight. Shara Betomax, who had played the famous outlaw Noon Speranza with such grace that afterwards every script had been gathered up and fired into a sun so that no lesser actor could ever sully the role. Shara Betomax, who had been cast as the lead in *The Saga of the Time Lords* precisely because she *could* steal the show from a hundred Daleks. Shara Betomax, who had the magnetism of a dwarf alloy star.

She was small, and she was slight, and each of her many wrinkles was as effortlessly elegant as the veins in polished marble.

'I never used to pour my own tea,' she explained, each word somehow sharp and soft at the same time. 'Normally, a show would furnish me with an assistant. Sometimes two. Alas, that was in better days. Now . . .' She sighed a perfect sigh. 'Now, I do panto.'

'I'm not much of a fan, either,' Rose said. She couldn't think of anything else to say, and it was far easier and more pleasant just to listen. Shara Betomax had that kind of voice. You could have cut up her syllables and used them as currency.

'Madame Betomax?'

The woman who popped her head round the door frame was dressed exactly like Shara, her silver robes crowned by one of those dessert-spoon headdresses. She held a walkie-talkie in her hand.

'Three minutes until curtain-up,' she said.

'Gabadine Tho,' Shara explained. 'My understudy. Gabadine, this is Doctor Tyler, an expert in Time Lords who management rather rudely teleported in on top of me.'

Rose started to apologise, but the actor shook her head minutely. Even her scorn was stately.

'Not your fault, my darling. The trials of my reduced station.' She trailed off, confusion crinkling her brow. 'Gabadine? What's the matter?'

The understudy had begun to shake. Her fingers drummed on the door frame. Something *moved* under her features, distorting them the way the passage of a shark ripples water.

'Time Lord,' Gabadine whispered through gritted teeth. '*Time Lord.*'

And then her features dissolved into a swirl of flesh.

Rose and Shara watched in horror as Gabadine's face became a foaming soup, her chin collapsing inwards, sucking in her hair like seaweed down a drain. More whirlpools of skin opened in her stomach and palms, joining and spreading until her whole body was a bubbling upright Jacuzzi full of boiling . . .

Similarities.

'Plastic,' Rose whispered, then grabbed Shara Betomax as respectfully as she could. 'We need to get out of here.'

They bolted.

Behind them, the Auton screamed a trilling, atonal scream.

As Rose Tyler and Shara Betomax ran, *The Saga of the Time Lords* began.

Rose knew the play had started because, as they had fled from the storeroom – just one step ahead of the staggering, slavering Auton – the loudest orchestra she had ever heard opened up seemingly right above their heads.

The noise was unbelievable. It physically vibrated her, like a struck bell. Rose swayed for a moment, reeling at the assault, before she remembered that she was fleeing and should really *keep* fleeing. It probably sounded very good if you were a few rows back, but at the minute all she could think was that she'd been in quieter air raids.

Shara grabbed her arm and pulled, dragging Rose through a set of double doors.

The din immediately lessened, though Rose's head still rang. She saw a mess of couches and tables, and realised they were in a green room – somewhere for cast and crew to wait in between being called onstage. The scatter of cups and plates on the tables gave the sense that the room had been very recently and suddenly evacuated, but whether that was because *The Saga* had started or because people were turning into Autons Rose wasn't sure.

'Help me with this!' Shara said, and the two of them pushed a couch in front of the doors they had just come through.

They were just in time. As soon as they stepped backwards, the whole door frame jumped, shaking under the wet pounding of two plasticky fists.

'Good thinking,' Rose said.

Shara Betomax tutted. 'Did not the Empress Magdalene defend the gate of her castle for three days armed with only a phase-sword and a hypershield?'

'I don't know,' Rose said. 'Did she?'

'No, actually,' Shara said. 'But I did when I was playing her, which is roughly the same thing.' Her brief look of amusement disappeared. 'That was Gabadine. We've been rehearsing together all year. I was talking her through a divorce. And she just . . . changed.'

'It wasn't Gabadine,' Rose said. 'It was an Auton. They like duplicating people. Was Gabadine sick recently? Absent?'

'Not a day,' Shara said, shaking her head. 'We've been in each other's pockets for months.' The look of queenly composure she had worn from the moment Rose had met her faltered. 'Do you . . . do you think the real Gabadine is alive somewhere?'

Rose placed a hand on Shara's shoulder, shocked at just how small and thin it was. 'It's very possible.'

'Then we need to figure out what this *Auton* wants,' the older woman said firmly. 'And stop it.'

'Them,' Rose said faintly. 'Stop them. It's usually a *them* situation.' A chill went through her. 'And, as for what they want . . .'

Forgive me, Doctor. I was not informed you would be attending.

The error in the psychic paper that had teleported Rose right into the path of an Auton.

The look on Gabadine's face, just before it had ceased to be a face and become a sucking nightmare swirl.

Time Lord. That was what it had said. *Time Lord.*

'I think they're after my friend,' Rose said. 'The Doctor. The *real* Doctor.'

The doors jumped again, so violently the couch was shoved a couple of centimetres back before they could right it.

'We need to find him,' Rose said.

She looked around. There was another set of double doors identical to the ones they had just come through, and a metal service elevator.

'Do you know where we are?'

Shara nodded. 'It's a simple layout – one circle on top of another. Above us is the stage. This level is all storage and dressing rooms. Through there –' she pointed at the other set of double doors – 'is the system control room.'

Rose's eyes narrowed. 'Is that where the teleporter controls are?'

'Yes.' Betomax stiffened as the cacophony above changed in tone. 'That's the overture finishing. I'm expected onstage soon.'

Life-and-death situations tended to provoke a lot of odd reactions, but even to Rose this was a new one. 'You can't seriously be thinking of going out there to *act*, can you?'

The doors shook again, the Auton keening against them with a fierce, animal need.

'The show must go on, my darling,' Shara said. 'You don't understand. I'm playing the Hand of Meg – the most important and mysterious figure in the Time Lords' origin story. It's the only role in this circus worth playing. My agent had to literally kill people to get it.'

Rose blanched. 'Really?'

Shara shrugged. 'Runner-up on *Dancing with the Stars*. No one minded. But it is *my* role, and I must play it. I need to be there to invent time travel. Otherwise, Rassilon can't betray me and lock me away in Harmony's Eye. It will ruin the whole second act!'

There was genuine panic on her face.

'I understand,' Rose said, as the Auton pushed its stretched-toffee thumb of a head through the join between the doors, gnarling at them through a melting mouth. And she *did* understand. It was Jericho Street all over again. Without Shara saying her lines, nobody else could say theirs.

Rose sighed. 'I can't believe I'm saying this but, if you just get me to the control room, I'll find my friend. He can stop this, and the show can go on. OK?'

Shara nodded, actual tears in her eyes.

She really is very good, Rose thought.

'Thank you,' Shara whispered. 'It's through here.'

They made their way to the second set of double doors across the room, flinching as, inch by creaking inch, the Auton forced the doors behind them open.

Rose's mind was racing. When had Gabadine been replaced? The last Autons she had faced hadn't exactly been experts at complex mimicry, and you didn't get more complex mimicry than *The Saga of the Time Lords*. How long had they been here? Actors playing actors, waiting for the right person to arrive.

Waiting for the Doctor . . .

Just as Rose had the thought, the elevator pinged. She and Shara turned to see two human stagehands in dark outfits step into the room. Both stagehands froze in horror at the sight of the bubbling, snarling Auton halfway through the blocked doorway.

'Oh, thank heavens,' Shara said. 'Gentlemen, please –'

Their eyes locked on to Rose.

'Time Lord,' they hissed in unison.

This time, Rose didn't wait to get a proper look. She just bolted, wincing at the liquid sounds of warping flesh behind her.

The double doors led out into another long, dingy corridor with more doors leading off it every few metres. It was some consolation that *The Saga* had apparently reached a quiet bit, with a single male voice, rather than an entire orchestra, rattling the architecture.

'That was Ribald,' Shara panted beside Rose. She even ran in a dignified fashion, like a startled flamingo. 'And Mern. I've signed autographs for them. Ribald puts me in my harness for the scene when I fall into the black hole. I *know* them.'

'They're not who you think they are,' Rose said. 'I'm not sure anyone here is.' Judging by the size and scale of the production, there could be dozens of Autons out there. *Why couldn't we have gone to a one-woman show?*

'That way!' Shara said, pointing at a door with a red light above it as, behind them, their three pursuers burst into the corridor in a chewing-gum tangle of grasping plastic hands.

The control room was small and square, and had that very deliberate clutter so often present in control rooms and workshops and garages – anywhere that very serious men and women wore toolbelts and organised screws by size and weight. Rose recognised it immediately from the TARDIS.

Unfortunately, most of the room was covered in Auton – a great, heaving mass the size of an elephant, if someone had spread an elephant like butter across one half of the room. Hands stuck out at odd angles. Faces, too – some human-sized and looking extremely perturbed, and others stretched out across the groaning bulk like distorted toffee sculptures. It would have been horrific if it hadn't all been clean and waxy plastic. As it was, it reminded Rose of the time she had tried to give her dolls a tan by putting them in the microwave.

'Time Lord!' it roared through twelve mouths at once. 'TIME LORD!'

'I'm really *not*,' Rose snapped back.

There might have been controls somewhere under the throbbing, gargantuan bulk, but there was no way Rose was going to go fishing for them. Betomax had pressed herself against the door they had come through, but already her feet were slipping and scraping as the Autons outside tried to get in.

I hate the theatre, Rose thought, then jumped as something twitched in her jacket. She reached into her pocket and pulled out her plastic ticket. It was tremoring so fast it was almost a blur.

The Auton-beast reared above her, drawing its great, soupy mass into a tsunami of smooth plastic flesh. The faces that still had eyes narrowed them, and the mouths that could open screamed at the top of their lungs, '*TIME LOOOOOORD!*'

And then it turned sideways and disappeared.

In its place, looking rather dishevelled, was the Doctor.

'Teleportation,' he said, then blinked. 'Sorry. Feels a bit weird if you don't finish the line.'

He blinked again, blearily, then whipped out his sonic screwdriver to point at the door. There was a deep *clunk* as it locked itself. Tentatively, Betomax stepped away. It didn't budge.

'Much better,' he said, then shot Rose a wry glance. 'And some people say the theatre is boring.'

Rose threw her ticket at him.

He snagged it out of the air with infuriating grace and held it up to the light. 'Brilliant things, these. At first, I thought there was a malfunction. But, by the third time I materialised inside a stationery cupboard, I began to suspect someone was trying to separate us.'

'Then how –' Rose began, but the Doctor had already tossed her back the ticket.

'I used the psychic paper to get us the tickets, and the tickets are all connected to the teleporter array. I backtracked that link to take control, and to find you. Simple.' He tapped a finger against his lip. 'Well, actually, it was incredibly complicated – but that explanation was really simple. Love a simple explanation.' He looked a little sheepish. 'Especially since it covers up the fact that I may have teleported a very large Auton to a very small stationery cupboard. But that's a tomorrow problem.'

He suddenly swept by Rose, bending his stork-like frame to gently kiss Shara Betomax's hand. 'Shara Betomax. Loved you as Noon Speranza. You know, I played Omega myself in a school play once. Female version too, actually –'

'Doctor,' Rose said. '*Autons.*'

'Yes,' he said, suddenly serious. 'It's not just the engineers, is it?'

'It could be everyone,' Rose said. 'Understudies, stagehands . . . According to Shara, they've all been perfectly normal for ages. Until –'

The door shuddered. The tiles on the floor began to buckle and shift as thick liquid pushed up from underneath.

'Until a Time Lord arrived,' the Doctor said. 'That was the trigger. The Autons kidnapped these people, replicated them, and have been mimicking them so closely that they might have genuinely believed they *were* those people until we showed up. Actors believing they're actors. Actors waiting for their cue.'

'This isn't a play,' Rose said, watching the seeping, creeping fluid grow a mouth and snarl. 'It's a trap. Waiting for a Time Lord to show up and spring it.'

'And now there's who knows how many in between us and the TARDIS,' the Doctor said. 'And Autons don't stop. They never stop. Shara?'

The actor had sunk to the floor, wrapping her thin arms round herself.

'All that work,' she said. 'All those rehearsals. And now it's all going to come grinding to a halt in front of a million people . . .'

'Shara,' Rose said gently. 'It isn't about the play any more. It's about –'

'That's it,' the Doctor said. 'Oh, Rose Tyler, you absolute genius.'

'Thank you,' Rose said. 'Wait. What?'

'These Autons have been in deep cover for who knows how long,' he explained. 'Rehearsing, practising, living *The Saga of the Time Lords* over and over again to get it right. That kind of complex mimicry leaves an effect. It etches the plastic. That's why they're coming apart so badly. They're resisting.'

'Doctor, what are you talking about?'

'You remember what it was like, don't you?' he said. 'Walking that stage, learning those lines, drilling it again and again until the line between who you *are* and who you *play* starts to blur?'

'I remember freezing,' Rose said. 'I remember panicking because I didn't know what to say next.'

'I know,' the Doctor said. 'And I'm sorry.'

'Why?'

'Because,' he said, 'the show must go on.'

'I don't like this at all,' Rose whispered.

It turned out that High Gallifreyan robes were extremely heavy. She had to keep them hitched up so she didn't trip, and the headdress kept making her think someone was behind her.

'I'd do it if I could,' the Doctor said, adjusting her collar one last time.

They'd retreated to the corner of the control room, the floor now shaking and buckling as, like floodwater, the Autons tried to push through. Even as Rose and the Doctor watched, a tile popped free and grit-flecked plastic began to ooze from the gap.

'But they sensed the vortex energy on you. To them, you're the Time Lord. That's the role they've given you, and you have to play it. Do you remember your lines?'

'I do.'

She'd watched him write them on a scrap of paper, and he'd reminded her of nothing so much as one of the Autons, his face scarily blank but for the flickers of something alien moving underneath. The fact that writing those lines – accessing those memories – had so obviously hurt him was what had made her agree to this in the first place.

Shara Betomax was a lot smaller and frailer without the bulky robe, but the look she gave Rose was worthy of several empresses.

'You're going to be fantastic, my darling. Break a leg.'

That was Rose's cue.

The Doctor pointed his sonic screwdriver at the teleporter controls, and – with one last look at the bubbling, growling flood making its way towards her friends – Rose turned sideways and disappeared.

When she snapped back into shape, she was standing centre stage.

Similarities, she told herself through the sudden and absolute terror. *It's just like the stage at Jericho Street.*

Except it wasn't. It really, really wasn't. Rose and the Doctor had been teleported away before they had got a proper look at the inside of the Masque Magestrix. She had thought the golden palace that topped the scarlet sphere was the theatre, but she'd been wrong. The sphere *was* the theatre – a hollow globe lined with a hundred thousand rows of seats, curving up and away on all sides. Miles of seats. *Millions* of seats. Millions of eyes, staring down at Rose, as numerous as the stars in the sky. It was so overwhelming that she could barely take in the majesty of the stage itself – a great circle covering the bottom of the sphere, vanishing off into the gloom.

Rose must have arrived during an exciting bit of *The Saga*. Maybe it was all exciting. She hadn't really had time to speculate. She was not the only person onstage by a long shot. There were holographic TARDISes flickering in and out of sight. There were projected constellations that would have made any Earth astronomer need a lie-down in a dark room. There were rust-red outcrops and golden cities, and a choir a hundred strong in robes of white and gold.

'IT IS I!' a voice roared.

Rose turned to see a large man in black robes, his voice as deep and smooth as a wardrobe made of chocolate.

'RASSILON, THE PRESIDENT OF TIME.' He stood on a floating platform, a great spiked claw on one hand. 'AND I SHALL BUILD AN EMPIRE THAT LASTS FOR TEN MILLION –' His eyes fell on Rose. 'TEN MILLION . . .'

The choir had seen her too. Some were murmuring. Others, she noticed, were beginning to twitch and shake as the sight of Rose triggered their Auton programming. A wing of holographic TARDISes above paused mid-dive. The orchestra cut off suddenly with a skidding, shrilling shriek.

'Um,' Rose said. 'Uh . . .'

Oh, God. It was Jericho Street all over again. The terror. The uncertainty. The ice in her veins, spreading and spilling out to everyone else like frost covering the surface of a lake. It was, she decided, a lot like the feeling you got when you missed a step on the stairs . . . but in front of a live audience.

Rassilon – no, the actor playing Rassilon, Remiere something – began to froth and dissolve. He took a staggering step towards her, claw outstretched. And, just when it felt like the silence couldn't stretch any longer, Rose began to speak.

She spoke of aeons. Of knowledge cut from the meat of the cosmos and pulled from the heart of black holes. She spoke of shining jewels, and binary stars, and golden cities under orange skies. She spoke of how majestic a civilisation could be when you gave them all the time in the world.

Every face was turned towards her, swirling as if stirred by her words.

Some of what Rose said was what the Doctor had told her to say, the lines he had prepared, but as she gained confidence, stepping out into the light of the holographic suns, she found words welling up inside her that demanded to be said.

Some were *her* Doctor's words – her first Doctor's – fresh in their pain. Others were scraps she had overheard, rumours of the later years, the harder years, the years when Gallifrey's arrogance and bravado had come home to roost. The Time Lords had all the time in the world, but the younger races, bright in their jealousy, lived more in their short time than any child of Gallifrey.

Bar one.

Rose didn't have Shara's voice, or Remiere's – a voice with gravity, a voice that drew you in. She hesitated. She halted. She became aware, crushingly so, of her dry throat, of every swallow and gap. But, somehow, it didn't matter.

People went to the theatre for lies, but Rose told them the truth.

Finally, she spoke of the ending. Of a moment – a single, simple moment – that was the culmination of all that had gone before it, the way a story was not finished until the last line fell into place.

The moment the Time Lords' saga ended and left a single soul alone.

The great, hungry vacuum of the Masque swallowed Rose's words, then swallowed her silence, until there was nothing at all but the eyes of the audience and her soft and ragged breath.

And then the whole theatre burst into thunderous applause.

The clamour was louder than the orchestra, but Rose didn't mind it as much. It beat down on her like summer rain and Rose closed her eyes and let it, feeling helpless and invincible and about eight years old.

When she opened her eyes, Remiere was beside her. His face had resolved, all hard and handsome angles, and he took her hand in one of his own. They bowed. It was what you did, when a show was complete.

Eventually, Rose raised her head. Remiere did not. The singers in the choir of Autons were slumping, sliding out of their robes in rivers of flesh. The audience's applause was still shaking the theatre. They evidently hadn't noticed. Perhaps they thought it was part of the show.

I suppose it is.

Rose saw the Doctor and Shara sitting in the front row. Shara was clapping, a small, dignified smile on her features, and the Doctor was smiling too, though tears ran from his face.

Her Doctor. Her sad, happy Doctor.

He hadn't changed a bit.

'Are you sure you don't want a lift somewhere?'

They had retreated into the green room, the floor littered with frozen puddles of deactivated Auton. Apparently, there was quite a queue for autographs outside.

Shara shook her head. She'd redonned her robe; it suited her. 'I think I'm going to stay here. We still have to find where the Autons stowed the people they mimicked, and I want to make sure they're all right. And get back to rehearsing, obviously.'

'I thought you didn't like panto,' Rose said.

A faint blush suffused Shara's features. 'Well. I must admit there is *something* about the spectacle. A sort of gaudy, horrific charm. And, after a few rewrites, I think *The Saga of the Time Lords* might be something really rather special.' She cast a shrewd eye at Rose. 'Especially if I could tempt you to a repeat performance?'

'Not even a little bit,' Rose said. 'But thank you. It was lovely to meet you.'

'And you,' Shara said, clasping Rose's hands in her own. 'Both of you. Very well done.'

She swept out of the green room.

'Doctor,' Rose began. 'I have two questions.'

'Hmm?'

'Firstly, is *Dancing with the Stars* actually still on?'

'Oh yes,' the Doctor said. 'Though now it's *Dancing with Actual Stars.* Massive fatality rate. What was your second question?'

Rose nodded at the doors through which Shara had just departed.

'Do you think . . .?'

'Well,' the Doctor said, 'the Autons were mimicking those actors so closely that their need to finish the show actually overrode their innate programming. You pretend to be someone for long enough, it can be hard to stop.' He leaned in conspiratorially. 'Plus, the *real* Shara Betomax once walked out halfway through a performance because the green room didn't have the right flavour of tea. I have to say, this Shara seems a lot more invested in her fellow actors.'

'So what happens when the real Shara wakes up?'

'I don't know,' the Doctor said. 'But I hope they sell tickets.'

After they had both finished cackling, Rose reached out and took his hand.

'It's not over, you know,' she said.

'What's not?'

'The saga of the Time Lords. You're still writing it.'

He took her hand. 'We both are, Rose Tyler.'

They twirled each other, and grinned.

'The show goes on.'

AFTER

'What did you think of the ending?' the girl asked, adjusting the fit of her delicate golden mask.

The theatre was empty now, the seats deserted but for a host of antlike cleaning droids. The unkind glare of the house lights picked out every stain and tear – another sight no ticket buyer was ever meant to see.

'I think employing Autons to lure out survivors of the war was risky,' the young man said. He had removed his silver mask and put it down on the seat beside him. Sometime earlier, a cleaning droid had whirred too close and made the fatal mistake of looking into his face. Now, it spun mindlessly in circles, making little whimpering noises, its optical sensors clawed out. 'We have bigger concerns.'

The girl sniffed. 'Only a Time Lord could wipe out a trillion timelines, and then try to use that to make you feel sorry for them later.'

As she spoke, she flickered; like a bad edit, a bleached negative that sizzled and cracked before becoming whole again.

'Time Lords have always been self-obsessed,' the young man said, impatient to be gone. 'It'll be the end of them.'

It was impossible to see beneath the girl's mask, but he knew that she was smiling.

'Not if I get there first,' she said.

2

FATHER OF THE DALEKS

1

It did not begin with the Doctor, of course, but he was there at the beginning, and for that Davros would never forgive him.

2

++ EXTERMINATE! ++

The cry blared from a thousand vocoders, a toneless thunder rolling from horizon to horizon. The Daleks spun down upon the world of Gryphon's Reach, fat cylinder after fat cylinder glowing with friction as they took their place in formation – bullets deciding where to strike.

As one, they dived, billowing dust from the Reach's endless grimy plains. From the command ship in orbit, Davros's scanners outlined a thousand red dots, which scattered and vanished as what little wildlife there was went to ground or simply died of shock at the majesty of his children making planetfall.

'Ex-loading coordinates of the facility,' Davros croaked, feeling that familiar thrill as the Daleks responded, like the memory of his long-lost limbs. Just for a moment, the cold confines of his command ship fell away – the empty halls, the snarled throne of wires and input feeds. Just for a moment, it felt as though he was striding the desiccated surface of Gryphon's Reach.

A father and his children.

An empire.

A family.

'Daleks,' he growled, 'exterminate.'

3

Christmas, on Lavellan.

'It amazes me sometimes,' Davros said.

It was evening. They had found a little café off one of the main squares. Most of the tables were deserted. The sky had turned a fantastic shade of violet, and the canopy of hard light above their heads was igniting each falling snowflake in a minute, dazzling flare.

Like a fleet making planetfall, Davros thought. *Like the end of the world.*

'What amazes you?'

A Lavellanese waiter, all feathers and tentacles, tried to hand Davros a menu, but he waved the waiter off. He never ate at these things. He rarely ate at all any more. Not since his . . . second reconstruction? His third? He wasn't sure. Somewhere along the line, digestion had seemed more trouble than it was worth.

'Christmas,' Davros said. 'Christmas on Lavellan. Why do they celebrate it? It's an Earth holiday, is it not?'

'Well,' the other man said, 'I imagine there's a story behind that.' He tapped his chin. 'Or maybe there isn't. Maybe it's just what happens when you're willing to share a universe. Cross-pollination. There might be a human colony somewhere out there celebrating the First Ascendancy of Lavel. Though you'd need a lot of feather boas, I suppose.'

'Like a virus,' Davros said. 'An idea pathogen. Carried not in the cells or the blood, but in the hearts and minds of those infected.'

He took a stylus from a pocket and absently began to scratch formulae on the tablecloth.

The Doctor frowned. 'They're going to make me pay for that, you know.'

4

The Kaled of Skaro – the ancient, bitter race to which Davros had once belonged, before he forged his own, superior people – were unsurprisingly fond of romanticising conflict. Davros's childhood had featured a succession of wrinkled, half-mad tutors preaching the glory of Skaro-That-Was, as if that planet still existed and hadn't long ago been reduced to an irradiated no man's land by a thousand-year war.

Now they were all gone, bar him. He was the last Kaled, and the Daleks – who were no more the descendants of the Kaleds than a pearl was descended from the grit that formed it – had no time for the past. Not when the future was there to be won.

++ EXTERMINATE! ++

A battle cry. A promise. A threat. An entire race and culture distilled into a single mechanical shriek spat in the face of the universe.

'Exterminate,' Davros whispered to himself in the clammy egg of his command throne. Drool had frozen on his upper lip. 'Exterminate.'

Gryphon's Reach was not the most illustrious beginning to a crusade, truth be told. Various races had conquered the dingy little planet over the aeons, in the way that one might examine a grubby penny before deciding it wasn't worth the trouble. It was a forgotten place. A nothing place. Remarkable only in how unremarkable it was – particularly to the Daleks, whose eyes, like the eyes of all predators, were drawn to movement and colour. There was little colour to Gryphon's Reach.

Not unless you knew where to look.

++ FACILITY LOCATED ++

++ COMMENCING ATTACK ++

The facility didn't possess a title, not that his children had asked. It was just a low dome built into the underside of a grey and crumbling cliff, its surface ridged with sensor baffles and perception filters that did nothing at all to hide it from the Daleks' newly upgraded sensors.

They should have come to me sooner. The Daleks had been combing this region of space for weeks, turning to him only when all of their options were exhausted. He could tell it cost them to do so. Admitting defeat was not in their design. But was that not always the way? They were his children. He was their fail-safe.

But no matter. They called. That was enough. That was always enough.

Davros pulsed a command, and a comms channel opened between him and the facility. Gloating was a bad habit, according to Kaled philosophy, but that didn't matter. Davros had rewritten all those lessons a long time ago.

Besides, he was lonely.

'Doctor,' he purred into the comms. 'We have come for you.'

5

Christmas, on Traxamere Beta.

The Lumineers Guild had outdone themselves this year. Each of the great crimson barges hanging over the capital had been strung with a hundred thousand lanterns, now hanging dark and deactivated against the swollen red globes like the pips of strawberries. Below the rooftop bar in which Davros sat, the streets were packed to groaning with excited onlookers, all here for the flicking of a switch.

'I don't understand,' he muttered. 'Why are you doing this?'

The Doctor stared into his drink. Tiny photoplasmic algae gleamed in its depths. Traxamere was a dark world with a weak sun. Light was many things here. Currency. Communication. And during this, the darkest day of the year, it became a celebration.

The Doctor took an experimental sip, the light spiralling and sparking down his throat. It made his new face gleam from the inside out. 'Not a daiquiri,' he said, 'but it'll do.'

'And why *you*?' Davros said. 'This young form. Come to mock me?'

'All your many reconstructions,' the Doctor said, looking out over the crowds with a rueful smile, 'and your skin is still always so thin. Always looking for insults, for challenges. Why can't I just be here to talk?' He set his drink back down. 'And I have been talking. Not to you, but to . . . me, I suppose. A few mes, actually. You know that we like talking.'

Davros grunted.

The Doctor looked around. There was something different about him. Davros could see it. Not his face – that changed all the time. But these meetings had rules, and one of those rules was that they always come alone. No allies, no minions, no traps, no threats. And, without an assistant to show off for, this Doctor was different. Quieter. Less prone to dramatics.

It didn't snow on Traxamere Beta, but there was a thrilling snap of cold to the air.

'That's what Christmas can be, sometimes,' the Doctor said. 'A time for talking.'

'But why you?' Davros repeated.

'Because I've never met you, and you've never met me,' the Doctor said, running a hand through his shock of brown hair.

Davros looked at him – the long coat, the bow tie, the childlike smile, and the old, tired eyes. *Why do I always rebuild myself exactly as before?* Every time he died. Every time . . .

'That limits me,' the Doctor continued. 'It limits what I can say about where you're going, and where I've been. But we decided it was worth it. That you might be more inclined to listen to someone you had less of a history with.'

'I have history with *all* of you,' Davros said quietly. 'You think I care what face you wear?'

The cold air was sour in his mouth. The oxygen separators in his chest were degrading, as they did every century or so. He would have to replace them. There was always so much work to be done.

'Do you know what I see, Doctor? When I look at you? At any of you?'

The Doctor shook his head.

'I see the look in your eyes the first time we met. All the way back on Skaro, when my children were in their infancy, and you arrived to take it all away before it could even start.'

Something dark passed across the Doctor's face. 'I didn't have a choice. The Time Lords –'

Davros waved his hand. It was aching, a spreading chill where metal and flesh met. *Why do I never build myself young?* 'We met, and just for a moment you threatened everything I had created. You held the controls of my life support in your hand, and you demanded that I destroy them or you would destroy me.'

'To know,' the Doctor quoted, 'that life and death on such a scale was my choice. To know that the tiny pressure of my thumb would end everything.'

Davros smirked to hear his own words in the Doctor's mouth. 'Your *casing* doesn't matter to me, Doctor. I never forget who I'm looking at.'

'So why accept my offer to come?' the Doctor asked. 'Why agree to meet me this Christmas? Or at Christmas on Lavellan? Or anywhere?'

Davros fell silent, staring up at the barges crowding the sky.

'Curiosity,' the Doctor said eventually. 'That's why I chose Traxamere Beta. The lights we're about to see are famous in this bit of the galaxy, and I've never seen them before. That's why I chose this Christmas, out of all the millions that are out there.'

The lights came on. They were so bright, Davros had to turn away.

'You've never seen them before either, I imagine,' the Doctor said.

Davros bristled at his certainty. 'How do you know?'

'Well, the place is still standing, for a start,' the Doctor said, his youthful grin painted red and green and gold by the celebrations above.

After a moment, Davros smiled back.

6

It didn't take long.

It never did, in Davros's experience. He could spend years planning. Years plotting, and hypothesising, and dissecting, ever dissecting the failures, both his children's and his own. But, in the end, victory and defeat always arrived in a single, narrow moment, like a dagger in the dark.

The facility on Gryphon's Reach had once been Krillitane, and it was in the business of invisibility. The winged, reptilian race were the opposite of the Daleks, in many ways. Davros had built his children to be superior, to be unique, to reject other life with religious zeal. The Krillitane, by comparison, were scavengers. Parasites. Thieves of DNA. They infiltrated other races, taking their forms and eating whole civilisations from within.

Word had reached the Dalek Empire that the Krillitane were a hair's breadth away from developing some sort of phase-cloak: true, complete invisibility. A tactical advantage no other race must be allowed to possess. That was the purpose of this invisible facility on an unremarkable world. That was the prize. And Davros had been summoned to make sure the Doctor could not take it from them.

++ ACQUIRE ++

++ ACQUIRE ++

The Daleks poured down the corridors of the facility, like wasps attacking a hive. The Krillitane fought back in their scattered, mongrel way – ambushes, scavenged weaponry, even herding genetically engineered warrior forms into the invaders' paths.

Davros's systems recorded every second of the conflict, every shot and scream and kill, but the scientist himself paid only half a mind. Davros knew the strengths of his soldiers. The power of his children. He held no concern for them. And yet . . .

'Doctor?' he hissed, fingers flicking over the controls so that his voice seeped from every single intercom at once. 'Allying with the Krillitane? I thought you had *some* standards.'

Nothing. No response.

Davros took a deep, shuddering breath, wincing as the compressor vents in his chest chugged and seized. He had been in the middle of a repair cycle when his children had called. They might have waited. He might have asked them to wait.

No. The business of empire called. And, when it called, Davros answered.

'Doctor,' he wheedled. 'I might show mercy . . .'

An hour since planetfall. Civilisations had fallen in less. Especially when the Doctor was involved. No one knew better than Davros that the Doctor loved to talk, and yet, in that hour, he had not said a single word.

Davros had engineered worry out of his children. To worry was to admit, however privately, that failure was an option. Not for the first time, he wished he had also done so for himself. For silence from the Doctor *was* worrying. Silence meant the Doctor had better things to do than talk.

++ EXTERMINATE! ++

Davros thumbed the controls. 'Keep focus, my children.'

Two Daleks fell to a proton blaster. Another exploded as a Krillitane warrior tore apart its casing. The reserve forces Davros had ordered to stay in the upper atmosphere were now spiralling downwards, their life signs spiking on Davros's screens as they scented blood.

Rage. Always, they raged. Getting bogged down in slaughter. Lashing out at the indignity of being opposed.

'The Doctor is the foe here,' Davros cautioned. 'This technology is the prize. Everything else is a distraction.'

++ EXTERMINATE! ++

They weren't listening. Too busy snarling and snapping at each other, baying like hounds on the hunt.

They are what you made them, Davros told himself, for what might have been the thousandth time. *You cannot resent the pure for being pure.*

And that was the truth of it. The heart of it. The other races of the galaxy scorned the Daleks for their maddened hatred of all other life, unaware that it was all their fault. The Daleks thought only of extermination because there were foes still to exterminate. Had the rest of life in the universe had the good grace to lie down and die, his children would be far more serene.

'Davros.'

And there he was. The co-author of Dalek rage. The midwife to their annihilating hate.

'Davros, you need to stop.'

That voice. It was always the same, no matter how different. Davros's boards lit up as weapons charged to dangerous capacity, as units pulled back from engagements or spun their casing crowns in berserk delight.

Now the Daleks listened. Now they focused.

Davros's chest compressors wheezed in and out.

'I'm giving you one chance, Davros. Call off your monsters. Retreat to high orbit. I don't want to –'

++ DAVROS ++

++ CREATOR ++

'Yes?' Davros breathed.

There was no capacity for emotional range in the voice of a Dalek. Davros knew that. He had designed them himself. But every time it came to this moment – this narrow moment between the Doctor, the Daleks and him – he imagined it trembled, just a bit.

'Do not waver, my children. Trust the augmented sensors I bestowed upon you. No matter what they have built here, he cannot hide from us.'

The uncertainty smoothed itself away. That was the job of a father.

++ THE PRIZE WILL BE FOUND ++

++ THE DOCTOR HAS BEEN ANTICIPATED ++

++ HIDING WILL NOT BE PERMITTED ++

The Daleks swarmed in, weathering the fire from the Krillitane defenders or ignoring it completely.

'Always running, always hiding,' Davros murmured into the comms. 'When will you learn, Doctor? Some problems can only be faced head-on.'

'I'm beginning to agree with you,' the Doctor responded, and then the world went black.

7

Christmas, on the Red Moon of Xhe.

'You're wasting your time,' Davros said. 'I'm not going to "see the light" or recognise some sort of virtue or value to all these civilisations you show me. You're *wasting* your time.'

'Time is the one thing I have lots of,' the Doctor said, pressing a pair of magnoculars to his lean face. 'What am I to do but waste it?'

Ahead, the first of the tribespeople tethered the great armour-plated beasts that were their mounts and homes. Vast, shaggy heads protruded from under spiked bone crests, staring blearily down at their keepers. Each one was the size of a city block – a mountain of flesh and shell that could house more than fifty people on its back. In the light of the red sky, they were the colour of dried blood.

'Then I must consider my time, if you will not.' The ground was uneven, cracked and baked by the unforgiving sun, and the anti-gravs of Davros's chair whirred as they sought to make sense of it. The plains of Xhe seemed to go on forever, red and desolate as a Dalek eye lens. 'Curiosity may sustain you, Doctor, but I have work to do.'

'Wait.'

Davros half turned, and then shook his head. The tribespeople were making camp. They hadn't seemed to notice the two men on the hill – one young and striking, the other folded over himself in a cramped bundle of limbs, his lower half encased in stainless steel.

The thin atmosphere pulled and dragged at Davros's lungs. When the first tribesman began to sing, his voice tremoring high and clear through the oxygen-starved air, Davros was unmoved.

'No,' he said simply. 'I won't wait. What am I supposed to be learning, Doctor? What puzzle am I supposed to solve? I have never understood this foolish obsession you have with Christmas, and I do not understand why it has brought us two thirds of the way across the known universe to this unforgiving nothing rock.'

'Because it's just a word.' The Doctor lowered his magnoculars.

It was the same face as before, but different. Older-seeming. Davros found himself wondering what those eyes saw from one Christmas to the next.

'I forget sometimes how incredible language is. The TARDIS translates, you see. Makes things simple.' The Doctor breathed out a long plume of cold air. 'But there are words – simple words – that you can say to a million different people in a hundred different eras, and to each person the word will have a meaning that is personal and unique.'

A tribeswoman had joined in, face lifted to the freezing sky. Another had turned a fragment of a shell into a drum, and was slapping out a rhythm with hard and breathless joy.

'Christmas is just a word. Here, it means singing. In other places, it means lights. It can mean religion, or family, or celebrating reaching winter's halfway point. It's a . . . selection box.'

'I don't know what that means,' Davros said. There was something about the song the tribespeople were singing, or the lack of oxygen in the air . . . He didn't feel like himself.

'It would take a surprising amount of time to explain,' the Doctor said. 'But you can choose the meaning of Christmas. You can build your own traditions, build it like an engine, so that it's entirely personal to you. You choose what it means. You choose the effect it has on the universe. There aren't many words like that. Words like Christmas.' His gaze fell on Davros. 'Words like father.'

Something in the intensity of the Doctor's gaze made Davros recoil. Something he had seen once, long ago.

'I am a scientist,' Davros snapped, angry at himself for flinching. 'I do not engage in ridiculous wordplay.'

'Don't you?' the Doctor said. 'You're still a Kaled, Davros, no matter how many bits you lop off or replace. All those lessons. All that philosophy. For a thousand years, words were the only thing your kind had to pass on to each other.'

'So?' Davros hissed. He didn't like this. He understood the mechanics of war. He could design weapons of destruction that would have terrified the generals who trained him. But, as always when he faced the Doctor, the Time Lord felt just a half-step ahead.

'Christmas can mean anything, Davros. So can father. But Dalek?' The Doctor shook his head. 'Dalek just means Dalek. A force of hatred. A force of destruction, of annihilation. And you are the only person who could make it mean something else.'

The gentleness had disappeared from the Doctor's voice. Instead, there was now hunger, the fierceness that shone through when wit met will and empires turned on the edge of a knife. He hid it well, mostly, especially when there was a human to impress, but Davros knew that ambition.
That anger.

It made the Doctor . . . bearable.

'I can stop the Daleks, Davros. I can beat them, time and time again. But you could *change* them.'

He knelt beside Davros, eyes bright and pleading wide, and Davros fought the urge to pull away, to hide the vulnerable controls of his systems with his hand.

'I've considered it,' he whispered. 'The thought has occurred.' His compressors wheezed in and out. *The atmosphere.* Yes. It was the thinness of the atmosphere. Nothing more. 'You are right in what you say. I have created them to mean one thing, and one thing only. They are not adaptable. They do not change, or learn, or grow. They are what they will be.' His voice quivered before he could straighten it out. 'But if I did change them, they would not be Daleks. They would not be my children.'

'But they don't love you, Davros.' The Doctor's voice was gentle again. 'They never will.'

'If they loved me,' Davros said, 'they would not be my children.'

He looked out over the plain, where a hundred tribespeople sang their hearts out for no audience but the desert, Christmas and two old men.

'It is beautiful, Doctor. Thank you for showing me.'

8

++ WE SUMMONED YOU TO COUNTERACT THE DOCTOR ++

++ THIS WAS NOT ACHIEVED ++

Gryphon's Reach shrank as Davros's command ship pulled away. There were still Daleks on the planet, firing again and again into whatever they could find, but Davros's work was done.

'Synaptic phase-cloaking,' he muttered. 'A mixture of Gallifreyan and Krillitane biotech, materialising *inside* the senses of the observer themselves. Sliding like a curtain between mind and nerve. I should have known. I should have –'

++ WE WERE UNABLE TO ACCESS OUR SYSTEMS ++

++ WE WERE TRAPPED IN THE DARK OF OURSELVES ++

++ IT WAS . . . NOT OPTIMAL ++

It had been torture. Cloaking technology was just that: a cloak. A barrier between the seer and the seen. That was why the technology was so rare. It was almost impossible to hide something so completely that no part of it could be detected.

The Doctor had not tried to hide the Krillitane. He had interfered with Davros and his Daleks' own systems, severing the links between their biological senses and their casings.

Hiding them from themselves. It had only lasted minutes, by Davros's internal clock, but for that moment – that terrible, eternal moment – every single Dalek in the fleet had been plunged into darkness. Deprived of their senses, shorn from the might of their machine bodies, and reduced to the wet nothing of their flesh existence. Bacteria in a Petri dish, trapped alone with their futile rage.

Some had self-destructed. Most had gone mad, though even Davros could admit that it was becoming harder and harder to make the distinction between which of his children were sane and which were not.

When the cloaking field had disengaged, the Doctor had been gone.

'I understand what he did,' Davros said, and it was true. He did, now that he had seen it. That was ever the issue. *Playing catch-up again.* 'Next time, we will not be taken by surprise.'

++ THERE WILL NOT BE A NEXT TIME ++

For just a moment, Davros was back in that darkness, his mechanical lungs wheezing and clattering, struggling to keep him alive.

'What?'

++ WE WILL NOT BE CONTACTING YOU AGAIN ++

'I don't understand,' Davros said. 'I know what he did. I can redesign you to defend against it. I can . . . I can help.'

++ WE DO NOT REQUIRE YOUR HELP ++

++ WE REQUIRE VICTORY ++

++ GOODBYE . . . CREATOR ++

The link went dead.

9

Christmas, on Alacracis IV.

Davros had already found a table by the time the Doctor arrived, weaving through the crowd in topcoat and tails. The bazaar was packed with last-minute shoppers, each stall glorious in festive finery of neon and crushed velvet. Merchants paced behind their stalls – demanding, cajoling – and incense burners coughed a thousand streams of smoke into the dark bowl of the sky, filling the air with a haze of cinnamon and soot.

Davros watched the Doctor make his way through the crush, stopping here and there to joke with a vendor or examine a piece of polished glass. He made it look very easy, as if he was genuinely interested in the price of glishfruit or the origin of a statue, despite being part of a civilisation so advanced that, by comparison, the people of Alacracis IV were insects grubbing in the dirt.

What am I missing? Davros asked himself. *Is there significance, and I simply do not see it?*

'You're early,' the Doctor said as he sat down.

The bazaar was full of little places offering mulled wine and pastries from a dozen different worlds. Davros handed the Doctor a menu he hadn't opened himself. 'I've been thinking about your offer.'

The Doctor lingered over his choice, before finally brushing his fingers across the menu's surface. An android waiter in the corner jerked as it received the order, then began ladling hot wine into a cup.

'I'm glad to hear it,' the Time Lord said.

'Things have to change.'

'I agree.'

'It is . . .' Davros paused. 'It is not easy to say this. It is harder to do it. But I have to admit that there is truth to what you say. You can continue to thwart my Daleks forever, but that will never change them. They will only hate more. Harm more aggressively. They know only one solution to being stopped, and that is to lash out more violently than before.'

The waiter placed the Doctor's drink before him, and the Doctor wrapped his long fingers round it. 'That's why I contacted you,' he said. 'I'm scared, Davros, of what might happen in the future, should we continue to clash.'

The wine smelled sweet. Delicate. Davros looked at the menu sitting in front of the Doctor. He could ask for some. He still possessed smell and taste faculties – they were useful for laboratory work. He could have a drink with the Doctor. His old enemy. His old friend.

It was Christmas, after all.

'I'm scared too,' he said instead. 'Something has to change.'

The tone of his voice made the Doctor meet his eyes, even as the first of the Daleks disengaged their cloaking field. Shoppers began to scream.

'Oh, Davros,' the Doctor said. 'Really?'

++ EXTERMINATE! ++

10

'I see you got it working,' the Doctor said.

They were surrounded. More than a hundred Daleks, some afloat, others hunched amid the flattened remains of stalls. The merchants and shoppers had all fled, and Davros could tell, even without his scanners and screens, that his children ached to turn and fire, to chase moving prey.

As always, however, the Doctor's presence had an incredibly focusing effect.

'It wasn't difficult,' Davros said. He shook his head, enjoying the moment. 'Working with the Krillitane, Doctor? For shame.'

'Rebels,' the Doctor said flatly. 'A splinter group who want no part of their people's expansion. I was helping them find a way to hide. A way to escape the Brood-Mother's eternal wars.' He took a long sip of his wine. 'Families disagree sometimes.'

'Except mine,' Davros spat. 'Is that it?'

++ CREATOR ++

Davros knew. He *knew* there could be no emotion bar hate in the voice of a Dalek, but he let himself imagine that his children were proud.

++ YOU HAVE DELIVERED OUR GREATEST ENEMY TO US ++

'Yes,' Davros said. 'Well. 'Tis the season. Isn't that right, Doctor?'

And there it was. The change. Davros had seen it before, and it was as profound as a regeneration. The tiredness vanished. The lanky shoulders rose. The chin lifted as if preparing to take a blow, or a bow. The Doctor had an audience now, and the compressors began to wheeze in Davros's chest.

'Do you know what's good?' the Doctor said. 'Do you know what's really very extremely good about this situation right now?'

++ YOU ARE SURROUNDED ++

++ YOU ARE UNARMED ++

++ NOTHING IS GOOD ++

'I'm always surrounded,' the Doctor said. 'I'm always unarmed. That's where I do my best work.'

He lunged to his feet and the front row of Daleks flinched.

'You know that, don't you, boys? That's why you haven't fired. You're afraid I've got some scheme or fail-safe, and the second you fire on me is the second that trap springs.' He grinned. 'Tell me I'm wrong.'

The silence stretched for too long before Davros broke it.

'This is foolishness, my children. He comes defenceless to these truces –'

'Exactly right,' the Doctor interrupted. 'No allies. No backup. Not a biscuit. Isn't that strange? Isn't that unnerving?'

'No!' Davros snapped. 'It isn't! Stop. *Stop this!*'

The Doctor continued as if Davros hadn't spoken. 'But this is Christmas, and I'm going to be generous. Here's my counter-offer.'

'Counter-offer?' Davros practically shouted. 'My children are not stupid, Doctor. Stop this theatre –'

++ THE CREATOR WILL BE SILENT ++

Davros froze. 'Who said that? Who said that to me?'

Not a single Dalek responded. Their focus on the Doctor was absolute.

'Families at Christmas,' the Time Lord said. 'They're always the same. Tell you what, boys. I'll let you kill me. I won't resist.'

He turned towards Davros, and his smile had disappeared.

'Just kill him too.'

Davros laughed, high and cracked and wheezing. 'You must be truly desperate, Doctor.' He shook his head. 'My children, this has gone on long enough. Kill the Time Lord.'

It was difficult, even for Davros, to read expression on a Dalek but, as the neon signs fizzled and the wine bubbled and boiled over in its mulling pot, it seemed that the hundred Daleks surrounding them might be suddenly lost in thought.

'Children,' Davros repeated. 'Kill him.'

With a low whine, fifty Daleks turned to point their weapons at Davros.

'No,' he whispered. 'No. You can't. You wouldn't.'

++ TO KILL THE DOCTOR ++

++ TO ACHIEVE VICTORY ++

++ THERE IS NOTHING WE WOULD NOT DO ++

'This is how you built them, Davros,' the Doctor said. 'This is how they were made.'

'Do not do this, Doctor. Do not *do* this.'

The Doctor spread his hands, a charlatan professing empty palms and innocence just before the climax of a trick. 'I'm not doing anything. This is on you. From the beginning, this was *always* on you.'

'Doctor, please –'

The Daleks fired.

11

Later, just a little later, when the smoke had cleared, the Doctor finished the last of his wine.

Sirens were blaring in the distance. The authorities of Alacracis IV, no doubt having detected the sudden absence of Dalek life signs, were rushing to show their control of the situation. Merchants were already returning, picking their way through the rubble. Shoppers too, lifting bags dropped in the chaos. Christmas, re-establishing itself in little spreading islands of calm.

The cinnamon scent of smoke still leaked from the incense burners, mingling with the smog from the broken Dalek husks.

'You didn't have a fail-safe,' Davros said eventually.

'Of course I did,' the Doctor said. 'I had you. Tell me, do they know you build them to self-destruct if they ever turn on you?'

'No.'

'Does it happen often?'

'I need to take precautions,' Davros said numbly. 'My children are unpredictable.'

'No,' the Doctor said. 'They're not. Merry Christmas, Davros.' He placed his cup back down on the little table. 'I hope we do not meet again.'

12

It was the day after Christmas.

Davros had instructed his servant creatures to bring the Dalek corpses on board. It wouldn't do to have the wider empire learn about his precautions, and the workshops deep within his command ship always needed new resources. He had Dalek models dating back to his very first experiments on Skaro, and there was usually much calm to be found in delving into his designs – assessing, improving, perfecting.

It felt like . . . conversation.

Now, though, silence seemed preferable, broken only by the whirring of Davros's chair as he drifted through the cluttered metal halls. It was time travel, in a way. Not the graceful sailing of the Time Lords, but a creaky, halting passage through the monuments of a failed life.

There, the dissected remains of a Supreme Dalek. Here, the arachnid chassis he had never quite been able to make work. Sensor globes and shoulder slats, dome lights and eyestalk after eyestalk after eyestalk, all looking at him with blank, rote hatred.

Distantly, he noticed that his engineered servants were following him, cowering and clicking at each other, unused to silence after a defeat. Rage was more common. Spitting curses. Making promises that next time the Doctor would not thwart him.

Next time.

Next time.

++ TO ACHIEVE VICTORY ++

++ THERE IS NOTHING WE WOULD NOT DO ++

Nothing, except listen to their father. Nothing, except trust him to know what was best.

'Is this all I am?' he whispered. 'Is this all I am for?'

Davros, the last Kaled. Davros, the scientist who had once dreamed of holding the universe in his hand. Davros, the father chasing the love of the creatures he had himself designed never to feel it.

++ WE DO NOT REQUIRE YOUR HELP ++

'Fine,' he said. '*Fine.*' A strange feeling was blooming in his chest. 'Live without me. Fight without me. Die without me. Ungrateful children. *Undeserving.* I contain more than you.' A fierce grin cracked his features. 'I always have.'

The words made him feel young again.

++ CREATOR ++

The voice thundered through the command ship.

++ WE REQUIRE YOU ++

++ WAR HAS BEEN DECLARED ++

++ WAR ON GALLIFREY ITSELF ++

++ A TIME WAR ++

++ A FINAL WAR ++

++ WILL YOU AID US? ++

For a moment, there was nothing but the sound of Davros's chest compressors wheezing in and out.

'Yes.' His voice cracked with a father's pride. '*Yes.*'

3

INFLICTING CHRISTMAS

WE
CREATE
FUTURES

'My name is Adeyemi Lawal. Let me show you what I can do.'

The audience went wild. It wasn't the words in themselves. Friedrich Zas had the morning slot, and he arrived on the stage via the prototype of Earth's first teleporter. Last night it was Lilith Decrois, who made her entrance by breaking both the world record for parachute-jumping out of a space shuttle *and* the skylight of the Convention Centre Dublin. Compared to that, simply stepping on to a dark, empty stage to deliver your presentation comes across as practically shy.

This was We Create Futures 2045, after all. At an event like this, you go big or go home.

Over the last twenty years, however, Adeyemi Lawal had made those simple words a battle cry. *Let me show you what I can do.* They were the mission statement of her company. They were emblazoned on the side of her satellites. When she began her life in the public eye, just a ten-year-old on VidTube, scavenging parts from the bins behind electronics stores and rebuilding them in her bedroom, they were the words she used to kick off every stream. Not a boast, she's fond of saying. A promise.

'I think a lot about memories,' she said, and a corner of her mouth quirked, just a fraction. This was, as any of her long-time viewers knew, the closest she ever came to smiling. 'Memories are what make us who we are. They are the foundations of our personalities. The basis for our relationships. The source of our hopes for the future. They are the filter through which we perceive. Every memory, no matter how small, has a purpose. Everything has a purpose. And, if it doesn't have a purpose –'

'We give it one!'

This too was one of her sayings. As soon as she said it, a thousand teenagers shouted it back.

'And yet,' she continued, 'memories are fleeting. They fade. They get confused. They blur into each other like ink on a damp page. What are we without our memories? What are we when they're gone?'

She fell silent and the room fell silent with her. Motes of dust spun in the single spotlight. A hundred articles were already being written, analysing every word, every pause, every detail of Lawal's short white hair and her sleeveless smock and the circuitry tattoos standing out pale on her dark, muscled arms.

'But what if we could save them? What if we could inhabit them? What if we could make them real enough to touch?'

Cameras flashed as an attendant ran out onstage to hand Lawal a circlet of metal. It was thin and silvery, too delicate to be called a crown.

'This hippocampal conduit taps directly into the memory centres of my brain, recording and copying every detail of a specific moment. The sounds, the smells, the textures. We do not just remember with our minds, my friends. We remember with our senses and our bodies and our hearts and our bones.' She donned the circlet. 'It is hard to put a memory – a *real* memory, a tangible one – into words, even to yourself. But, with the help of the minute hard-light holographic emitters placed around this room, I don't have to. I can make it real.'

She snapped her fingers, gunshot loud, and just like that Christmas bloomed.

A thousand gasps were suddenly visible, as plumes of smoking breath disturbed air that was now filled with swirling, drifting snow. Tinsel wove itself out of nothing, inching across surfaces like caterpillars, and wreaths flowered on every door. The stage was no longer empty. Instead, Adeyemi Lawal was now standing in the centre of a cosy little living room. It wasn't anything fancy – certainly not what you'd imagine as the home of one of the world's greatest inventors. The hidden holographic projectors had not just replicated the sagging couch and the mismatched chairs, but the slightly balding tinsel and the cloudy stain halfway up a wall where someone had inexpertly painted over some mould.

However, for the reaction of awe it elicited, it may as well have been the Palace of Versailles. Even as a child, Adeyemi Lawal was famously protective of her privacy. Whole forums were dedicated to puzzling out details of her life, from obsessively investigating serial numbers on the components she stole to attempting to work out her country of origin by the plug sockets half-glimpsed in her videos. All to no avail, of course. Figuring out something Adeyemi Lawal doesn't want you to know would mean outsmarting her.

And now, casually, she had invited them right into her head.

'This is Christmas in the apartment I grew up in,' she said, after an instant's pause, 'and I can call it up whenever I want. A frozen moment of time. A memory made real enough to touch. A present to myself.'

Then, to yelps of surprise from the audience, Adeyemi Lawal – inventor, philanthropist, master engineer, a woman so poised and precise that a single raised eyebrow can earn its own news cycle and stock fluctuation – took two steps and flung herself on to the couch like a kid just home from school. The hard-light projection shimmered, before stabilising once more into worn fabric and sagging springs.

Again, that lightning flash of amusement.

'Any questions?'

'Doctor, why are we here?'

Bill Potts had been to some amazing places with the Doctor. She'd walked on the frozen River Thames two hundred years before her own birth, and had run for her life under alien suns. She'd faced Dryads and Ice Warriors, and capitalist algorithms in space. She'd even had a date ruined by the Pope.

Compared to all that, you could be forgiven for wondering why Dublin's convention centre had been next on the Time Lord's list. It wasn't that there was anything wrong with the place. It was quite a nice building, actually – a gargantuan glass cylinder ringed by neon, jutting up from a concrete base into the sky at a forty-five-degree angle like the focusing ring of some huge sci-fi space cannon. (Sci-fi space cannon had been Bill's first guess as to why they were there, in fact. So far, unfortunately, that did not seem to be the case.)

'We Create Futures, Bill,' the Doctor said, pointing at the huge banner overhead. 'Which, yes, doesn't make a whole lot of sense seeing as everybody creates a future if you wait long enough, but it's a catchy title for an inventors' conference all the same.'

He peered through his sunglasses at the milling crowd. Bill had almost got used to him wearing the glasses constantly. This was made easier by the fact that, somehow, they'd managed to find a crowd of people that the Doctor *didn't* stand out in – which was sort of a miracle in itself.

The convention centre's foyer – the base of that huge glass cylinder – was packed to groaning with hundreds of people. Most were teenagers; thrilled and nervous in equal measure, some in school uniforms and some in what Bill could only describe as 'inventor chic' – clothes as colourfully mismatched as the boxes of scientific equipment they carried. Then there were the parents, who mostly just looked nervous;

laden down with more equipment, with presentation boards and flipcharts and schedules they checked about once per minute, hurrying their charges into one line or another for registration.

'Everyone here's an inventor?' Bill said. 'Some of them look like they're still in school.'

'That's why I like it,' the Doctor said. 'We Create Futures is where young scientists gather to impress some of the biggest companies and innovators in the world. I've been meaning to come for years. Every teenager here is hoping to be selected and sponsored. Oh, look at this!'

A cluster of drones was dancing through the air, assembling themselves into a single robot before breaking apart again without missing a beat. The Doctor raised his hands, stopping just short of touching them.

'Wireless hive mind, compressed-air hovering system, totally green energy – fantastic!'

The fourteen-year-old girl operating the controls went pink.

'And then, over here – come, come!' He bounded – actually bounded – across the display-room floor, dodging between the crowds to a booth where a set of complicated graphs and equations danced across a screen. 'This is . . .' He paused, peering closer. 'This is . . . What is this?'

The young man behind the booth glanced up from his notepad. 'An algorithm proving why time travel is impossible based on paradox theory, extrapolated string fusion and Wittgenstein's secret love of poetry. Don't worry if you don't understand it. It's for Adeyemi Lawal, not –' he indicated them lazily with a hand – 'you know. Civilians.'

The Doctor looked at the graph. Bill looked at the Doctor.

Finally, he gave the young man a slow, wide smile. 'Marvellous. Wonderful work. Very good. Although . . .'

'Although?'

The Doctor tapped one of the equations. 'Here. You've forgotten to carry the two.'

The colour disappeared from the young man's face. 'What? Where?'

The Doctor shrugged. The young man leaped to his feet, squinting at the screen, lips moving frantically and silently.

'You know, I met Wittgenstein once,' the Doctor said, gently placing his hands on Bill's shoulders and steering her away. 'Lovely man. Great whistler. Whistler, ironically, completely useless. But when you can paint like that, what does it matter?'

'Oh my *God*,' Bill said. 'That's why you're here. You're looking for show-offs.'

'Nobody likes a show-off, Bill,' the Doctor said, picking a speck of imaginary dust off his black velvet frock-coat. 'That's just a fact.'

'Yes,' Bill said. 'But you're deflating the show-offs by *showing off*. Tell me that's not the only reason we're here.'

'It's not the only reason,' the Doctor said. 'Of course not. I just like to . . . keep an eye on these things. Keep track of who's inventing what and when. Innovation and disaster go hand in hand – just look at my outfit. It's always worth knowing who's impatient for the future to arrive.'

The air of excitement in the foyer suddenly doubled as the auditorium ahead opened, and a flood of people streamed out, excitedly chatting.

The Doctor neatly snapped a pamphlet from a woman's hand, ignoring the annoyed look that followed. 'Adeyemi Lawal,' he said. 'Who's that?'

'Projectors 11A through E were a little slow in compensating for my movement,' Lawal said, watching the last of the audience file out. 'And let *Innovation Quarterly* know they misquoted me. I said "*our* senses and *our* bodies", not "*your* senses and bodies".'

Carl took down her words. After five years, it didn't surprise him at all that his employer's presentation had been over for less than three minutes and she was already editing the world's response. This was what working for Adeyemi Lawal was like. That's what made it so thrilling.

'Inspired last-minute change on the memory, Ms Lawal,' he said, handing her a glass of water. 'Tying the idea of memory to Christmas was a stroke of genius. We're already seeing it track very well across social media channels.'

Something unreadable flickered over her face. 'Yes. Well.' She looked down at the circlet. Lights winked on its surface like gems. 'Physical, transmittable, viewable memories. The *potential* of it. Psychological breakthroughs. Crime-scene walk-throughs. The teaching possibilities . . . And what they respond to is Christmas.'

She placed the circlet down on a little table on the stage.

'I don't understand people, Carl. Give me circuitry any day.'

Carl didn't say anything. There wasn't anything to say. There was a sense, when working for Adeyemi Lawal, that she viewed conversation with other people as little more than a blank whiteboard to work her thoughts out on.

'Now, I have some inventions to assess, do I not?'

Carl nodded, relieved they were now on safer territory. 'Yes, Ms Lawal. Then another private demonstration for the investors later. Shall I keep the room as is?'

'Yes. No one in or out, please.'

Lawal swept from the room, her assistant following her, and the door closed behind them. As soon as it did, the door to a maintenance closet at the back of the room opened, and a figure slipped out.

The figure was small and slim, and moved with the practised caution of a prey animal, pausing every step to cock his head and listen, freezing every time distant chatter or laughter from the rest of the conference seemed too close or too loud. He knew that, even now, various Lawal Inc. security staff would be guarding the auditorium doors. That was why he had been sitting in that maintenance closet all morning, waiting for Lawal's presentation to end.

This was not the first presentation the figure had attended, despite the fact that his name and face were at the top of every Lawal Inc. security officer's watchlist. Idly, he wondered what the consequences would be if he was caught. The thought thrilled him, as it had many times before.

He reached the stage, turning to the empty auditorium to first make a fair imitation of Lawal's stiff poise, and then a long and flourishing bow.

Then he picked up the circlet and placed it on his head.

Once more, the holo-emitters whirred and clicked, filling the room with the colour and lights of Christmas. The figure paced, taking in every detail of the snow, the tinsel and the wreaths, before stepping into the memory of that cosy little apartment. He stared for the longest time at the discoloured patch on the wall, the caution in his frame replaced by trembling, contained rage.

As he stared, the discoloured patch began to grow.

'I remember her!' Bill said, staring up at the huge display from which Adeyemi Lawal stared sternly back. 'From my time. She'd just started her company. I guess it went well. Will go well.' She gave the Doctor a sidelong glance. 'Should I buy shares?'

'Oh, absolutely,' the Doctor said distractedly, thumbing through a pamphlet marked with the white-raven logo of Lawal Inc. 'The space–time continuum loves it when you exploit future knowledge for personal gain. I've got whole rooms in the TARDIS brimming with money.'

'What?' Bill said. 'Really?'

'No,' the Doctor said, throwing her a withering glance.

'Just, you do have kind of a Scrooge McDuck thing going on . . .'

'Purely coincidental.' The Doctor closed the pamphlet with a snap. 'She's making memories real. Real enough for others to see and touch. That sounds dangerous.'

'Does it?' Bill said. 'Why? Being able to consult your memory sounds really great, actually. I'd love perfect recall. Especially coming up to exam time.' She paused. 'And, you know, if you lost someone. When you lose someone. It'd help you remember them.'

The Doctor's voice softened. He knew exactly who Bill was referring to. 'I can understand the desire, Bill, but it's the method I worry about. Memories aren't the kind of thing you can pin down. How did we meet?'

Bill frowned at the sudden change of topic. 'You called me to your office. You had noticed that I was sneaking into your lectures, even though I just worked in the kitchen.'

'There's no *just* about working in a kitchen,' the Doctor said. 'Kitchens are great. They're the heart of things. And what is your first memory of me?'

'You were . . . I don't know. It's hard to say what I thought of you then, after everything we've done since.'

'Exactly,' the Doctor said. 'That was our first meeting. But remembering it now is totally different, because of what's happened in between. You no doubt remember me being wise and mysterious and charming –'

'You threw a book at me,' Bill interrupted. 'Or to me. You wanted me to catch it, but I remember feeling like, if I hadn't, then you might have decided I wouldn't be your student at all. I remember feeling . . . tested.' She paused at the look on the Doctor's face. 'It's OK, Doctor,' she said. 'I passed.'

'But that's what I mean,' the Doctor said. 'Which is right? Was I testing you? Was I judgemental? Was I cross? Or was I fascinated? Impressed? Was I just throwing you a book because that was the quickest way to get it across the room to you? Which of those memories is the correct one?'

'They're all correct,' Bill said, after a moment. It should have felt strange, an academic discussion on the nature of memory at a science conference twenty-odd years in the future, but, then again, class was in session. It always was.

'Exactly,' the Doctor said. 'There's no such thing as perfect memory. Everything is filtered. Interpreted. Rewritten over and over again. An ex texts you out of nowhere on New Year's Eve, and you suddenly forget all the horrible things they did. You remember an argument as being calm and controlled, and all the other person remembers is trying not to cry.' He looked again at the pamphlet. 'Hard-light hologram. A projection that feels real. Giving one person's memories form and weight is a very dangerous thing to do indeed. You never know exactly what you're going to get.'

That was when the screaming started.

Bill was learning a lot about screams in the company of the Doctor. There were the screams of soldiers facing something they'd never dreamed they would face. There were the screams you screamed in a dark and creaking house when your friends were vanishing left and right. There were the screams you gasped when your oxygen was running low.

This scream was a contagion. It dropped into the room like a rock into a pool, spreading ripples of panic out through the crowd. People started to turn, to push, to shove, trying to flee, while ahead the crowd contracted inwards like a balloon under a needle seconds before the fatal pop.

And then the moment broke, the crowd shattered, and Bill and the Doctor were left facing a monster.

When Bill was a kid, her teacher had told her that birds evolved from dinosaurs. She had found that hard to imagine – birds looked so harmless, with their fat little bodies and their springy, hopping legs. *Bit of a glo down*, she remembered thinking.

She regretted thinking that now. The creature before them was like a missing evolutionary link – a bird on a prehistoric scale, lanky and raw-boned, halfway between a velociraptor and a crow. It was amazing how different you could feel about a bird's twitching, juddering movements when its talons were savagely sharp and as long as your arm.

But that wasn't the strangest thing. It wasn't even the *second*-strangest thing. The second-strangest thing about the creature was that it was carved from ice. Every inch of it – from its gangling limbs to its bat-like folds of skin – was made of a dark grey ice that thudded with an internal crimson light. Flecks drizzled off the creature as it moved, flecks the grey-black of mould. The kind of colour that would make you call your landlord at once.

No. The *strangest* thing about the creature was that it had the face of Adeyemi Lawal.

Another creature emerged from the auditorium, then a third; half flapping, half stumbling, barely able to keep themselves in the air. Both of them had Adeyemi Lawal's face too, delicate features distorted by mouths of long, sharp fangs. They seemed just as upset about the situation as the audience – fumbling like baby birds finding their way around a nest. Then, as one, they lunged, delving into the fleeing crowd.

One grabbed a woman a little older than Bill, then pivoted in mid-air to snap its wings open and take off. The crackling beat of its wings blew people off their feet in a storm of ice flecks.

The second screeched with a voice like a glacier calving, and pounced on an old man, dragging him up into the air with ragged beats of its wings.

'Doctor!' Bill shouted. 'What do we –?'

It was exactly the wrong thing to do. The third of the creatures turned to her, its human head bobbing on that pterodactyl neck. Bill had just enough time to see the two other monsters dive back towards the auditorium – prey clutched tight to their scrawny chests.

Then the third was upon her. Claws closed round her wrist and shoulder. A nightmare head hissed cold spittle into her face. Then, with a heave that nearly wrenched her arm out of its socket, the beast took to the air. Bill's stomach plunged into her toes. Her view of the conference-centre foyer spun crazily, from the fleeing crowd to the rippling banners to the shocked look on the Doctor's face.

Then cold, and dark, and rushing flight.

In a conference room three floors up, Adeyemi Lawal was changing lives.

'Impressive,' she said to fourteen-year-old Andrea Borg from Malta. 'I could see myself investing in this,' she said. 'Carl, get a preliminary contract written up. Who's next?'

The assistant walked the young boy to the door, then checked his clipboard. 'John White. Theoretical presentation on why time travel is impossible –'

'No,' Lawal said. 'I don't have time for people telling me things are impossible.' She frowned. 'Can you hear . . . screaming?'

The sentence had barely left Lawal's lips when two of her security detail burst in the door. Attacks weren't unheard of at We Create Futures. There were always overzealous fans. Protesters uncomfortable with the speed at which the future was arriving, who felt it should be left where it was. That was why Lawal's security carried sleek white non-lethal stun guns of her own design.

'Your helicopter is on the roof, Ms Lawal,' Carl said. 'We can have you out in –'

Lawal looked around. 'Where's Ebi?'

Carl went grey. There was no point in apologising. Apologies ranked lower with Adeyemi Lawal than compliments. 'He didn't show up for breakfast, Ms Lawal. We were hoping to have him located before you –'

'Noticed he was gone,' she finished, then opened her briefcase to reveal her own gleaming stun gun. 'I see.'

Bill had just enough time to scream before the darkness folded away like a vampire's cape and she landed in pure white snow.

Rolling awkwardly on to her back, trying to rub life back into her arms where the creature's claws had clamped them, Bill looked up and saw the ice-gargoyle bank in mid-air, then turn back lazily, flapping its great wings before vanishing once more into the dark sky of . . .

How long were we flying? Unless Bill's eyes were lying, they were no longer in the convention centre. They certainly weren't in the auditorium the creature had dived into only moments before, unless the place had undergone *serious* redecoration.

Before Bill, a snowfield stretched as far as she could see – a featureless, pristine wasteland as white as the sky above was black. This wasn't Dublin. She was pretty sure this wasn't even Earth, because she couldn't imagine an expanse of snow – not even in the Arctic – that was this inhumanly, perfectly untouched.

Just thirty metres away, an immense tower rose up to scrape the sky like a jutting piece of rib, its curving length carved entirely from ice and white, white snow.

Bill was the kind of person who liked asking questions. She liked categorising things. Finding answers, or the gaps where answers should be. That was what the Doctor had seen in her. And right now the answer she was getting to all of her questions was 'fairy tale'.

Not because the landscape was jolly and colourful and benevolent – it wasn't. The ice blocks of the fortress behind her were black with frozen dirt, and their edges looked sharp enough to cut you to the bone. The landscape in front of her looked fantastical, but in the old sense of the word – it looked like a Brothers Grimm story, or the nightmare that might have inspired it, hundreds of years ago when every winter hid bears or wolves.

No, it was like a fairy tale because it wasn't real. Bill knew it wasn't real, because the wind blizzarding flecks of snow upward didn't touch a strand of her hair. The snow under her feet was as crunchy and satisfying as anyone could ask snow to be, but it had the temperature of dandruff or packing foam.

Hard-light hologram. That was what the Doctor had said. *A projection that feels real.*

'Star Trek holodeck,' she said, above the howling of the not-wind. 'Cool.'

She was in some sort of illusion. She might even just be in the auditorium, metres from safety. *Or you could be on the roof. You could be standing on the edge of a lift shaft.*

Memories weren't always trustworthy. Bill hadn't needed the Doctor to tell her that. Now, she found herself in the unenviable position of having to treat them like solid ground.

'Less cool,' she said. 'Very much less cool.'

And then she saw the other impact craters in the snow, the footsteps leading away towards the tower, and realised that if there were other people here, they would need her help.

Bill set out.

In the foyer of the convention centre, Carl was watching a tall, lanky Scottish man shout into a pair of sunglasses.

'Come on! Calibrate!'

The man was the only person still inside. Everyone else had been moved outside and was now pressed up against the building's great glass doors, staring in at the hundreds of inventions and presentations they had been forced to leave behind.

A security guard had approached Lawal and Carl as they entered.

'We tried to throw him out,' the guard said.

'And?' Lawal asked, fixing the stranger with that intent stare.

'And he shouted at us.'

'Ms Lawal.' The man was coming towards them, putting his sunglasses into a pocket. 'Big fan. Especially of the way your memory projector has metastasised into a full-on mini universe of horrors.'

He pointed at the door to the auditorium. It no longer opened out onto a room full of chairs. Instead, what lay beyond was a howling white wilderness, the inky black sky dominated by a bulging moon. Carl started as a bristled, colossal *something* began to inch its immense crimson bulk around the glowing silver orb with a soft and sinister rasp. 'Is that . . . tinsel?'

A sudden blast of wind that none of them actually felt blew snow across the carpet, where it fizzled away to static.

'Tell me,' the stranger said. 'Bug, or feature?'

'Get him out of here,' Lawal said, as if simply saying the words deleted him from the equations already running in her head. She turned towards the doorway leading to the seemingly infinite plain and stowed her stun gun at the small of her back.

'Hippocampal encoding,' the man said quickly. 'That's it, isn't it? You need as much detail as possible, so you're connecting directly to the brain's unconscious memory centres. Lifting it right off the disc.'

Lawal held out her hand and Carl passed her a tablet, on which she made notes with sharp, delicate strokes of her nails. There was a guard at each of the stranger's shoulders now, their confidence bolstered by their boss's presence.

'This isn't a human memory,' the stranger said. 'It can't be. But people remember all sorts of things. They remember bad dreams. They remember pain, and pain colours things. Pollutes them, like an oil slick across fresh water. And this machine makes all of that real. Real enough to touch. Real enough to kill.'

For a long moment, the only sound in the foyer was that of Lawal's nails clicking on her tablet.

'And it's self-updating, isn't it?' he continued. 'Like a videogame landscape, resolving round the main character every step they take. The people taken in there could wander that place for years. They could starve to death, metres from the exit.'

'That won't happen,' Lawal said. She still hadn't looked up from her device.

'No?'

'No,' she said. 'We're going to go in after them.'

'Then you need my help,' the stranger said.

'Do I?' she said calmly. 'And why is that?'

'Because whoever is in there doesn't like you very much.'

Carl gasped. He couldn't help it. Even the security guards winced.

Now, the scientist raised her head. Her smile was fractional and humourless. 'I do not, as a rule, care about who likes me and who doesn't.'

'I can imagine,' the stranger said. 'But, if your projectors are active, someone's feeding them the landscape of their unconscious mind. A landscape that includes flying white monsters.' He pointed at the banners above them, each one emblazoned with the white-raven logo of Lawal's company.

'A rival,' Carl said. 'I know Elon Musk was tweeting –'

'It's more personal than that,' the man said. 'The creatures had your face. You can't tell me that's business. That's –'

Lawal held up a hand. 'I already know who it is.'

The man looked surprised. 'You do?'

'Yes,' she said, and that fractional smile disappeared. 'It's my son.'

There was a doorway set into the tower, barely more than a sliver between two massive blocks of ice. Bill approached it warily. It took effort, real effort, not to test every step with her toes before she took it. *Hard light*, she told herself for the hundredth time. If it looked real, it was real.

She had to turn sideways to slip through the gap. As she did so, a jut of ice caught her jumper and tore it.

Real enough, she thought, and was not reassured.

Inside was a bare space. The floor was cobbled with ice-glazed stones, the ceiling disappearing off into darkness.

The walls were dark stone beneath a film of frost. Archways led off to other rooms, the intricate carvings on their surfaces twisting as if being worked on by invisible sculptors even as she watched. She moved closer, and faces emerged from the stone, blurry and half finished. They almost looked like . . .

'Give them a minute.'

Bill jumped and spun round. Behind her back, the empty chamber had changed. The gap through which she had entered the tower had vanished, and the room had rearranged itself into a spectacularly long hall, its limits lost in shadow.

At its centre was a throne of sharp black ice, and sitting on that throne was a boy.

He couldn't have been more than twelve, and was dressed in a We Create Futures hoodie and jeans; the red of his sweatshirt almost too bright in the gloom. There was a trail of We Create Futures stickers up his arm, as if he had stuck them on one by one, out of boredom.

Gleaming from his temples was a silver circlet.

'Give what a minute?' Bill asked carefully.

'The carvings,' he said, pointing. 'They up the resolution when you're looking at them, then lower it when you're not. Saves processing power. The holo-emitters really aren't meant to be stretching so far.'

'Huh,' she said. 'You seem very well informed.'

He shrugged. 'This is all coming from me. My memories. All I have to do is focus on them and they become real.' He tapped the circlet on his brow with the kind of exaggerated nonchalance that Bill recognised as pretty much standard issue for an adolescent schoolboy. Or for the Doctor, come to that.

She adopted the same air too, folding her arms and looking around at the icy architecture. So what if she'd been kidnapped by pterodactyl-esque creatures with the face of a famous inventor? So what if she'd been lost in a living illusion that looked like a cross between Narnia and a heavy-metal band's album cover? Fear was just another tool at your belt. That was another lesson she'd learned with the Doctor. *Use the fear when it's useful. Ignore it when it's not.*

'So,' she said. 'Is this a good memory or a bad one?'

'All I have are bad memories,' the boy said. It was the kind of thing you said when you were twelve, and Bill had to remind herself that it didn't make it any less true to him. There had been times in her life when she would have said the same thing and would have been telling the truth. She didn't want to think about what her memory landscape would have looked like then.

He leaned forward, suddenly animated. 'What do you do? What were you bringing to the conference? Robotics? Energy efficiency? That last one is really what we're looking for.'

We? 'Bit of everything,' Bill said, unsure what the right answer here was. 'Had a poetry lecture last week.'

The boy scowled. 'Poetry? That's stupid.'

Bill shrugged. 'You'd be surprised.' As it turned out, the Arcturan ambassador had been quite partial to Byron, and had ended up letting the Doctor and Bill out of the guillotine in return for an introduction. 'You're looking for energy scientists? Why?'

'To stabilise the projectors, obviously,' he said. 'They can't keep up something this complex for long. I've disengaged the safety protocols, but eventually that's just going to blow us all up. So someone who could fix that would be good.'

'Oh,' Bill said. 'Sure. Obviously.'

And maybe it was talking about science. Maybe Bill's brain had been working away on it in the background and was only now providing an observation. But Bill had seen that expression before. It seemed like invention ran in the family.

'I'm Bill,' she said. 'And I know what you mean about bad memories.'

There was a crack in the boy's nonchalance. Bill could hear it.

'Ebi. Ebi Lawal. What do you know about bad memories?'

'Lots,' she said, and meant it. 'Lost my mum when I was little. There was a long time there when I couldn't sort out the bad memories from the good. Took a while, but eventually I was far enough away from them . . . and her . . . to see that there were good memories to be had. Now, it's those good memories that keep me going on the bad days.'

The darkness behind Ebi shivered and warped, like a stain of poisonous black mould on the air. 'Really?'

'Yes,' she said, laying the word down as carefully as she had laid down her steps when she wasn't sure what was real and what was fake. 'Believe me.'

He nodded slowly. 'I think that's the problem.'

'What is?' Bill asked.

The curtain of darkness pulled back. Bill saw row after row of cells, barred with ice. Most were empty. A handful were not. She saw the woman and old man who had been taken when Bill had. She saw a dozen of those icy gargoyles clinging to the walls of the tower, clicking and chirruping like bats.

And she saw that the boy did not sit on a throne at all. He sat in the lap of Adeyemi Lawal.

Not the haughtily precise woman from all the banners, but a twelve-foot-tall replica carved out of the same gritty grey ice as the tower itself. As Bill watched in horror, the throne's ice ran and re-formed into the folds of a long black gown. Long fingers curled protectively round the boy, and a face appeared, hard and sharp as a temple idol, crowned by translucent spikes of obsidian and jet.

'My mother's right here,' the boy said.

'Think of a hall of mirrors at a funfair,' Adeyemi Lawal said. She was stalking between discarded inventions as she spoke, lifting them, examining them, and then setting them down again. It reminded Carl of her earlier assessments, deciding who to invest in and who to reject. The crowd outside clearly thought so too, their awed murmuring audible even through the thick glass.

The stranger – the *Doctor*, as he had introduced himself – was watching her too.

'The hallways loop back and forth,' she continued. 'And though you're not *physically* that far away from other people, they are hidden by the bends and the curves of the loops, even as the reflections create the *image* of distance around you. You could be standing just metres apart, yet –'

'Seeing something completely different,' the Doctor said, still book-ended by Lawal's security detail. 'That's good. And accurate. I like that. Normally my explanations just sound good, and any resemblance to what's actually happening is coincidental. I might save that one for later.'

Lawal knelt to pick through a nest of cabling.

'Also,' he said. 'You want the one to your left. With the red duct tape.'

She looked up. 'Excuse me?'

He pointed. 'And you'll want the trans-ecliptic resonator from that box over there. Noticed it when I came in. Plus that hyper-attuner matrix there.'

Lawal's eyes narrowed. 'You think you know what I'm building.'

'I *know* I know,' the Doctor said. 'Someone inside the projections doesn't see the whole picture, but the network of emitters has to, or the whole thing doesn't work. They have to know exactly where the people inside the projections are, so they can arrange the image around them. You're trying to hack into that network to locate Bill and your son.'

'No,' she said. 'I'm going to momentarily interrupt the signal so I can see where they are for myself. And I don't need your help,' she said, though Carl noticed she did reach down for the red-marked cabling.

'I got to read up on you a little bit,' the Doctor said. 'You've been doing this for a long time. Working on your own. Being the best. Being the smartest. Other people just get in the way, don't they? Unless you need an extra pair of hands to pass you a tablet or hold a torch or get impressed by your timeship.'

'Timeship?' Lawal asked.

'The point is, you're wrong. You're not wrong about a lot, but you're wrong about this. Other people don't get in the way. They're another viewpoint. And that viewpoint is always useful. I can help. I *need* to help.'

'Why?' she said.

'Because one of the many, many people who taught me that lesson is in there, and I need to get her back.'

There was a long moment of silence, and then she let out a sigh, throwing the Doctor the tablet she was holding. 'The blueprints are all there.'

Carl stepped forward. 'Preliminary and proprietary, of course, so you'll have to sign a non-disclosure agreement.'

The Doctor stepped round him as if he wasn't there, eyes fixed on the screen of the tablet, which had begun to flash red. 'Now, I'm not a scientist or anything . . . Oh wait. Yes I am. Tell me, just how large an explosion should I be associating with the words "power source critical"?'

'My God,' Carl said. 'That could take out the entire block.'

'Don't be dramatic,' Lawal said. 'Just the building, I imagine. And everyone in it. Doctor?'

'Yes?'

'Get to work.'

'Did *she* send you?'

The world had shimmered and changed again. And, while Bill couldn't say she exactly missed the grimdark tower with its leering carvings and icy shadows, at least it had made more sense than what was now before her.

The apartment wasn't much bigger than the one Bill shared with her foster-mum. It was rundown in a warm, lived-in kind of way, the couch sagging beneath its throws, the walls painted blue several tenants ago. It had been decorated for Christmas, clearly on a budget – the tinsel limp and the wreath yellowing at the edges. With the practised eye of a student renter, Bill could see the places where somebody had slapped on another slightly mismatched coat of blue to hide the marks and spills.

The tower had been trying to be scary, in a very twelve-year-old kind of way, but the failed normality of the apartment was far more frightening. It wasn't just that only three walls of the room had materialised around them, like a doll's house. It wasn't even the Ice-Mother looming over them like a grotesque puppetmaster ready to play make-believe.

It was the stain that consumed one entire wall, bubbling black under its skin of paint, pulsing like a telltale heart.

'I *said* –' the boy sat up on his perch, and the bruise of mould frothed and popped – 'did my mother send you?' His voice was tight with paranoia. He seemed to have forgotten that he'd been the one who kidnapped Bill.

None of this is real, she thought. *All of it is real.*

'No,' she said. 'I didn't even know she had a son.'

'That's the problem,' he spat. The Ice-Mother growled in sympathy, a bass rumble that set the whole structure shaking. Bill was trying very hard not to look at the towering monster. Looking at her made the fear a lot harder to control. Worse, it made her think of her own mum, and that made her equal parts sad and angry. The circlet glinted on the boy's head. *He has no idea how lucky he is.*

'What's the problem?' she asked, trying to figure out a course of action.

'Nobody knows I exist,' he said. 'Mum says it's a security issue. She says our lives should be our lives. The world should be kept at arm's length. That's why we still live in her crummy old apartment. That's why I get tutored instead of going to a real school. She spends her life presenting at expos and conferences and media events and I sit in the hotel room like a . . . phone charger. Ready for when she needs me and abandoned when she doesn't.'

'*She forgot your birthday. Remember that?*' The Ice-Mother should have sounded evil. She should have sounded like a vicious avalanche. But she didn't. She sounded small, and hurt, and frustrated. She sounded like Ebi.

Bill knew that inner voice too. *Why is it always easier to remember the bad, rather than the good?*

'Yeah,' Ebi said. 'I remember.'

'*You were nine. She was launching a new phone design. Do you think she even remembers that she let you down?*'

'Why don't you ask her?' Bill said.

The Ice-Mother's head whipped round with a hiss of dislodged frost. Ebi scrubbed the back of his hand across his eyes. 'What?'

'You can ask her,' Bill said. 'That's not a luxury everybody has. Your memory is one side of the story. Do you know hers?'

It was the wrong thing to say. Ebi jumped from the Ice-Mother's lap, stalking forward with fists clenched. 'That's *all* I hear! That's the only version that ever gets told!

She even used this place in her presentation, like a . . . a . . . prop. Like a movie backdrop for her origin story, when really it's –'

His voice caught in his throat, just as the whole chamber suddenly dissolved in a snowstorm of static. For just a moment, Bill saw the whole auditorium through rippling veils of translucent hard-light. She saw how close the door was, and how it might as well have been on the moon. She saw the Doctor, and Adeyemi Lawal bent over a bolted-together collection of antennae and circuitry, and she saw the look on the inventor's face when she spotted her son and the monstrosity looming behind him.

'Is that . . .' Lawal's voice was faint, though whether that was due to distance or horror Bill couldn't tell. 'Is that how you see me?'

And then they were gone. Bill rushed forward, but came up short against a wall of stone.

'Ebi,' she said. The Ice-Mother was growing, her fingers sharpening to claws, great jagged icicles rising like armour from her shoulders and chest. 'Listen to me. If you don't stop, then your story will be the one that gets told. You win the argument. She is who you think she is.'

The boy scowled. 'Good!'

'Well, that's just it. Do you want her to be?'

Another blizzard of pixels, through which Bill could see the Doctor and Lawal, closer now, fighting to get through. She had to give them time. She had to make Ebi *see*.

'Do you want to be right about your mother? Do you want this to be the version of her that's true?' She stepped closer, careful now, aware of the Ice-Mother's eyes boring into her, the memory-creature now nearly half the size of the tower itself. 'Because I remember my mother as a saint, Ebi. I remember her as the best person I ever knew, and I would give all those good memories up if I could have one *new* moment with her today.'

Ebi was close now, close enough for Bill to see the pain in his eyes.

'If I had the chance to choose between memories and a real mother, no matter how real those memories felt, I know which one I'd pick.'

'Ebi!'

A hand found Bill's shoulder, and she whirled to find the Doctor. He caught her up in a hug, then composed himself. 'Well done, Bill.'

'You heard us?'

'All of it,' he said, looking past Bill at the Lawals. 'I hope she heard it too.'

The tower had vanished, replaced by a million swirling pixels. Now there was just the apartment, the pulsing void-black stain, and the gargantuan, growling Ice-Mother.

'Ebi,' the real Adeyemi Lawal said. Her composure was gone, replaced by bitter anger. 'Stop this right now.'

'This memory,' he snapped, pointing at the stain. 'You took this memory. Last Christmas, when we fought and I threw a glass at the wall. You took that, and you used it as promotional material.'

The stain, Bill thought. Just a tiny thing, and yet it had grown and grown until it was a darkness big enough to drown them both.

Lawal shook her head. 'That's not . . . that isn't . . .'

'To embarrass me. To make me feel bad.'

'Carl thought I was using it as well,' she said, and wiped a hand angrily across one eye in a gesture that was so like Ebi's earlier it made Bill's heart hurt. 'But I didn't mean for that memory to come up at all. It's just been eating at me for this long, and I haven't been able to think of anything else.'

'Because . . .' Ebi's voice was suddenly uncertain. 'Because of what I did?'

'No,' she said. 'Because of how badly I reacted. Because of how badly I always react.' She shook her head. 'I'm sorry.'

'It's OK,' he said, looking up at the mountainous form of the Ice-Mother above them, her blades looming like sickle moons. 'I'm sorry too.'

And then he reached up to the circlet and snapped it in half.

After the darkness of the winter hellscape, the sunshine outside was terribly bright. Bill pulled out her own sunglasses, and she and the Doctor found a bench to sit on. Security was trying to stop people from going back into the convention centre en masse. Lots of people were taking photos.

'Do you think they'll be all right?' Bill asked.

Bill had been expecting a tearful hug when the holographic landscape had dissolved, but the Lawals weren't that kind of family. Instead, the two of them had just stared at each other, as if Bill and the Doctor weren't there. That was the thing. The day had been saved, all right. *Today*, at least. Everything else is up to them.

The Doctor shrugged. 'I think they have a better chance of it now that they're actually talking, instead of just remembering all the horrible things they've said to each other. After that, it's up to them. Which is how it should be.'

'Just for a second in there,' Bill said, 'I thought I might have had it easier having a mum who's just memories. I'd win every argument. She'd always agree with me. But after seeing the reality . . .'

'You have both, Bill,' the Doctor said. 'Never forget that. Now, what say I bring you to an actual sci-fi space cannon?'

Bill grinned. 'I'd like that.'

'Good. Now, your typical sci-fi space cannon works like a funfair hall of mirrors . . .'

4

FOR THE GIRL WHO HAS EVERYTHING

RUN
314

Section 314 of UNIT sits under the Tower of London, and both of its doors are locked.

The first door is located behind a modest reception area seemingly no different from the reception area of Section 315 next door, or indeed from any other reception area in this part of the Tower. The grey of the floor tiles and the beige hue of the ceiling lights are standard government issue, as are the cheap plastic chairs in a line against the wall. The reception area is windowless, which is not uncommon, and a single vent keeps stale air in weak rotation around the glass-fronted counter and the three free-standing shelves at the back.

A casual observer might note the OUT OF SERVICE sign on the ticket dispenser and the skin of dust on the counter and conclude that Section 314 does not see a lot of traffic. They might assume that the department is forgotten, or neglected, or that it has no purpose at all. However, that conclusion would be a mistake. This is not the fault of the casual observer. This room has never seen a casual observer, and no casual observer has ever seen it.

Section 314 is the Grey Archive, and it is one of the most dangerous rooms on Earth.

It is not the only archive beneath the Tower. There is the Red Archive – the list of entities that have threatened Earth before and may do so again – and the Blue Archive, where every transmission between humans and alien-kind is pored over for future diplomatic advantage. There is the Black Archive – the ultimate repository for extraterrestrial technology deemed lethal enough to be locked away forever.

Section 314's abandoned atmosphere is more than a disguise. It is a mission statement. Beyond the careful blandness lies the most advanced equipment government money can buy, operated by the sharpest minds UNIT can hire, borrow or steal. Every inch of the archive – from the secrets lurking on its shelves to its curated facade of neglect – has been built to the precise specifications of the greatest and most paranoid minds of the human race. All for one simple purpose: to test extraterrestrial artefacts for use, value and danger.

However, despite all this, despite the extensive perimeter defences and the inner precautions against accident or contamination or disaster, the design of the Grey Archive has one fatal flaw.

Section 314 has two doors.

Its designers are only aware of one.

And, at 7.28 p.m. on Christmas Eve, the second door unlocks.

17:56.

Petronella Osgood is annoyed.

Not at the clock. She likes the clock. The clock is one of hers. Built from prototype psychic paper and scavenged Nestene plastic, it shows you the time. Which, yes, is a clock's basic purpose – nothing hugely special there – but this clock reads *you* as you read it, and shows you whatever time you need to see, anywhere in the galaxy. There are further uses too, once Osgood figures them out. Word is the top brass is thinking of implementing it UNIT-wide. Osgood is proud of the clock. It isn't bad, for her first month on the job.

No, what Osgood is annoyed at is mostly Christmas and slightly herself.

'It's not going to go any faster if you keep staring at it, Osgood,' Douglas calls from his desk. His briefcase is on his lap.

'Unless it does,' Blair adds. He has edged his chair outwards, hunching over his briefcase in the manner of a sprinter waiting for the starter's pistol. 'Does it?'

'No,' Osgood says wearily. 'At least, I don't think so. I still have a couple of tests left to run.'

'Well,' Niki says, stretching, 'if they're not done now, they can wait until after Christmas. It's two minutes to six. I say we call it. Happy holidays!'

Everyone bolts, grabbing coats and stowing work tablets in desks. Osgood doesn't blame them. From where they are, the reception area is at least half an hour's walk away.

Architecture inside the Grey Archive is . . . complicated. Not as you enter, of course. Section 314's reception appears as government issue as they come. It's only when you make your way to the shelves that things get . . . well, UNIT. Walking past the shelves takes you to the back of the room in three long strides. Walk *between* the shelves and you end up somewhere else entirely.

Between the first and second shelves there is a corridor so long it shouldn't fit beneath the Tower of London, let alone in the room you just left. This corridor leads to the office in which Osgood now sits: an open-plan sprawl of blocky analysis equipment and recently abandoned desks, each with its own little dash of personality – a potted plant, a family photo.

But it's walking between the second and third shelves that yields the real treasure: mile after mile of storerooms packed with crates and chests and artefacts of alien origin. The more obviously dangerous of these sit in lead boxes or hang in the glittering beams of stasis-lock. Others languish in government-issue cardboard boxes – partially because cursory scans have declared them inactive, and partially because there is only so much lead to go around.

The Grey Archive is understaffed and underfunded. The only thing they're not short of is room, thanks to experimental spatial-folding technology borrowed or stolen from a race so advanced it gives Osgood a headache. Whatever the source, this technology has given the Grey Archive the architecture of a fairy tale. Turning a corner then turning back won't necessarily return you to the same spot. Doors disappear if you approach them from the wrong direction. Clearance here is less about passcodes and access cards and more about learning the routes of an ever-changing maze, about keeping a living map in your head.

It's weirdly poetic, in the way that only old and tired government institutions can be – the Grey Archive's business is uncertainty, so much so it's baked into the very walls. Only the Chief Scientific Officer of UNIT knows how big the Grey Archive really is, but speculation puts it at roughly the size of London.

Niki pauses at the door. 'You sure you don't want to come for a drink or something?'

Osgood's phone pings. She doesn't need to look at it to know what it says. 'I'm actually quite happy here. Thank you though.'

Niki sighs. 'Just don't get lost. And, Petronella?'

'Yes?'

'Merry Christmas.'

In a storeroom deep in the Grey Archive, there is a black metal box that looks a little like a coffin and a little like a womb. The green liquid that fills it has been inert since UNIT acquired it in the incident referred to as 'The Sontaran Stratagem'.

At 19:05 the liquid begins to bubble.

At 19:15 it begins to seethe.

And, at 19:28, the surface of the liquid is broken by a hand that turns in the air like a flower seeking light.

The box is a Sontaran cloning pool. From above, it very much resembles a door.

Osgood's phone pings again. Nova must be getting desperate.

Sister.

Ping.

You're being unreasonable.

Petronella Osgood is not being unreasonable. She is very rarely unreasonable, actually, because the Osgoods are an old UNIT family, and to them reason is important. Reason is why Petronella Osgood did her Christmas shopping in October, but now has fifteen new messages from her sister, who didn't.

Ping.

Look, I just forgot, OK?

Ping.

And I don't have time to go in to town now. You know what it is like on Christmas Eve!

Nova Osgood is entirely unreasonable. Being unreasonable suits her. The laws of physics touch Nova Osgood lightly. She gets away with stuff in a way that Petronella never has. It's something to do with her hair, and her dimple, and most likely something to do with her name, which, like her smile, is a blinding cosmic event.

Petronella is a scientist. It would be unreasonable for her to think that names had anything to do with personalities, which is why she tries not to think about how her sister's name refers to something fleeting and spectacular, while Petronella is a Dutch name that means 'rock'.

Ping.

This happens every year. *Every* year.

There's an air of healthy competition in the Osgood household when it comes to Christmas presents, and every year Petronella Osgood comes out on top. There is planning. There is research. She takes it *seriously*. But, every year, Nova doesn't.

Petronella, please! Just nick Dad something from the office!

Frank Osgood isn't UNIT. He could have been. Their father has built things in his shed out of old radios and bits of string that would put half the UNIT staff to shame. He's never explained why he didn't apply, why he'd rather spend his time building electron telescopes and scanning for evidence of aliens than ask any one of a dozen family members who could not only provide said evidence but also probably a home address. But maybe that's the reason. Maybe he *likes* the mystery, and UNIT is all about taking the mystery apart.

Either way, it's this odd little detail that makes Petronella go the extra mile when it comes to her dad's Christmas presents. She sources rare photographs of suspected alien activity. She finds blueprints for Mars probes that don't officially exist.

But she never, ever steals from work.

This Christmas, she managed to source the journal of US pilot Kenneth Arnold, the very first civilian to report seeing a UFO. There are hundreds of confiscated pilot reports in the Grey Archive, but she found this one using her own contacts and her own money, because doing otherwise would be cheating. Cheating is Nova's thing. Petronella, like her namesake and unlike her sister, is extremely subject to the laws of physics, and this Christmas she has decided to use this to her advantage.

I'll go have a poke around the storerooms where there's no phone reception, she thinks. *And if that makes me miss Nova's messages, well . . . it's hardly my fault, is it?*

Stealing things from work. The *idea.*

The green liquid bubbles and froths.

Sontaran technology, like everything about the Sontaran Empire, is deceptively simple. They are a clone race, grown in their millions and imprinted from birth with a hunger for war and victory. As such, their technology is designed to be efficient. Intuitive design is essential when you're born on a battlefield.

The UNIT technicians seeking to deactivate the cloning pool were easily able to locate and remove its power cube. The biodata storage drive came out as easily as the magazine of a gun.

However, Sontarans also believe in fail-safes. They believe in victory at any cost. Any clone can be a hero. Any defeat can be a door to revenge. All cloning pools are designed with a backup generator and reserve biodata, kept at minimum power to avoid detection. At full capacity and with a living, connected source of DNA, Sontaran cloning pools can create a near-perfect copy. In the absence of these essential components, however, this particular cloning pool has created monsters instead.

No two are alike. The pool did whatever it could with the scraps of code rotting in its servers. One clone is hideous, with muscly human-length arms dragging behind its squat Sontaran frame. Another is so tall it scrapes the ceiling, spine curved like the blade of a scythe. The third crouches low on knuckled feet, its two heads blinking brand-new eyes.

And the fourth simply waits as the pool gives a final, churning gurgle. Something bobs to the surface of the liquid.

It is a simple spiked disk. Cloning pools cannot produce metal, so it is made of hard Sontaran bone.

A mark of rank. These things are important, culturally.

The fourth clone picks it up and affixes it to its bare chest.

'Sontar,' it slurs, 'ha.'

Turn right, then left at the end of the corridor.

Osgood consults her tablet, scrolling through page upon page of confiscated alien tech. By her count, she has taken 113 turns into the archive's vast stores, each change of direction like a link in a chain.

Take the second door. No, the third, because it's a Tuesday after six.

Osgood steps through the door, closes it, then opens it again on a completely different corridor from the one she just left. She finds herself wondering, as she often does, whether the spatial-folding technology simply replicates the same fifty feet of corridor, or whether UNIT spends an utterly ludicrous amount of money on grey carpet.

The little storeroom she enters isn't technically her office. She's too junior to have one of her own. However, nobody seems to have noticed the little desk she's set up between teetering stacks of boxes, or the prototype Nestene clock she's hung on the wall, or the little Christmas tree her dad gave her.

Everyone on the team has their areas of interest. Douglas likes weapons. Niki has written fascinating studies on Abzorbaloff tech. And everyone but Osgood scrambles for the 'good' stuff, the career-changing artefacts. Anything that might get them noticed by the Chief Scientific Officer. Some technicians treat the Grey Archive like a stepping stone. An airlock. A place to pass through to get to their next assignment.

There's a lot of . . . tat in the Grey Archive. That's why they need so much room. Everything that comes into contact with aliens must be analysed. There are as many boxes here dedicated to Cardiff quarry gravel as there are potentially world-ending threats. That's why Osgood loves it. She has exactly the same amount of interest in a Silurian tea-set as she does in antimatter drives.

More than that, this *is* an airlock. It's transformative. It's a monument to how anything can be changed by a brush with the majestic.

This is a place where rocks meet the sky.

With a smart little flourish of her sleeves, Osgood selects a random box from the stacks surrounding her desk. She could just look up its barcode on the tablet, but sometimes it's nice to do a lucky dip. You never know what you might find.

'After all,' she says to herself, 'it's Christmas Eve.'

That's when she notices that the clock has changed.

Which is not, by itself, a reason to panic. Changing is what clocks do. Except that now, instead of Nestene-plastic numbers on a psychic-paper face, its display is flashing a single word.

RUN.

RUN.

RUN.

It is, Osgood realises as the first monster kicks down the door, telling her the time.

Elsewhere, the fourth clone is exploring.

It has discovered, first of all, that there are barriers to victory. This is not unexpected. The cloning pool had no access to a live subject on which to base its clones, and no Sontaran mainframe to educate them. Compromises had to be made. The fourth clone, human and handsome and more intelligent by far than its siblings, is that compromise. It does not know where it is. It knows nothing about the Grey Archive, or humanity, or Earth. It understands hardly anything of the empire that created it, bar the necessity for victory.

But it is an extremely quick learner.

Now, it stalks through the corridors, occasionally sniffing the air. Everything looks the same. Grey carpet, white walls, storeroom after storeroom packed with locked crates or boxes containing equipment that seems either useless or lacking in decent Sontaran simplicity.

There are trees too, which the clone finds strange – trees set up in corners and hung with glowing bulbs. *Frivolous*, it decides, after eating a couple. *Frivolous and deserving of destruction*.

Nevertheless, for the purpose of navigation, the clone memorises the placement of every sparkling wall hanging and every flashing light. It has never heard of spatial folding, but it can tell that there is something wrong with the architecture here, and it is already devising countermeasures.

There is always victory to be had. All the clone must do is find it.

Its siblings have been sent out in different directions, to return with their own data. They probably won't. The fourth clone knows this, and the knowledge pains it. It was created apart from them, and despite their programmed understanding of rank and obedience, their base hungers will undoubtedly lead them off course.

The fourth clone is very smart, and very alone. This is the way of those chosen to lead.

It smiles suddenly as a thought occurs to it, then it turns gracefully on a heel to pad back the way it came. It has a very good memory. Retracing its steps is easy. Tilting its head back, it lets out a long, low roar.

Maybe its siblings will hear it and return. Maybe they won't.

But, if the fourth clone finds the pool's power cube, it can make all the siblings it needs.

Osgood has always meant to clean her storeroom one day. The fact that she hasn't saves her life.

The beast is massively muscled. The door doesn't slow it at all. What does slow it, however, is hitting the three crates of dwarf-star alloy stacked in front of Osgood's desk. There is a particularly nasty snap as the creature rebounds. The crates don't even shudder. Osgood winces. She doesn't know a lot about dwarf-star alloy, except that once she stubbed her toe on it and felt it for weeks.

RUN, the clock flashes at her. *RUN*.

Oh, right. Yes.

It's too cramped in here to run, so Osgood has to do a sort of awkward sideways scamper between the boxes and out past the monster as it writhes on the floor. It's only at the door that she pauses, wondering whether she should also take the clock.

I knew there were other uses, she thinks with surprising calm. *Maybe I should –*

That's when the second creature grabs her from behind.

Osgood's feet leave the ground. She spins, catching a lazy, panoramic view of a snarling thing filling the corridor behind her, and then she lands in a graceless explosion of pain.

It threw me, Osgood thinks from the floor, and for a second is absurdly glad Nova wasn't there to see it. *I can't believe it threw me.*

It is gaunt, and sinewy, and so tall it needs to hunch over to keep clear of the ceiling. Something about its squat skull strikes Osgood as familiar, but inevitably her gaze is more drawn to the blood dripping from its claws. There is pain, sharp and sudden, in her left arm.

The creature advances . . . then freezes, as a distant roar echoes down the hallway.

Osgood freezes too. It is not a sound one might imagine coming from a human throat.

The creature blinks at her through blood-marbled eyes, then turns and pads away. The squat monster follows, pausing only to pop its shoulder back in place and give Osgood a resentful glare.

She resists the urge to apologise, then gets up herself.

Horrible creatures leaving? Good, she thinks. *Horrible creatures leaving because they've been summoned by something worse? Less good.*

This, Osgood decides, would never happen to Nova.

The fourth clone does not look up at the sound of footsteps. Instead, it continues to glare miserably at the crates it has torn apart.

Drip.

Nothing.

Nothing but trinkets and baubles. Each one stinks of failure. Of defeat. There is no greater curse. No greater fear for a race that is bred for victory.

Drip.

This place is enormous. Deserted. They could search it for years and never come close to finding the power cube. The bone disk affixed to the clone's chest feels heavy as a neutron star. It was created to find victory, and instead –

Drip.

With adder-quickness, the fourth clone reaches out to catch the drop of blood before it hits the floor. Slowly, very slowly, it raises its head.

Sontaran features are not built for a wide range of expressions, and yet somehow the second clone manages embarrassment. It raises its bloody claw and points back the way it came.

There is someone else here.

Someone native to this place. Someone who knows how it works. Someone who will share the location of the power cube, and then the clone will ram an empire's worth of soldiers down this grey little planet's throat.

'Go,' the fourth clone growls. Words are coming to it. That is good. It will need them for the interrogation. 'Bring them to me.'

Petronella Osgood is taking stock.

She is also hiding under a table in the storeroom beside her office. It isn't a long-term strategy, but it's the only thing she can think to do right now. It's Christmas Eve. The place is deserted. Her phone doesn't work and the messaging software on her tablet is locked to internal. An external attack should have activated the perimeter security system, but it clearly hasn't, and Osgood has no idea how to activate the system herself.

I've . . . Her arm hurts a lot. She is fighting tears. *I've only been here a month.*

She takes a puff of her inhaler, and the familiar chalky taste calms her enough to peel back her tattered sleeve and take a look at her wounded arm.

OK. OK. It isn't life-threatening . . . Although, the sight of it spins her head a little. *Focus.* She needs to clean it. Bind it. There's probably a risk of infection too, but Osgood is going to have to survive first.

I should be at home. The thought stings her as she rummages through boxes, looking for bandages. *The house all thick and soft with the smell of mulled wine, things burning because Dad's distracted by thinking about how to redesign the oven.*

And Nova – *bloody Nova* – would have her feet up, and Petronella would be peeling the –

'Sontarans,' she says aloud, suddenly remembering the taut olive skin and domed heads from her Major Alien Threat briefings. 'They're Sontarans.'

Clone warriors. Class 5 Aggression Rating. But Sontarans are all short . . . Aren't they? The thing that had thrown her was anything but.

This is something new, or something old come again, or something she hasn't got the clearance to know about, running around the most dangerous warehouse on Earth. And all that is standing in its way is Petronella Osgood, tear-smeared and anxious, one whole month on the job. Not Douglas, who spends his spare time practising with Ice Warrior swords, or Niki, or her dad. What is she supposed to do, just stumble upon –

Osgood stares into the box.

There isn't anything special about the scarf, except that there seems to be rather too much of it. In the washed-out light of the Grey Archive, its bright yarn seems to almost glow.

Osgood is alone. She is facing an unknown foe, with unknown plans, and has nothing to defend herself with. She is out of her depth. She is in grave danger.

This, she decides, *is what being in UNIT is all about.*

One end of the scarf is tied tight round her arm to slow the bleeding. There's still about five metres of it left, so Osgood picks up some scissors . . . and then, on some unknown impulse, decides to wrap the excess round her neck instead.

It's time to go to work.

Simplicity, the fourth clone thinks. *It all comes down to simplicity.*

That's why enemies underestimate the Sontarans. Other races love complexity. They wear it like a badge of honour. The designers of this place obviously believed complexity would protect them but, as always, simplicity cuts through.

It's the blood. The identical stretches of corridor might fool normal scanners, but all the clones have are their claws and their senses and – like any predator worth its salt – they can smell the prey's blood in the air. It is, the fourth clone imagines, a delightfully simple solution. A Sontaran solution.

It looks forward to meeting one some day.

The creatures lope along a corridor, pausing every so often to sniff and snort. It is so dead and grey here that the smell of fresh blood stands out on the air like scarlet paint on a white wall. They follow the smell through cluttered storerooms and conference rooms, turning left and right almost by instinct.

The prey must be panicking. It's left smears on nearly every doorway they pass.

The fourth clone freezes, hand hovering above a door handle. There's a fingerprint of human blood on it. That was why it chose this door over the other three in the room. Stepping backwards lightly, it motions the third clone forward. The clone obeys, the growls of its two heads not quite in sync, seemingly unworried by its siblings taking positions as far away as possible.

It sniffs at the blood, then it turns the handle.

Many races have invented gravity bubbles. There is a whole room full of them in the Grey Archive. Osgood has chosen one with RAF printed on the side. It feels like a good omen.

And, as the third clone opens the door, it activates, and a device meant to propel a Mark IV Spitfire through the vacuum of space ignites in the confines of a government-standard corridor.

Osgood doesn't stop to watch the results. She is already running, as fast and as quietly as she can.

The fourth clone sighs, picking himself up off the floor. Ahead, where there was once a wall and a door and a very briefly surprised clone, there is now a perfect sphere carved out of the architecture. He wonders briefly whether the device *im*ploded or *ex*ploded . . . And then he wonders when he started thinking of himself as a *he*.

A few centimetres away, the floor ends in a ragged fringe of carpet. Exposed wiring sparks. Masonry dust drizzles from the ceiling. Carefully, the clone leans forward.

What he should be looking at is the floor below. That's how buildings work. But instead there is an infinite ravine of corridors, all attaching and reattaching to each other like surgery conducted by invisible hands. It looks a little like clockwork, except clockwork doesn't churn reality and make you want to throw up.

A few metres across the gap, the corridor continues. There is a spot of blood on the carpet.

Mocking them.

Enticing them.

It's too much for the first clone. Growling hungrily, the squat creature flings itself across the gap and down the corridor like a cannonball of muscle and stringy drool.

'Gravity bubble,' the fourth clone murmurs, watching his sibling smash down a door head first. 'Provides gravitational lift by anchor-linking to the planet's core. I imagine activating one in the midst of a complex spatial fold is rather like poking a stick through the spokes of a bike.' He thinks for a moment. 'Except that the stick is gravity. And the bike is the universe. It's punched a hole right down through the maze.'

The second clone is almost vibrating, caught between the desire to serve and the desire to hunt.

'What . . . mean?'

The fourth clone realises he has no idea. That's the problem when a cloning pool isn't drawing on a live subject for inspiration. It has to use other DNA to plug the gaps. Just as his siblings are a meld between Sontaran biodata and whatever else was in the pool's servers, so too is he a mixture of scraps and fragments and . . . memories. Memories that are not his. Memories of arrogance. Of anger. And of loneliness, so deep and bitter the clone can taste it in the back of his throat.

It is a horribly familiar feeling.

Victory.

Victory must be found. Victory will cure him. The longer he and it are separated, the more his head begins to feel like the swirling vortex below. The more he feels like he might come apart.

'It means,' he says eventually, 'I know how to catch them.'

It is beginning to occur to Osgood that there is such a thing as a plan being too successful.

You want them to chase you, she reminds herself for the fifth time, rummaging through another storeroom for something – anything – that might be useful. *If they're chasing you, they're not thinking about all the alien technology they could be chasing instead.*

Somewhere distant, the squat clone lets out a bestial roar. There is the sound of a door smashing inwards, and another howl, this time of utter frustration.

Two corridors away, Osgood thinks, kneeling under a desk to pick up a polished silver sphere and compare it to the image on her tablet. *Or three maybe?*

There's something a little reassuring about the fact that, for an advanced race of warrior clones, her pursuers don't seem interested in technology more complicated than the claws on the ends of their fingers. Then again, Osgood's only been here a month, and she managed to turn a gravity bubble into a landmine with five minutes and a hairpin. She dreads to think what someone with any actual experience might be capable of.

No, focusing on her is good. *Or it will be, if this is what I think it is . .*

Osgood knows she's been tremendously lucky so far. Her tablet has a list of everything in the archive, but anything really nasty is above her clearance level, a fact which never bothered her before but now feels like a serious gap in her CV. So, she is relying on the archive's rather fantastic backlog, and hoping there are dangerous things here nobody has got to yet, or things that were deemed un-dangerous that she can *re*-dangerous.

What's worrying her is that she seems to be quite good at it.

And then the squat clone bounds on to the desk above her head, and all her other concerns go and hide.

The wood creaks under the clone's weight.

Osgood goes rigid. Afraid to move. Afraid to breathe.

In contrast, the clone is deafening, even at rest. Osgood can hear its sinews flexing under its skin. She can hear the meaty crunch of its joints as it lowers itself into a crouch. She can even hear its heart, bludgeoning itself against the barrel of its chest.

That doesn't sound healthy, thinks the part of her not inwardly screaming in terror. *How long do clones live?*

There is one connector left on the device in her lap – a device that, along with gravity bubbles, would probably be locked away somewhere if the archive wasn't extremely behind. All Osgood can do is stare down at it, even as a long line of drool extends into view from the creature perched inches above her head.

She could just do it. She could just click it in. The plan had been to leave it on the floor for the creature to find, but that's not going to work now.

I'll throw it.

Osgood has only the barest idea of the device's range, but even if she is caught in its effect, isn't that better than dying?

I can't die at Christmas, she thinks, grasping the connector in her shaking fingers. *It'll ruin it for Dad.*

And that's when the tablet in her pocket lets out a cheerful little beep.

A number of things happen in quick succession.

First, Osgood bangs her head on the bottom of the desk.

Second, she slams the connector home and flings the device as far away from her as she can.

Third, the clone lets out a shriek like a strangled cat and lunges so powerfully after the little silver sphere that it upends the entire desk.

Predator instincts, Osgood thinks, with a hint of triumph, before suddenly realising there's about to be what one can only describe as an 'area of effect', and she'd be best off outside of it. She dives across the floor just as the creature, neat as an acrobat, snags the device out of the air and spins to face her, a mad grin on its squashed Sontaran face.

'Weapon!' it barks, holding the silver sphere high.

'Actually,' Osgood says, as it starts to vibrate, 'it's a memory filter.'

'Actually,' Osgood says, as it starts to vibrate, 'it's a memory filter.'

'Actually,' Osgood says, as it starts to vibrate, 'it's a memory filter.'

'Actually,' Osgood says, as it starts to vibrate, 'it's a . . . memory filter,' she finishes, and then shivers from toe to nose as if she's just been dunked in cold water. Everything is swimmy and strange for a moment, then snaps back into focus.

'Must have been on the fringe of it,' she says out loud, more to make sure her brain is working than anything else. 'Which means . . . Oh.'

The squat clone is standing in front of her, still holding the silver sphere. Every other second, it twitches. It has, she realises, the exact expression of someone who has walked into a room and then promptly forgotten what they came in for, over and over again.

'Sorry,' she says, then backs slowly out of the room.

*

Three corridors later, Osgood remembers her tablet. She ducks into a storeroom, inwardly cursing herself for not thinking to put the device on silent when she was hiding from monsters. When she pulls it from her pocket, there's a missed call on the messaging server. The internal server. There's someone else in the archive.

Osgood opens the server – checking the tablet's volume first – then returns the call.

It rings once, twice . . .

Please be security. Please be security.

'Hello?'

Osgood swallows. 'Hello?'

'Please help me!'

The voice is male and terrified. Osgood doesn't recognise it, but that doesn't mean anything. The archive is a big place.

'Stay calm,' Osgood stammers, wondering whether she is speaking to the speaker or to herself. *What do I say? What am I supposed to* – 'What's your name?'

There is a pause.

'Luke. Luke Rattigan.'

'Hi, Luke.' Osgood winces at her own forced cheerfulness. 'I'm Petronella. Listen. We're under –'

The next voice she hears is a low, burbling growl.

'No more chasing. No more tricks. Now, you come. Or we kill this boy.'

The line goes dead. A moment later, a location ping comes through on the server. Osgood stares at it for a very long time, and then brings up the search function on her tablet.

A casual observer might find little difference between the reception of Section 314 and that of Section 315 next door, or indeed from any other reception area in this part of the Tower. The grey of its floor tiles and the beige hue of its ceiling lights are government issue, as are the cheap plastic chairs in a line against the wall.

The swirling vortex the gravity bubble punched through its floor, however, is not.

Petronella Osgood has never really been any good at casually observing things. On her first day here she noticed the tremble in the air, the subsonic hum of hidden machines. And now, stepping out from between the second and third shelves into the reception of Section 314, Osgood can't help but notice that the hum has changed to an angry buzz.

Luke Rattigan stands on the edge of the vortex, dressed in a lab coat, slacks and a slightly mismatched jumper – basically the closest thing the Grey Archive has to a uniform.

The creature hunched behind him is the curved-spine scarecrow who threw Osgood so casually earlier, its head a grinning lump of sinew and meat. It has Osgood's blood on one hand, and Luke's throat in the other.

'It . . .' Luke can barely get a word out around the thing's long fingers. 'It wants a Sontaran power cube. It says if you find it, they'll let us go.'

Osgood's fingers are white where they grip her scarf.

'Want,' the beast growls. 'Want . . .' It pauses, and something Osgood could swear is embarrassment crosses its face. 'Want the . . .'

'The cube,' Luke finishes helpfully. 'Do you know where –'

'Do you think this is the original?' Osgood asks.

The monster blinks. Luke stares at her in shock.

'The corridors. The maze. Did it all start here, before they stretched it out? Or is this room a copy of somewhere else too?'

The creature's claws flex on Luke's neck.

'Petronella, please.'

Osgood takes a careful step towards them. She can feel vertigo wash over her from the swirling vortex between them. It looks like it goes on forever.

'And, if it's a copy, how would we be able to tell?'

The terror vanishes from Luke's face, replaced by a serene, dead calm. It's frightening to watch. Like stagehands emptying a stage.

'How long have you known?'

'I have a good memory for briefings,' Osgood responds. 'Luke Rattigan was a human accomplice to an attempted Sontaran invasion a couple of years ago. That's where UNIT got the deactivated cloning pool that must have made you all.'

'So that's who he is,' the clone says. He's handsome, in a reptilian kind of way. 'That makes sense.' He reaches up and taps his skull. 'It's a little jumbled in here. I have memories. Just fragments, churning around and around. Feels wrong. Feels right. *Luke.*' One of his eyes is twitching. 'And the pool won't be deactivated for long.'

'Well,' Osgood says. 'Yes. I think that was one of Helen's. She's probably going to be in trouble. How are you feeling?'

Luke flinches at the question. The monster is staring at him too, growling like an idling engine, like the unseen machines in the walls.

'The briefing on Sontaran invasions was pretty comprehensive,' Osgood continues. 'Though it didn't mention that they sampled the original Luke's DNA. I wonder, did he know? Luke Rattigan, a prodigy at eighteen, pretty much as smart as the human brain would allow. You look like him. Exactly like him, in fact. And I think you're probably as smart as him too, or you wouldn't have worked out how to get here.'

'The gravity bubble ripped a hole straight down through the spatial folding,' the clone says. 'Navigating by it was easy. Working out how to use the tablet I found was harder, but Luke liked things like that. I think.'

'Very impressive,' Osgood says, trying to keep her voice from shaking. 'What are you, two hours old?'

'I'm clever,' the clone boasts. His smile is bright and chilling, but his jaw is clenched. 'I'm very clever. I am the last, best chance for victory.'

'Ah.' Osgood is at the vortex's edge. She can feel the floor tiles under her feet quiver and warp. 'You don't know then.'

The clone starts forward, before catching himself. Osgood notes the sweat on his brow, the tension thrumming a vein in his neck. 'Know what?'

'That you lost,' Osgood says. 'The original Luke, that is. He lost, and the Sontarans lost, and you ended up just being tat in our archive.'

A long, low growl oozes from between the clone's perfect white teeth.

'I mean, you can't be blamed. I don't even think the original Luke knew who he was dealing with, and you're just an . . . artefact. A recovered save. You couldn't have known.'

'But I *will* know,' the clone hisses. 'You will find us the power cube, and we will switch on the pool, and I will not be alone, and then I will have victory. Perfect victory. Sontar-ha!'

He shouts these last words, and Osgood shrugs nonchalantly, more scared than she's ever been in her life. 'Luke hated being alone too.'

The boy stares at her. There is a genuine, actual monster hunched behind him, a terrible nightmare of claws and blood-red eyes, but Osgood's gaze is fixed on the quiver in Luke's lower lip.

'It ate at him. Made him do terrible things. Search for allies in bad places.'

Petronella Osgood is a reasonable person. Sweeping dramatic statements are more of a Nova thing. But she knows, with an entirely unreasonable sense of certainty, that she will never forgive herself for the words she is about to say. 'I misspoke earlier. I'm sorry. Luke did find victory.'

The clone's voice is childishly hopeful. 'He did?'

'He did,' Osgood says. 'At the end. He found people he was willing to sacrifice himself for. That's how you win. You fight for people.'

Osgood takes the Sontaran power cube from her pocket. It hadn't been that hard to find, in the end. Nobody had thought to lock it away. The technician's note in the manifest on her tablet had said it wasn't dangerous at all.

Luke's eyes widen in shock.

'Victory means nothing if you're alone,' she says, and then she tosses the power cube into the vortex.

The clone doesn't hesitate. He lunges after it, with a predator's grace, and vanishes into the vortex without a word. There is a noise like the feeling of missing a step on the stairs, a smell like the sound of cricking your neck, and something hits Osgood in the chest. She catches it by reflex.

It is a medal, formed of hard white bone.

She looks at it for a moment, then she hears a growl.

'Oh,' she says, as the other clone rises to its full height, spittle hanging from its jaws. 'Oh dear.'

Spatial folding or not, the sound of the shot in the confines of the office is deafening. The beast stiffens, a look of very human surprise on its utterly unhuman features, and then topples forward into the vortex too.

Standing behind it are two soldiers, and UNIT's Chief Scientific Officer.

'Ms Osgood,' Kate Lethbridge-Stewart says, her arms folded. 'Can I have a word?'

'We monitor everything,' Stewart says. 'Well, of course we do.'

They are sitting in her office, which does not have grey floor tiles but polished dark wood. Osgood finds this reassuring. She doesn't particularly want to see the colour grey ever again. This may require a career change, but that feels like a January problem.

A cardboard box sits on the desk between them.

'Everything,' Osgood repeats a little hollowly. She isn't sure how she feels about people knowing what she's just done, even though she is convinced it was necessary.

'Well, yes,' Stewart says. 'Your sister is texting, by the way. She's decided to say that your present is from both of you.'

'Luke –' Osgood begins, but Stewart waves a hand.

'That wasn't Luke Rattigan.'

Osgood has only met Stewart once before, at her very first briefing, when the Chief Scientific Officer gave a five-minute speech about duty that Osgood can still recite by heart. She looks mostly the same as she did then – ice-blonde hair, features sharpened by intellect and alertness. She is, however, now wearing a Christmas jumper, which Osgood finds extremely jarring.

'Sontaran clones don't work fantastically even when they are connected to the host they're copying. He was degrading, even if he didn't know it.'

'I think he knew,' Osgood says.

'Sontarans,' Stewart says, shaking her head. 'All that technological advancement and the only thing they succeeded at was making a Luke Rattigan even unhappier than the original.' She checks a sheet in front of her. 'It took the pool years to rebuild enough scrap DNA for four clones, especially with its processors running low enough to avoid detection. Actually birthing them was what finally spiked our graphs.' Her Christmas jumper has a periodic table done in snowflakes. It says *OH, CHEMIS-TREE*.

'I've always been against the spatial-folding idea. It's nice for storage, but far too complicated in the long run. Lowers response time too, because we have too many corridors to traipse down. I like what you did with the memory filters, though. Must remember that. Ha.'

She says this last without a single trace of humour.

'Can I go home now, please?' Osgood says in a small voice. The bone disc is warm in her hand. *I think I know why you didn't sign up for UNIT now, Dad. Mysteries are safer, sometimes. Mysteries don't smash down your door.*

Stewart snaps to. 'Yes. Of course. And, in January, I'm going to speak to your team directly. About reassignment.'

Osgood stiffens. 'Really?'

Stewart nods. 'I'm putting the Grey Archive on indefinite hiatus. Not your team, of course. We'll be keeping you all on retainer. Spread you out among the different departments. But I think the archive itself will be shelved until we can figure out a better system.'

Osgood isn't sure whether or not that requires an answer, but she is extremely relieved she hasn't lost anybody their job.

'And you'll report directly to me.'

'Sorry?'

'You handled yourself very well,' Stewart says, tapping her lip with a finger. 'I think I could use that initiative.' She's lost in thought. 'I mean, if thieves invade the Black Archive, it just detonates a nuke. Simple, yet effective.'

Osgood checks her phone. It's working again. There are a lot of messages, mostly from Nova. That's a small thing she can focus on, instead of the last thing Stewart said.

'I should go, ma'am.'

'Oh, yes. Of course.' Stewart stands up and shakes Osgood's hand. 'Good work.'

Then she picks up the box containing the Grey Archive and locks it in her desk.

Later, Petronella Osgood sleeps more deeply than she ever has in her life and, like every Christmas morning, she is woken by Nova bouncing on her bed.

'When did you get home?' Nova asks, and then, without waiting for a response, points at the neat stack of presents by the door. 'And you never answered my question. I just assumed it was OK to pop both our names on Dad's card and –'

Petronella looks down at the spiked medal of bone in her hand. It is small and pale, and she would rather not be alone with the story of it in her head. At least, not until she goes back to work.

'You know what?' she says. 'Keep it. I'm going to give him something else.'

5

VISITING HOURS

'Drop your weapon!'

It wasn't the largest gun that had ever been pointed at Rory Pond, but he had to admit that even saying that spoke to some pretty poor life choices.

'It isn't a weapon,' he said wearily. 'It's stuffing.'

He tweaked back the baking tray's tinfoil. The crisped scent of breadcrumbs and sage wafted through Stormcage Containment Facility's visitor clearance area for just a moment, before the air filters whisked it away.

The guard leaned closer, breath snorting out from between its metal fangs. Rory hadn't seen this design before. Last year it had all been holograms – sleek and bright and cheery, like a prison crossed with a mobile-phone shop. The year before, Stormcage had gone digital. Rory found it hard to explain what it felt like to be converted to an email attachment, except to say that he really didn't want to feel it again.

This year, it seemed that Stormcage was favouring the direct approach. The guard was eight feet of pale, ponderous muscle, its face a glittering mass of lenses that clicked and rotated, painting a triangle of targeting lasers over the centre of Rory's Christmas jumper.

'Stuff-ing?' the guard growled.

You couldn't blame it for being confused. Most visitors to Stormcage travelled light. It was a bit like an airport – nobody wanted to spend an hour emptying their pockets for the scanners while everyone else in the queue glared at them. This was true whether you were spending a cheeky weekend in Lanzarote or visiting the most secure prison of the fifty-second century.

And yet, it *was* Christmas.

Rory didn't know if Stormcage got a Christmas. He imagined it might be low down on the list of priorities when you were guarding some of the most dangerous felons in the universe. So, every year, he and Amy tried to bring Christmas to them. Or, at least, to one inmate in particular: their daughter, River Song.

The visitor clearance area was a vast concrete square painted a dazzling antiseptic white. Hulking brutes – much like the one currently pointing its gun at Rory – guarded gleaming white doors that led to what Rory hoped were offices and not interrogation rooms. He had a sudden unpleasant image of the turkey they had cooked being searched for contraband. The poor thing had been through enough already.

'It's just food,' Rory said, indicating the shopping trolley behind him, laden down with roasting dishes, plastic containers and tinfoil-covered bowls. 'And it's already cooked, so lasering it is overkill. I could make you a plate, if you like? Just a little one?'

Just a little plate was Amy Pond's solution to all problems arising between the twenty-fifth of December and the fifteenth of January. They still had leftovers from last year.

I wish Amy was here.

Suddenly, every single guard in visitor clearance snapped to attention, bulky weapons slamming against their chests. Rory turned to see a figure entering through a door, hand raised in greeting.

'Rory Pond.'

The man *gleamed*. That was Rory's first thought. His suit was a pressed and perfect white – a blinding non-shade that blended in so thoroughly with the white walls that, for a single, unnerving second, all Rory saw drifting towards him was a disembodied human head.

'Henrik Chyll, Chief Psychiatrist.' A hand appeared, again seeming disconnected by the brightness of the suit, and after a moment of juggling baking trays Rory took it.

You could say that being a nurse was the opposite of being a soldier. Rory certainly would. He had been both. But there were similarities, and being both a nurse and a soldier had given him a sort of radar for the people who ended up in charge.

There were the kind people – or, rather, the *tired* people. The leaders who were tired from trying to be kind in a job where there was often no kindness to be had. The leaders who cared about those they led. Then, there were the tyrants. The sell-outs. The leaders who saw those they were responsible for as a number, or a nuisance, or both.

Which, Rory wondered, *are you?*

Chyll wasn't so much handsome as he was well assembled; his dark features sharp and alert, his eyes a deep and clever brown. He was smiling, open and friendly, and yet there was something a little too precise about the expression, as if he'd learned it from a book.

'Where is your lovely wife?'

'At home,' Rory said. 'Her mother's not well.'

Amy would be better at this. Rory had seen his wife stare down Daleks, defy presidents and argue with reptiles from the dawn of time. She'd even broken Raymond Chetterley's nose in fifth form when he had tried to glue Rory's hand to a school locker. That might have been the moment when Rory fell in love with Amy, except for all the other moments that had come first.

'So sorry to hear that,' Chyll said. He didn't *sound* sorry. He sounded like he was saying the kind of thing you said when people told you other people weren't well. It was like having a conversation with a scalpel. 'I trust your transit was satisfactory?'

That was a complicated question to answer. Travelling from the twenty-first century to the fifty-second had been as smooth as could be expected, in that Rory and the Doctor had only been diverted twice for life-threatening adventures. Rory knew he shouldn't complain. It had taken him a while to realise that, in terms of space travel, taking your first trip in a TARDIS was like doing your driving test in a Ferrari.

Prison policy had dictated that Rory make the final approach alone, in one of Stormcage's own transfer ships – a blunt bullet of a vessel that stank of sadness and sweat. *That* was something to complain about, except Rory never would.

He would have walked there, if he'd had to. It was what you did when you were a parent.

'A Christmas dinner!' the psychiatrist exclaimed with a dry clap of his hands. Even that seemed calculated to draw Rory's attention to the echoey vastness around them. 'How marvellous. Doctor Song is very lucky to have you.'

'Oh, I don't know about that,' Rory said, with his best British *must-get-going* smile. 'But you're very good to say.'

Chyll waved the guards back. 'I apologise for my boys' dedication. They can't help it.' Again, that mathematical smile. 'It's how I designed them.'

Tyrant, then. Amazing how it never took long for people to show you who they really were.

'May I accompany you to her accommodation?' Chyll phrased it like a question, but they both knew it wasn't.

Rory found himself thinking of the conversation he'd had with Amy after their visit last year.

'I hate it there,' Amy had said.

'I know.'

'I hate River being there.'

'Me too.'

'But I understand why she has to be there. Everyone thinks she killed the Doctor. If she wasn't in prison for it, then his enemies would

hunt him and her. And, yes, she breaks out all the time, and he visits her, and I understand. All right? I do.'

'I don't,' Rory had said, taking her in his arms. 'I mean, they've explained it, and they're happy with it, and that's important, but it doesn't mean I understand it. So I don't feel bad about being upset about it. And neither should you.'

'Mr Pond?' Chyll was still smiling, neat as the signature on an eviction notice. 'Shall we?'

The conveyance cart hummed, and Henrik Chyll hummed along with it.

The black beetle-like craft descended through wide white tunnels, and Rory soon realised that the glare of the psychiatrist's suit came from some sort of internal illumination. Like a portable searchlight, and with rather the same effect – deepening shadows, freezing security officers in place, bouncing from blade edges and gun muzzles so they seemed dazzlingly sharp.

Steel door after steel door spooled out before them, neat as the notches on a measuring tape.

'Brandon Sadness. Megatheft.'

Occasionally, Chyll would call out the occupants of the cells they passed, like the lift announcement in a posh department store.

'Hynern Oshhovo. Two thousand counts of murder. Such a busy boy.'

'Star Felon. Really, with that name, I don't know what they were expecting.'

He smirked at that. Rory didn't. Instead, he busied himself with checking the food, or absently counting the stencilled black numbers on the prison wall. This was something he had learned in long shifts at Royal Leadworth Hospital – if you couldn't topple a tyrant, the least you could do was not give them an audience.

It did not go unnoticed. The ghost of annoyance appeared on Chyll's mechanically precise features, as the cart purred into a huge service elevator, the platform corkscrewing downwards. Somewhere in the distance, a muffled siren wailed and was immediately cut short.

'I imagine,' Chyll said eventually, 'I do not need to explain that I am a powerful man.'

Then why do it? Rory thought.

'And not just powerful, but respected. The strategies outlined in my papers on the criminal mind are now standard practice in many facilities. I have interviewed utterly villainous individuals. The Butcher of Bamond, Amon the Destructovore. These are –' his hands fluttered – 'celebrities. And being the man to document them provides its own celebrity too.'

Rory pretty much always wished Amy was nearby, but now the pang was particularly sharp. He'd read once that sharks could smell a single drop of blood in the water from a hundred kilometres away, but that was *nothing* compared to Amelia Pond realising she had just gained the upper hand.

'River,' he said. 'You want to interview River.'

'Doctor Song is proving stubborn,' Chyll said reluctantly. 'Records of her . . . adventures are either confusing or outright contradictory. Her background is somewhere between unknown and completely unbelievable, and even our medical scans cannot seem to agree as to her genetics. I am *still* receiving word that she is out there in the universe, despite knowing that she is imprisoned here!' Again, the fluttering, like birds trying to escape. 'Put simply, she is *frustrating* – which means that the man who finally tells her story will be famous. I would like you to convince her to cooperate.'

'I think,' Rory said, because it was probably a better response, on the whole, than punching Chyll in the face, 'she's probably quite happy telling her own story. Why would she want you to do it?'

The hands stilled in that shining lap. 'Because I can set her free. Or, at the very least, aid her escape. You know, I have always considered our transfer ships an accident waiting to happen. Practically prehistoric in terms of security. Why, all it would require is a little inattention on our part and a prisoner could be light years away.'

'River doesn't want to escape,' Rory said carefully, adding *permanently* in his head. Stormcage was protection for her and the Doctor both. 'And she'd be hunted even if she did. You can't prevent that.'

'Can't I?' Chyll said mildly. 'For her to be hunted, someone would have to report her gone. If she is *believed* to be here, surely that is as good as being here, no? Christmas at home, Mr Pond. Wouldn't that be nice?'

They made the rest of the trip in silence.

Stormcage was vast. It took another thirty minutes of bleached-white gantries and wide concrete corridors before they approached Cell 426 in Cell Block Humanoid 3.

Imprisonment came in many forms here, just like the prisoners; cell design had to be flexible when you were imprisoning hyperspace wyverns and Saturnian light-vampires and people who took whole planets for joyrides. River Song's cell, much like River herself, had started out relatively normal – just a polished-stone square fronted by everything-proof glass and bookended by two hulking guards. However, that had very swiftly gone out of the window once they had put River Song inside.

Now, Cell 426 was an archaeologist's dream. Every inch was piled with the tat and treasure of a thousand cultures, like all of history colliding in a space the size of Rory's first apartment. Priceless French wardrobes had been stacked five high along one wall, their drawers yanked out and converted to bookshelves. Gems the size of baby potatoes glittered among stacks of tattered paperbacks – mysteries, and romance, and adventure, and crime. And sitting in the middle of it all, reclining on a mound of duvets like a dragon on its hoard, was River Song.

Doctor River Song.

Also, Professor River Song, quasi-Time Lord River Song, and Universe's Most Wanted River Song, depending on the day you met her, and sometimes on the day she met you. She was also Rory's daughter. The order of items on that list worried him sometimes.

'Merry Christmas,' he said.

'And to you, father dear,' she said, shaking out her explosion of curls. 'I got your message. Is Amy's mother OK?'

Rory gave her a small smile. 'You can call her Gran, you know.' He thought for a moment. 'Maybe not to her face.'

River grinned back, a tad awkwardly. They had spent relatively little time alone with each other, for father and daughter. River had been kidnapped as a baby by the Church of the Silence, taken from Rory and Amy and shaped into a weapon aimed straight for the Doctor's heart. It was complicated – and Rory wasn't great at complicated. He was, he knew, possibly too simple a person to be running around different timelines and futures and planets, but he knew he was going wherever Amy was going, and that was that. River had gone somewhere he couldn't follow just ten minutes after she was born, and by the time he did find her (by way of a thousand confusing interactions before and after her birth) he was so far behind he didn't think he would ever catch up.

'It's good to see you,' River said. 'Really. And – is that Chief Psychiatrist Chyll?'

Her smile turned tigerish. Rory had seen Daleks die in front of a smile like that.

'I told you, Henrik,' she said. 'I write theses. I don't star in them.'

'River Song,' Chyll said. His hands were fluttering again. 'I thought we had cleaned all the contraband out of your cell.'

She picked her way across a pile of broadswords to lean against a vase the size of Rory. 'What contraband?'

Chyll gave Rory a long-suffering look, which Rory avoided by glancing warily into Cell 427 across the corridor. As always, it was pitch-black and silent; a cube of darkness like the tank of some strange deep-sea fish. He'd always meant to ask River who was in there, but it felt somehow rude to do it within earshot.

The guards snapped to attention as Chyll disembarked from the cart, and River's smile disappeared.

'You know he's wired them to do that? Synaptic controllers surgically implanted in all of their heads so he can pull their strings.' She shook her head scornfully. 'Sometimes, Henrik, I think if you didn't have captives to experiment on you'd probably experiment on yourself.'

Chyll's words replayed in Rory's head: *They can't help it. It's how I designed them.*

'You're hardly in a position to take the moral high ground,' Chyll snapped. 'Or you wouldn't be trapped on the other side of those bars.'

River indicated the trove of artefacts around her with a lazy wave of her hand. 'Do I look trapped to you?'

The lights went out.

Rory's vision exploded in purples and blues as the overheads cut off with a series of snaps. The guards' needle-thin targeting lasers vanished. Even Chyll's suit shut off. The corridor was plunged into darkness so complete that it felt like Rory's brain had suddenly been dropped in ink.

'Stay still, everyone,' Rory said reflexively. He had been a guard once. Amy had been imprisoned somewhere, and Rory had spent a very long time guarding her, with sword and axe and blade and bow and knife and fist. He tried not to think about it too much. That's why he liked Leadworth – a place so relentlessly normal you couldn't help but be normal too.

But you didn't spend centuries being a prison guard without gaining an instinct for when things had gone terribly wrong, and it took a conscious effort to pull his hand away from his hip, where a sword had hung for the best part of those two thousand years.

'River?'

'Getting a torch!'

'Good.'

It was so *dark*. Not the dark of night, which wasn't really dark at all – not with the moon and light pollution and a million other things to break up the black. This was the dark of a hole. The dark of a grave. The kind of dark you only got underground.

Someone was whimpering.

'Chyll?' Rory said. 'Is this a power outage?'

No answer.

'*Chyll.*'

'Stormcage works off a geothermal siphon.' River's voice was muffled. It sounded like she was rummaging through dozens of scrolls. 'Unless someone found a way to turn off the planet's core, it isn't a power outage.'

'Then what is it?'

Stormcage answered for her.

Unmoored and disorientated by the blinding dark, Rory felt as though every other one of his senses had spun into overdrive. Gears ground. Vibrations stung his boot soles and chattered his teeth. He flinched backwards as a deafening rasp echoed from the vague direction of River's cell. He had no idea what it was, until he heard it again, and again, and again, chasing itself through the corridors of Cell Block Humanoid 3 like a legion preparing for war.

The doors.

The cell doors were opening.

Alarms began to howl. Screams rose with them. A hundred, a thousand, overlapping and competing; the joyous, chaotic symphony of prisoners smelling freedom in the air. It very nearly drowned out the sound of Cell 427's door retracting into the wall behind Rory, then a voice swam out of the blackness, thick as bubbling fat.

'It isn't a power outage. Is it, Chyll?' said Prisoner 427.

Henrik Chyll's suit had rekindled in slow and sickly flashes, painting his skin the colour of a corpse.

'It's a prison break.'

It occurred to Rory, as Prisoner 427 burst from its cage in a blur of limbs, that *humanoid* was a far broader term that he had originally thought. He had just enough time to register snapping jaws and wet, glistening muscle before he threw himself past the cart and into River's cell.

The creature hammered into the cart with one meaty shoulder, rocking the half-tonne vehicle up on two wheels before it righted itself with a deafening slam. Chyll shrieked. Rory flung a baking tray. And Prisoner 427, fully twelve feet of scales and serrated crustacean limbs, reared up to its full, ceiling-scraping height, clacking its mandibles like a hungry man at a buffet.

That was the first and last mistake of its newly freed life.

The light of River's blaster would have been blinding even if the darkness hadn't been near total. As it was, it felt like standing beside the birth of a star. Rory rose to his feet holding a broadsword, just as everything above Prisoner 427's neck came away in light and noise. Drizzling fluid, it curled in on itself like a dead spider, flattening the cart as it fell.

'Dad?' River asked eventually. 'Are you OK?'

'It was only the sprouts,' Rory said. 'I'm fine.'

'That's contraband,' Chyll whispered.

They found him at the feet of one of the guards, neither of whom had moved a muscle during the fight.

Synaptic controllers, Rory thought. *They need Chyll pulling the strings. If they're on the same circuit as the rest of Stormcage, then every guard in the prison might be down.*

'Blasters are contraband,' Chyll muttered. 'Swords are contraband. *Sprouts* are contraband.'

'Chyll,' River said. 'Focus. Stormcage's systems have failed. We could be looking at a mass outbreak –'

'They haven't failed,' Chyll retorted. The chance to contradict River had snapped him at least partially out of his trance. 'Not all of them. Life support is working, obviously. The alarms are working. It's only select systems that are down, which means . . .'

Chyll raised a hand to stroke his right sleeve. Trails of soft light followed his fingertips before fading back into the cloth, and suddenly an image appeared across the folds of his suit. Bent and distorted by his arm underneath, it was still recognisable by its white concrete as somewhere inside Stormcage.

'The cameras are untouched,' he murmured. 'Of course they are. They probably want this on public record. To bring

Stormcage to its knees – well, that's career-making, isn't it? And criminals love the dramatic.' Something ugly darted across his face. 'Isn't that right, Doctor Song?'

'What are you looking for?' Rory asked, before River got her blaster out again. He had retrieved and switched on some battery-operated Christmas lights from the trolley he and Amy had packed, and was wrapping them round his arm as a makeshift torch.

'Control of the prison network can only be taken from the panopticon – that's Stormcage's nerve centre, on level three,' the psychiatrist explained. The image on his suit panned silently, before coming to rest over banks of computers and glowing screens. '*There.*'

Figures hunched over keyboards, cloaked in the white garb of Stormcage technicians, their body language unmistakably terrified. Pacing behind them was a creature so large it only appeared in fragments – a swirling cloak, elongated limbs, an elephantine skull underneath a jagged wire crown.

Rory's voice was hushed. 'Who . . . who is that?'

'Isolde Rubel.'

River stiffened. 'This is where Rubel ended up?'

'Only after I pulled a lot of strings,' Chyll said proudly. 'Fascinating individual.'

'That's one way of putting it,' River said. 'But how did she escape?'

'Looking for tips?' Chyll said sardonically. 'I don't know, Song. She could have been planning this for months. The woman is a genius. A polymath. Biologist, roboticist, geneticist – utterly dedicated to pushing the limits of what the body can achieve. Particularly her own.'

'And others',' River said darkly.

'Well,' Chyll said, 'I do try to avoid using the term "mad scientist".'

They watched the colossal skull turn this way and that, surgical scars gleaming. Some of them looked fresh. Some looked home-made.

'At least, not without making my own diagnosis,' he added.

Rory took River by the arm and led her away from Chyll, who was still stroking the sleeve of his suit like a puppy yearning to be let back into a room.

'Can we call the Doctor?' he asked.

River shook her head. 'Last we spoke, he said he was going to find the exact nanosecond when Christmas Eve became Christmas Day and park there to have a nap.' She grinned. 'Besides, this could be fun. A little father–daughter time.'

'River, I'm holding a broadsword. It doesn't *feel* like father–daughter time.'

Rory had met River before he'd conceived her. He'd seen her at the death of the universe. He'd seen her taken from him and her mother, and then he'd seen her reappear with secrets and a smile. But he'd never seen her look hurt.

'Doesn't it?' she said.

Rory turned to find Chyll hovering behind them, the images on his suit now replaced by that sickly flashing glow.

'So, let me get this straight,' Rory said. 'Control of the prison can only be wrested back from this . . . nerve centre. This panopticon.'

'Yes.'

'Which is currently being guarded,' Rory continued, 'by a notoriously mad scientist?'

'*The* mad scientist,' River offered unhelpfully. 'The worst this century has to offer.'

Chyll tapped his chin. 'Hmm. One could make a case for Magnus Greel being *slightly* ahead in terms of general unpleasantness, but, for all intents and purposes, yes, I would have to agree.'

They digested this in silence for a moment.

'River?'

'Yes, Rory?'

'Would you like me to make you a little plate?'

The ham tasted funny.

River was scrounging in her cell for ammunition. Chyll was trying to plot some sort of route to the panopticon that wouldn't run them directly into any brawling inmates. And Rory was absent-mindedly chewing a cold piece of ham and wondering, *Is this just Christmas now?*

He had always wanted kids. Some nurses didn't. Working in a paediatric ward could do that, sometimes. It was hard to see families on their worst days. On helpless days. On days when you could do nothing but say 'I'm sorry' over and over again. Rory had seen a lot of frightened parents in his time. Sometimes he thought that having a kid was like keeping your heart outside your chest – open, exposed, at the mercy of the world.

So you did little things. You put tinsel on ECG machines. You sprayed non-toxic snow on all the windows. You kept a smile on your face no matter what. You pretended everything was normal and the universe made sense, in the hope that you might somehow make it true.

Rory took another bite. The ham always tasted funny in the hospital too.

'Can't be easy.' Chyll eased himself to the floor beside Rory, his skin grey and washed out in the half-light of his suit.

Rory didn't say anything. He just chewed. Maybe he would get to like the taste. People could get used to anything.

Chyll waved his hand, indicating the dark corridor, the open cell, the wailing alarms. 'I doubt this is anyone's ideal Christmas.'

Rory shrugged. 'I've had weirder,' he said, before realising with a start that it was true. *At least the whole thing with the space sharks had snow.* He eyed Chyll warily. 'I'm not going to convince River for you.'

'I didn't think you would. Honestly, I can't imagine the lengths you'd have to go to in order to convince River Song to do anything.'

I can, Rory thought. *I've seen it.* Amy had explained to him just what River had gone through after her abduction. The training. The brainwashing. There had been a flow chart.

I wish Amy was here.

'You know,' Chyll said gently. 'I see families at odds here all the time. Families who have nothing in common. Families who have let each other down. Sometimes it helps to –'

'Right, you two.' River was loading her blaster with heavy, gleaming rounds. 'I've got six more shots in this. Rory, you have a . . . broadsword. And, Chyll, you have a route.'

The psychiatrist nodded. 'I can swing us round the riots on level two, using the cameras to scout ahead. With a little luck, we can avoid most of the prisoners until we get to the panopticon.'

'And Rubel?' Rory said grimly, getting to his feet. 'Do we have a plan for her?'

River cocked her blaster. 'I'm going to shoot her. See if that works.' She stared at them for a moment. 'What were you two talking about?'

'Nothing,' Rory said, and wondered suddenly why he had lied.

Once, not long after Rory's long guard of Amy had ended, the Doctor had taken Rory to a room in the TARDIS that he had never seen before and poured him a drink. It had been a very strange experience. Not just because the Doctor didn't really understand humans, or because he didn't understand liquor and had poured them something that ate through both the glasses and the table. Mostly, it was because the gesture had the awkwardness of your dad giving you a long-overdue talk about girls.

'Do you ever wonder,' the Time Lord had said, 'why I occasionally – very occasionally, mind you – come across as a tiny bit scatterbrained?'

'No,' Rory had said truthfully. 'I thought you were just being scatterbrained.'

'Thank you for that.'

'Sorry.'

'I'm trying to help.'

'I know.'

'The reason, Rory, that I might occasionally be a little scatterbrained,' the Doctor said, 'is because I have a long memory. And people can get lost in memories. Too much detail. The past, acting on the present. So I try to stay in the present, and only go looking for the memories I need.'

The conversation had always stayed with Rory, particularly because that was the moment the acid-chewed table had chosen to collapse. He couldn't remember every single moment of his two-thousand-year service, and the memories he did have were more like brushstrokes of a painting – all texture and colour and feel, blurred from one angle and crystal-sharp the next.

Their passage through Stormcage had a similar feel; creeping past Amon the Destructovore, as it took on thirteen Draconian warriors at once, breaking bodies with every swing of its fists. Fighting back to back with Silurian corsairs against a shoal of squirming, flashing Rutan, their sizzling tendrils scorching nonsense patterns in the white concrete walls. Running hand in hand with River, and even Chyll once or twice, the psychiatrist's suit flashing in time with the ever-shrieking alarms.

I hope these memories fade properly, Rory thought. He had enough memories of war zones already.

He couldn't have said how long they had been fighting when Chyll found them a looted infirmary, its floor strewn with scattered bandages and the remains of nurse droids.

'May I?'

Rory was trying, one-handed, to patch up a cut on his arm when Chyll knelt beside him. Rory flinched, instantly scanning for River, and the psychiatrist gave him an amused look.

'She's covering the front door. Four rounds left, by my count. And you should let me help with that. I am a doctor.'

'And I'm a nurse,' Rory said.

He'd lost some of the Christmas lights from his trembling arm. That was something the movies left out about fighting – swinging around a lump of metal for any length of time turned even trained muscles to jelly.

'I didn't know that,' Chyll said.

Rory cursed himself inwardly.

'Well. I defer to your professional opinion.' Then Chyll added, 'In this, and in the matter of River.'

'Sorry?' Rory said. It was actually extremely difficult to patch yourself up one-handed. They didn't teach classes on it or anything.

'You know what's best for her,' Chyll said simply. 'And you think her place is here.'

'I don't think that,' Rory said hotly. 'She does. And –' He stood up abruptly, leaving his arm untended. 'Let's go.'

They plunged back into the fray, River giving Rory a look of surprise as he barrelled past her with his sword held high.

Don't tell him anything, Rory reminded himself with every sword thrust. *Even if he's keeping us all alive.*

That was another awkward truth. Stormcage had become too chaotic to cross without at least some fighting, but Chyll's cameras had led them round the worst of the brawls. Without him, they might already be dead.

That doesn't mean he's right.

We could be at home right now.

If River wanted to be.

Fleeing from a heated duel with Star Felon and a motley crew of allies brought Rory, River and Chyll to the dim sanctuary of an abandoned cell, just a few corridors from the panopticon itself. Chyll accessed his suit, once again bringing up his camera feeds. The scene hadn't changed: the cowering technicians, and the lurking, patchwork monstrosity, drool hanging from her elongated jaw.

'Why is she still there?' River murmured. 'She has control of the shuttle bays. She should be making her escape.'

'Does it matter?' Chyll retorted. 'Perhaps she intends to use Stormcage as a base. Recruit the prisoners as a private army, take control of our –' he paused, straightening his tie – 'admittedly brilliant medical facilities.'

'Oh, fantastic,' River said. 'You two can open a practice together.'

'Guys,' Rory said. 'Could we focus on a plan?'

Chyll manipulated the image with deft strokes of his fingers.

The panopticon was a circular room, divided into a series of concentric circles by clicking, thrumming machines. At their centre was a computer twice the size of all the others, its console studded with screens that pulsed in time with Chyll's suit.

'If I get to this console, I can shut the doors. Activate suppression fields in common areas. Activate the guards. We can take Stormcage back.' He frowned. 'Providing Rubel doesn't stop us first.'

'Leave that to me,' River said.

'What does that mean?' Rory said, unable to keep the frustration from his voice. 'You can't just charge in and leave us playing catch-up. That's not how this should work.'

River sniffed. 'I know how attacking the panopticon of a mega-jail works, *Dad.* Do you?'

'No,' Rory said. 'I guess I don't. All I know is that Amy and I spent a lot of time making a portable Christmas party for you and now it's back at your cell, presumably being eaten by Alfred the Destructovex or whatever he was called.'

River looked hurt again. 'I know this isn't the Christmas you wanted –'

'This isn't Christmas at all,' Rory said. 'This is tinsel draped over an ECG machine.' He sighed. 'It doesn't matter. Fine. Let's charge in.'

'No,' River said, and now she looked angry. 'This is definitely the time for you to have a tantrum. I'm sorry you're spending Christmas in prison, Dad, but this is where I live. Battle and danger and gunfights. I didn't ask you here. You were the one who wanted a family Christmas.'

'Well, sometimes this doesn't feel much like a family, either.'

Something exploded in a nearby corridor, followed by delighted prisoners hooting and cheering. It was a stark reminder that the war zone hadn't slowed down because they had. If they didn't take the panopticon soon, there might not be much of Stormcage left.

River's voice had turned icy – that cool, considered tone that made even the Doctor stop in his tracks. 'You see, that's the thing about family. You don't get a choice.'

'*You* have a choice, though, don't you?' Rory said. 'You're choosing to be here, instead of –'

'Instead of helping Chyll?' River said flatly. 'I suppose I am making that choice, yes.'

The psychiatrist was suddenly very concerned with the play of light on his sleeve.

'Well then,' Rory said, abruptly standing. 'I guess we all have to make the choices we think are right.' He turned to Chyll. 'We get out of this, I'll help you write your paper. I'll tell you anything you want.'

He lifted his sword and charged.

Rory didn't look round to see whether they were following him. He simply ran, pelting down that final hallway and smashing open the doors leading into the panopticon. It looked much as it had on the screen – circle upon circle of gleaming white consoles, presided over by the monster herself: Isolde Rubel.

She was even more terrifying in person than she had been on screen – at once hulking and exaggeratedly slender, every trace of humanity removed and replaced by layer upon layer of flushed muscle and hooked bone. Mechanical arms had been grafted alongside her biological ones, each ending in a forest of surgical implements that whirred and gnashed and gleamed. Her head was the size of one of Stormcage's shuttles, a blunt, fanged wedge crowned by spurs of wire, with red gleaming eyes glaring from deep-set sockets.

'Ah.' Rory's charge turned into a slightly awkward jog. 'Hello.'

Rubel lunged.

A metal fist caught Rory in the chest, flinging him clear across three consoles before he slammed into a wall. His sword hit a second later and stuck in the wall just above his head, quivering like a tuning fork.

It is possible, Rory thought, as the mad scientist stalked towards him, *that dramatically charging in might have been a mistake.*

'Listen, as one medical professional to another –'

Isolde said nothing. Instead, she vaulted over the first console, fingers leaving visible dents in the metal, and kicked the next one aside.

Rory couldn't help but frown as he scrambled to his feet, ducking a sweeping blow from a scalpeled paw. Normally – and, again, it worried him that he could say *normally* about situations like this – villains liked to explain, or boast, or preach as to why them killing him was quite a good thing, actually, and he really should be on board.

He wasn't sure why this was. Maybe they didn't get to chat much with their acolytes. Maybe they thought it might somehow put their victims at ease. Either way, Rubel's bedside manner was leaving a lot to be desired. Rory wasn't an expert in figuring out facial expressions at the best of times, especially on faces so impressively reconstructed, but did she look . . . confused?

It was the wrong thing to be paying attention to. Rory's back hit another wall. He tried to dodge left, but a tentacled set of pincers slammed into the metal and blocked his path. He turned right, but another arm punched deep. Rubel lifted a third to strike him down – then flinched as River's first blast took the limb off at the elbow. The monster spun, stained white coat floating around her, as River and Chyll rushed into the panopticon. River aimed to take another shot. 'No!' Chyll shouted. 'Don't!'

Rubel hesitated. She actually hesitated, though whether it was in the face of River's blaster or the shock at Henrik Chyll actually showing some bravery, Rory wasn't sure. Either way, just like Prisoner 427, Rubel's hesitation bought them a second to move.

'Now!' Rory shouted, and River spun on a heel, putting her last blast directly into the console to which Henrik Chyll had directed them.

'No!'

The console exploded in a flower of sparks. A shudder ran through Stormcage's bones, as if the facility itself had been shot, and the huddling technicians flickered and vanished in wisps of smoke. Isolde Rubel froze mid-turn.

A clear voice rang out through the suddenly silenced alarms.

++ SYSTEM INTERRUPT CANCELLED. BACKUP SYSTEMS REASSERTING THEMSELVES ++

Chief Psychiatrist Henrik Chyll sighed, patting down his now-black suit. 'How long have you known?'

'That you were faking, you mean?' Rory said.

He put a foot against the wall and, with some effort, managed to drag out his sword. Rubel had really thrown it quite hard.

'Dad figured it out,' River said with no little pride. 'He got suspicious after Prisoner 427's convenient hesitation. And then your merry dance through Stormcage kept us in in *some* danger, but never enough that we might actually die.'

'You're a control freak,' Rory said.

Rubel was still frozen, arched like a scorpion in a museum exhibit. Rory had no desire whatsoever to get close to the monster, but even from across the room he could see the faintest tremor in the mad scientist's tangle of limbs, as if she was straining with every fibre to be free.

'I know the type,' Rory went on. 'A massive system failure with no backups that goes just wrong enough that we have to join forces? Didn't feel right at all.'

Chyll spread his hands, offering once again that scalpel grin. 'All in the name of science, dear River.'

'You knew I wouldn't open up to you,' River said. By Rory's count, she had used her last round on the console, but being unarmed only made her *twice* as dangerous as anyone else in the room. 'So you thought you could convince Rory to tell you my story instead.'

'And didn't I?' He turned to Rory. 'You seem like a reasonable, baseline human. Far too baseline to have produced something like River Song. You're nothing alike, and my offer still stands.'

Rory spun the broadsword in a lazy figure of eight. Chyll's eyes couldn't help but follow the point as it hummed through the air.

'I was a Nestene duplicate for two thousand years,' Rory said. 'I watched Rome burn, and put the Twelfth Cyber Legion to the torch. I put Hitler in a cupboard.' He took River's hand. 'We're more alike than you think. Oh and, before you start writing a thesis on me, I also know how medical papers work.'

River's smile was tigerish again. 'If the greater medical community was to find out that your interviews were conducted with synaptic controllers, you'd be ruined,' she said. 'Why, you could have been making them say anything. I could tell you that I'm a child of a TARDIS raised by a fanatical church to kill the universe's last Time Lord, but instead I married him and faked his death, and now I use your prison as free accommodation while he takes me out on dates . . . and you wouldn't be able to publish a single word.'

Chyll's smile disappeared.

'Merry Christmas, Henrik,' she said lightly. 'I'll be in my cell. You should probably get all this cleaned up. I wouldn't like to be near Rubel when the paralysis wears off.'

*

Later, after little plates and large plates and crackers and – yes – tinsel, Rory put his arm round River, careful not to reopen his cut.

'I'm sorry for what I said.'

River shrugged. 'He needed to believe you were close to caving. But . . . I do understand. This isn't the Christmas you were expecting. Or the daughter.'

'I don't think anybody gets the kids they expect,' Rory said. 'And you've had a lot of people try to make you into a lot of things. Me, I wouldn't change you for the world.' He looked down at his plate. 'Unlike this ham.'

River's expression turned sly. 'You know, I don't think security by the kitchens will have fully recovered . . .'

Rory set down his plate and lifted his broadsword. 'You read my mind'

AFTER

'Wake up, Henrik. It's your lucky day.'

Chyll sat up with a start. He hadn't been sleeping, in point of fact. Sleep had been eluding him, ever since what he was rather carefully referring to as 'the incident'. 'Incident' sounded better than 'jailbreak'. It certainly sounded a lot better than 'failed attempt to manipulate a troublesome prisoner'. The problem was, what Henrik called it wouldn't matter once word got out. That was the nightmare that kept him from sleep.

'Who's there?' he snapped, looking around and trying to rub the ache out of his head.

A form resolved out of the darkness. A porcelain oval, polished and pale, floating in the blackness like a leaf on dark water.

No. Not a leaf, Henrik realised, as two slits opened and blinked. *A mask.*

'How did you get in here?' Chyll said, trying to keep a note of panic from his voice. 'My guards, they should have –'

'Stopped us?' A second mask appeared from the gloom. The voice was light, like a little boy's. 'They tried. In this and in many other timelines. Not hard enough, unfortunately. Lucky for you, though.'

'Lucky?' Chyll's mouth was dry. 'What do you mean, lucky?'

'Because, in another timeline,' the first mask said, its voice soft and female. 'River Song killed you. You pushed her too far by going after her family, so she put a round through your skull.'

The panic button. It was beneath his pillow. He could press it easily. And yet, something stopped him. Fear perhaps, or curiosity – that foolish curiosity that had got him into this mess in the first place.

'She killed me?'

'Then,' the first mask continued, as if Chyll had not spoken, 'there was the timeline where Rory killed you. Several timelines, in fact. He *is* an interesting one. We're watching him quite closely.'

Press the button, you fool. They could be anyone.

Chyll's hand was still at the back of his head. There was a pain there – tight and piercing and impossible to ignore. He found himself having to think *around* it rather than through. 'What are you talking about?' he said.

'And then there were the many, many timelines where your own prisoners broke free, and the things they did –'

'Sibling,' the second mask said. 'Enough. You don't need to worry about those other timelines, Chief Psychiatrist Chyll. Because you're in this one.'

'And what timeline is that?' Chyll said, still trying to find the source of the pain . . . and then froze as his fingers found a cold little bulb of steel.

A synaptic controller. Funny – when he'd designed them, he hadn't given a lot of time to wondering what wearing one would feel like. *You can't get too wrapped up in that kind of thing*, he remembered thinking. *It gets in the way of the science.*

'The timeline,' the boy said, 'where you tell us everything we need to know about Professor River Song.'

6

WE WILL FEED YOU TO THE TREES

'Don't think of it as death,' I say, checking the shackles on the Doctor's hands. 'Think of it as being in service to a miracle.'

He doesn't answer, and I don't blame him. Our ways probably seem fair old-fashioned to an outsider, and he looks outsider to his core, with his long coat and his wide hat and his vest covered in question marks, of all things. The good people of Outsmawe wear sturdy wool and good leather boots. Simple clothes. The kind that will take care of you if you take care of them. We're not question-mark kind of people.

It's winter. The sky is that blue you only get on winter mornings, glassy and glacial, a blue so blue it'd hurt your eyes.

We pick our way through the outskirts of the village, past the squat cottages and the haggard sheep huddled in their barns. The Doctor follows me sullenly, a chain linking my hand to his bound wrists, and the little question-mark umbrella he refused to leave behind.

Hard to blame him for the sulking, either, if I'm honest. It can't have been an easy night, tied up before Elders' Keep as the villagers chanted and the fires roared and the torches burned themselves to pluttering stubs. I don't know why all the ceremony is necessary. Except I do, of course: it's the way we do things here. That's a good enough reason for anything.

The Outsmawe road is crowded, and it doesn't take a genius to see that we're the only two heading *out*, while everyone else is heading *in* – a huge queue of farmers and families beating a path to shelter behind the village walls, their arms laden down with supplies. The Doctor watches them as we pass. Clever eyes. Question-mark eyes. Outsider eyes, I imagine, though he is the first outsider I ever met.

'Expecting a harsh winter?'

Winter. It's an old word, a word from the before times, the mythic times when it is said that we sailed here on great ships across a black and icy sea. These days, there are only really two seasons here in Outsmawe – Succour, the easy time, the time of planting and harvesting and preparation, and Siege – the time when we hope those preparations are enough.

Siege comes every year, and Succour is getting shorter all the time.

We walk, and soon the ground begins to rise into the first of the Uppsmarch hills; humped and hairy with brambles, the soil pale and pinched with cold. Every so often I hand him my waterskin, and he drinks, sharp eyes never leaving mine. It's been hours since the crowds on the road dwindled and, with one last look around the deserted horizon, I take a thin gold ring from my pack and slip it on my finger. The Doctor watches that too.

'I'm a traveller,' he says eventually, his breath a little ragged from the slope. 'I crashed here. I have no quarrel with your people. With any people, really.' He frowns. 'All right. That isn't completely true. But usually I have to at least know what's going on before I end up in chains . . .'

I think he's used to being listened to. It isn't because he's a big man, because he isn't. It isn't because he's an Elder, because he's not – though there are enough laughter lines and worry lines on his sharp face that I wouldn't like to guess his age.

I think maybe somewhere else he's somebody. That's what it is. Somewhere else, he speaks and people jump to. You can see it in the way he stands – hands resting on his lapels like a schoolmaster or a priest – and you can hear it in his voice, fast and particular as stitching thread. He's somebody, wherever he's from.

Well. We're in Outsmawe now.

'If you could at least tell me where we're going –'

We come to the top of the first hill. I lift my hand and point.

The Doctor's gaze follows my finger. 'What is that?'

My wife had a little book once. It wasn't strictly allowed, not by the scripture, but the little glimpse of it I got didn't look too ungodly at all – just a fat stack of pages full of stories about monsters and heroes and cities where the buildings and the bodies were so tightly packed that it never got quiet and never got cold. A silly little thing. Not worth all the trouble it caused.

I remember it had a picture of a forest, and in that picture the forest was green.

I shouldn't have been surprised. Outsiders are wrong about nearly everything. The scriptures tell us so. A green forest, trees all narrow at the bottom and fat at the top, laid out neat as houses in the street. There were *flowers*. There were shafts of light coming down.

Our forest is not green. It is not neat. There are no flowers between the trees, because those fat old monsters are jealous and choke out all the light. Our forest is black and angry, and it weighs down the horizon like a mountain range, or a bruise. If you squint, you can see the teams of cutters desperately trying to halt its advance.

'That's what Sieges us,' I say. 'And, every year, it is a miracle when we survive. That, Doctor, is how your death will serve.'

As we approach, the world gets wilder. Technically, this is all reclaimed land. The cutting teams march out at the start of every Succour, fighting and bleeding the stubborn trees to clear ground for the farmers to grow their crops.

But you couldn't call it civilised. Even though the land's been cleared, and soil stands bare where turnips and tatoes have been hastily grown. There are still stumps everywhere, pushing through the earth like warts. Vines try and trip you with every step. Roots stand out like veins in a madman's neck.

Every Siege, we hold less ground. Every Succour, fewer things grow.

'You're really not even curious?' the Doctor asks. Frustration is plain on his face, like I'm a student failing to grasp the obvious. 'A box falls out of the sky, a man falls out of a box, and your Elders just decide to chain him up and send him to die? Is that how you treat all the strangers who come to your village?'

Ours is not a complicated faith. It dates back to the before times, the Great Voyage, when a soul was chosen each year to serve and die so that the rest could live. Now, though the Voyage is over, the tradition remains. Siege comes, and the forest advances. Only a life's service can hold it in check, buy us a little breathing space until next Succour.

It's a trade, just like life in Outsmawe is a trade. That's what the Elders tell us. We all have to pay to keep the trees from our door. There is no room for selfishness in a Siege.

'I don't know nothing about a box, sir,' I say mildly. I shouldn't be talking to him at all, but I was raised polite, and it's hard not to talk to someone who will not stop talking at you. Besides, what does it matter where he's going? 'And yes, that is what the Elders do with strangers.'

He stares at me. 'Why?'

'Because that means a year when one of us doesn't have to go.'

The Doctor draws himself up, which doesn't take long. He really is a small man.

'Now, listen to me, madam,' he says gravely. I don't think I have ever been called madam before. 'If this . . . strange forest is waging some sort of war on your people, I can be of far more assistance alive than dead. I've travelled the known universe, I've –'

'Can you hew?' I ask, pointing at the cutting team nearest to us. They're totally intent on their task. Siege is nearly here. Already the branches are shivering; or jerking out of the path of the axe. Another couple of hours maybe, and these scarred, sweating men and women will sling down their tools and run, laden down with the firewood we'll desperately need when the temperature falls and writhing, slashing vines are scratching at our doors.

'I'm more comfortable with an umbrella,' the Doctor says, and I snort.

'Not much use here.'

We're close enough now to the forest's edge for me to make out the tree trunks, each one wide as a barn, the bark stone-grey and stone-tough. Sheets of moss hang down like green waterfalls, blurring where one tree ends and another begins until you could be forgiven for believing that it is all *one* tree, a single organism growing outwards in all directions until the whole world is wrapped in its roots, a near-solid mass of tangled, vicious life.

'It's beautiful, in a way,' the Doctor says quietly, which just shows how much of an outsider he is. 'You humans have a thing about forests. A fear of them, or a love. I think there's a part of every human that remembers when forests were all you knew, and you lived and died under the eyes of trees.'

He sounds so much like her in that moment I have to fix my gaze on the forest edge until the blurring in my eyes goes away.

That's when I see it. The tremble in the trees.

'It isn't that I don't understand the concept,' the Doctor is saying. 'Plenty of human cultures attempt to bargain with nature. Samhain, the Viking *blót* sacrifices, Marzanna, the Chimú tribes . . .

The cutting teams have noticed it too. Some are backing away. Others are stuffing a last few logs into sacks. A few are already running.

'But nature isn't a thug you can buy off or bribe.' The Doctor is *still* talking. 'You're putting human motivations on a natural process. Forests can't be bought off with a sacrifice.' He smirks. Actually smirks. 'What's the going rate for a Time Lord, anyway? A few extra turnips?'

The forest erupts. The motion is stilted and painful as a birth, the entire forest edge advancing with a flexing, deafening creak. The rear line of cutters simply vanish. Those caught on the fringes shriek as branches lunge like snakes, tangling in limbs and hair and lifting them bodily into the green and hungry dark. The others drop their tools and flee.

'That's . . . impossible,' the Doctor says in horror. 'That's . . .'

'Siege. In two days, all this land will be covered by trees. In a week, the forest will be at Outsmawe's walls. Unless we do as tradition demands. As we have always done, from the years of the Great Voyage to the long years living at this monster's edge. Someone is chosen. They are taken to the forest. They serve. They die to soften the Siege.'

I don't say it to hurt him. I don't say it to frighten him neither. It's just the way things are. It's what we learn as children. It's what they told me when they took my wife away. If I were a braver woman, I would have asked who reported her for reading that infernal book, but the lessons of our childhood are deep and strangling roots.

We don't question. Not in Outsmawe. Questions are for sinners.

And everyone around here knows where sinners go.

There are no roads by which you enter the forest, and the fact that we can enter at all proves it is a thinking thing. It's no accident, the gap we find where a dying tree's slow, mulchy descent has pushed its smaller siblings out of the way. It's no coincidence that the ground here is clear of bush and scrub.

The forest knows we're coming, and it has given us a path.

Beneath the trees, it's the difference between watching a lake from the shore and swimming in its depths. Outsmawe has a music – the wind's whistling shriek and the chop and clatter of the cutting teams – but in here there is nothing but the groan of trees and the cacophony of birds. Thousands upon thousands of them flit and dart above us, chattering like raindrops as they shelter from the cold.

It is the only thing about the forest I do not hate. Nature quiets itself when humans are nearby, for fear of being found. Here, the birds are fearlessly and delightedly loud.

'Explain it to me,' the Doctor says. He's noticed the path the forest is leaving. I can almost hear his mind working beneath his sweat-streaked brow. 'Explain how the process works.'

'I don't know what more I can tell you.'

'Because you don't want to, or because you don't know?'

There's no fear in his voice. I'm used to fear. I expect anger or bargaining or quiet acceptance. It's a lot like grief, being chosen for the forest, except the person you're grieving for is yourself. Instead, he sounds curious.

'The sacrifice of a human slows the growth of the trees. Stops them overrunning your village. Does giving two people stop it entirely? What if you give it a short person? Does that only slow it a little? What about a family? What about a child? If the deal you've made with this forest is going to claim my life, I should at least understand the terms.'

His words dig into me like burrs. Speculation is the province of the Elders, but we've all noticed that Sieges are getting longer, and Succours shorter, as if the sacrifices we give are pleasing the forest less and less each time.

'Curiosity,' I say leadenly, 'is a sin –'

He laughs, hard and flat. Birds flit closer, amused at the sound. 'I've already been marked for sacrifice. Is there more trouble I could be in?' His eyes turn shrewd. 'And what about you?'

'Me?'

'Why are you here? I'm here because I'm a sinner, apparently. What about you? Is this escort detail a privilege? Or a punishment?'

He is too small a man to be frightening, and yet I find myself backing away from the iron glint in his eye.

'Are you the one who does it? Is there a bloodstained altar and a knife somewhere in our future?'

'No!' I snap, shocked at the thought.

'Then who? A high priest? A druid? Does the forest do it itself?'

'I don't know, I –'

Now, he could be an Elder. His voice rings out, sharp and commanding, certain, even when questioning, even when digging at the very roots of what I believe to be true.

'You've brought people out here before, you've let them be *sacrificed*, and you don't *know*? What do you do when this "miracle" starts? Do you watch? Do you look away?'

It's already started. The Doctor thinks he is clever. He imagines this forest as merely the ground on which individual trees lie, and not a mind that watches and waits and decides. The heart of our faith. The centre of our seasons. The chooser of who lives and dies. For all the Doctor's questions, he has not listened at all.

He hasn't noticed the birds have stopped singing.

'Goodbye, Doctor,' I say, snapping my end of the chain round a low-hanging branch, leaving him tethered tight. 'I have to go.'

'Back to your wife?'

His voice is idle. Almost cruel. His fingers trace the shape of one of the question marks on his vest.

Do not be drawn in. I have left many people in this place. Villagers I knew. People I liked. Sometimes I think the forest does not open a path to make it easy for the sacrifice to get here. It does so to make it easy for me to walk away.

I am not curious. I am not a sinner. I have no desire to see what happens when the forest takes its due.

Not again.

'How did you know I was married?'

'So you *are* capable of asking questions,' he says, once again the schoolmaster. 'Good. Let me tell you what I know.'

'That's not what I asked –'

'You're human,' he says, 'but this isn't Earth. The soil isn't right. The winter's too . . . cinnamony. But the trees around you are Earth natives, and you're baseline human, so this must be a colony world.'

'So?' I snap. The words he's saying – *Earth, colony* – mean nothing to me. *But the stories do say we travelled*, a treacherous voice whispers. *We sailed here, on ships of great iron.*

'So,' the Doctor says, each word needle-sharp, 'I'm guessing First Great Human Migration. Twenty . . . fifth century. I can tell it by the stitching on your tunic and the way you drop your R's. They genetically engineered the trees they brought with them to be hardier, to grow quicker – but I've never seen anything like this. Unless . . . what did you call it? *Service*. In service to a miracle. Why not call it sacrifice? Why not call it what it is? Why are you all so convinced it's the only way?'

'It *is* the only way,' I snarl. The trees are shaking. Something is coming, and it is nearly here.

'You don't believe that.'

'I do.'

The Doctor throws up his hands helplessly. '*Why?*'

'Because it has to be.' All the fight goes out of my voice. The shaking has stopped. Everything is quiet now, as if the forest is listening too. 'I'm no scholar. I just do what I'm told. And if this isn't the only way, it means that all those people . . . our fathers, our mothers, our wives, our husbands . . . their sacrifice meant nothing at all.'

It's no answer, and he knows it. But whatever question he was about to fling at me has no chance to leave his lips.

From out of the green shadows they come – twice as tall as humans but silent for all that size, towering bodies woven from vines and twisted wood. They look like the dolls Outsmawe children bind together from twigs – fat-bellied and skinny-limbed, with bobbing heads of bark. The children call them angels. The Elders call them servants, because there is no holier thing than serving the purpose you were given.

Roses bloom where their eyes should be.

The claws of the forest servants close around the Doctor, snipping his chain like shears, and he does not fight as they bear him away.

He just stares at me, as she did all those years ago.

I make my way back, the path the forest cleared for me already becoming overgrown. The Doctor's umbrella is in my hand. He dropped it when they took him, its red handle bright against the gloom. Shoots are struggling through the soil. Ivy links like fingers, and I have to pick my steps.

Is this escort detail a privilege? Or a punishment?

When I arrive back at Outsmawe, the Elders will be waiting. I'll receive an extra ration to make up for my exertion. A fair trade, for the work I do.

You've brought people out here before, you've let them be sacrificed, *and you don't* know?

Magdela, last year. She was pious. She went when she was told.

Gunthre, the year before, who was old – older than me – and ready to do his part.

Timon, who fought and begged and bargained, as if there was anything he could give me that the Elders wouldn't take.

This is my duty, and I perform it for the village.

What do you do when this 'miracle' starts?

It is proper night now beneath the trees. Moonlight stabs down like silver thread. The forest's edge is much advanced since this morning, but it is not long before I see flashes of open ground ahead, tatters of red cloth and tools discarded in the cutting teams' frantic rush to escape.

I will be at Outsmawe by morning. The Doctor's death will hold back the Siege. Until next season. And the next. And maybe some day, the bitter questions I hold in my heart will be asked, and then I will be sent here too, to have them answered.

Something glitters at the base of a trunk, half hidden by climbing vines. I kneel, tucking the umbrella under a strap of my pack, and brush away leaves. The glinting thing is already half buried. In a day, it will be like it was never there.

My fingers wrap round the handle and pull.

I don't know what lies at the forest's heart. I don't know what happened to my wife, or what is happening to the Doctor, and whether interfering with it will doom Outsmawe, its Elders and my faith.

But, as I stare down at the axe in my hands, I realise I am curious to find out.

*

If entering the forest the first time was like slipping into a lake, now it is like trying to sail one under a storm. It does not want me to return for the Doctor. Branches gouge. Roots squirm underfoot. It feels as if every burr and thorn is seeking my flesh, and the tough woollen clothing of Outsmawe proves no defence at all.

The axe is a different story.

The forest cuts me, and I cut back, hacking a path through bush and vine. Lift and fall, slash and crop; a lifetime of fear and anger in each and every blow. It is punishing – the most punishing thing I have ever attempted in my life. My arms weep sweat. My cuts ooze blood.

If the forest's attention were not so squarely on its sacrifice, I think I would have made no headway at all. But, like a great beast absently flicking away flies as it feasts, the forest's mind is elsewhere, and so, step by aching step, I advance. The axe is weapon and compass both – after a lifetime of following orders, *resistance* becomes my guide. I take the most tangled route, go where the branches knot the tightest to try to force me back.

I cut, and I hew, and I climb, and I crawl.

Hours pass. Days, maybe. I begin to think I'm dreaming when I see the great metal shapes jutting from the undergrowth – fragments like debris from a wreck. Some are nearly invisible beneath coats of moss. Others are so tall they fight the trees for space. Sometimes the ground beneath my feet is soil. Other times it is a dirty, artificial white material I have never seen before. In some places the white material is peeling back, and I see iron underneath, more iron than I have ever seen in one place.

Iron ships, I think blearily. Is this where they came to rest?

And then the half-blunt axe, now as much a part of me as my hands or my heart – hits nothing but air. My exhausted eyes refocus. There is space here to breathe. There is soft grass underfoot, broken only here and there by the swelling of roots. No, not roots – cabling. A tangle of white pipes that pulse and purr.

I freeze. A forest servant, three metres of bulbous body and skeletal limb, steps *over* my kneeling form without so much as a whisper. It reaches its talons, each one long as a child's arm, up into the canopy, and I have to scramble as cut branches begin to rain down.

It's pruning the trees. Caring for them.

I see another on its knees, repairing a stretch of broken pipe with swift, smooth motions of its fingers, and then another three working as a team to fell an entire tree, blade-fingers flashing as they take it apart. The tree does not resist them, as I have seen with the cutting teams. Instead, it falls with something like relief.

In the silence that follows, I hear a voice.

'You know, it'd be far politer to first explain why you're killing me, and then kill me. Don't you think?'

The Doctor. Still asking questions. I could laugh, if I had the breath. Instead I push my wobbly legs into a run.

I find him in a clearing, beneath the largest tree I have ever seen. You could have fit the entire village of Outsmawe within the circumference of its massive trunk, its bark as thickly wrinkled as the folds of a brain. I have seen trees grow up and around tools, submerge them in their flesh, but this tree is so huge that it has gathered up and swallowed up great pieces of the broken iron ships so they jut out like thorns.

At its base, about head-height off the ground, there is a great horizontal slash. Like an axe-scar, two metres tall and thirty across. White pipes spill from the gap in their hundreds to sink deep into the earth, and when light pulses from inside the scar the pipes pulse too.

This is the heart of the forest. This is the tree from which all other trees grow. And beneath it lies the Doctor, with a forest servant's hands round his throat.

'On reflection,' he croaks, one hand jabbing weakly at the air, 'I think I'd prefer an altar.'

I start forward, axe raised, but as I do so another servant drops from the canopy above, landing hard on the hooked talons of its feet. It rises, fully a metre taller than me, head bobbing on its stem neck, and lunges with a scything hand. Blocking the blow with the axe nearly throws my old body from its feet.

'Doctor!' I shout, trying to circle around to him and keep my attacker at bay. 'What should I do?'

The Doctor clips the creature attacking him across the face, and when it rears back I catch my first proper glimpse of what's happening. The forest servant isn't strangling him. It's pushing him into the roots beneath the tree. The bark has opened like cracked, dry lips and is trying to suck him down with fitful gulps, like an Elder working a lozenge beneath their gums.

'RENEWAL.'

The voice comes from everywhere and nowhere.

'RENEWAL REQUIRES SERVICE.'

The forest. The forest is speaking, and its voice is so world-shatteringly loud that beside it the Doctor's is barely a gasp.

'The pipes! Cut the pipes!'

He must be mad. There are hundreds of them. Where would I start?

And then I see – deep in the gap of the gargantuan tree, the pipes come together like veins into a single artery, thick as a waist. I don't know if my axe will even dent it. But I have to try.

A wild swing makes the nearest servant jerk back, bemused and wary. I don't think they fear me at all, but I think the forest has a long memory, and this place has suffered under the simple technology of an iron cutting edge. More servants are gathering now too, sickle claws gleaming with sap.

Move, woman. I hear the words in her voice, and I run like I have never run before.

I vault across the tangle of roots swallowing the Doctor and leave half the skin of my palms on the rough bark as I half climb, half scramble my way into the cut above. A clawed hand hooks the back of my coat, and I fling it off clumsily before the servant can use it to drag me from my feet, then turn to bring the axe hard into its face, sending it staggering into the path of its siblings.

It buys me a handful of heartbeats. I clamber to the heart of the cut, and raise my axe above the drumming, pumping pipe.

'Do it!' the Doctor shouts. Only his head still remains exposed. 'Now!'

'How did you know?' I ask.

The servants are forcing their gangling bodies into the cut. One swipes, the talons passing so close they ruffle my hair. I don't know what flows through this artery, but it may as well be faith, the faith of a hundred generations all the way back to the black sea and the iron ships. Those first people, one a year, who sacrificed their service so that others could live.

'How did you know I didn't believe?'

'Because you still mourn her,' the Doctor says.

I bring the axe down.

And it stops, an inch from the skin of the pipe.

'ATTEMPT TO HARD-INTERRUPT MAIN GROWFUEL PUMPLINE DETECTED. WOULD YOU LIKE TO ACCESS SETTINGS?'

'Yes!' the Doctor shouts. 'Very much so!'

I tug on the axe, but it won't move. Something invisible is holding it dead in the air. The servants have stopped climbing over each other too, pulling themselves out of their tangle to stare back at where the Doctor is emerging from his coffin of roots.

Tentatively, I let go of the axe. It stays hanging in the air.

'These old terraforming systems are robust,' the Doctor says, panting. 'Practically indestructible. All sorts of defences built in if you try to interfere with them.'

'Doctor, what are you –'

He bends down to pick up his umbrella from where it came free from my pack, dusting it off with the back of a hand. 'Thing is, they're here to make your world liveable. If you *do* try to interfere with them, they assume you've got a good reason. So they do the software equivalent of letting you speak to the manager.'

My expression makes him grin. 'Terraforming, my dear, is the act of making an inhospitable world *hospitable.* Standard equipment for a colony ship. It's a complicated process. You need a machine that can change the soil, a machine that can change the air, a machine that can even change the seasons. Machines that won't pollute the land while they're doing it. You know what I call a machine like that?'

I shake my head numbly.

'A forest.' He waves his umbrella around him. 'But this one isn't doing its job. The machine is broken. It needs . . . well. It needs a service.' He places a hand on one of the forest servant's chests. It cocks its head like a dog expecting a rub behind the ears. 'There's a seed of truth in every religion. That's what makes them so pervasive. And your people have been talking about *service* for years. Sending someone to the heart of the forest. *Ritual* is just another word for *interface*, after all. I thought it was a sacrifice at first. So did you, though you didn't use the word.'

I step back from the floating axe, out to the lip of the cut in the tree. From my vantage point, I can see more forest servants loping from the trees – a hundred, two hundred – their wickedly bladed limbs hanging loosely by their sides. The roses in their eye sockets shiver in the breeze.

'Not angels. Not demons. *Gardeners.* That's what the forest was asking for. Servants, to care for it. I don't know what happened to the original colonists – whether your records were damaged, or time and hardship just made you forget, but it's no wonder the seasons are out of sync if you've been overfeeding the machine without . . .'

'Without what?'

Jabbing his umbrella into the soft earth so it stands unaided, the Doctor slips his hand into his pocket, then withdraws it to reveal a whirring metal tool.

'I wondered why you didn't call it sacrifice. It's an odd little detail – a little holdover of truth from before things became so clouded. I love details like that.' He smiles. 'It isn't sacrifice, if you know they're coming back.'

The tool in his hand purrs, and the pipes tremble and twitch. I flinch as the axe suddenly falls harmlessly to the ground. The forest servants clutch their heads as if in pain, or in release. Those long, branchlike fingers tighten and pull. Bark peels away in curls of grey. Petals fall like snow.

'Organic exoskeletal life-suits,' the Doctor says. 'The ultimate healthcare package. It's a machine meant to bring life. It doesn't want anyone to die.'

The closest servant splits like a nutshell, and a person falls out, shaking, blinking like a newborn. The massive frame of the creature begins to disintegrate into ash and particles of bark, and the person looks up with utter confusion on their face.

It's Magdela. Last year's sacrifice. 'I was dreaming,' she says, half to herself. 'I was dreaming of a forest.'

'FACTORY SETTINGS RE-ESTABLISHED. TERM OF SERVICE – ONE YEAR.'

Bark splits with a sigh, and the hollow of roots that nearly swallowed the Doctor reopens. I look down from the gap. Something sad has entered the Doctor's eyes.

'I'm sorry,' he says. 'I've reset it so it will release on the year, instead of just holding them. That should stop the out-of-control growth as well. But the forest still needs maintenance. It still needs a servant.'

Servant after servant cracks open, men and women spilling out on to the grass. And among them . . .

There are flowers dusting her shoulders. There are petals in her hair. I reach my hand up, suddenly conscious she hasn't aged a day. But I am old, I am old now with the waiting . . .

And then she smiles. She smiles like springtime.

'It's all right,' I respond. 'I know what I have to do.'

Next winter isn't that far away.

7

CHRISTMAS WITH THE PLASMAVORES

'It is a French name,' said Henri Plasmavore, and smiled so widely you could see every tooth in his head. 'Very common.'

'Very normal,' added Madeleine Plasmavore. She was smiling too, but she had no teeth at all. 'Very human and normal.'

They filled the doorway of the Sullivan home like jelly in a mould – a pair of squat, fleshy rectangles in identical black button-up coats. Henri had a red scarf crimping the dead white skin of his neck. A beret had deflated on Madeleine's scalp. Other than that, it was surprisingly difficult to tell them apart.

Catherine disliked them on sight. This was not an uncommon reaction for Catherine. It wasn't that she had anything against people, on principle, but she had simply decided six months ago that she had met enough of them and didn't need to meet any more. There was a quota. She had reached it. Her father had tried to explain to her that there wasn't a quota, actually, and, even if there was, she couldn't have reached it because she was nine. This was just one of the many things on which Catherine and her father did not see eye to eye.

'And your car broke down?' Maurice Sullivan was small, for a dad. He dressed in oversized cardigans, even in summer, and his receding hair stuck up in tufts, as if waving for help.

Maurice needed help with a lot of things. He had to be reminded to take his anxiety medicine. He sometimes worked so hard he forgot to eat, and Catherine had to remind him to do that too. The only reason there was a stubby little Christmas tree in the corner was because Catherine had reminded him it was Christmas, and she wished she'd had the presence of mind to also remind him that you didn't open the door to strange people at midnight on Christmas Eve.

But now he had, and the Plasmavores loomed over them both like the twin halves of a Venus flytrap about to snap shut.

'Engine trouble,' Henri Plasmavore said. His voice was flat and nasal, more like a photocopy of a voice than the real thing. 'Isn't that right, Madeleine?'

'It is right, Henri.' Madeleine's voice was strange in an equal yet completely different way – a soft and rustling whisper that sharpened without warning on certain letters, like finding thorns in dry grass.

Behind them, the storm raged. It wasn't a good storm. Good storms were snowstorms and thunderstorms. This was a *bad* storm, full of shrieking wind and sideways rain. Catherine could see the dots and flecks of rain besieging the hallway's honey light, even with two flesh rectangles blocking the door.

Maurice peered at the strangers. 'I'm not much of a mechanic, I'm afraid. But if you'd like to come in and wait while you call someone?'

The Plasmavores' smiles widened. 'We would.'

They didn't speak at the same time. That would have been creepy. Instead, they spoke slightly out of time with each other, which was worse.

'Dad . . .'

The Plasmavores' eyes lowered. Catherine ducked further behind Maurice's leg.

'Yes, Catherine?'

She could say something. She *should* say something. There was something off about the Plasmavores. Something artificial. Their eyes glittered without reflecting the light.

Their skin had a peculiar shine, like fingernails or teeth. Alarm bells were jangling in Catherine's head.

If she did say something, Maurice would listen. Most adults didn't. They said things like 'not now' or 'shh, the grown-ups are talking'. This was especially true when it came to Catherine, who liked sharing facts about scorpions and horror movies, and planning what to do in the event of a zombie apocalypse. She had it on good authority from the kids in her class that liking these things made her 'weird', which was fine, because in Catherine's opinion not planning for a zombie apocalypse made you an idiot.

Maurice wasn't a perfect dad. He forgot things. He burned dinners. Sometimes Catherine felt that *she* was parenting *him*.

But he never called her weird.

Maurice looked down at her, his eyes kind and a little weary. 'Is everything all right?'

Catherine forced a smile. 'Yes, Dad.'

Henri Plasmavore grinned down at her. 'Marvellous,' he purred. 'Amélie?'

The two Plasmavores separated wetly to reveal the small shape of a girl standing behind them, just where the Sullivan porch light gave way to the dark. She was Catherine's age, as blonde as Catherine was dark, her hair a complicated mass of ringlets bouncing and eddying in the wind. Rainwater glistened like diamonds on her bright yellow mac.

'Amélie Plasmavore,' she said, brushing a drop of rain from her little button nose before sticking out her hand for Maurice to shake. 'How lovely to meet you!'

That clinched it for Maurice. He shook the little girl's hand, half grave and half smiling, then hurriedly beckoned all three Plasmavores inside the cramped little hallway. Amid the confusion of limbs and unbuttoning coats, Catherine found herself face to face with Amélie, who gave her a dazzling smile. She didn't look like the older Plasmavores, with their square heads and pressed, waxy grins. She looked like one of those German girls in old-fashioned storybooks who lived on the top of mountains and were eighty per cent dimple.

People aren't always like their parents, Catherine thought. That made her a little sad, so she stopped thinking it. 'Let me go put on the kettle, Dad?'

Maurice squeezed her shoulder. 'That's a great idea!'

'What a sweet child,' Madeleine said, as Catherine scampered to the kitchen.

'Oh, Catherine's not sweet,' Maurice said, and though he was joking the words snagged Catherine for a second on her way up the hall. 'She's Catherine.'

'All children are sweet.' Amélie's laugh was like the tinkling of bells. 'If you get the seasoning right.'

By the time the Plasmavores had removed their coats and hung them up in the hallway, Catherine had laid out a spread on the coffee table in the sitting room. The Sullivans' house was small, but Maurice liked to say it was 'compact'. You didn't need a lot of space when everything had its place. That was another thing Maurice liked to say.

They'd moved into the little two-up two-down after . . . After.

Catherine had her bedroom – a dark cave walled with books about witchery and urban legends and military tactics. Maurice's bedroom was mostly an office, where he wrote his books on local history, with a cot bed in the corner. Downstairs was a little kitchen – polished to as much of a gleam as the worn counter would allow – and the sitting room, with an overstuffed chair and two-seater couch that was just long enough for Catherine to lie flat out.

The Plasmavores sat on it with a creak.

The un-jangly part of Catherine – the part 'making an effort' – had hoped the Plasmavores would look less creepy out of the storm. Unfortunately, the cosy setting of the Sullivan sitting room only made Henri and Madeleine look more out of place, like finding a pair of slugs in a lunchbox.

'What a nice little home,' Madeleine Plasmavore said.

'Very nice,' Henri Plasmavore added. 'Very little.'

There was something sly in their tone, but Maurice didn't seem to notice. He was bad at noticing things. Sometimes, Catherine wished he was better at it.

Only Amélie, sitting on the couch with her feet not quite reaching the floor, looked like she belonged in the heat and the warm. Beneath her yellow mac, she was wearing a crinkly white dress with blue ships on it the exact colour of her huge eyes. The material made a soft *shushing* noise every time she moved, as if even her dress was polite.

'I think it's perfect,' she said.

'Thank you,' Maurice said, standing up to pour the tea. 'It's not much, but we make do.' He smiled wanly. 'Charity-shop chic, I like to call it. Sugar?'

He pointed at the little sugar bowl Catherine had laboriously filled from a dozen tiny packets. It wasn't stealing. People put them out in cafés – whole boxes of them. Maurice had told her, as sternly as he was able, that it *was* actually stealing, and money being tight didn't mean they should break rules, but they both knew his heart wasn't in it. Now, Catherine emptied all the packets of sugar and salt she stole into Tupperware bowls so it was a little less obvious where she'd got them.

'Nine sugars please,' Amélie said.

'None for us,' said Henri. He looked around, smacking his lips as if tasting the air. 'And it's just the two of you?'

Maurice froze mid-pour. 'I . . . yes. Catherine's mother passed away six months ago. A car accident.'

He always said it in the same way: a single toneless blurt, like someone reciting a phone number. That was how Catherine said it as well. It was a bit like a phone number, when you thought about it. Something you had to hand out to people, so they knew how to talk to you.

After six months, it felt like Catherine had heard every possible response to the news that her mam had died. However, this was the first time anyone had clucked their tongue as though they'd found a hair in their food.

'How very inconvenient,' Amélie said. She frowned a pretty little frown. 'I mean, what a waste.'

Silence, for five long ticks of the clock on the mantelpiece. Then, like a switch, Maurice's smile returned as if no one had said anything at all.

The jangling in Catherine's head intensified. She wanted Maurice to say something, except Maurice never said anything. He didn't say anything when everyone at the parent–teacher meetings fell quiet as they entered the room, then started whispering after they'd left. He never talked about the letters Catherine knew got sent home whenever she got into fights with kids who thought she was weird for not having a mam. And he didn't say anything when strangers barged into their Christmas and sniffed at Mam's absence like it was somehow the Sullivans' fault.

'Have you called a repair service?' Maurice asked.

'We have,' Henri Plasmavore said, 'but it'll be the morning. I'm sure we can find a hotel nearby . . .'

The dots landed like breadcrumbs. Like a lure. And, as Catherine knew he would, Maurice picked them up.

'Oh, well, you must stay here! If you don't mind an air mattress?'

'Like a sleepover!' Amélie said, clapping her hands in delight.

Catherine's eyes narrowed. She didn't realise that was a real thing children did. *Maybe clapping their hands is what happy children do?* She resolved to do it more in future, particularly around therapists.

'Just like a sleepover,' Maurice said, and the way he looked at Amélie sent a pang through Catherine's heart. She knew he'd like her to have friends. She owed it to him to try.

'Amélie could sleep upstairs with me?'

She raised her hands to clap them, then felt a bit silly, so she put them down again, masking the gesture by lifting up the little plate of snacks she'd prepared. 'Would you like a cracker? Or a crisp? They're salt and vinegar –'

She might as well have offered garlic to a vampire. Both Plasmavore parents flinched backwards, as if struck. Amélie had gone so completely still that Catherine found herself checking the plate to see if she'd accidentally included a tarantula.

'No,' Amélie said in a high, tight whisper. 'No, thank you.'

Henri placed a hand protectively in front of his daughter. 'Amélie has to be *very* careful about her salt intake.'

'Oh,' Catherine said. She set the plate down, feeling very bad. Normally, Catherine didn't worry so much about being nice. But Amélie was sitting right there, curls practically glowing, her polite little dress shushing them all, and suddenly Catherine wanted to be the best possible person she could be. 'Why don't I just –'

'Throw them out?' Amélie suggested quickly. Her sunny smile had reappeared.

Catherine stared forlornly at the plate of crisps and then, with a quick look at her dad, picked up the plate and went to the kitchen. She had just put the plate down on the counter when she heard her dad approach, sticking his head round the door frame.

'You couldn't have known, pet,' he said.

She shrugged awkwardly, and that made him awkward too. Normally, Maurice was the one person Catherine wasn't awkward around. But that was the thing, wasn't it? He'd invited other people in.

They stared at each other a little longer, then Maurice ducked back to deal with their guests. Catherine wasn't sure whether *very careful about salt intake* meant *mild allergy* or *throw out immediately*, and suddenly felt very worried about all her carefully-collected Tupperware bowls of salt, but after taking a very quick look behind her, she stuffed a few crisps into her mouth. This wasn't a wasteful house.

When she turned to leave, Amélie was standing right behind her.

Catherine jumped. She couldn't help it. The Sullivan kitchen was very small – just a nook really – and Amélie was standing *very* close. Somehow her dress hadn't made any noise at all.

'Your dad said you would show me upstairs to your room,' she said. 'Shall we?'

Catherine didn't say anything. This was partially because it seemed silly and babyish to say that normally Maurice would have tucked her in, and partially because her breath smelled of salt and vinegar, and she didn't want Amélie to keel over and die.

So, instead, she nodded and tried to smile through her clamped-shut mouth.

'Good,' said Amélie.

Catherine hadn't read one of those old German storybooks for ages. She tried to remember if the smiles in the illustrations were always so sharp.

'*Goodie*-good.'

Catherine was at the top of the stairs before she realised she was having a sleepover. A *sleepover*, with a girl her own age. This was good. This was normal. This was . . . What was the word her therapist kept using? The word that made her teeth itch? Oh yes. This was *integrating.*

'So, this is my room . . .' Catherine said, pushing open the door and waving for Amélie to hop up on the single bed. Most of the room was taken up by a groaningly full bookcase, the floor an obstacle course of boxes the Sullivans hadn't the room to unpack.

As always, Catherine felt calmer as soon as the door was closed. This was where she was allowed to be herself, where teachers and therapists couldn't poke and prod and ask her to be happy when she wasn't.

It was strange to have someone else in here with her.

'Let me see,' Catherine said, a trifle nervous. 'Oh, these are good! Dad gets me a book about war every birthday.' She handed Amélie a thick hardback, its edges festooned with brightly coloured stickers. 'I've marked all of the really good gory bits.'

She rummaged a bit more.

'Ooh! Here's a spell book Dad bought me at the crystal shop in Temple Bar.' She held up another book, this one bound in russet leather and inexpertly etched with symbols. She leaned forward conspiratorially. 'I don't *think* the spells are real. Also, most of them seem to be about "mindfulness", which I think is like happiness but quieter. I was hoping for fireballs or curses. And then *here* is my collection of fancy-smelling candles. Want to sniff?'

Amélie shook her head.

Catherine shrugged. 'They're nice. I'm not allowed matches to light them. But I guess that means they'll last forever . . .' Catherine trailed off as she saw that there was no expression at all on Amélie's face. 'Is . . . something wrong?'

'No,' Amélie said eventually. 'It's just not what I expected a little girl's room to look like.'

'Oh,' Catherine said, and put the candles down. 'OK.'

'I was expecting it to be pretty,' Amélie explained. 'You know. Frills and stuff. Like these.' She plucked at the ruffs of her dress. 'And to have lots of nice things. Not weird books about armies killing each other and candles that smell like dead flowers. And is that a throwing axe?'

'I won it,' Catherine said in a small voice. 'In a competition.'

Amélie Plasmavore made a face. 'And those decorations in the sitting room. Did you make those yourself?'

There was a large, awful lump making its way up Catherine's throat. No words would fit around it, so she just nodded instead.

'No wonder they look so ratty. Couldn't you just have bought some? Big glittery ones. Or . . . or those shiny foil ones that fold out into banners.' Her eyes had lit up again. 'I *love* Christmas. It's so indulgent. A feast for the senses. We don't have anything like it where I'm from.'

'They don't have Christmas in France?' Catherine asked, confused.

This wasn't going the way it was supposed to go. Catherine had seen sleepovers in movies. Catherine would show Amélie the things she loved most in the world, and then they would lie under a duvet, and tell secrets, and eat popcorn, and braid each other's hair. None of these were things that Catherine actually enjoyed, obviously. She was happiest on her own. But it was normal to enjoy those things, and so she was determined to try.

Unfortunately, it seemed that Amélie had decided to stop trying completely. Oh, she was still smiling – that blank, pretty smile, wide as the gleam of light on a knife blade – but the expression didn't match the words coming out of her mouth.

'I'm not French, you stupid girl,' Amélie Plasmavore said with idle cruelty, biting off each word with a clack of her perfect white teeth. 'I'm a blood-drinking alien from the depths of space. And I *think*,' she said, looking around her, 'that when I've drained you and your father dry this house will be a perfect little lair. After some redecoration, of course.' She smoothed the front of her dress as if brushing away crumbs. 'Little children should be sweet, after all.'

Catherine stared at her for a long moment. 'You're an alien.'

'A blood-drinking alien,' Amélie said. She seemed to be enjoying herself. 'Yes.'

'From space.'

'That's where aliens generally come from, yes.'

'Oh,' Catherine said. 'Then I shouldn't feel bad?'

Amélie frowned. 'Bad about what?'

Catherine hit Amélie as hard as she could in the face with her book.

The Plasmavore shrieked, tumbling into the narrow space between the bed and the wall.

Catherine was already yanking the door open and scrambling out on to the landing. *Dad*, she thought. *I have to protect Dad.* Maurice would forget his own head if Catherine wasn't there to remind him. Alien monsters were definitely beyond him.

Madeleine Plasmavore was standing at the top of the stairs.

Catherine skidded to a halt on her stockinged feet, mere inches from the huge woman's outstretched hands, but Madeleine made no move to snatch her. Her pale, clammy fingers hovered in the air, still as a statue's, curved into hooks as if frozen mid-grab.

Heart hammering in her chest, Catherine looked closer. The smug twist to Madeleine's features had disappeared, replaced by a dreamy slackness. She didn't appear to be breathing. Madeleine Plasmavore had clearly *been* moving, but then she'd stopped.

Like a powered-down screen, Catherine thought. *Like she's been switched off.*

Catherine hadn't even heard Madeleine coming up the stairs, even though their house had such thin walls you could usually hear the neighbours going up the stairs two houses over. Madeleine had been silent as a snake.

And then she'd just *stopped.*

Catherine was only a passing student in school. She daydreamed a lot. She really only listened to the parts of her classes that featured war, the supernatural or death. Numerous report cards had pointed out that this was likely to hold Catherine back in later life, but had failed to predict that her later life would involve a fight with aliens.

Blood-drinking aliens. From space.

And, though Catherine wasn't great on her times tables and had little to no interest in verbs, she had read enough about monsters to recognise when knocking out the leader shut down the troops.

Madeleine Plasmavore stopped just as I hit Amélie.

Even as Catherine had the thought, Madeleine suddenly twitched back to life. Her head came up, the waxy flesh of her face stumbling through a series of expressions.

Booting up. Start-up protocols.

Madeleine's eyes focused on Catherine, then narrowed. She smiled her toothless smile. But that wasn't why Catherine's blood went cold.

Knocking out the leader shuts down the troops. So, if Madeleine's awake . . .

There was a quiet noise. It sounded very much like a *shush.*

Catherine dragged her gaze away from the looming Madeleine to see Amélie perched like a spider on the ceiling above her, blonde curls hanging down like grasping claws.

'Merry Christmas,' the Plasmavore hissed, and lunged.

Catherine Sullivan woke to her father apologising.

'I'm so sorry, Catherine,' he whispered. 'Oh, God. I'm so sorry.'

Her whole body ached, but worse than that was a sensation she could only describe as 'faded', like a drawing that had been partially rubbed out. She felt blurred and jointless, her thoughts just scratches on paper. There was a point of pain on the side of her neck.

They were in the sitting room. Maurice was in his chair, bound with loop upon loop of garden hose as if trying to do his very best caterpillar impression, an image that would have made Catherine laugh had her thoughts not been so muddled.

She tried to lift a hand to rub her eyes, but couldn't. She was tied up too.

Amélie Plasmavore was sitting on the floor, carefully ripping all Catherine's carefully made decorations to shreds. Madeleine Plasmavore stepped in from the kitchen and tossed a pair of scissors to Amélie, who caught them without looking.

'Much better,' the little creature said, and promptly snipped a Christmas star in half.

'I'm sorry,' Maurice said again. He was shaking his head. 'I should have –'

'Oh, do be quiet,' Amélie said sharply, then gave Catherine a look of mock consternation. 'He's been like this for hours. How *do* you put up with it?'

The blurriness was wearing off, but that wasn't why Catherine was quiet. She was quiet because she didn't know what to say.

Amélie's smile widened. 'I'm not complaining, mind you. Things are so much easier when the prey doesn't struggle.' Her smile withered. 'I've been prey long enough. Running from world to world, just one step ahead of . . .' She shook herself. 'Well. Not any more.'

She reached inside a pocket of her dress and took out a long tube. At the sight of it, Catherine felt the twinge in her neck pulse in sympathy.

It was a straw.

'We're . . .' Catherine's voice was scratchy and weak. 'We're not going to make much of a meal for the three of you.'

Amélie smirked. 'If you were a civilised race, I'd be insulted.' She indicated Madeleine with a lazy wave of her hand. 'Don't let their wit fool you. Henri and Madeleine are Slabs. Bodyguards with just enough of my psychic imprint to pass unnoticed among the lesser life-forms. I'll admit their current forms are not as . . . artistic as I'd hoped, but a quick resculpting and they'll be perfect.'

'Perfect what?' Catherine asked.

'Perfect parents,' Amélie said. 'A perfect mum and dad for you.' She shrugged. 'Or close to perfect, anyway. My ship is being tracked. I had to take what I could get.'

The creature that had once been Henri Plasmavore stepped out of the kitchen.

The clothes were still Henri's – the coat, the scarf, the ugly brown jumper – but now they hung loose on Maurice Sullivan's frame. *No*, Catherine thought, *not Maurice's*. This wasn't her dad. It wasn't just the tufts of hair combed back in an approximation of neatness. It wasn't just that there were fewer frown lines crowding his eyes and mouth.

It was the fact that he looked happy. That was what really turned Catherine's stomach. There wasn't one, single change she could point to – even if she hadn't been tied up.

It was everything. It was his shoulders, straight and unhunched. It was the way he laced both hands comfortably round his stomach instead of fretting them up and down his chest.

This was the Maurice who used to take Catherine on climate marches, the dad who baked terrible fig rolls for every school fundraiser and took her out for walks during good storms or stayed inside and let her put sprig-like braids in his hair. This was the Maurice she didn't have to constantly look after. The Maurice who remembered things. The Maurice who stuck up for her at school and started planning for Christmas around the thirty-first of March.

This was her dad before she had lost her mam.

'See?' Amélie said delightedly. 'Huge improvement. Slabs are extremely programmable, especially when there's a live subject to copy.'

'That's . . . that's what you're going to do to me,' Catherine said. 'Copy me with your . . . your Slab.'

Amélie had that little knife-point grin again, shiny and sharp. 'Well . . . yes and no. *I'm* going to be you, Catherine. A much better you than you are, by the looks of it. A properly perfect little girl. And the process is far more enjoyable than messing around with Slabs.'

'It is?' the real Maurice asked haltingly.

'Oh yes,' Amélie said with relish. 'We Plasmavores have an expression.' She twirled the straw round her fingers. 'You are what you eat.'

The two Maurices stared at each other. Catherine couldn't blame her dad for being so stricken. It was like looking into a mean-spirited funhouse mirror – a reflection not distorted but *improved.* A better version of yourself than you could ever be.

She wondered what Amélie would look like, when Amélie was *her.*

'Of course,' Amélie continued, 'there's one *little* problem.'

'Problem?' Maurice whispered faintly, and Catherine noticed with a chill that the Slab-Maurice moved his lips almost in time with the real one.

'Yes,' Amélie said patiently. 'A problem. I'll be needing a picture of Catherine's mother. For Madeleine to copy.' She was suddenly on her feet, skittering closer on her little white shoes to tap Maurice on the knee with the straw. 'Quickly now.'

Catherine spat at her. It was half defiance, and half a ludicrous hope that any leftover salt-and-vinegar in her spit might somehow burn Amélie. Unfortunately, the Plasmavore simply dodged out of the way, quick as a snake, and snapped the metal straw she was holding across Catherine's face in a thin, stinging line.

'Nice try,' the monster hissed. 'I do respect anger a lot more than grief. And nicely observed on the salt. As dear Henri said, I have to be *very* careful about the amount I take in. That's why humans are so delicious. Your blood gets the balance *juuust* right.'

She turned back to Maurice. 'Come on then, weeper. Where are the photos?'

Maurice was staring at Catherine, his eyes red from crying. The sight made Catherine irrationally angry. He was her dad. He was supposed to be looking after her, and yet she was the one doing all the fighting. It was *typical.*

'Cupboard above the sink,' Maurice said. Catherine's eyes narrowed, and he gave her a minute shake of his head. 'The box at the very top.'

Amélie's laugh was a high little tinkle. 'Wonderful.'

'Don't you touch them,' Maurice snapped, but his heart wasn't in it, and Amélie just snickered again. 'Get one of your . . . one of your creatures to do it. I don't want *you* touching them.'

'No?' Amélie purred. She took a dancing little step towards the kitchen, a kitten playing with its food. 'Stand down, Slabs. I'll fetch them myself.'

'Be careful,' Maurice whispered. 'It's all a bit precarious up there.'

Amélie cackled. 'Are you really giving me advice right now? Grow a spine, human.'

She disappeared round the corner, and Catherine heard the squeak of little shoes on plastic as the Plasmavore scrambled up on the counter, then the creak of the cupboard door.

'Top shelf,' Maurice said, his eyes on Catherine. 'The box at the back.'

There was a rustle, and Amélie Plasmavore pulled on the box so hard that it and several Tupperware bowls of salt came down on her head.

Catherine didn't see what happened next, but she heard it, and that was enough. Every pane of glass in the house shattered as the shriek of a dying Plasmavore bored through Catherine's brain. It was so loud and went on for so long that she was almost convinced she'd be hearing it forever, and then it dried up, like a slug under salt.

Henri and Madeleine looked extremely confused for a moment, then fell flat on their faces.

'I didn't realise you knew I kept them there,' Catherine said eventually, through the ringing in her ears.

Maurice shrugged as much as his bonds would allow. 'It's not a big house, Catherine.'

More silence. Catherine bit her lip.

'I'm sorry,' Maurice said, and this time it was quieter and softer and smaller than all the apologies before, but somehow bigger too. 'I'm sorry you've had to do so much. I'm sorry I haven't been a dad to you for a while. It's my job to keep you safe.'

'It's *our* job,' Catherine said. 'Mam is gone, but we're still here. We have to keep each other safe.'

Maurice smiled sadly.

Then the door banged open so loudly Maurice fell off his chair.

Standing in the doorway was *another* stranger. He didn't have the sheer mass of the Slabs or the plastic prettiness of Amélie Plasmavore, but there was something in his wide, wild eyes and frantically orbiting hands that made Catherine think *alien* as well.

It seemed to be the night for them.

'Salt,' he said dramatically, 'can overload a Plasmavore's circulatory system.'

He paused, taking in the scene in front of him.

'The Slabs are down,' he said, and Catherine could swear there was disappointment in his voice. 'Did I do that? I don't think I did that.'

'No,' Catherine said. 'We did. Now, are you any good at knots?'

8

A GIRL CALLED DOUBT

When the Cybermen came to Agrippina, everything changed.

Change was the one constant, amid the chaos of the invasion. There had been so many news broadcasts, so many panicked voices – government statements, arguing reporters, experts and anti-experts referring to the Eleventh Cyber Legion as an army, as a plague, as demons, as the end of days. The only thing these competing opinions actually did agree on is what the Cybermen were there to do.

Conversion.

The Cybermen had converted Agrippina in a whole host of ways. It had been a planet of blue skies scrubbed clean of cloud by strong winter winds. Its cities had been long avenues lined by crocuses and neat plazas of marble so white it was hard to tell where the stone ended and the snow began. Agrippina Primus, the capital, had been a city of churches – not just the towering Cathedral Majoris at the city's heart, but dozens of little chapels and shrines and places of worship, each as unique as a loved one's smile.

Now, most of Agrippina Primus's avenues are rubble. The perfect lines of the plazas are cratered by bombardment, and the sky and the snow are grey with ash. From the top floor of the abandoned warehouse in which they've made camp, Doubt can see that many of the churches still stand but, instead of reaching proudly for the sky, their steeples now list to one side like a company of punch-drunk knights.

'All the crocuses are dead,' she whispers. It is the first time she has spoken aloud in days.

'Get away from the window,' Sergeant Terrick growls from beside the fire. He is the largest human being Doubt has ever met, and the quietest – a huge brute of a man whose eyes stare out, bleak and bright, from a face permanently darkened by camouflage paint and soot.

'We have to keep in cover, Doubt,' Memnes says. His voice is kinder. This is how it always works with the sergeant and the scientist: Terrick growls; Memnes smooths.

'The further we get into the city,' Memnes adds, 'the likelier it is we'll run into any steelers the legion left behind.'

Steelers. It's as good a name as any for the Cybermen. It describes what they are, and what they do.

Doubt pulls back from the blown-out window but does not apologise for her carelessness. She's only been part of the resistance for a short while, but she's already noticed that the extra second it takes to say sorry is a second you could be using to fall back in line. You don't apologise. You correct your mistake.

The other members of the squad have set up a chem-fire in the centre of the room, with boxes stacked around it so that the light doesn't escape. All the boxes are still in shrink-wrap. A vending machine in the corner is somehow still running. There are mugs in the sink. If you were to ignore the broken windowpanes – shattered like all the others in Agrippina Primus – then these soldiers would be the only sign that the war had happened at all.

'Feels strange, this fire,' Raoul says, rubbing their gloved fingers. It isn't really a fire at all, of course, but a crunch-pack of chemicals that, when mixed together, produce a warm purple glow. 'Not quite heat, but the *feel* of heat, you know? The dream of it.'

'Better than nothing,' says Badoris. Her pulse rifle sits disassembled in front of her, and she is trying to scrape some charry build-up from the barrel. Badoris does this at every opportunity. Doubt isn't very experienced with pulse rifles, and has no idea whether the residue affects the gun's performance or whether the slender, fussy woman just doesn't like knowing that it's there. 'And at least *they're* reliable.'

Memnes doesn't rise to the insult. He was some sort of scientist before the war. He doesn't talk about it much. But, whatever he was before, he is resistance now. There's a raw recruit in every patrol, to get them trained and ready to fight. Baptism of fire – they will learn or they will die.

In a way, the Cybermen are converting them too.

'Save your breath,' Terrick says. 'You'll need it if we're going to win the war.' There's a touch of irony in his voice. *Winning the war* has become a little joke among the soldiery, simply because it can't be done.

The Eleventh Cyber Legion converted Agrippina into a place near-unliveable, reduced it to ruin, and left it riddled with thousands of steelers they didn't think – or didn't want – to take with them. And, when the bulk of the legion moved on from this planet, they took the war with them to a new one. Doubt doesn't know where those Cybermen have gone, or whether other resistance movements are having more luck. Most likely they're all dead, or near enough.

Conversion, Doubt knows, is just another word for killing.

Winning the war means something else to patrols like this. The day you find a food cache. The day you find ammo for your pulse rifle, or a miraculously undamaged charging station. The moment you find a survivor who somehow made it through the invasion. Cans of preserved fruit and battered sleeping bags wouldn't have been cause for a parade in peacetime, but now they are what victory looks like in the city of Agrippina Primus.

The soldiers start putting out the fire, rearranging the boxes so it looks like nobody was ever there. Doubt helps, ignoring the sour look Terrick gives her. There's no use trying to figure out why the sergeant doesn't like her. The available evidence suggests he doesn't like anyone at all.

As she moves to leave, something silver winks at the corner of her sight. When she turns, there is nothing there.

The patrol moves through dead Agrippina Primus, up along the old docks, the piers now sitting high and exposed after fat Cyber-Collector ships drained the harbour dry. They scramble over defences – first the expertly laid ramparts of steel reinforced by energy-shield generators, and then the hasty barricades that were thrown up after the ramparts failed.

Badoris leads from the front, taking the squad from cover to cover as methodically as a child joining the dots. Doubt follows, then Memnes, still awkwardly holding the rifle Doubt has never seen him fire, then finally Raoul, playing the scope of their sniper rifle smoothly over broken windows and storefronts.

Terrick is . . . somewhere. He never stays too long with the squad, instead looping out in constant circles like a moth circling a flame, directing Badoris from defensible point to defensible point. Doubt will be watching some flutter of movement – cloth in a breeze, the scampering of a rat – and then suddenly the sergeant will be there, glaring and motioning with a jerk of his fingers to keep her eyes on the path ahead.

It's hard. Harder than he makes it look. Doubt has lived here her entire life, and every time they turn a corner she sees some new scar created by the Cybermen. She's been to Julius Café. It's supposed to have bright-red awnings outside and a host of stray cats out the back because Master Julius never closes his bins. The Domitian shopping district is supposed to be a tinsel-laced throng of people at this time of year, a wall of noise that always used to make Mother grab Doubt's hand extra-tight before they plunged in, like divers meeting a wave. These places shouldn't be empty. They shouldn't be rubble.

Doubt keeps expecting one thing – *remembering* one thing – and seeing another. She doesn't like it. It's as if the city is arguing with her.

Again, a silver flash out of the corner of her eye. She turns, but there is nothing. Nothing except the snow and the ash and the rubble like exposed bones, and the squad is moving too fast for her to be able to look properly.

It's nothing, she thinks. Silver is everywhere these days.

That's the worst thing about conversion. Doubt lost people in the war. They all did. She understands loss. The gap it leaves, that can be impossible to fill. It isn't that the Cyber-Leader and his legion killed Agrippina. It's that they killed it, and it's still here.

An hour later, they see their first Cyberman.

The steeler is standing in the shadow of a burned-out post office, facing the front door as if it has just knocked and is waiting for a response. The street for thirty metres around is covered in the charred remains of envelopes. Ash drifts on the breeze.

Doubt wouldn't have noticed the steeler at all if Terrick hadn't abruptly stepped out of the shadow of a truck to halt them, his rifle already trained on the lone silver figure. He doesn't say anything. He doesn't need to. Memnes and Badoris immediately turn to form the nine and three points of a clock – Memnes a little clumsy – while Raoul spins to cover their six with their steeler-killer sniper rifle.

Since Doubt is the newest to the squad she simply crouches, her pulse rifle up and panning. The thought of firing it makes her ill.

Cybermen aren't people, she tells herself. *Not any more.*

There is a huge government-issue poster on the side of the post office, and it shows a plucky Agrippinan youth in a peaked cap, dead Cybermen piled at her feet. The slogan reads UPGRA-DEAD: THEY'RE NOT WHO YOU KNEW. There were hundreds of these posters back at the start of the war – back when everyone thought the war could be won, and the news was still full of people asking for some sort of cure for conversion. 'What will we do with all the people the Cybermen have converted?' they asked. 'How will we change them back?'

Doubt heard scientists tried cures. Tried their own forms of conversion. By all accounts, it did not go well.

Nobody asks those questions any more. Now, there are just the posters, damp and faded beneath the ash, and the nickname that the soldiers have given the trudging metal monsters. *Steelers.* The undead come to steal you away.

And this steeler *looks* dead. It looks like it has been dead a while. It looks like it died in the war, back when the resistance had access to weapons more complicated than pulse rifles or pistols. Something high-powered and non-standard – a spatial cutter or positron cannon – has caught the steeler on its left side, scooping away a third of its body in a neat semicircle beginning at its lower hip and ending just below its chin. Like an ice-cream scoop, slicing one whole side of the steeler away. Snow has collected in the wound.

The steeler's one remaining hand is still moving. That's what caught Terrick's attention. It is gently tapping at the post-office door.

Threat minimal, Terrick signs with a flick of his fingers. Sign language is one of the first things you learn for these patrols, though Doubt finds it hard to get her fingers to make the shapes.

Hold fire, the sergeant adds, and then there's a knife in his hand, its edge glittering blue with an unstable molecule field. A veteran's weapon, designed for killing steelers. Terrick, Doubt knows, has been killing steelers for a very long time.

The huge man vanishes into the shadows, reappearing just a few seconds later at the far end of the street, just six metres from the ruined Cyberman. It does not notice, still sleepily *tap-tap-tapping* on the door.

Do we have to kill it?

The thought comes out of nowhere, and Doubt is immediately angry at herself for having it. Of course they have to. It's a *steeler.* It's a monster. It died when the Cybermen converted it, and all Terrick is doing is finishing the job. There are thousands of steelers like this on Agrippina, all left behind because Cyber-Leaders weigh every choice they make against the energy required. If it takes too much effort to repair a single Cyberman, the legion simply leaves it behind. That's why Agrippina will never be unconverted. The Cyber Legion didn't want to waste the resources to fix these steelers, but the resistance does not have the bodies to destroy them all.

The Cyberman tapping at the post-office door was a person once. They had a life. They had friends. They had family. But the monsters that stole them and took them apart don't even want them any more.

What a waste, Doubt thinks. *What a terrible, stupid waste.*

The sergeant is only a metre or so away now, a shadow inside a shadow, his knife behind his back so as not to catch the light. A sudden flurry of wind peels some snow from the windowsill by the Cyberman, and then there is that flash of silver again – just a tiny line glinting in the cold winter sun.

Did you used to work here? Doubt wonders, her eyes on the steeler's reflection in the dark glasswork of the door. *Did you come back because something in you thought the war was done?*

She pities the monster, then. The war will never be over. Oh, it might be won, some day, out in the stars, but the war will always be here on Agrippina, because the abandoned Cybermen will always be here.

Then Terrick's blade darts out –

A sound suddenly shakes the air, a low drone as menacing as a wasp, and deafeningly loud –

And the steeler catches Terrick's knife in the vice of its hand.

'Contact!' Badoris snaps. No sign language this time. That's how Doubt knows they're in trouble. 'Aerial contact!'

Memnes fumbles off his safety. Raoul racks a round into their rifle with a dry clack, turning with Badoris to follow the moaning purr as it circles above them, invisible behind the press of buildings.

It sounds like breathing. It sounds like the low and dangerous growl of a predator just out of sight.

Terrick doesn't bother wrestling with the creature for control of his knife. Instead, he lets it go, and drives his huge knee right into the Cyberman's damaged side.

Nothing. Not a tremor. Not a flinch. Instead, the steeler crushes the knife between its fingers and clubs Terrick on the side of the head. Suddenly Terrick is on his knees, the most confused Doubt has ever seen him, his mouth and eyes comically wide.

Doubt doesn't even think. She drops her shoulder and charges. The steeler has just enough time to turn before she puts it through the stone wall. It's the last straw for the post office. The whole structure, already sagging like it's been punched in the stomach, collapses in on the Cyberman with a roar. Dust billows over Doubt, and, through it, she realises that the sound of the unseen predator has vanished.

Doubt holds her hand out to Terrick, but the sergeant doesn't take it. Instead, he pushes himself to his feet with a groan. A bruise is already darkening the side of his neck. He was lucky the Cyberman was damaged. A punch from a steeler can break a person's neck.

For a moment Doubt has the distinct feeling that she's forgotten something, but for the life of her she doesn't know what.

'Sergeant . . .' Memnes points at the ground. Silver insects glint on the snow, scrabbling on their backs from where the building's collapse has dislodged them. As the squad watches, the little creatures right themselves and assemble into a neat line, then burrow under the snow only to reappear near the rubble.

They look like they're searching.

'What *are* they?' Badoris asks quietly.

'You're the scientist,' Terrick says to Memnes, somehow managing to make it sound like an insult.

'I was a surgeon, actually. Not that . . .' He sighs. 'You don't care.'

'No,' Terrick and Badoris say together.

Memnes crouches, looking closely at the squirming, creeping line. 'I have heard stories. Cybermites. Repair insects seeded in the ground after an invasion. One mite builds another, then those two build four, then eight, then sixteen. It can take months. Years, even, as the swarm looks for minerals. Like ants searching for food. Eventually, the swarm reaches critical mass, and they start to . . . well. Do what they were made to do.'

Doubt is kneeling right where the mites are disappearing into the rubble. They're tiny, so small it's hard to believe they're machines. Their shells are bright and shiny, as if brand new. She wonders whether they'd bite if she touched them. She wonders –

There is a click.

'Doubt,' Badoris says, her voice gentle.

Raoul and Memnes are looking at Doubt, too, and both have the oddest expressions on their faces. They all have their rifles up. In that instant, it is unclear to Doubt whether they are pointed at the line of insects or at her.

'I think you should step away,' Badoris says. 'They might be dangerous.'

Doubt gets to her feet, and just like that their expressions return to normal.

Don't apologise, Doubt thinks. *Correct.*

'They're more than dangerous,' Memnes says, uncharacteristic determination in his voice. 'We need to find where they're coming from. The heart of the swarm. If we don't shut them down, they could start rebuilding the broken steelers. A new legion, rising from the rubble. I don't know about winning the war, but if they're not stopped we'll lose it for good.'

The silver insects still glitter and shine, but now it is the dangerous brightness of something poisonous and revolting.

'Fine,' Terrick says. 'New mission. We find the source of the swarm, and we shut it down. Memnes, you take Doubt back to base.'

'What?' Doubt says. 'No! I can help!'

'With respect, Sergeant, you may need her. You may need both of us.'

Badoris and Raoul exchange glances. This is the first time any of them have heard the scientist stand up to Terrick.

'You said this swarm repairs Cybermen,' Terrick snaps. 'I'm not risking bringing a recruit like Doubt anywhere near that. Or a recruit like you, for that matter.' He glares down at the smaller man. 'A *surgeon.* Was that what you were . . .'

'Doubt?' Memnes says, without breaking the sergeant's hateful gaze. 'Can you tell which direction the mites are coming from?'

'That way,' she says without thinking, pointing to the east, further into the city.

'We need her,' Memnes says. 'You need her. And you need me, if this is going to work.'

Terrick holds the eye contact a second longer and then angrily shakes his head.

'Fine. Let's go.'

Doubt follows the silver flash, and the squad follows her. Every street they cross brings more of the shambling steelers – some walking in circles like wind-up toys, others scratching absently at their metal skin. Some stand as still as statues, staring upward as if waiting for the legion to come back. All are damaged. Limbs are missing. Great chunks have been carved away from chests and heads. Doubt sees a Cyberman, fully cut in half, dragging itself along a snowy street.

All of them are on edge, listening for that predator purr, but the whickering noise does not return.

Every so often, Terrick grudgingly consults with Doubt about which direction the insects are swarming in. They're strange moments, taut with stress because of the hostility radiating from the sergeant like heat from a flame. But there is pride there too. Doubt finally feels useful. Feels she is finally helping in a way she could not before.

'What are you going to do?' Badoris asks that evening. 'You know, after the war?'

The squad has made camp in a department store, the floor awash with trampled tinsel and confetti. Torn-down banners wish everyone a merry Christmas and promise peace to all.

Outside, the city is barely recognisable. The fighting was fiercer this far in. Whole blocks have been destroyed, towers ripped down, skyscrapers decapitated to make way for the Cybermen's own constructions: steeples covered in circuitry, spindly sensor platforms, blocky facilities that stand stiffly on thousands of short silver legs. Agrippina has lost its entire air force. There hasn't been an aerial photograph of the city taken since the first weeks of the war, but Doubt can imagine Agrippina Primus – with its jagged jigsaw of human and Cyberman architecture – looking not dissimilar to a snow-filled Cyberman skull.

Memnes has been watching Doubt. He thinks she hasn't noticed, but she has.

'Go back to work, I hope,' he says in reply to Badoris. 'Figure out how I can be of use. You?'

Badoris has her pulse rifle disassembled again. 'I was a teacher. Hopefully, I'll be one again.'

'Don't let Terrick hear you talking about this,' Raoul calls from their post at the window, though in a rare display of relaxation they have taken off their helmet and let their fabulously long red hair hang down to their waist.

'You don't have retirement plans?' Memnes asks.

Raoul snorts. 'I follow the sergeant.'

'Doubt,' Memnes says suddenly, 'what about you?'

Being asked feels like a badge of honour to Doubt, like she's one of them at last, and so she shrugs the way Badoris did. 'My mother and sisters were taken to one of the rural civilian hideouts up the coast. I'll go there. Follow the coast until I find somewhere green. Maybe plant something and make it greener.'

It's Raoul who smiles first. 'That sounds lovely, kid.'

'Yeah,' Badoris chimes in. 'I like that a lot.'

'What are you talking about?' Terrick asks, emerging from the shadows at the back of the store. There's a strange, frantic energy to the big man now. After so long scouring the city for ration packs and fuel cylinders, he finally has a real mission. A real war to fight.

'Nothing,' Memnes says. 'Did you catch any sign of the aerial contact?'

Terrick shakes his head. 'I didn't know the steelers still had an aerial presence on Agrippina. We'll have to be even more careful, moving out.'

'A storm is coming,' Raoul says from their perch by the window. 'Might provide cover.'

The sky is far darker than it was moments ago – a black swirl. Storms never used to come this quickly. Some effect of the invasion, a poisoning of the atmosphere. Just one more thing the Cybermen left behind them.

Nothing to them. Everything to us.

The silver flashes are nearly everywhere Doubt looks now, tiny threads like strands of a spiderweb. She shakes her head. For a second, her thoughts feel gappy and distorted, twisted like the clouds outside. The air feels strange and, even though the wind is rising, motes of ashy snow hang in the air as if suspended in the fluid of a snow globe.

'We should get moving,' she says. It's as though the threads are pulling at her, as though following them has tangled her up. She wonders if the same energy that has infected Terrick now fills her. 'Shouldn't we? I feel like . . . I feel . . .'

The storm breaks.

It isn't loud. Snowstorms never are. But the air outside is suddenly blinding, churning white, puffing like static, and with it comes a roaring, rushing silence, an un-noise that drives all thoughts from Doubt's head.

It makes the wheezing sound from earlier very easy to hear.

'Run,' Terrick shouts. 'Run!'

They run, and the noise chases them.

Terrick shoulders through the back door of the department store, checking his corners as Raoul and Badoris rush past. Doubt and Memnes come next, stumbling and uncertain, and Doubt flinches as Terrick pushes her into the lead, her mouth and eyes suddenly filling with gritty grey snow.

'You said you know where you're going,' the sergeant snaps. 'So go.'

Doubt runs, and the squad runs with her, through snowfall so thick and urgent it's almost solid. The noise comes with them – a warbling, wandering buzz. It sounds a little like Doubt's mother, the angry hum she used to make when she forgot what she was saying in the middle of a sentence. A searching noise. An insistent noise.

Doubt tries to look up and see its source, but the storm is so fierce that when she does her eyes fill with snow and she has to scoop them clean.

They run down streets, and across plazas, and through parks where everything living has died. By some miracle, there are no Cybermen in their path. Maybe the flying thing scares them away. It scares Doubt – scares her in a way she has never been scared before.

And then, out of nowhere, looming through the storm like the prow of a ship, is the Cathedral Majoris, battlements and spires stretching skywards. It is gigantic and awe-inspiring, and it appears so suddenly Doubt freezes in her tracks.

Doubt always loved the cathedral. It wasn't usually open to citizens; reserved for ceremonies of state and high society. At Christmas, though, the doors would be flung wide, and every soul wishing to celebrate was invited in. She remembers the queues, remembers showing up hours early and waiting in the cold. She remembers the hawkers selling hot wine and toasted chestnuts until the grim-looking altar servers chased them off. She remembers the towering doors inlaid with so much gold leaf that it was hard to see the wood underneath. Doubt used to trace the patterns with her fingers the way one might follow rain down glass.

Now, however, this is a cathedral to something else entirely. The gold leaf has been hacked away, a king's ransom piled like discarded wrapping paper in the snow. The neatly trimmed hedges have been torn up and replaced with tangled gardens of cables, some sparking uselessly. New metal spires have risen around the cathedral's steeple, crackling with energy, sending intermittent fingers of lightning up into the atmosphere.

And every inch of the cathedral pulses with a mat of writhing Cybermites, shimmering like the scales of a beast too big to exist. There are enough of them to rebuild an entire legion. Enough to *be* a legion, all by themselves.

This is the heart of the swarm.

Why, Doubt wonders, *does it feel like coming home?*

It takes Terrick and Memnes together to push just one of the cathedral doors ajar, both of them nervously eyeing the millions of Cybermites buzzing and clicking just metres from them. But the mites seem to have no interest in the soldiers, instead climbing over each other in great hanging drifts like sleeping bees.

The squad staggers into the long body of the building, shivering and patting snow from their shoulders. Snow has mounded across the flagstone floor. Statues have been toppled. And yet, despite the destruction, the great stained-glass window above the altar remains intact. In a city where every window is broken, it could almost be a miracle – if not for the fact that dozens upon dozens of steelers are standing before the altar like penitents. Each one is nearly invisible beneath a wriggling skin of Cybermites.

'They're being repaired,' Memnes breathes. 'We're too late.'

Metal heads twitch. Hands clench and unclench. Occasionally, there is a low moan, somewhere between the cough of a jammed printer and the mutter of a prayer.

Badoris, Terrick and Raoul have their guns raised, but even Doubt can tell there's no point. They'd all be dead before they had the chance to reload.

'What do we do?' Raoul whispers. They sound afraid. Doubt has never heard them sound afraid before.

Why am I not afraid? Doubt wonders. For a moment the snow-globe feeling returns, her thoughts a swirling, staticky soup. Something is unfolding inside her head, revealing itself like a skull beneath melting snow.

'They're not repairing,' she says, and knows it to be true. 'They're searching.'

'Searching,' Memnes repeats. He sounds fascinated. 'Searching for what?'

'All the Cyber-Leaders are gone,' Doubt says. 'There's nothing to unite all the steelers left behind. When the legion left, it took the war with it. These units are broken. Empty. Soldiers with no orders. Bodies with no minds.' She thinks of the Cyberman tap-tapping on the post-office door. 'Abandoned. Alone. Waiting for the Leaders who discarded them to tell them what to do.'

Anger rises in her, then. The war for Agrippina was hard-fought. Hard-won. Resources expended. Units downed, damaged, and then just left behind. What a waste. What a stupid, terrible waste. It offends her. Offends the very core of her.

Why? Why does it make me so angry? A shadow passes behind the final, unbroken window. Out of the storm comes that whirring, wailing noise again. Their pursuer knows they are close. It will not let them do what they came here to do.

Why did I think 'hard-won'?

The stained-glass window explodes.

Shards rain down. Snow rushes in through the gap, and with it comes a shape – not a Cyber-creature, not some waspish steel monster come to convert them to death. It's a box. A battered blue box that thrums and spins, landing with a crash between the steelers and the squad.

There is a long, shocked silence.

Then the door opens, and a man falls out.

'You,' he says accusingly from the floor, 'are all in serious trouble.'

The man is blond. He is wearing white and red. There is what appears to be a stalk of celery pinned to his lapel. It's the first green thing Doubt has seen since entering the city, and the sight of it oddly gladdens her heart.

'Except you, my dear,' he says, catching Doubt's eye as he climbs to his feet. 'You're not in trouble at all.'

'Who are you?' Terrick snarls, rifle raised. 'What is that box? Where did you come from?'

'All wonderful questions,' the man says, smoothing the vegetable on his lapel. 'But I've a better one.' He points at Doubt. 'Why doesn't she know who she is?'

'What is he talking about?' Doubt says, but before the sentence leaves her mouth the entire squad, all but Memnes, are pointing their guns at her. 'What . . . what are you doing?'

'I'm sorry,' says Memnes. He looks sorry – his rifle slung, his hands held out as if reaching for hers. 'But we wouldn't just reprogram steelers for routine patrols. It's been about finding the swarm. It's *always* been about finding the swarm. You were our best chance.'

'What . . .'

'You and all the other Doubts.'

Doubt takes a step backwards. Flagstones crack under her tread.

There's a raw recruit in every patrol.

Terrick's inexplicable dislike for her, from the very day they met.

The ease with which she had slammed that steeler through a wall.

What will we do with all the people the Cybermen have converted? The people had asked. *How will we change them back?*

'I have a mother,' Doubt says suddenly. 'I have sisters –'

'What are their names?' the newcomer asks from behind her.

'I . . . I don't . . .'

'When did you join the resistance?' he continues. She can see he is trying to be gentle, but the questions just highlight how little she knows. Her brain is a bombed-out city. There are craters. Gaps, where answers should be. 'Where did you fight? What age are you? What did you do before the war? What are you going to do after?'

The Cybermites are humming dangerously now. Snow drools from the steelers' slot mouths.

'My mother and sisters were taken to one of the rural civilian hideouts up the coast. I'll go there. Follow the coast until I find somewhere green. Maybe plant something and make it greener.'

It's exactly what Doubt said earlier. Word for word. Like a line in a play. Why is it only now that she notices that? Why is it only now that she can hear her voice as a mechanical growl?

'I don't hate a lot of things,' the blond man says, 'but I hate that you gave her an afterwards. That, I think, was especially cruel.'

'It wasn't hard,' Memnes says, and it's somehow worse to Doubt that he can say such things and his voice still sounds the same. 'We needed an early-warning system against the emergence of a repair swarm. A few memories hidden there. A few more created. Steelers all want orders. We just told this one to be a girl.'

'A surgeon. Was that what you were . . .'

Doubt looks down at her silver chassis, at the great gleaming paws of her hands, and she screams, and she screams, and she screams.

In the silence that follows, the click of Terrick chambering a round is very loud indeed. 'We found the swarm. Mission complete. Badoris – set the charges.'

Badoris looks from Doubt to Terrick. 'Sir . . . what about –'

'*Now.*'

'Sergeant . . .' Memnes begins, but Terrick has his rifle raised and pointed.

'I agreed to have that thing in my squad in order to find the swarm, and now we've found it. So now we don't need –'

'No.' The stranger, the blond man, steps in front of the gun. 'I'm the Doctor, and I won't let you do this. I came to Agrippina to help. To try to rebuild. And then I found out what the resistance was doing –'

'How dare you?' Memnes snaps. Raoul's eyes widen. None of them have ever heard him so angry. 'What we did was necessary. There are thousands of Cybermen on Agrippina. What happens if the Cyber-Leaders come back and start giving orders again? What happens if they repair a Cyberman enough to take that role –'

'That's why I'm here,' the Doctor says simply. 'I'm here to do what you should have tried to do the moment you realised you could make a Cyberman think for themselves.' He turned to Doubt. 'What do *you* want to do?'

For a moment, Doubt is as frozen as any other broken steeler.

'I could give you a big speech about how you're a person. And how you have choices. But you already know you're real. It's the humans who have forgotten. So what do you want to do?'

'Get out of the –' Terrick takes a step sideways to get a clear shot, but the Doctor steps with him. The barrel of the pulse rifle is darkly streaked with soot, and leaves a black scar across the pristine white of his coat.

'She's a person,' the Doctor retorts. 'You made her a person again. You stole her back. You can't abandon her now.'

'Sir?' Badoris says. Her gun is up too. It's pointed at Terrick. 'I think we should hear him out.'

Raoul stares between them both. 'We're not doing this. Tell me we're not doing this. Doubt is one of us. Sort of. Kind of. We *know* her.'

The Cybermites buzz and trill.

'It isn't a her,' the sergeant says. 'And I'm not risking them coming back. You think some of them haven't gone rogue before? You think she's the first Doubt I've had to put down?'

'Then help us find an end to it,' the Doctor says.

'No!' Every part of Terrick trembles except the hand that holds the gun. Doubt is reminded of him inching towards the damaged steeler earlier – life and death balanced on the point of a knife. 'Not until it's over. Not until they're gone. Not until we *win*.'

'We've already lost,' Memnes says, and lifts that never-before-fired gun.

Just as before, Doubt moves, faster than thought. Everything becomes static. Becomes snow.

When the drifting flecks clear, Doubt is on her back and the Cybermites are swarming. Wings unfold, light as glass, and a million silver insects boil upward into the arch of the cathedral like a tornado turned on its head, with Doubt lying in the eye of the storm.

'Sorry,' Terrick is whispering. He and Memnes have both dropped their guns. Raoul and the Doctor are shouting, though they can barely be heard over the burr of wings. 'Sorry.'

Doubt feels the tiny legs of a Cybermite land on the edge of the wound in her chest. Then another. And another. There's no pain. Why would there be?

It slips inside, and Doubt gasps as repairs begin.

When the legion left, it took the war with it. These units are broken. Empty. Soldiers with no orders. Bodies with no minds. Abandoned. Alone. Waiting for the Leaders who discarded them to tell them what to do.

There are no Cyber-Leaders any more. Just a lone steeler, who can think for itself.

Doubt pushes past the human memories in her head, reaching down and down into herself until she finds the parts the surgeons buried. Cold steel and connection.

'Don't apologise,' Doubt says dreamily. 'Correct.'

My mother and sisters were taken to one of the rural civilian hideouts up the coast. I'll go there. Follow the coast until I find somewhere green. Maybe plant something and make it greener.

Doubt speaks, and the swarm listens. It is a simple order. Maybe Terrick will destroy the swarm. Maybe the Doctor will be able to stop him. Doubt doesn't know. But there are thousands of broken steelers in the city, the city of her birth, a city with not enough humans to rebuild what has been destroyed. If the swarm can reach them, she can give them a last order, a final order, an order that might just end the war at last.

Plant crocuses.

9

A PERFECT CHRISTMAS

'It's a plot,' Vastra said morosely as she stared at the Christmas stocking. 'And I will not allow it.'

The Christmas of 1885 at 13 Paternoster Row in London was to be as conventional an affair as possible, considering the circumstances. Vastra was aware this might involve extra effort on their part. Neither she nor her Sontaran manservant, Strax, had grown up with the holiday, what with her being a reptilian detective from a prehuman age and him being a bloodthirsty clone. They had, as Vastra's wife, Jenny, put it, rather a lot to learn.

Personally, Vastra could see the advantage to being a stranger to the holiday (she refused to use the term 'alien to', as she was Silurian and therefore more of an Earthling than any johnny-come-lately mammal). It meant she was in the unique position of being able to treat human traditions as a sort of buffet, choosing those that intrigued her and entirely ignoring the ones that did not.

There was a purposeful note to Vastra's optimism, though neither she nor Jenny had said as much. Even Strax was aware of it. Last Christmas had been a sombre affair. A revived Silurian priestess had sought to lure Vastra away from her human-adjacent life with murder and nostalgia. There had been . . . tension. Vastra and Jenny's relationship had survived, of course, but it had been a closer thing than either of them liked to admit.

And so, Vastra was determined to pursue this year's festivities with a precision bordering on the scientific. Exhaustive research had been completed. Popular publications of the day had been consulted for recipes and trends. Traditions had been assessed and advice sought, particularly from children, who seemed to have a natural talent for ritual whimsy. A whole host of provisions had been ordered. Finally, and most importantly, a master list had been compiled – a document as detailed as any legal case Vastra had ever assembled, in this age or her own. It ran to forty-eight pages, not including appendices and diagrams.

The Christmas of 1885 was going to be one to remember.

'You know,' Jenny said, 'it's possible you're taking this a little too seriously.'

Vastra raised a scaled eyebrow.

December had dressed the city of London in winter's white, but inside their drawing room it was pleasingly warm, thanks to the advanced heating system that Vastra and Strax had devised. Fat vines climbed the walls, lending the air a rich, smoky scent. Jenny was perched on a stool, effortlessly balanced as she adjusted strands of tinsel. Personally Vastra did not see the appeal of tinsel, but this was what humans did at Christmas and so it would be done.

'I am not taking things too seriously,' Vastra said, trying to keep a most unseemly note of petulance from her voice. 'I am simply approaching your culture with the appropriate respect.'

'Very much appreciated.' Jenny flashed Vastra her pirate's grin.

Vastra fought the urge to return it. 'And,' she continued, glaring at the stocking on the mantel, 'my own particular research has led me to believe that stockings are a plot to limit the size and scope of possible gifts. You simply cannot fit anything of note inside one. It is a conspiracy.'

'I see,' Jenny said, jumping down from her stool. 'And do you have evidence for this?'

'Not as such,' Vastra admitted. 'But I have spoken to Henry Wainwright from number eleven, and he believes my theory.'

'He does?' Jenny gasped, putting a hand to her breast. 'And tell me, my love, how old is Henry? Nine?'

'Twelve,' Vastra corrected haughtily. 'Not that it matters. Satsumas, Jennifer. They are giving children *satsumas.* It is, frankly, a matter of human rights. I have a mind to warn the authorities.'

'Do not warn your foes!' Strax barked as he stormed through the door, his voice muffled by a stack of boxes. 'You will lose the tactical advantage.'

'Yes, thank you, Strax,' Vastra said wearily. One of these days the door was going to fall off. 'Didn't you say last week that surprise was the weapon of cowards?'

The Sontaran paused. Vastra could practically hear the wheels turning in his skull.

'Tactics evolve,' he said finally. 'The warrior who stops learning is as good as dead!'

'Glad to hear it,' Jenny said. 'Did you get everything on the list?'

'The raid was successful!' Strax placed the stack of boxes on the table and triumphantly waved a sheaf of papers.

'Resistance was utterly futile. I left a veritable bloodbath in my wake.'

Jenny cleared her throat.

'And by that,' Strax muttered, 'I mean I paid for the goods and services I required in the manner of a functional member of society.'

'Very good,' Jenny said. 'And what's –'

'Did you get the correct herbs for the goose?' Vastra interjected.

'Yes, madame.'

'And the breadcrumbs for the stuffing?'

'Yes, madame.'

'What about the wine?'

'*Yes*, madame.'

'Because I specified an 1858, and if you or the vintner has supplied an inferior year I will –'

'My love?'

Vastra lowered her voice. 'I would just like things to be perfect. We have a plan.'

Jenny gave the kind of nod one might give someone who is a hair away from agreeing to release hostages. 'And it will be, my love. Don't fret.'

Vastra looked away, then frowned. 'Strax, what's that box up there on the top?'

'Ah,' Strax said. 'I visited the feeble human constabulary on the way home.'

'The bobbies, you mean. The police,' Jenny said.

Strax shrugged his meaty shoulders. The effort to re-educate the Sontaran was . . . ongoing. As far as Vastra was aware, the closest Strax's culture came to Christmas was the ceremony in which they were given their first grenade. Not murdering shopkeepers was actually a sign of great progress.

'A pickpocket was nearly apprehended in Spitalfields Market this morning. The constable failed. *Pathetic.* Only managed to drag off the ruffian's coat.' He scowled. 'His superiors weren't even going to execute him for his failure!'

Horror entirely failed to appear on Vastra's face.

Strax sighed. 'Well, the commissioner had the coat put aside for you. Not as a case. There isn't one, really. But as a –' his face screwed up – 'mental exercise. Which I, of course, told him was a waste of time and the recourse of useless intellectuals . . .'

Strax disappeared into the kitchen, still muttering, and Vastra lifted the coat. The commissioner was fond of such things – little cases and curios, oddities and wonders. Sometimes she wondered whether he thought he was testing her. *That* was amusing. The hunters under which Vastra had learned her arts made Scotland Yard look like a nest of hatchlings. Armed with only her senses and a blade, she had hunted criminals at a time when the world was younger and more violent than these greyly civilised times. Any measure that could be taken of her had been taken a long time ago.

'I'm afraid I'll have to decline.'

Jenny's eyebrows rose.

'What?' Vastra said. 'It's Christmas. It's the holidays. And I do not wish for anything to intrude upon our time together.'

Now it was Jenny's turn to frown. 'That's not like you.'

Vastra looked stung. 'Not letting things interfere?'

'No,' Jenny said. 'You just like a challenge, that's all.'

The coat didn't look like a challenge. It was just a ratty old grey topcoat. One sleeve was matted with dirt as if its owner had fallen often, and badly. There was a frayed hole in one shoulder. *Moth-eaten*, Vastra supposed. She'd rarely seen a garment so desperately unloved.

'Besides,' Jenny said coyly, 'I like watching you at work.'

Some cold little knot in Vastra's stomach eased. It felt like a long time since her wife had smiled at her like that.

'A man,' Vastra said. 'Obviously. Previously wealthy, but now fallen on hard times. This coat was in high fashion ten years ago. If its wearer was still wealthy, he would have replaced it.'

Jenny sniffed. 'That's easy. Come on now, my love. Impress me.'

Vastra knew she was being baited. That didn't make it any easier to resist.

'He's stopped treating his skin condition,' she said airily. *That* made Jenny sit up straighter. 'There's strawberry oil staining his collar, but the stains are at least a year old. Can't afford it any more. Sudden weight loss, too. You can see it from the wear on the buttons. An illness, perhaps.'

'Madame Vastra?'

Strax had poked his head round the door frame.

'Yes, Strax?'

'Can I offer a theory?'

This was unexpected. 'If it's about shooting the butcher,' Vastra answered. 'Then no. I do not think it will "put fear into all the others, therefore improving our chance at successful commerce".'

'A theory on the *coat*, Madame Vastra.'

Vastra waved a hand for him to continue.

Strax gave the coat a long and serious look. Not for the first time, Vastra had the disturbing thought that the Sontaran's cheery brutality might only be a cover for a very sharp mind.

'I think that the coat's owner might be all those things you mentioned, madame. But the person who was wearing it during the scuffle at Spitalfields is probably a fifteen-year-old human child. A beggar, about five feet tall, with red hair and an impressive knowledge of local sailing curses.'

There was a long silence.

'Strax,' Vastra said. 'What makes you say that?'

'I just caught her trying to climb in the kitchen window, madame. Hit her with a frying pan.'

He looked at their shocked faces.

'Would you like to question her?'

'Want my coat.'

The girl was fifteen years old, as Strax had said, and unkindly constructed, it seemed, from string and sinew and straw. Every detail of her looked to be battling with itself – from her broad face to her long, gawky limbs, her hair a shock of angry ginger flattened where Strax had introduced her to the frying pan.

It hadn't seemed to slow her down any. When she had regained consciousness, she had immediately started flailing at Strax like a trapped daddy-long-legs but without, Vastra had noted, screaming or panicking. Panic would not have been an undeserved reaction to being treated by a Sontaran nurse, but instead there had been an eerie calm on her freckled face as she struggled. As if she had already decided nobody would come at the sound of her screams.

The look of someone who knows they have to save themselves, Vastra had thought.

Now, the girl sat in the centre of the table, fists cocked as if ready to give them all a bloody nose.

'I said,' she repeated in a thick Irish accent, 'I want my coat. Are ye deaf, as well as being . . .' she trailed off, scowling, 'whatever ye are?'

'I'm a *nurse*,' Strax said, his tone offended. 'And you are a patient. A patient with a mild concussion, by my estimation.'

'A concussion *you* gave me.'

'Well, that's neither here nor there –'

'Please stop,' Vastra said mildly.

She had donned the veil that allowed her passage through human society and now appeared to be no more than another British high-born. The girl glared at her. Vastra knew that look. It was the look of someone who had decided to prioritise escape over explanation.

'Why were you breaking into our home?' Vastra asked her.

'You've got me coat,' the girl snapped. 'I saw the bobby pick it up, and I waited outside the police station until I saw this . . . gremlin bring it back here. It's mine. You're thieving from *me.*'

'Well,' Vastra said, 'that must be a novel turnaround. And *is* it your coat?'

'I were wearing it, weren't I?' the girl said coldly.

'Then you are more than welcome to it,' Vastra said.

Strax and Jenny turned to her in surprise, but Vastra had already tossed the girl the battered old topcoat. The urchin couldn't help but flash a toothy grin as she snatched it out of the air, but the grin soon disappeared as she ran her fingers under the collar.

'Is there a problem?' Vastra asked.

'I . . . well . . .'

'It's your coat, you said,' Vastra said. 'And now you have it back. Unless . . .'

The girl scowled.

'Unless what?' Jenny asked.

'Unless she's just checked the thief's pocket in the collar and realised there's something missing. Something the bobbies didn't find.'

Vastra held up her hand. A gleaming ruby pendant slithered out from between her fingers, bouncing on a thin golden chain. The stones had the heat and hue of a Jurassic sunrise, red as freshly spilled blood.

Inside the largest of the rubies was a shadow, long and slim, trapped like a fly in amber.

'Give it to me!' the teenager demanded.

'Do you know what this is?' Vastra asked.

Her tone was still calm, her face without expression, though as soon as she'd found the pendant her mind and heart had started racing, thoughts swirling like the snow outside. *That thing. Here. How is it possible?* All she had wanted was a perfect Christmas. That's all. A Christmas to replace the one that had gone bef–

It was the gap in Vastra's attention that the child needed.

She lunged forward, snagging the pendant with her long fingers. Strax and Jenny both tried to grab her, but there was something evolutionarily advantageous in gangliness after all, and her lanky frame slid in between them like a knife between ribs.

She flung the door wide and was gone, out into the crystal cold.

They stared after her.

'Vastra?' Jenny said. 'Are you all right?'

It took Vastra a moment to respond. 'Yes. Yes. Of course.'

I could just say nothing. The thought came to Vastra shamefully quickly. She could just say nothing, and they could stay in, and drink wine, and cook a goose the size of Strax. It could just be Christmas.

'Strax,' Vastra said finally. 'You know my rules on appropriate weapons?'

'Nothing above a Grade Two,' the Sontaran said promptly. 'No grenades, nothing orbital, nothing likely to put a hole in the Earth's crust, no –'

'Consider the rules withdrawn,' Vastra interrupted. 'Load for war.' She drew her curved sword from its place in the umbrella rack. 'We're going out.'

'Madge O'Sullivan! I bring good news!' the nine-foot-tall cyborg sang joyously, then it opened fire.

The golden cannon of its left arm turned night to day with a beam of dazzling light, turning snow to steam and the shopfront of Downey's Greengrocers to sizzling ruin. The cyborg's other arm, a flared tube reminiscent of the trumpet of a gramophone, followed up with a searing blast of blue-white plasma.

No response was forthcoming.

This late on Christmas Eve the streets were deserted, the snow softening even the electric whine of cycling barrels to a dull burr.

The marble mask of the cyborg's face was as fixed and expressionless as the sarcophagus lid it resembled. It panned left and right, scanning for prey. Steam vented from the slot of its mouth. The sculpted panels of its chest rose and fell, like the pedals of a church organ, with the beating of its mechanical hearts. It was huge – a Renaissance statue brought to life – and it sang with the overlapping voices of a children's choir.

'Increase volume!' it yelled cheerily. 'Repeat exaltation!'

This time, it brought the building down. Plasma-chewed joists collapsed. Masonry boiled away to vapour. Walls fell drunkenly against each other, and a small figure detached itself from the shadows and leaped for cover.

'Aha!' The cyborg chortled as it took aim. 'Blessed are the meek!'

'Foolish robot!'

The cyborg swivelled on the brass gimbals of its waist to see Strax marching towards it, topcoat flaring like an angry schoolmaster.

High above on a rooftop, Vastra winced. *So much for a stealthy assault.*

'Meekness,' the Sontaran continued, 'is disgusting! A feeble tactic intended to pull on the heartstrings. Reject mercy, lest it be used against you!'

The cyborg cocked its head, dainty as a bird. 'Goodness,' it said eventually, then its stone features split into a huge and terrible grin. 'A debate!'

That was when Vastra hit it with her missile launcher.

The explosion didn't kill it. The Papal Mainframe built their Sacristan kill-bots to be durable – Vastra knew that from personal experience. But the impact did drive the cyborg to its knees, cracking away its marble face to reveal the clicking prayer wheels within.

It was still kneeling when Vastra approached, and fire had found its way inside its chest. Burning paper fluttered against its translucent ribs.

'Thou shalt not . . . sha-a-alt not . . . *shalt not* –'

'Steal,' Vastra finished. 'And, in that, we do not disagree.'

She brought her blade down in a neat arc.

Vastra was still staring down at it when Jenny plonked Madge down in front of them. The edges of the young girl's coat were singed, and she was missing some of that dandelion aura of hair.

'You missed the head,' Jenny said, a tad sullenly. 'I told you I'm the better shot.'

'And I told *you* to stay at home,' Vastra said. 'I don't want us falling behind on our plans –'

'That's not how we do things,' Jenny said, cutting her off. 'And besides, if I had, this little one –' she scrubbed her hand through Madge's curls – 'might have got away.'

'What is it?' Madge whispered. All the defiance had left her. Real fights tended to do that, Vastra mused.

'A Sacristan,' Vastra said quietly. 'Assassin android of the Papal Mainframe.'

'The what?'

'A church,' Vastra explained, and pulled back her veil. There didn't seem much point in keeping it on any more. 'A church from the fiftieth century, to be precise. A church that takes the theft of its holy relics very, *very* seriously.'

'I didn't steal from no church,' Madge said. Her eyes had widened at Vastra's features, but she seemed to have decided that the still-smoking cyborg in front of them was the more pressing issue. *Smart girl.*

'It isn't the pendant I'm worried about,' Vastra said. All that planning. All that *effort.* She had been worried about devising the perfect Christmas. Now, the biggest concern was surviving it.

'It's the TARDIS key inside it.'

'But it's just a *key.*'

They sat in the kitchen of 13 Paternoster Row. Madge had grudgingly accepted a cup of tea, and her eyes were fixed on the door as if she expected a charging cyborg to crash through it at any moment. It wasn't a bad instinct. Vastra was warring with something similar.

'All keys are just keys until you slip one into the correct lock,' Vastra said. 'And then, with a single turn, all sorts of things can be unleashed.'

The key was only really visible if you held the gemstone against the light. It wasn't anything showy: just a standard silver twentieth-century key, a touch battered and scratched. On first examination, the only thing truly remarkable was how it had managed to end up encased in a ruby.

That's not even close to the strangest place you've been, though, is it? Vastra thought. When she considered the places this scrap of metal had been, the things it must have seen, she felt, briefly, a strange kinship with it. Depending on the calendar, she was either approaching standard Silurian middle-age or older than all of human civilisation. It was a lonely feeling.

'This is the pendant of Tasha Lem, Mother Superious of the Papal Mainframe. She fought with a friend of ours called the Doctor at the Siege of Trenzalore.'

Madge's eyes narrowed.

'Fought *with* or fought *with*?'

'Yes,' Vastra said simply. 'She gave her life to protect an awful lot of people. For her service, she was buried with one of the most precious things in the universe. Not the pendant – though I'm sure you could sell that too – but a key. A key to a TARDIS, a ship that can travel through time and space.'

'Dunno what one of those is,' Madge said, shrugging, 'but can you get it out so I can sell the stone?'

Jenny fought a grin. Vastra scowled.

'Unless you have access to the kind of high-grade fiftieth-century molecular folding the Mother Superious's attendants would have, no.'

'I told you, I didn't take it from no Mother Superior.' The teenager had wrapped her long fingers round her teacup as if trying to store the warmth for a cold tomorrow. She was quite obviously focusing on the parts of Vastra's explanation that she could understand. 'It was a man in the street, looking around hisself like he was asking to be robbed. He didn't even see me when I bumped into him. Got a wallet and the pendant.'

'A new wallet, I imagine,' Vastra murmured.

Madge started, then nodded. 'How'd you know?'

'You can always tell a time traveller by the contents of their pockets,' Vastra said. 'Or the lack thereof.'

'You robbed the *Doctor*?' Jenny said.

There was a most unseemly look of amusement on Strax's face.

'He could have been a doctor,' Madge conceded grudgingly. 'Though I never seen a doctor without at least a few coins in his pocket.'

'I don't believe it was the Doctor,' Vastra said thoughtfully. 'He is . . . frivolous, but I don't believe he is frivolous enough to miss being pickpocketed.' *And you're a hungry child*, she thought, looking at Madge. *The Doctor notices children first of all.* 'But it has to be a time traveller,' Vastra continued. 'Tasha Lem died in the fiftieth century and was interred with this pendant.'

'Interred?' Madge said. 'Like in a grave?'

Vastra had always thought it looked like a snowflake. She'd only seen pictures, of course – her own run-ins with the Papal Mainframe meant she gave their territories a wide berth. But, when Tasha Lem fell at the Siege of Trenzalore, a great fleet of morimentum ships had been dispatched to a hundred freezing worlds, and each one had returned lugging a thousand tonnes of ice. Just carving the tomb had taken thirty years. A small price to pay true homage to the last, late Mother Superious.

'Yes,' Vastra said. 'A grave defended by a whole battalion of Sacristans who are no doubt on their way.'

'I didn't steal from no grave,' Madge snapped. 'I wouldn't –'

'I know,' Vastra interjected. 'But someone did, and then *you* robbed him.'

She tried to keep her voice steady. It would be easy to be angry. Easy, and pointless. The girl didn't know any better. Her world was moment to moment, meal to meal. She had no understanding of other worlds, of strife like the kind that had come to Trenzalore. But Vastra did, and the thought of that terrible war reaching out across the centuries and touching her wife and her Christmas didn't make her angry.

It made her afraid.

'So, we try and find him then,' Jenny said, pouring more tea into Madge's cup. 'Hand him over to the Sacristans so they go home.'

Vastra shook her head. 'The Sacristans won't care who did the thieving. They'll hunt whoever has the pendant.'

Tasha Lem had fallen at Christmas – another Christmas, a long way from here – and she had not been the only one. It wasn't just the pendant, though that was bad enough. It wasn't even that possessing such a key gave you access to the TARDIS, one of the most wondrous and dangerous ships ever built, though that in itself was a prize worth almost any cost.

It was the simple fact that the key was a piece of the Doctor, and any time a piece of the Doctor stayed in one place for too long the universe converged. Time Lords had their own gravity. Being too close could get you crushed.

Well. Not this time.

'I'll take it.' Vastra scooped up the pendant, slipping it into the pocket of her own coat.

'What?' Jenny and Madge said together.

'I'll leave London. Draw the Sacristans away. And then I'll contact the Doctor, and give him back his key.'

She looked at their shocked faces.

'It's too dangerous to stay here. We could be bringing great danger down on not just Madge, but on London. On the planet.'

'Where will you go?' Strax asked.

Vastra grabbed her veil from its hook. 'When are we? 1885? Alexander Bell should be on his second prototype by now. A few days in his lab and I might be able to rig up something capable of reaching the –'

'*We* could do it,' Jenny said. 'We've psychically linked to the Doctor before.' There was an odd expression on her face. 'We could do it together.'

Vastra shook her head violently. 'Psychically linking makes us vulnerable. It's too risky when we are being hunted. I must do this alone. You three will stay here. Continue with the Christmas list.'

'Pardon?' Jenny said incredulously, but Vastra was already pressing the stack of papers into Strax's hands.

'We're a little behind schedule, but I'm sure Madge can take over my duties, and if you jump to paragraph nineteen, subsection twelve –'

'So you're just leaving?'

'Jenny, I have to. That key is a link to the TARDIS. A link to the Doctor. I can think of fifty alien empires that would want it. I can think of monsters that would burn this entire *world* just to get their hands on it.' She forced a smile. 'I won't have your Christmas ruined by an intergalactic war. It isn't on the list, after all.'

'I don't *care* about Christmas.'

Vastra stared at Jenny for a long moment.

'That's not very in the spirit,' she said finally. 'Now, if you'll excuse me, I have to pack.'

Time and space bent. The snow drifting through the dark alleyway froze mid-fall, then began to rise upward, flakes spinning in a thousand gentle collisions. A pinpoint of ice-white light appeared. It tore itself in half to become two, then four, then sixteen, and finally a storm.

The blizzard of lights exploded outwards, rotating in a slow, perfect arc, then crashed together to form two massive kneeling shapes.

'Good news,' they whispered through unmoving lips.

Ammo-loaders rattled. War hymns began to throb from inside their ornate chests.

'We bring good news.'

When Vastra came back downstairs, the house was empty.

That hurt. She had hoped Jenny would understand. There was a focus of thought that came with being a detective. With being a hunter. The Sacristans achieved it through zealotry and cybernetics, but it had been drilled into Vastra since the day she was hatched.

Jenny would understand, once they were safe. First, though, Vastra had to make sure she *was* safe.

She patted the pocket of her coat one last time, her sword and bag hanging from a shoulder, and felt the hard shape of the pendant within. Such a tiny, tiny thing. It would be good to see the Doctor again. He'd understand that she had to leave to protect Jenny. It was, she imagined, a choice he had made with his own companions many times.

The storm had worsened, which was a small blessing. Deserted streets meant a much lower risk of innocent casualties should the Sacristans attack. They obviously had some ability to track the pendant. That was good. Vastra wanted them to be able to find her.

The Silurian moved through flurries of white, her breath smoking against the inside of her veil. The world was silent but for the papery rustle of snow and the fizzing glow of the street lights.

It should have felt peaceful. Vastra had been raised for the clean purity of the hunt. She had been looking forward to that moment when everything fell away, when you became your senses, when you became your footfalls and your breath, and that shining thread of your quarry's trail.

More than that, the time alone to think should have been a relief. Vastra was off. She *knew* she was off. She hadn't been thinking straight for months, not since she'd started keeping that damned list in her head.

Not the Christmas list – that laboriously assembled battle plan – but the list Vastra had been keeping in her head since last year. The list of missteps and silences between her and Jenny. The pauses, the occasional frowns, the awkward jokes that didn't quite land. Vastra sometimes thought of them as clues, or footprints, but they were what they were – all the signs of the fault she'd introduced last Christmas when she'd momentarily been a fool.

I hate Christmas, she thought.

'GOOD NEWS!'

Vastra ducked just as a fat line of light turned the snowstorm to spinning flecks and hissing steam. She went low, tracking the beam to its source a moment before it winked out, only to be replaced by the bark of a missile launcher. A wagon, tucked snugly beneath a tarp, went up in a bloom of flame and smoke.

Move.

Her limbs were sluggish in the chill. She should have anticipated that. *You've been distracted*, she thought, scrambling behind a snowdrift on hands and knees, pausing only to draw her sword. The cyborg was a dim shape up ahead, lit only by the street light and the lamp-glare of its single flaring eye.

You became complacent. You believed in your own invincibility, and so you came alone –

'THOU SHALT NOT STEAL!' came the voice, deafeningly loud. A voice from *behind* her. 'THOU SHALT NOT DESECRATE A TOMB!'

Oh. Oh *dear.*

Vastra had just enough time to scramble backwards as, with a crunch of golden pistons, a second cyborg landed directly in front of her. This one's face was a golden mask, its expression radiant as a saint's.

'Suffer not,' it crooned, and spun a burning scarlet blade through each of its six hands, 'the sinner to trespass.'

Vastra raised her own blade, and said a small prayer that the steel would hold.

Then the cyborg bunched its backward-jointed legs and leaped *over* her, before barrelling down the street.

Vastra stared after it, then jumped as a voice spoke near her ear.

'Cold getting to you?'

'Jenny!' Vastra's voice was half a snarl. 'Don't sneak up on me! I could have –'

'Could have what?' her wife retorted. 'I could never have snuck up on you before. Or swapped the pendant out of your coat pocket for one of mine without you noticing. You're distracted, Vastra. Why *is* that?'

Vastra's hand flew to her pocket, even as the first cyborg let out a whooping blurt of song and rattled down the street past them.

'Jenny, who has the –'

'Strax,' Jenny said. 'For now. He is *not* enjoying the feeling of retreating from an enemy, but I sold it to him as a set of tactical feints and I think he was able to make peace with it. Maybe the re-education *is* taking hold. But that's not who I'm worried about.'

'Jenny –'

'Vastra,' Jenny hissed. 'You and I are *fine*. Really. We'd even be happy, if you weren't desperately overcompensating with forty-eight pages of carefully planned Christmas traditions.'

Vastra stared at her.

'I know last Christmas was hard. I know we were shaken by it. But I also don't need to be protected. That's not how we do things. Just like we don't run to the Doctor before we talk to each other. And I don't need this Christmas to be perfect.'

Jenny slipped her hand into Vastra's. Her wife. Her beautiful, razor-sharp wife. Vastra's Silurian tutors would have been *terrified* of her.

'I just need us to face it together.'

'Jenny, I'm sorry –'

Another explosion. Snow caught fire then peeled away to steam. Not responding must have been *killing* Strax.

'Don't be sorry,' Jenny said. 'Be smart. None of this makes sense. Someone goes to all the trouble of stealing a rare pendant – a pendant containing the key to the TARDIS, no less – and comes to our time just to let themselves get *pickpocketed*? And then doesn't come looking for the pendant themselves?'

Vastra's eyes narrowed.

'Go on, my love,' Jenny said, grinning. 'Impress me.'

Then it clicked. It all just clicked. The worries clouding Vastra's head vanished, and she saw what she had been missing with the clarity of a hunter sighting her prey.

We don't run to the Doctor before we talk to each other.

It's just a key.

'Jenny,' Vastra said, and kissed her firmly on the mouth. 'You are a genius.' And then she stood, cupping her mouth with her hands. 'Sacristans!' she yelled. 'Sacristans of the Tomb of Tasha Lem!'

For a moment, there was nothing but the rasp of the storm and the clatter of reloading. Then the sword-wielding guardian padded through the dark, two of its six arms folded across its chest.

'Confess?' it trilled with the voice of an angel. 'Confess?'

'Not exactly,' Vastra said. 'You came here for the pendant of Tasha Lem, yes? That's what you're hunting?'

It cocked its head like a bird.

'Would you like it back?'

*

'How did you know they'd accept?'

It was the night before Christmas. They'd returned home to 13 Paternoster Row to find the back door open. Not only that, Madge and most of their provisions were gone. That was fine. The food was with someone who needed it, and that was the main thing.

'They're hunters,' Vastra explained. 'All they care about is their quarry. Had I not been so muddled with . . . Well. Had I been thinking more clearly, it would have occurred to me earlier.'

Strax frowned, placing plates of beans on toast down in front of Jenny and Vastra. 'What would have occurred to you?'

'Thank you, Strax,' Vastra said. 'A veritable holiday feast.' Her blood was slowly unfreezing, though that had more to do with Jenny's hand on hers than the central heating. 'That calling the Doctor would have been the worst thing we could have done.'

'Why?' Jenny asked.

'The key,' Vastra explained. 'He's never really needed one, I suspect. And . . .' Vastra paused, fork halfway to her mouth. She had briefly considered not sharing her deduction with Jenny and Strax. She didn't want to scare them.

I just need us to face it together.

'And keys are just keys, until you slip one into the correct lock.' Her earlier humour had fallen away, and now she spoke in a low and quiet voice. 'You said it yourself, my dear. A thief sharp enough to break into the best-defended tomb in the galaxy just *lets* themselves get pickpocketed? And then the key just *ends up* in the possession of one of the few people who could contact the Doctor? A person who could *summon* the Doctor?'

'The TARDIS,' Jenny whispered. 'They were after the TARDIS.'

'What good is a key without the thing it unlocks?' Vastra said. 'Poor Madge was nothing more than a pawn – putting the pendant in our hands and the Sacristans on our trail so that we might bring the Doctor and his TARDIS here. Returning it to its tomb means that it is once again under guard, and far away from the blue box it unlocks.'

'So Madge is safe now then,' Jenny said. 'Good.'

'Indeed,' Vastra said. 'Thus partially making up for her stealing our goose.'

Strax harrumphed.

'Are you sure?' Jenny asked, and there was just the slightest hint of uncertainty in her smile. 'The shops are all closed. We'll be on half rations until Boxing Day. It's hardly an orthodox Christmas.'

Vastra looked around the dim little kitchen. When the snowstorm cleared there would no doubt be questions asked about certain property damage nearby. There was a skinny little urchin girl out probably trying to either eat or flog three people's worth of Christmas dinner.

And, somewhere and some*when* beyond that, a mysterious foe had gone to quite a lot of trouble to use Vastra and her family as bait to steal a time machine.

Right now, though, it was warm, and they had food, and Vastra's wife was holding her hand.

'You're right,' Vastra said. 'It's perfect.'

AFTER

On a rooftop opposite 13 Paternoster Row, the individual known in this time and place as Madge sighed, laying her sniper rifle at her feet.

'They're not calling him,' she said.

The reptile was smarter than she had imagined. Madge gave it less than a day before they found the listening device she'd secreted beneath the dining table. By that stage, of course, she would be long gone.

'Good,' the boy snapped. She had never seen him so angry. That made her feel better. Anger made you strong. 'Researching the Time Lord's allies is one thing, but actively baiting them? You're risking *everything*.'

Today's mask was iron – a lump of metal roughly hammered into a disc and strung with black leather. He threw hers to her, hard enough to rock her on her heels. As she settled it over her face, she felt 'Madge's' features dissolve away. Maintaining a human face was an effort now. There were days when she could barely remember her real face at all.

'I've told you,' he said, voice softer now. 'We don't want the Time Lord's wrath. Not when we're this close. Not when . . .'

Not when there's so little of us left.

'Fine,' she said. 'Have it your way.'

He was right, of course. Their goal was not petty theft, but something far greater. They could afford to be patient.

Soon, they would have all the time in the world.

10

MISSING HABITAS FROND

SCOTTISH CROWN JEWELS STOLEN

The Scottish Crown Jewels, known more formally as the Honours of Scotland, were stolen by an unknown group of thieves. The jewels, comprised of a crown, sword and sceptre, are usually kept on public display in Edinburgh Castle. Superintendent Horrinthal had this to say about the crime . . .

'Excuse me, I believe you are in my seat.'

It was a day of firsts.

Normally, Habitas Frond, forty-six, of Prestongrath, Scotland, was not the kind of gentleman to complain about a stranger pinching his seat on the train. It happened often enough to Habitas Frond that he knew this about himself. It was as if seat-stealers could tell without ever having laid eyes on him that, upon finding someone in his assigned place, Habitas Frond would do nothing but awkwardly clear his throat, then go and stand somewhere else.

'Madam,' he said again, when the woman continued to stare out of the window. 'Excuse me?'

Habitas was also not the kind of gentleman who would move a *woman* from his seat, in usual circumstances. Habitas Frond liked to believe himself a chivalrous sort, even towards a woman who had seen fit to ignore the reservation card slotted in the seat's headrest and was now seeing fit to ignore him as well.

Then again, Habitas Frond thought, he had never been fired on Christmas Eve before today either.

A day of firsts indeed.

'Madam!'

The woman wore a plum-coloured skirt and jacket, her hair a skewered bundle above a dark and lazy smile. A governess, perhaps, by the arctic starch of her collar and the prim little topper on her lap.

Slowly, very slowly, she turned away from the window to look at him.

Frond involuntarily took a step backwards.

The woman's clothes said 'governess'. Her smile said 'snake'.

'Missy,' she said. 'My name is Missy.'

For God's sake, Frond told himself. *Get a hold of yourself.*

It was the last service out of Edinburgh on Christmas Eve, 1909. Frond had tarried later than usual, but he had booked a seat ahead of time to make sure he would have space amid the early celebrators and late shoppers. Was he going to have to stand for the next hour? Was it not shameful enough that he would be arriving home to dear Elizabeth and little Ben with the news of his dismissal?

It's Christmas. How much was one man supposed to take?

'Missy? Missy what?' he said, with what he considered to be a fair attempt at sternness.

'Just Missy,' she said, adder smile sharpening. 'Like Hamlet. Or Cher. Can I help you?'

'I believe,' he said, clearing his throat, 'that you are in my seat.'

A set of complicated expressions flickered across Missy's face, like the rotating images of a nickelodeon, before settling on an innocent curiosity so complete that Frond began to believe he had imagined the dark grin preceding it.

'Oh, how *awful* of me,' she said, immediately gathering the bag at her feet and making to stand. 'How could I –'

Frond flushed as people turned to look. 'Oh, well, it's not quite as bad as all that –'

'No, no, what an awful transgression. I am mortified, Mr . . .'

'Frond,' said Frond. 'Habitas Frond.'

That smile reappeared momentarily, like a nosy neighbour peeking through the curtains. 'Of course it is. Marvellous name. Now now, sit! I'm sure this lovely lady –' she indicated the small mushroom-shaped old woman in the single seat facing Frond's – 'won't mind sharing her seat.'

'I do indeed mind,' the old woman croaked. 'I booked this seat too, you know, and –'

Missy whispered something in the woman's ear. It was hard to make out exactly the expression on a face comprised mostly of wrinkles and liver spots, but all of a sudden there seemed to be just enough room for Missy to perch beside her.

Missy adjusted her hairpins, giving Frond a dazzling smile. 'All sorted, and no need to call your comrades in the constabulary. Isn't that nice?'

'Yes,' Frond said, then frowned. 'Wait. How did you know I was a policeman?'

'*Was' being the operative word*, he added morosely in his head.

'Detective novels,' Missy said. 'My one and only weakness. And, though I do not claim to be any great talent at the art, observing people has become a hobby of mine. A little game I play with myself.' She held a hand to her face, whispering as if imparting some great secret. 'I can also see your hat in your bag.'

It felt good to laugh. 'Well now, I think the department would be much improved by your presence!' Frond said, then his smile faltered. 'And, as of today, there is a new vacancy, I regret to say . . .'

'Oh, Frond,' Missy said, all trace of amusement gone. 'Really? How awful! I did not mean to make fun –'

He waved her off. 'You couldn't have known, detective skills or not. I only received word this evening, and, in truth, the superintendent was probably right to let me go.'

'I don't believe that for one second,' Missy said, patting him on the knee. 'Why, if I quit every time I failed, I'd never get anything done. Have you considered, perhaps, that any of those moments you perceive as failures could be entirely the fault of others?'

Frond thought about the time he had hailed a carriage to get out of the rain, only to leave the hard-won confession of the Beresford Strangler behind him in the cab. He thought about his subsequent reassignment to the Edinburgh

Constabulary's new forensics lab, and the accidental combination of chemicals that had resulted in an evacuation of the entire street. He thought about his forgetfulness. He thought about his distractedness, and clumsiness, and his absolute lack of an eye for detail.

And then he thought about this most recent calamity, and how it put all others into the shade.

'You are very kind,' he said as the whistle wailed, and the engine throomed, and the 21:02 service began to depart. 'But I'm afraid it's true. You've seen the papers?'

Missy clutched her bag tight. 'The theft of the jewels? Of course. Shocking.'

Frond sighed morosely. 'Shocking indeed. And I'm afraid to say – all my fault.'

It occurred to Frond, midway through relating his sad tale, that the superintendent might not have appreciated Frond sharing the events of last night with a civilian. However, on reflection – and after four sips of brandy from the flask in Missy's bag – he decided he hadn't appreciated being fired, so they were probably even.

'So there we were,' he said, a little flushed in the cheeks. 'Ten of us, the best the superintendent could grab from the night shift. The jewel thieves had gone to ground in the

Infirmary Street Baths, and he said we hadn't a moment to waste.'

Missy was rapt. 'You must have been so excited!'

Frond mostly remembered being nauseous. His expertise as a detective did not lie in confronting cornered criminals. Were he being honest, he wasn't entirely sure where his expertise *did* lie, but it certainly wasn't standing in a freezing alleyway at midnight, torch in hand, desperately hoping that if the thieves did make a run for it, they did not make a run for it towards *him*.

'Very excited,' he repeated. 'Yes. Unfortunately, the thieves were too canny, and as the surrounding constables stormed the baths, they managed to somehow slip away unnoticed.'

Missy tutted. 'But that's hardly your fault, is it?'

'*Ye-es*,' Frond said. It was a lovely conversation, and the brandy was just excellent, and he saw no point in ruining either by going into too much detail. 'Well. I imagine the superintendent needed a scapegoat for his own failure. Yes. That's it. I'm just a scapegoat! Superintendent Horrinthal likes to *play* the hard-bitten detective, stamping around crime scenes and chewing on those awful cigars, but really he is at the mercy of politics, the papers and public opinion.'

'How very awful,' Missy said, shaking her head. 'Truly despicable. And, tell me, was there any evidence found at the scene? Any leads the police might be following?'

'Hmm?' He thought for a moment. Surely there had been . . . 'Yes! I think there was. Truth be told, I was not paying much attention.' His features hardened as he remembered Horrinthal castigating him so thoroughly that he had to tell himself it was the cigar smoke making his eyes prickle with tears. 'Oh! This is something that could fit in one of your detective novels. A red leather glove was found at the scene. Flashy little thing. Other than that, I believe my . . . *former* colleagues are stumped.'

Missy nodded slowly. 'I suppose that's no longer your problem. You could nearly call it a relief.' She looked up as the train began to slow in anticipation of the first stop. 'This is me, I'm afraid. What a pity this was so brief! But lots to do, I'm afraid. Lots to see.'

'Ah,' Frond said, a little tipsy. 'A gentleman friend, perhaps? If I am not being too presumptuous to ask.'

Once more, that nickelodeon flicker. 'Not this time, I'm afraid. Though Scotland does remind me of him. Unfortunately, I fear he might never visit again, so caught up is he with affairs on Darillium.' She said the last with not a little venom.

'Darillium,' Frond repeated. 'I do not believe I have heard of it. Far East?'

'Sort of east,' she responded. 'Little bit east. More *up* than anything else. Without him, I find myself just wandering, trying to find things that amuse me –'

Her next words were drowned out by a sudden shout from the conductor. There was some kind of kerfuffle on the platform outside – two men struggling with each other, their features lost in the shadows of the platform's intermittent lights. Passengers were standing, wiping condensation off the windows, trying to get a better look.

The conductor shouted again. 'Thief! Thief!'

The second of the men bolted down the platform, leaving the first man staggering in his wake. Frond flinched as Missy grabbed his shoulder.

'Oh, this is perfect!' she said.

'It . . . it is?'

For a small woman, Missy really was surprisingly strong, her iron grip levering him out into the aisle. 'Of course it is! A chance to prove your quality, Frond. Go. Go!'

He went. Frond *hated* running. He had the stamina of an ageing sheep and the crumpled posture of a half-glued envelope. It took him just a single step out into the cold air of the platform to realise that he hadn't a chance of catching up.

And yet, something about the way Missy had looked at him galvanised his sagging frame, pushing him into a struggling, lopsided sprint.

A chance to prove your quality.

'Hey!' he shouted, immediately regretting it when the combination of exertion and empty lungs prompted him to splutter and wheeze. 'Stop!'

The ruffian showed no sign of doing any such thing. He was nearly at the end of the platform now, slamming both hands on to the ticket barrier and fairly vaulting it in a single bound.

Oh, well, I'm not doing that, Frond thought, and gratefully began to slow, before realising that he had left his bag and briefcase on the train. He lumbered back the way he had come but it was too late. The train doors had closed and, just as he reached for the handle, the carriages lurched into movement. A frustrated moan escaped his lips. His presents!

My hat, he thought forlornly, and then turned to find Missy making her way down the platform towards him. She must have been right behind him as he departed the train.

'Frond? Any luck?'

No, Frond thought. *Not lately.* It took him a moment to realise that she was talking about the thief, and then all Frond could do was shake his head.

Missy sighed. 'Not to worry. I've taken a look at the corpse – from a distance, obviously. I know my crime-scene etiquette. I think –'

Frond held up his hand, suddenly very certain that he had missed a fairly important part of the conversation. 'I'm so sorry, Missy. The *what*?'

'The corpse, my dear constable.'

She stepped aside, and Frond saw a crowd of shocked bystanders. At their feet, the man who had been robbed was lying face down in a spreading pool of blood.

'I'm afraid there's been a murder.'

'It's all right, everyone!' Missy said, shooing back the crowd. 'He's a detective.'

'Oh, thank God for that,' Frond said, fighting for control of his stomach with two pasties, a ploughman's lunch and four generous sips of brandy. Then he realised she was talking about him and felt sick all over again.

Maybe it was Missy's confident tone. Maybe it was that it was late on Christmas Eve and they all had homes to go to. Either way, they dispersed quickly, giving Frond, Missy and the corpse a wide berth.

'Yes, yes, go on, shoo shoo,' Missy said, following them a little ways up the platform before doubling back. 'Police business. Very important.' She patted Frond's shoulder. 'That was all right, wasn't it, Frond?' She grinned. 'I kind of enjoyed it actually. Maybe *I* should get myself a box.'

Frond had no idea what she was talking about, and decided that she must have been in shock. Frond could relate. He had been to crime scenes before – he was a detective, after all. It was just that, by the time he arrived, a lot of the work had been done. There were sheets over things. Someone had usually been over it with a mop.

And, though the air was cold and the wind was rising, blood was not a shy smell. It was a heavy smell. A purposeful smell. One that got right up your nostrils and into your brain so that your own blood thumped in reply.

'You should go on with them,' Frond said faintly, indicating the last of the departing passengers. 'This is no place for a lady.'

Missy was still smiling. *Why is she smiling?* 'You're *very* kind, Frond, but this isn't my first body.' She thought for a moment. 'Apologies. That sounded quite accidentally suspicious. What I meant to say was that I have a little experience with medicine. From my gentleman friend. He's a doctor by trade, as it happens. Do not worry, Frond. Blood holds no fear for me.' She scampered over to the body, slipping a toe underneath it to turn it over. 'Now, let's see . . .'

'Missy, wait –'

Frond didn't want to see. He didn't want to see the man's staring eyes and slack mouth, all painted a deep, dark crimson. He didn't want to see, because he knew from bitter experience that he wouldn't *see* anything. When other constables looked at crime scenes, they saw traces of soil on the edges of boots, and smudged fingerprints, and lipstick stains on collars. All Frond tended to see was the incident report he'd have to write if he vomited during a live investigation. Again.

'Missy, we should really just call for –'

'Hmm . . . there isn't much evidence,' Missy said, tapping her chin exactly like a detective from a pulp crime serial.

Frond felt a wave of relief and fought the urge to tap his chin too. 'Really? I was . . . I was just thinking that. We should call the station and –'

'All I can see is a thirty-two-year-old dock worker with a wife, two children, a relatively serious gambling debt and a weak left lung.' She cocked her head. 'Nope – right lung. Sorry.'

Frond stared at her in amazement. 'How can you tell all that?'

'Medical knowledge,' she said offhandedly. 'Can diagnose a patient from a mile away.'

'With gambling debt?'

'Frond,' Missy said patiently, 'I know your razor-sharp constable's intellect might get tangled up on every minute detail, but the trail is going colder than the body. Can you see anything at all that might be a lead?'

Frond struggled to remember his training. 'We should look for the cause of death.'

'Oh, that's not interesting,' Missy said. 'It's blood. He's been bloodened. Blood-out syndrome. Too much outer blood. Not enough inner blood.'

'With respect, Missy, I believe you may be in shock,' Frond said. 'Looking for the cause of death is really Chapter One.'

Missy seemed about to say something, then her features once again settled in that fixed, supportive smile. 'Right you are, Habitas. Go on, then.'

'Oh,' he said. 'I . . .' He knelt as close as he dared, trying to ignore the warm, thick smell still rising from the body. It all seemed to be coming from –

'A puncture wound,' Frond said. 'In the neck. He was stabbed by something thin and sharp. Like a needle or a . . .'

'Look at this!' Missy said suddenly. She withdrew her hand from the corpse's pocket to reveal a sheet of paper and a piece of leather as red as the man's still-escaping blood. 'Isn't this a . . .'

'A glove,' Frond said distantly.

'A red leather glove was found at the scene. Flashy little thing.'

There was the nausea again. Not the simple, direct queasiness of seeing blood on the *outside* when it should have been on the *inside*, but the bilious terror of being out of his depth. He'd felt it when the superintendent had dragged him out to corner the thieves. He'd felt it standing in that alleyway, terrified he would actually have to *do* something rather than disappear into the background like he always did.

'It could belong to anyone,' he said distantly. 'Plenty of people have red gloves –'

'No, Frond,' Missy said, her eyes shining with fierce delight. 'It's a *clue*. Of course it is. He was just stabbed on a train platform! Perhaps this was a quarrel between the gang who stole the jewels, and now one of their number is fleeing with them in hand!'

'Missy, I don't –'

'*Come now*, Frond,' she said, grabbing his hands. He winced at the feel of the cooling blood on her fingers. 'This is a lead! A lead you managed to *find*. And I'm sure there's more if we look.' She handed the sheet of paper to Frond, and knelt by the body once more, rummaging again through the pockets.

Frond looked down at the paper. There was an address hurriedly scrawled in the corner, half obscured by a bloody fingerprint.

Throw it away. The thought was quiet and desperate, and Frond flinched when he heard it in case Missy somehow heard it too. That was the thing about being bad at finding clues. It meant you didn't have to *do* things. Clues were just more chances to fail.

Missy sat back on her heels. 'Nothing more in his pockets. Oooh! Is there anything written on the paper?'

It was windy. He could just let the piece of paper go.

'Frond?'

The sky was black cloth, stars scattered like flecks of lint. Wind was raking the trees. If Frond squinted down the tracks, he could just about see the lights of the train disappearing into the darkness. Somewhere down that line was Elizabeth. Patient Elizabeth. Elizabeth who deserved better than a failed constable for a husband.

'I have told you already,' Frond said haltingly, 'I am no detective. Not any more. The truth is, I am not sure I ever was.'

'What do you mean?'

'Superintendent Horrinthal was right. It was my fault the thieves escaped.' He sighed heavily. 'All I had to do was guard the alleyway to which I was assigned. Everyone else was trusted to storm the Baths. And I . . .'

'Frond?'

'I went to get a bag of chips.'

Missy's eyebrows rose. 'You did what?'

'I went to get some chips,' he said. 'Nausea makes me hungry. When I came back, the thieves had escaped, and Horrinthal was, understandably, furious. If this is a clue, and if this is somehow connected to the theft of the jewels, then we would be far better off calling in the *real* detectives. I no longer have the authority to solve this crime. Nor, I fear, the ability.'

'That remains to be seen,' Missy said. She stepped forward to look into his eyes, the edge of her dress brushing the lake of congealing blood. 'Doesn't it? Tell me, Frond, what happens if you *do* solve it? What happens if you chase this thief – this *killer* – and apprehend him? What does that make of your ability, in the eyes of the superintendent? In the eyes of the public?'

In the eyes of Elizabeth, he thought. *I'd be . . . I'd be a hero.*

It might have been the cold air. It might have been the brandy. But Frond suddenly felt an unfamiliar fire kindling in his chest.

No, not a fire. A question.

Why not? Why not me?

Habitas Frond, the hero.

'A day of firsts after all,' he said, handing Missy the piece of paper with the address. 'Let's go solve a murder.'

*

The fires of confidence burned strong in Frond all the way through hailing a coach outside the train station and, indeed, most of the way back into Edinburgh. By the time they were rattling across the cobbles of Old Cowgate Street that inferno had begun to flicker. By the time the cab pulled up outside the address, they were naught but smouldering coals.

'I wonder, Missy, have we thought this through?'

'What's there to think about?' she said, before opening her bag and having a speculative look inside. 'Hmm . . . Frond, could you . . .'

'Oh, yes, of course,' he said, and paid the driver, wincing at the meagre handful of change he received in return. 'I just think we're being a bit hasty –'

But Missy had already departed, and all Frond could do was follow, shivering at the winter fog's icy caress. The cobbles were slick and treacherous with frost. A wall of white swallowed the street in both directions, submerging the buildings like ice cubes in milk.

And ahead – the Balelight Bar. Even when open, it was a grim institution; three floors of grey stone stacked untidily on top of each other like a child's playblocks, precariously held together by the looping staircase from street to roof. Now, all the lights were off, and the splintered wooden door was closed. The building and its denizens had cropped up enough in police reports that Frond had recognised the address on the bloodstained paper immediately. All sorts of illicit dealings went on at the Balelight. *Perhaps the two men were on their way to sell the jewels before one betrayed the other. Maybe this was where the gang laid low after the theft. They could be waiting for me just the other side of the door . . .*

'What am I doing here?' he asked, face grey and waxy with sweat. 'If the superintendent knew I was attempting a solo investigation he'd kill me! I should have taken the evidence to him. He would –'

'Snap it out of your hands,' Missy said. 'Wouldn't he? And tell you to get out of his way as he claimed all the credit. Like he always does, am I right?'

Frond nodded.

'Unless you show him.' She smiled encouragingly. 'Unless you show them all.'

She was right. *Damn the superintendent*, Frond thought. Missy was right! This was his chance to redeem himself. To save Christmas for his family. What was a little fear next to that?

Frond gritted his teeth, reaching for the handle. But before his hand could close upon it, the door jerked open, and a pale flabby face stared out from the space between frame and door. A pair of rheumy red eyes widened in panic, as they took in Frond and Missy.

'You! No . . . no!'

The man bolted.

'Stop!' Habitas roared, and plunged into the darkness of the bar, not waiting to see if Missy was following. The inside of the Balelight was a dank cave; the bar itself little more than a plank of wood laid over two kegs beneath shelves of dusty bottles and cigar tins. Drunk on the unfamiliar taste of both exercise and adrenaline, Frond did not notice the fleeing man tipping over a stool until it was far too late, and proceeded to plant his foot squarely between the stool's legs, pitching himself forward with a manful yelp.

I hope Missy didn't see that, Frond thought, face and shoulders a mass of pain as he struggled back to his feet. He looked around, but there was no sign of her. *Good.* This was men's work, he told himself, and, besides, the villain had made a cardinal error in fleeing upstairs. There was nowhere for him to run. Frond could ascend at his leisure. His limping, aching leisure.

The Balelight's first floor was a miserable little two-room apartment – just a cot bed, a battered chest and a washbasin of plates glued together with food and neglect. There was no sign of his quarry, but the back window was open.

The staircase. Frond cursed, but the thought of showing up the superintendent was encouragement enough, and he was out and on to the narrow, rickety stairs before common sense caught up. Step by creaking step he climbed, praying the rusty iron pins holding him up would not fail, until finally he stumbled out on to the roof with a gasp like a drowning man breaking the surface of the sea.

'Oh, hello, Frond,' Missy said, from the opposite side of the roof.

'Missy! What are . . .'

'Shortcut,' she said, pointing at the staircase from the street. 'Would you believe, he only went and fell off the roof?'

Frond rushed to her side. The man's descent had sliced through the fog like a knife through fat, and he now lay at the bottom of a shrinking tunnel of mist, his life leaking out into the cobbles.

'He lunged at me,' Missy said, giving the corpse a disapproving look. 'I think fear of the long arm of the law – fear of *you*, Frond, and your impressive pursuit – had driven him quite mad.'

'What do we do?' Frond said hollowly. It was an unworthy thought, but he found himself mourning his chances of revenge more than the criminal. *And solving the case, obviously,* he reminded himself, though that and embarrassing Horrinthal had become rather entwined in his head.

'What any detective does,' Missy said. She didn't sound discouraged at all. 'We look for clues.'

Unfortunately, the only evidence they uncovered was that the man who had fallen was Sidney Evans, barkeep and proprietor of the Balelight, and that he had not cleaned since some time before the Boer War. Frond searched (Missy supervised) but they could find no sign of anything that hinted at the identity of either the buyer or the gang, nor the location of the jewels. Exhausted, frustrated and increasingly aware of the long and expensive trip home ahead of him, Frond eventually gave up, slumping down on a bar stool and giving the one that had tripped him a desultory kick.

'Elizabeth will be in a panic,' he said. 'Ben will be wondering where his father is. This is pointless, Missy.'

'There must be *something*,' Missy said. She was examining bottle after bottle in turn and then placing them before her on the plank that served as a bar. 'For our sakes.'

'Yes,' Frond said absently. 'Wait. What?'

Missy looked surprised. 'Well, there's the body outside, Frond. Two bodies, really. I'd say we really have to solve these crimes, because otherwise the only connection they have . . . is us.'

Frond stared at her in horror. 'Us?'

She was right, he realised. Being present at multiple crime scenes wasn't suspicious for a detective, necessarily, but Frond wasn't one any more. It would not be that difficult, were one equipped with certain prejudices, to look at Frond's impromptu investigation and come to the entirely wrong conclusion.

'Oh God. Oh *God*,' he said, hopping up off his seat. 'We have to find something. And quickly. I just don't even know what we're looking for.'

'A connection,' Missy said, lifting down one of the polish tins that served the Balelight as an ashtray. 'That's all. To a buyer. To another member of the gang. Perhaps even an inside man. It is an ambitious theft to pull off without some kind of advantage . . .'

She looked into the tin, and her eyes widened.

'Frond. Look at this!' She dumped the contents of the tin on the bar, painstakingly picking away the crushed butts of home-rolled cigarettes and lifting out a charred brown cylinder.

Frond looked at it. 'It's a cigar butt.'

'*Yes*,' Missy said. 'And we know that the thieves must have had inside help to steal the jewels.'

'Do we?' Frond asked. Things were moving a little fast for him. 'I mean, that's just a guess –'

Missy had that smile again. Like this were a game, or the plot of one of her detective serials. 'You're getting bogged down in self-doubt again, Habitas. Your instincts got us this far, didn't they?'

'That isn't . . .'

But it was. Wasn't it? The barkeep had killed himself rather than face Frond. He must have been guilty. And cigar butts often turned out to be clues. He had definitely heard that somewhere. It did stick out, among the cheap rollies. That had to be something, didn't it?

It had to be. The alternative was Frond answering some hard questions about the two bodies so far this night. Horrinthal would enjoy raking Frond over the coals. He couldn't let that happen.

'So our inside man,' Frond said slowly. 'He smokes . . . cigars.'

Missy nodded patiently. '*And* must have access to the castle. Perhaps high up in government or . . .' She let the pause stretch out, until it became clear Frond had nothing to add.

'Or?'

She sighed. 'Or law enforcement, Frond.'

*

This time when Frond knocked, the man on the other side of the door did not attempt to flee. Then again, Superintendent Marcus Horrinthal was not the kind of man who fled from anything. It was that bloody-minded tenacity that had carried him first through military service and then to become the highest rank law official in the city.

Six feet of rugged muscle, topped off by a moustache stained the colour of weak tea by a lifetime of smoking cigars, glared down from the doorway at Frond. He was no less intimidating for his dressing gown and slippers.

'Frond? What in blazes are you doing here?' His eyes narrowed as he saw Missy hovering behind Frond. 'Tell me you didn't bring your wife here to plead your case?'

'Excuse me?' Missy said.

'A moment of your time, superintendent,' Frond said quietly. 'That's all I ask. Can I come in?'

The superintendent harrumphed like a descending portcullis. 'Fine. But only because it's Christmas.'

Frond had never been inside Horrinthal's home before, but it was much as he'd imagined – rich, dark wood and a plethora of animal heads, mounted on the walls alongside the pistols and hunting rifles that might have felled them. The superintendent bid them follow into his office at the front of the house, clearly eager to get rid of them as soon as possible.

'So,' Horrinthal said, closing the door. 'Why, can I ask, are you interrupting my Christmas Eve?'

'We'll ask the questions around here!' Missy barked, slamming her hands down on the desk.

Horrinthal and Frond both stared at her.

'Sorry,' she said. 'I've always wanted to do that.'

'Who *is* this woman?' Horrinthal snapped. 'I demand an explanation.'

'I think an explanation would do us all some good,' Frond said.

And he reached up to take a pistol from the wall, before pointing it squarely at the superintendent.

Missy laughed, clapping her hands. 'Oh, well done, Frond!'

'Frond,' Horrinthal said leadenly. 'Have you gone mad?'

'I feel as though I have,' Frond said. 'From the moment that gentleman was stabbed on the station platform, I felt like I was in a dream. Or a story where none of the details quite fit together until you have the single piece that connects them all.'

'Habitas,' said the superintendent. 'I don't think you realise . . .'

Frond allowed himself a moment of improper enjoyment at the forced softness in his tone. Had you asked Frond before tonight, he might not have believed Horrinthal even knew his first name, so used was he to roaring *Frond!* like a general saddled with a first-day recruit. *So many insults over the years. So many minor mortifications.*

He jabbed the revolver at the superintendent, who abruptly went quiet.

'I realise enough,' Frond said, and then he aimed the gun at Missy's head. 'Don't you think?'

'Oh,' Missy said, and smiled a viper's smile. 'Plot twist.'

'I am ashamed it took me this long,' Frond said.

'Yes, well,' Missy said, 'you are an astonishingly bad detective.' She sat on Horrinthal's desk, kicking her heels like a child waiting to be collected from school. 'I thought I'd literally have to draw you a diagram.'

'You killed those men,' Frond said. 'You *killed* people. Why?'

'I'm *bored*,' she said simply. 'And the Doctor seems to get such a little kick out of picking up you people as pets, so I thought I'd do the same. If it makes you feel better, you kept my attention longer than the last crew.'

Horrinthal had gone puce. 'Will somebody *please* explain what is going on!'

'Oh, you are tiresome,' Missy snapped, before her frosty smirk returned. 'No wonder Frond despises you. He spilled out all his woes to me, and I thought I would give him a little Christmas miracle to solve. I tell you: we were lucky we witnessed a mugging, otherwise that little old lady was going to get it.'

'A mugging,' Frond said with dawning horror. 'On the platform. That was all it was.'

Missy withdrew one of her long hairpins, and Frond tensed as he remembered the puncture wound in the first victim's neck. 'Oh, nobody writes detective series about *muggings*, dear Frond. So, I spiced it up a bit.'

'But . . . but . . . the jewels,' Frond said. 'The thief we chased. The red glove, and the address. The barkeep who dived off the roof rather than deal with us. *All of it.*'

'As I said, you kept my attention longer than the last crew.' It wasn't a viper's smile, Frond was realising. Vipers had motives you could understand. Missy's grin was . . . alien. 'You'd think they would have been grateful, considering I lent my considerable experience to helping them steal the jewels, but then they betrayed me. Well – I betrayed them first, obviously, but it was a close thing.' She tutted. 'Poor Sidney at the Balelight probably thought he'd got off clean, but then you came along and I thought, why not kill two birds with one stone.'

'You're a monster,' Frond said.

'What I am, Habitas, is annoyed we didn't even get beyond Act I.' Missy rummaged in her bag. 'I had a whole bunch of other clues I was going to fabricate. There was even a subplot about you turning out to be Horrinthal's son. That was going to be really exciting –'

'He's not my son!' Horrinthal said incredulously.

'Give me fifteen minutes with your DNA,' Missy said, 'and there isn't a doctor in this whole century who can prove otherwise.' She sighed. 'I'm *bored*, Frond. I told you that. I'm at a loose end. I've tried exploring. I've tried conquering. I cured a bunch of diseases, and then turned them back into diseases again. The last time my pulses got above two hundred was escaping from Skaro. I need someone to bounce off, and the person I like bouncing off most is currently enjoying quiet married bliss in an utterly boring corner of the universe. So I'm *helping*. Don't you feel *helped*, Habitas Frond?'

'Frond!' Horrinthal snapped, with that parade-ground snarl that Frond had hated since the moment he'd first heard it. 'Listen to me –'

'Shut up,' Frond heard himself say, then immediately flushed. 'I mean, I . . .'

'No, no,' Missy whispered. 'That's exactly right. This doesn't change anything, Frond. I can come up with some very convincing evidence for Horrinthal being the murderer, and you can be the one to take him in. Think of how impressed everyone will be. Think of how impressed Elizabeth and Ben will be. Isn't that what you always wanted?'

Frond opened his mouth, then closed it again.

'Frond, you idiot,' Horrinthal said. 'Tell me you're not listening to –'

Slowly, very slowly, the gun swung round to point once more at the superintendent.

'This is your Christmas miracle, Habitas Frond,' Missy whispered. 'All you have to do is take it.'

How much is one man supposed to take?

'Frond, I order you to –'

In the confines of the office, the gun sounded very loud indeed.

'Hmph,' Missy said.

Frond dropped the gun in horror, as both he and Horrinthal stared at the wisp of smoke that rose from the hole in the wall.

'Only you, *Frond*,' the superintendent said, the relief in his voice mingling with contempt, 'could be so incompetent as to miss at such a short –'

A hairpin materialised in his throat. Horrinthal gagged, fingers clamping round his neck, but the pin was sharp, and it had gone in deep. With a gargle, Superintendent Marcus Horrinthal fell backwards, taking a chair with him as he went.

'He's not wrong,' Missy said, lowering her hand. 'I however, am an excellent shot.'

'Oh my God,' Frond said. 'You . . . you killed him.'

'Well someone had to,' she said. Her smile had disappeared, replaced by a very governess-like look of disappointment. 'And now I find myself bored all over again.'

'Wh-what do you mean *bored*?' he stammered. He had tried to kill Horrinthal. What was wrong with him? How could he have been so stupid? 'We have to fix this. We have to . . .' He looked down at his commanding officer. There was really quite an appalling amount of blood, and the smell was even more forceful than before.

'I didn't do anything,' he said suddenly. 'It was *you*. I wouldn't have . . .'

'Yes, you would,' she said. 'You tried to. That's the problem. I could offer the Doctor the moon and the stars and he'd turn them down if it'd hurt a single hair on someone's head. That's why I keep trying. That's what makes it fun. You're not supposed to just *give in*.'

Elizabeth. Ben.

'What . . . what are you talking about? You said that we were going to –'

'Oh, there'll still be a crime scene,' Missy said. 'A really entertaining one at that. For the masses, at least.'

She reached up and withdrew another of her hairpins.

'That's the problem with substitutes. When I try to bounce off them –' she came at him, laughing – 'they break.'

11

A DAY TO YOURSELVES

WISH YOU WERE HERE

The engines roared, and time roared back, washing over the hull of the TARDIS in waves of icy blue and burning gold. Reality unfolded for the spinning wooden box, funnelling it through a storm of seconds, then folding back into place as neat as wrapping paper.

The Doctor swept through the doors, wearing his best and fiercest grin.

'Hello,' he said grandly. 'I'm the Doctor, and I'm here to save the world.'

'That's nice,' said the receptionist. 'And, tell me, do you have an appointment?'

The Doctor's grin faltered, then he rallied, straightening the lapels of his black leather jacket. 'Well,

I'm a time traveller,' he said jauntily. 'I don't really *do* appointments.'

That usually got a reaction. It was one of the Doctor's favourite details about the universe outside Gallifrey, as well as one of the things he found most confusing. Time travel was, to Time Lords, about as exciting as the postal service. It was mostly cheap, mostly reliable, and everyone used it. Yes, sometimes it took an awfully long time to get to the desired destination, and sometimes things went spectacularly wrong but, all in all, it was just a thing that happened, and you were a bit weird if you talked about it too much, particularly at parties. Non-Gallifreyans, however, genuinely believed time travel was magic, while ignoring the far more impressive inventions of their own cultures. Such as, for example, a delivery system where one paid a pound to have a folded piece of paper inside another folded piece of paper taken from Bingley to Guam.

If the receptionist was impressed, he was doing a very good job of hiding it. His wrinkled face was set in the grimly pleasant expression common to all receptionists when dealing with the unwashed, appointment-less masses. This was another little detail the Doctor found interesting: whether you were dealing with a nine-foot-tall receptionist samurai on Hegetory Prime or the planet-sized Appointmentrix of the Wailing Twelve, there was a *look*. They all had it. He'd always meant to take a weekend to investigate why, but he'd presumably have to make an appointment to do so.

'I'm afraid you need an appointment. We have a very packed morning here at Moveomax Holiday Cards,' he said, checking the inlaid screen on his desk.

His name tag said WINSTON. Winston was not a nine-foot-tall receptionist samurai, disappointingly, but Moveomax Holiday Cards was apparently the kind of company that invested in their employees, and eight segmented metal arms branched from his shoulders, each one stamped with the Moveomax company logo.

'Ah,' the Doctor replied. 'I understand. Except, wait. Because I don't.' He looked around. 'Isn't there some sort of . . . emergency you need help with?'

The receptionist followed his gaze around the waiting room. Moveomax Holiday Cards was at the forefront of the twenty-fourth century's holographic personalised greeting-card industry. The Doctor knew this fact because it was emblazoned on the wall in migraine-bright letters. Below these letters was a small, hard couch, a coffee table with a framed selection of bestselling cards and a potted plant. *Dracaena marginata*, the Doctor guessed. Unfortunately, aside from the plant being a little underwatered, there was a distinct lack of emergency to be had.

'I don't think so,' Winston said. 'Sorry.'

The Doctor's frown deepened. 'Well, I don't mean specifically in here.' He tried once more to inject some jauntiness into his voice. 'I don't really do office emergencies. Generally, the emergencies I fix are a little more . . . global.'

Winston sniffed. 'We trade on seventeen planets, you know.'

'Oh no,' the Doctor said hastily. 'I didn't mean to insult you.'

He was getting frustrated, and took a moment to remind himself that getting frustrated was good, actually. Frustration, he had decided, was something this version of the Doctor was going to feel a lot, because frustration meant he wasn't winning. The Doctor had won a war recently; now he never wanted to win anything ever again.

He picked up the little flip calendar sitting on the receptionist's desk. It was Moveomax-branded, and the picture of Santa on the front was animated, moving back and forth and waving at the Doctor. The Santa was Moveomax-branded too.

'It's the twenty-third of December, isn't it?' the Doctor said. 'In the year 2321? And this is the planet Eirene? Galactic coordinates 51–2–89–14:02? Past the wobbly red star and that comet with all the yellow bits?'

'This is Eirene, and that is the date,' Winston confirmed. 'I'm not one hundred per cent sure about all the other words that you said.'

'OK, good,' the Doctor said. 'Marvellous. Fantastic. It's just . . . you're really supposed to be getting invaded right now.'

The receptionist checked his screen again.

The Doctor waited patiently, or as patiently as the Doctor ever waited for anything. This meant that he fidgeted a lot, unfolded and refolded his arms several times, and absent-mindedly worked out Eirene's axial tilt based on the position of the sun and how long it had been since Winston's mechanical arms had been tuned up.

Winston's fifth and sixth arms readjusted his glasses. 'I'm afraid I don't have anything under "invasion".'

'Really?' the Doctor said. 'It's a Gnarlmind invasion, if that's any good to you? Kind of like rats, but worse. Giant rats. In spaceships. Think it's supposed to kick off around two?'

The receptionist thought for a moment. 'Oh! Oh, yes. Large rat things. I remember now.'

'Phew,' the Doctor said, sagging with relief. 'So, if you could just point me to –'

'It's all been sorted actually,' Winston said. 'Thank you very much, though.'

'Sorted?' the Doctor said. 'What do you mean, "sorted"? It isn't a printer jam.' He caught himself. This frustration thing was taking a while to get used to. 'Sorry. It's just there's supposed to be about forty-three million of them. I had this whole big speech prepared about how, in the face of a horde, it only takes one person to make a difference. Who sorted it?'

'A man,' Winston said. 'He didn't have an appointment, either.' His eyes drifted across the Doctor's battered leather jacket. 'Though he was better dressed. He had a suit. Brightly coloured shoes. More . . .' He cleared his throat. 'Taller hair.'

The Doctor rubbed his scalp self-consciously. Some said regeneration was a lottery, but at least with lotteries you got to enter once a week and try your luck again.

'He didn't leave his name, unfortunately,' Winston continued. 'It was all a bit exciting. But he did have a box. A box just like yours, actually.'

He pointed at the TARDIS.

'Oh,' the Doctor said. '*Oh.* I *see.*'

'Now that I think of it, he said someone might be dropping by.' Winston laced four hands pensively under his chin. 'And I believe he left you a . . .'

He turned to the shelf behind him, retrieving a blue pinstriped envelope with a single word scribbled on the front.

When he turned back round, the man and the box were gone.

Oh well, the Doctor thought, as the TARDIS plunged once more through the vortex of everything that was, will be or could be. *Bound to happen sometime, right?*

It was. It definitely was. The universe was large – really, truly, gigantically large – but it wasn't so large that coincidences didn't happen. He was always running into people from his past. And from his future, come to that. He'd even run into himself a few times, though that was usually only on special occasions. It was what happened when you had very specific interests – a bit like comic books, or Chibolg Mega-Stamps. There just weren't that many people interested in the same thing, so you inevitably ended up crossing paths with one another.

It stood to reason that, eventually, another version of himself would accidentally poach his adventure.

'Bound to happen,' he said, out loud this time.

The words echoed around the control room. There was nobody else to hear them. The Doctor usually travelled with people. Travelling with people was half the fun. If Peri was here, or Jo, or Sarah Jane, they could have had a laugh about the stiff, confused look on Winston's face. If the Brigadier was there, the Doctor could have had a laugh about it and the Brigadier could have scowled at him good-naturedly. Leela might have offered to stab Winston, and they could have had a jolly old laugh about that, too.

'I'd even settle for Adric,' the Doctor said glumly.

This was no good at all. It was nearly Christmas, or at least it had been on Eirene. The Doctor decided then and there that it would be Christmas for him too, because one benefit of living in a time machine was that you had Christmas pretty much on tap.

'I'm going to save someone's Christmas,' he said jauntily, and that made him feel a little better. He needed to put things out of his head. Move on. Keep moving, as far as he could.

'Bound to happen,' he said again, and pulled a lever to take both him and the thought away.

Wind moaned through the Crystal Sphere of Zed Trief.

No one knew who had made the sphere, or set it spinning through the void. It was one of this sector's great mysteries: where had the night-black sphere come from? Who had carved the mirror-smooth tunnels through its core?

To some cultures on neighbouring planets, the sphere was a bad omen, appearing at the end of every year like a miserable aunt. To others, it was a symbol of the universe's fundamental impermanence, how even beings powerful enough to create such a sphere could be forgotten in time.

To the Cult of the Breaking Sunset, it was home.

Dark and mysterious rituals required dark and mysterious spaces, so the fanatical brotherhood had plumbed the depths of Zed Trief, turning its chambers into chapels, fortifying its surface, installing stolen weapon platforms. The sphere had been a bad omen. Now it was a fortress.

Or so the Doctor had heard, anyway. He neatly bypassed every single one of the cult's security measures by materialising the TARDIS right in the middle of the sphere's great central chamber. More specifically, he materialised it right on top of the Grand Hierophant's black stone altar, knocking over some very ornate candleholders.

A thousand cultists paused mid-chant. The Hierophant, already a little top-heavy because of her crown, fell off her chair.

'Hello!' shouted the Doctor.

For all their many faults, the cult had picked an excellent spot to hold their sinister get-togethers. This was the largest chamber beneath the sphere's surface – a great circular cavern large enough to hold several football fields (should the Cult of the Breaking Sunset ever decide to get a match going) and so acoustically perfect even the slightest whisper carried.

'I'm the Doctor, and I've come to stop your terrible plan!' He paused. 'You *are* doing a terrible plan, aren't you?'

Silence. The Doctor rubbed the back of his neck. 'And the entrance? The entrance was OK, wasn't it? Sorry, it's been a bit of a morning.'

'I thought it was very good,' the Grand Hierophant said from the floor. Her features, like those of her congregation, were hidden beneath the hood of a voluminous black robe. The Doctor liked black robes. No self-respecting cult skimped on the robes.

The Grand Hierophant sat up, straightening her crown. 'Although . . .'

The Doctor hopped from one foot to the other self-consciously. 'Although?'

'I'm not quite sure we *are* doing a terrible plan, unfortunately.' The Grand Hierophant had the careful, surprisingly smooth voice of a community-club organiser, the kind of voice that took notes on meetings, got the proper insurance and remembered to put out biscuits. Good voices were also necessary when it came to running cults.

'Well, you would say that, wouldn't you!' the Doctor crowed triumphantly. 'You're the Cult of the Breaking Sunset. Worshippers of the universe's ending. You've chosen the last days of the thirty-third century to steal the Globe of

Unmaking from the vaults of the Shemi-Goroth, and now you're going to use it to punch a hole through reality itself!' He took a breath. 'Aren't you?'

The Grand Hierophant had the grace to look embarrassed. 'No. Sorry.'

The Doctor sat down hard on the lip of the black stone altar. 'Oh,' he said. 'I had a suspicion. Didn't see a Globe of Unmaking anywhere.' He picked at a bit of congealed candle wax with his finger. 'Can I ask why not?'

'Well, for a start,' the Grand Hierophant said, 'we're not the Cult of the Breaking Sunset. We're the Order of the Knotted Fate.'

'Blessed be,' said the congregation.

'The Cult of the Breaking Sunset were the last tenants. Left the place in an awful state too, I don't mind telling you. We recycled the robes because, well, they're nice robes, but we threw out all the skulls and candles because they weren't really in keeping with the whole Knotted Fate thing.'

'Blessed be,' said the congregation again.

The Doctor gave them a look. 'And so *you* stopped them?'

'Oh my, no,' the Grand Hierophant said. 'We just moved in when it looked like they weren't coming back. I wasn't actually here but –' she looked around, then pointed at a hulking figure in a hooded robe identical to all the other hooded robes in the chamber – 'you were, Clodus, weren't you?' She leaned in conspiratorially. 'Clodus *was* in the Cult of the Breaking Sunset. Now, he's on the side of the Knotted Fate. Aren't you?'

The huge figure shrugged. 'Just like keeping busy, your grace.'

'What happened?' asked the Doctor. He was getting frustrated again. This was what happened when you tried to go somewhere specific, instead of taking the universe how it came. Getting your dates wrong, well, that wasn't the worst thing. There were a lot of dates. It was hard to pick the right one. But he'd always wanted to see a Globe of Unmaking, a piece of technology that made a TARDIS look young. But now the globe was gone, like so much else, and the Doctor had missed it.

'A man came,' Clodus said, scratching his head through his hood. 'He interrupted the Elder Magnificant just as she was about to activate the globe, then gave the whole cult this big dramatic speech –' Clodus pointed – 'right where you're standing. And then it turned out that he'd done something to the globe's circuitry and, rather than poking a hole in the universe like it was supposed to, it just unmade itself. He said it was –' the Doctor could practically hear Clodus's brow furrowing in the depths of his hood – 'cascade polarity reversal.'

'Cascade polarity reversal,' the congregation repeated as one.

'After that, we all started thinking that maybe it was fate that the universe hadn't ended, and then me and the boys thought maybe we should find a new cult –'

'Order,' the Grand Hierophant interrupted. 'Order sounds better, Clodus.'

'As you say, Elder Magnifican–' Clodus cleared his throat.

The Doctor was sure that, within the confines of her hood, the Grand Hierophant was scowling.

'Um. Grand Hierophant,' Clodus went on. 'And, by the time we thought to look for him, the man was gone.'

'And tell me,' the Doctor said, pinching the bridge of his nose. 'Did this man also have a blue box?'

A ripple of nods went through the chamber.

'We thought about adopting it as a symbol,' said the Grand Hierophant. 'But then we thought about the other thing he said, and we decided that this might be more appropriate.' The Grand Hierophant pulled down her hood, revealing a face as wrinkled and shiny as an old apple, her hair a dandelion mass of white wispy curls.

The other cultists pulled their hoods down too.

They were all wearing bow ties.

'Bow ties are cool,' the Grand Hierophant said a little sheepishly, but the Doctor was already flinging open the doors of the TARDIS. Then he turned as if a thought had just occurred to him. 'Did he say anything? This stranger?'

The Grand Hierophant held out a red envelope. 'He gave me this. In case – and I quote – "the grumpy one with the big ears" showed up.'

The Doctor stared at the envelope suspiciously. 'What is it?'

'I think,' the Grand Hierophant said, 'he called it a Christmas card.'

The TARDIS spun. Outside, whole aeons flew by. Flocks of minutes whirled like spooked sparrows. Centuries pattered like raindrops against the doors.

The inside of the TARDIS was just as complicated as the vortex swirling around it. The Time Lords had built the TARDISes, but it was more accurate to say they had *grown* them. Planting a seed didn't mean you knew where every bud would bloom or where each vine would curl. There were places in the TARDIS that even the Doctor didn't know. There were rooms he had never been in.

There was one room he thought he might never go in again.

The door to this room wasn't dramatic or forbidding. It wouldn't have passed muster with any cults for dark and mysterious deeds. It was just a door, no more intimidating than the envelope in his hand, and that just went to show how misleading such things could be.

I should know better, he thought.

It was incredibly dangerous to contact your past self. Even the Doctor, who was curious in the way stars are hot and ice cream is cold, did his best not to meddle in his own timeline. Even the slightest knowledge of the *next* changed the *now*. A single bow tie could destroy the universe.

'Twice now,' he said. He'd gone back and retrieved the envelope from the receptionist on Eirene, mostly so he could glare at it. '*Twice*. And they're *writing* to me.'

What were they thinking? Never mind reading the card – just *having* it was a Class Four Felony. He dreaded to think what the Time Lords' Chancellery Guard or the Celestial Intervention Agency would have said about that. Gallifreyan law enforcement got really *ratty* about anyone messing with timelines. That was one of the reasons why the Doctor had enjoyed it so much.

Time Lords were so solid. So sedate. The TARDISes had given them a doorway to every picosecond and planet that ever was or would be, but the Time Lords looked at those door frames and saw picture frames instead. Like the universe was just a painting on a wall – faintly interesting, but mostly decorative. So intent on taking their time, when all the Doctor wanted was to take time and *do* something with it. That was the seed the Time Lords had planted in him.

'And look how that ended up,' he said, and gave the closed door in front of him a sad little smile.

That was all over now. The Doctor would have quite relished being dragged up on charges in front of his peers – again – but there were no more Class Four Felonies to be charged with because there were no Time Lords to do the charging. There was just him. Only him. And it frightened him to death getting a card like that, because it meant that maybe this loneliness would last forever. Maybe, somewhere out there among all the minutes and seconds was a version of himself so alone they were desperate enough to send him *cards*.

The Doctor knelt, and carefully pushed the envelope under the door. It could sit there forever, for all he cared.

'You're the last person I want to talk to,' the Doctor said, and went back to the TARDIS's control room.

One lever hadn't been enough last time. Now he pulled two, just to be sure.

Unfortunately, not listening to yourself cuts both ways.

The Doctor flew to the Ark of the Gammazed – that famed, failed expedition beyond the borders of the dying twenty-ninth galaxy – only to be gently told off by the ark's captain, who was 'doing fine, thank you,' since a nice traveller had pointed out the flaws in the Gammazed grav-acceleration design before they caused catastrophic engine failure.

A third card took up residence in the TARDIS. The Doctor pushed that one under the door as well.

Next, the X-Particle Mines. The Doctor had always wanted to visit the X-Particle Mines. It was said that, in the deepest tunnels, there were shapes. Shapes that whispered under the clatter of tools and the gasp of the particle collectors. Shapes that promised you things. Shapes that stole you away.

When the Doctor arrived, however, he learned that a nice woman in a blue box had not just rescued the missing particle miners, but had also convinced the miners *and* the shapes – revealed to be particle miners from another dimension tunnelling into this one – to strike for better holidays. Now the disappearances had stopped, and everyone got Sundays and Christmas off. Which was nice.

The Doctor left with a plate of turkey, the beginnings of a monstrous headache, and a fourth Christmas card. It was very like collecting Chibolg Mega-Stamps, he realised, in that you swiftly wanted to kill everyone else who was doing it.

That was when he had a fantastic idea.

*

The Forty-Fifth Chibolg Mega-Stamps Convention was held at the Zhudash Plaza Hotel, on the sprawling city-world of Ghent. It was the most famous event concerning Chibolg Mega-Stamps – which meant that if you were *in* the hobby it was the event of the year, and if you were *outside* the hobby you had no idea it existed. This led to annual confusion among the Zhudash Plaza's other guests, who for one weekend a year found themselves sharing the hotel with very intense beings from all over the universe who wore garments with slogans like IF YOU WANT ME TO LISTEN, TALK ABOUT MEGA-STAMPS or I WAS COLLECTING MEGA-STAMPS *BEFORE* IT WAS COOL! (The Doctor, on witnessing the latter T-shirt, briefly considered visiting this mythical time, but decided there were some areas of history too distant for even him to visit.)

There had been a time in Ghent's history when it had not been a city-world, but that was long forgotten. Now, every square metre of the planet was covered in shining neon towers and oiled-brass citadels. They marched not just over the land but across the oceans, the great floating raft-districts spreading like oil slicks. Forests had been bulldozed. Mountains had been planed flat. All for the ever-growing Megapolis of Ghent.

A hundred billion people lived in this city, and what little sky existed above the vast super-skyline was filled with circling, swooping atmosphere scrubbers, spindly as dragonflies. Their wide, thin wings were complicated arrays of smog-sieves and ash-collectors and they hummed softly as they drank in pollution and exhaled crisp, clean air.

'You know they have to keep moving?' the Doctor said, to nobody in particular, slinging first one leg over the hotel balcony rail, then the other. 'It's the way they're designed. They never land. Never stop.'

Behind him, the opening ceremony of the convention continued. The organiser – a twitching, hissing Voord whose rubbery black skin contrasted sharply with the distinctive white gloves of a Mega-Stamp collector – was giving a speech. People sipped drinks and chatted. This was a big occasion in the world of Mega-Stamps. Everyone who was anyone was there.

I should go make friends, the Doctor thought. He was good at making friends, most of the time. Though that might have been because he usually tried to make friends when things were exploding and, if you spoke like you were an expert on *why* those things were exploding, people tended to listen. And, often, he did know why they were exploding, which worked out well for everybody.

Now, however, he just couldn't bring himself to do it.

It was funny, he thought. He'd spent so much of his life running from his home world, but, now that it was gone, it was like the ground had been stolen from under his feet.

The roof of the Zhudash Plaza Hotel was 284 floors above the busy street below. Wind plucked aggressively at the Doctor's STAMPS? STAMPS!! T-shirt. He thought about saying something clever, but then decided that there wasn't much point if there wasn't anybody around to hear it. Then he pushed himself off the balcony.

It was a long fall, but Zhudash Plaza had not skimped on its safety protocols. The Doctor had barely plummeted ten floors before the hotel's lawsuit-avoidance hardware spun into life and caught him in a focused anti-grav field.

I could say something clever now, too, he thought.

Instead, he took out his sonic screwdriver and convinced the window opposite his floating form that it should be a door instead. The translucent gel that served Zhudash Plaza as glass opened in a neat circle, and the Doctor drifted through, feet touching down lightly on the carpeted floor.

'Hmph,' he said.

Suite 2V34 was an immense warren of complicated art and plush furniture, all carved from materials so rare they could have bought whole tower blocks anywhere else on Ghent. Wall-mounted screens played local Christmas-music videos on mute. The suite had its own kitchen, tucked away behind a holo-screen in the corner. The Doctor could hear the armed guards outside in the corridor, and gave serious thought to knocking something over so they'd rush in to capture him and he'd have someone to talk to.

He decided against it. They would have enough to deal with in a moment.

The Forty-Fifth Chibolg Mega-Stamps Convention would eventually become known as the Mega-Stamps Massacre, because the Fraternity of Keepers (who did not go for robes, but did have very sharply tailored tunics) was about to steal the Mega-Stamp commemorating the crowning of Chibolg Emperor Glin. A fierce war would break out in the wake of the theft. The hotel would be locked down for months.

That was why the Doctor was going to steal the Mega-Stamp first.

He made his way to the huge desk in the centre of the apartment, scanning it with his sonic screwdriver until he found three slight discolorations on the wood.

'Voord finger oils,' he murmured disinterestedly.

He held out three of his own fingers in roughly the same arrangement, pressing down on the stains until a secret hinge clicked and a panel slid back, revealing a tiny square in a glass display case.

'The Chibolg,' the Doctor said, 'built the most efficient postal service in the universe. It became a species obsession – hunting for innovation, improving response times, training legions of staff – and then they all just disappeared. Vanished one day. Total mystery.'

Nobody exclaimed shock, or seemed impressed, or used this as an opportunity to tell the Doctor something about their experiences with the postal service. Nobody said anything, so the Doctor continued talking, because it was better than being silent.

He swept his sonic down the little square, then nodded. 'I thought so. Sentient ink. That's where the Chibolg went. Everything they were, everything they are, rendered into data and written on paper. They began posting themselves.'

He smiled. It was the first genuine smile he'd had in a while.

'And why not? You build this amazing thing – of course you're going to use it. Why have something so marvellous and *not* use it to go everywhere and see everything? Why spend any time at home at all?'

He looked closely at the little square. The tiny threads of ink were writing and rewriting themselves constantly.

'I suppose home is what you make it,' the Doctor said, and lifted the glass display case. 'I suppose it only feels like home when you can't go back.'

There was a series of clicks.

'You're early,' the Doctor said, turning round to find seven guns pointing at him. 'I wasn't going to trip the secret alarm for another three minutes.'

'Hello, sir,' the leader of the security team said. The visor of her helmet danced with a glowing crosshair. 'My name is Squad Leader Quell. We'd like you to stand down, if you don't mind.'

'Hi, Squad Leader Quell,' the Doctor said. 'Nice to meet you. I probably won't stand down, actually, if it's all the same to you. I think I'll escape with this Mega-Stamp so it can't be stolen, thus preventing all-out war.'

'That does sound nice,' the soldier said. 'And what do you plan to do after that?'

The Doctor shrugged. 'Don't ask me this early. I never know this early.'

'He said you'd say that.'

The translucent gel of the windows shimmered and became diamond-hard. Armoured panels crashed down over all the doors. The other members of the security team moved like the jaws of a trap, surrounding the Doctor and covering the doors.

There was a long moment of silence.

'Was it the bow-tie one again?' the Doctor said. 'Because I –'

'I don't know anything about a bow tie, sir,' Quell said. 'This gentleman had a bit of an accent, sir. Sort of an angry accent. He –'

The Doctor waved his hands. 'Don't be specific! I can't know specifics. I'm trying to forget the specifics I've already heard!'

'Sorry, sir.' The Doctor had never seen someone so apologetically point a gun before. The crosshairs on Quell's visor flashed as she blinked. 'Our orders are specific. He's going to deal with the kerfuffle outside, and you're going to put your feet up for Christmas.'

'I'm *what*?'

'He says you need a break. That's what Christmas is for.' Quell indicated the plush surroundings. 'This suite is practically impregnable. He paid quite a lot of money for us all to train in a very expensive restaurant on Darillium, sir. He really thinks you should take some time off, sir. He said he was trying to be nice.'

'House arrest,' the Doctor said disbelievingly. 'House arrest as a Christmas present.'

The security guard looked distinctly uncomfortable. 'I'm sorry, sir,' Quell repeated. 'He said you'd understand why he couldn't say more. He said there's a room in the blue box you won't go into, and he says he knows why.'

The Doctor let out a long sigh. 'All right. *All right.* Just let me . . .' His eyes narrowed. 'So you're all highly trained, are you? Best equipment in the universe? Probably kitted out with all sorts of enhanced sensors, right?'

The security guard nodded. 'Best money can buy, sir. Magnification of all five senses. I can hear the atmosphere scrubbers sighing two hundred feet up. I can hear the bell at reception. They're really very strong sensors, sir.'

'Wonderful,' the Doctor said. 'Fantastic.'

He pointed his sonic screwdriver at the wall-mounted screens.

'How loud do you think these go?'

Later, the Doctor sent Quell and the whole security team boxes of chocolates as an apology. In their thank-you notes, they assured him their hearing was definitely going to come back.

They also sent him a fifth card.

And *later* later, when the adrenaline had worn off and the silence had returned, the nervous energy that the Doctor usually poured into bad jokes and rescuing the universe propelled him, as it always did, to the door. The door he wouldn't open. The door he hadn't opened since trading his former self's clothes for a battered coat and the first T-shirt he could find, old boots crunching on a carpet of broken glass.

'OK,' he said. 'Fine.'

He opened the door and stepped inside.

There were many phrases on Earth that did not translate to Gallifrey. One of those was the notion of a walk-in wardrobe. The costume room of the TARDIS was not a walk-in wardrobe; it was a walk-about wardrobe. A walk-for-miles wardrobe. Even the Doctor didn't know how far it stretched. Sometimes he wondered whether the TARDIS was always quietly adding to it because it liked dressing him up in new clothes.

There were a lot of mirrors in the costume room. All of them were broken.

'I'm sorry about that,' he said.

The TARDIS did not respond, but the grumble of the engines smoothed just a little at his words.

'I don't even really remember doing it. My memories are fuzzier than they should be.' He stuck a finger in his ear and wiggled it. 'Timelines grating off each other. My future selves changing things. Messing around. Messing things up.'

He looked down at the floor.

The Time War. Gallifrey's ending. The version of himself who did these things, and all the other versions who were to come.

'I worry they're still grieving.'

He noticed there was a broom in the corner. It hadn't been there before. The timeship could have repaired all the mirrors itself, folded away the broken glass as if it had never been there, but the TARDIS knew the Doctor. It knew moving was better than standing still.

The Doctor began gently sweeping up the glass.

'The old things feel different. My adventures don't feel right. It's like Gallifrey was always *there*. It was my forwarding address. It was the star I guided myself by, even when I didn't agree with it, or didn't approve of it, or defied it entirely. Where do I go from here?'

Something caught in his broom. He looked down.

It was another envelope. Small and scuffed and brown, tucked underneath one of the largest shards of glass.

'If I don't want cards from my future selves,' the Doctor said, 'then I definitely don't want one from *you*. I left you behind. You're the me who did this. This is your fault, and now I have to clean up the mess.'

He snatched up the envelope, angry now. Angry enough to tear it open and pull out the card.

It wasn't a Christmas card.

It was small, and Moveomax-branded. The little shape on it spun and sparkled in its field of black.

The Doctor stared at it. He had seen a lot of planets. There were square planets. Living planets. Planets made of song. He was from a planet that was as red and orange as a fire agate – so red you could almost feel its heat from space. The planet on the card was blue and green. Not particularly impressive. Not particularly large. The script on the card read WISH YOU WERE HERE.

The Doctor looked around the room, at the costumes he had worn and might wear, and then he looked at the one place he had always gone no matter how lost he felt.

'Home,' the Doctor said. 'A place that always needs saving.'

He closed the card.

'Merry Christmas to me.'

12

THE PARADOX MOON

POLICE BOX

1

Before

23 June 2007, UNIT Aircraft Carrier Valiant

It was the Master's utopia, so of course it was the end of the world.

Geneva was burning. Tokyo was aflame. The President of the United States of America had just been vaporised live on TV. A demented Time Lord had conquered the Earth, and a rift had opened in the sky – a blood-red scar the length of a continent, disgorging a rain of invaders that giggled as they killed.

Extravagant, Sibling Same thought. He was on his knees, gasping at the cold metal deck. Everything felt too real and not real at all – the warble of alarms, the tremor of marching feet, the crackle and pulse of distant guns.

Just for an instant, he saw the grating *through* his fingers, as if he were on the verge of fading away.

Get up, he thought. *This is nothing. You survived the war, didn't you?*

It was an ironic little mantra. Technically, *nobody* had survived what a grateful universe was now calling the Last Great Time War. Technically, it had never even happened; wiped from existence by a do-gooder Time Lord and their truly colossal sense of entitlement. A fitting end for a war in which time itself had become a battleground, so torn by constant interference that eventually you couldn't even trust one second to follow the next.

Staggering to his feet, wiping drool away with a translucent hand, Sibling Same set out, trying not to think about how the red light of the alarms was painting him crimson from the inside out. There was a lot of commotion. Soldiers were running. Civilians were panicking. He could hear radio chatter and intercom announcements, coming fast and loud and panicked:

'Repeat, repeat! The Doctor has been captured!'

'This is London! We're under siege. Oh God, what do we do?'

And then, over everything, a voice, thunderous with manic satisfaction. The voice of a child with no limits to its spite or its hunger:

'– *and I looked down upon my new dominion, as Master of All* –'

For a weak, sentimental moment, Sibling Same wished he could tell them: None of this had ever happened. Oh, it was happening right now, obviously – people were dying, a world was on fire – but it wouldn't be happening for long. Someone was going to turn the clock back, and cut away this timeline the way a child might snap a dead twig. Like a gardener. Like a god.

Sibling Same limped to a closed metal door and forced it open. He was still weak from the effort of breaking into a timeline about to be undone. Beyond, cast in a halo of scarlet light, was a blue police box with its door wide open, hundreds of cables spilling out into towers of machinery that pulsed a deep, infernal red.

Gardens were meant to be plundered, he thought, moving forward. That was a mantra, too. *Gods are meant to be robbed.*

*

2

Now

Possibly December, definitely the Shadow Proclamation HQ

'It's the moon, if you must know,' the Shadow Architect said, a note of accusation in her voice. 'But I know nothing about any distress call.'

She had a good voice for accusation, the Doctor thought. Of course, that was practically a job requirement. The Shadow Proclamation bound nearly forty thousand planets in a shared agreement of laws, jurisdiction and cooperation, and at the centre of that viciously complicated tangle was this pale, chilly office and this pale, chilly being.

The Shadow Architect was lean and graceful, with skin the colour of parking tickets and eyes the shade of drying blood. It was hard to tell, behind that praying-mantis poise, but she looked just as confused to see the Doctor as the Doctor was to see her.

'Well, I didn't show up just to say hi,' the Doctor said, mostly to the Architect but also, crucially, to the eight Judoon guards stationed around the cavernous marble office. 'No offence.'

'None taken,' the Shadow Architect said icily. The Judoon kept their weapons raised. There was no love lost between the Doctor and the Proclamation. It wasn't that the Doctor didn't approve of laws as a general concept, but she was also very aware that law was a fragile thing, and it changed depending on where you stood. Right and wrong, and kindness and mercy, on the other hand, were portable, durable and, in the Doctor's opinion, valid just about everywhere.

The Shadow Proclamation did not approve of the Doctor at all. This was for many reasons. The Doctor popped up in strange places. She didn't recognise any jurisdiction but her own. Worse, she was a living symbol of that half-mythical age when law and order had in fact been the provision of the Time Lords. That hadn't ended well for anybody, least of all the Time Lords themselves.

'I had a whole day of minor maintenance planned,' the Doctor said, pointing at her TARDIS in the corner of the room. 'Nothing major. Just little tweaks. TARDISes are a lot of work. Like jellyfish.'

The Shadow Architect placed a long graceful finger on her temple. 'Excuse me?'

'Not in shape, obviously. And you'd be hard-pressed to find a jellyfish that contained a library, though I could tell you stories. But because a jellyfish isn't just one creature – it's part of a collection of creatures that all support each other. Just like a TARDIS. Translation matrix, chameleon circuit, ambiguous resolver . . . It's a full-time job keeping them all going. What's the word? Oh, it's a great word . . .'

'Siphonophores,' one of the Judoon grunted, before looking slightly sheepish – an impressive feat for a humanoid rhino. The Architect gave them a long, appraising look.

'Fam-inals,' the Doctor said. 'Easier to say. *Point being*, I have things to do. I'm only here because I received a distress call.'

'And I am telling you,' the Shadow Architect said, 'that we did not send it.'

She rose from her seat, bidding the Doctor follow her through one of the office's many gloomy archways. On the other side, standing out against the headquarters' faded marble glory, were banks upon banks of data-monitoring equipment.

All of it was aflame. Some terminals sparked sulkily under drifts of anti-fire foam. Others blazed defiantly, their screens and keyboards blown out. Parchment-skinned acolytes ran back and forth, trying to splice cables or recover charred read-outs, but it was clearly a lost cause.

'Our entire communications network is down,' the Architect said. Her long fingers twitched, as if she could feel all that information slipping between them. 'We cannot contact our fleets, and our member planets cannot contact us. The Shadow Proclamation is blinded, Doctor.'

It clearly stung the Architect to say this, and the Doctor could understand why. The Shadow Proclamation was a blunt instrument – slow, unwieldy, and as subtle as a brick to the face when it came to matters of right and wrong – but it also mainly, *mostly* managed to keep a certain type of peace. It was certainly better than nothing, but now *nothing* was exactly what nearly forty thousand worlds were getting.

'It's the moon,' the Architect said again, pointing up through the chamber's transparent domed roof to the white orb above, murky and pearlescent as a blinded eye.

'What's wrong with it?' the Doctor asked.

'We don't have one,' the Architect said simply. 'Or we didn't, until about six hours ago. It just *appeared*, and the resulting gravitational distortion blew out every single defence shield and communications array we had. We're lucky it didn't shatter our headquarters completely. As it is, it will take us months to rebuild.'

The Doctor stared up at the rogue moon. 'Where did it come from?'

'We do not know.'

'Has it tried to communicate with you?'

The Shadow Architect scowled, once again pointing at the ruin of their communications equipment. 'We sent a data-boat up, but there's been no response. Further data-boats are in transit to our closest outposts. A fleet will be raised to blow this thing from the sky. Unless our own guns come online and do it first.'

'Do you always have to enforce the law at the barrel of a gun?' the Doctor said. 'Is there, in fact, a law against moons showing up out of nowhere?'

The Architect frowned. 'I imagine there is. At the very least, you need a permit. Why? What are you proposing?'

The Doctor grinned. 'Let me take a look.'

'Absolutely not!'

'Why not? I'm *supposed* to be elbow-deep in some artron cabling right now. The door on the TARDIS is a little stiff from our last crash-landing. Two of the showers are producing chocolate instead of water. That's fewer than normal. I have lots to be doing.'

'If you're that busy, then why do –' The Architect's eyes narrowed. 'Oh. You want a distraction.'

The Doctor shrugged. 'I didn't become the time traveller I am today by thinking about *maintenance.* Takes all the fun out of things. Neatening things, doing accounts, tying up loose ends – that's boring. No offence.'

'None taken,' the Architect said again. It didn't sound any more believable the second time around. 'Doctor, you seem to be forgetting that you have no authority here. Your presence is unasked for. The Shadow Proclamation does not call on time-travelling vagabonds who cause just as much chaos as they prevent. We enforce treaties. We lay down sanctions. We raise armies if need be. We do things *properly*.'

The Doctor sighed. 'The thing about "properly" is it discounts all the things that are *not* proper. Like moons showing up out of nowhere. This seems like a very *improper* situation, honoured Architect. Let me take it off your hands.'

The Shadow Architect stared at the Doctor with eyes that had judged civilisations and found them wanting. 'Doctor,' she said, 'do you know something we don't?'

'Perish the thought,' the Doctor replied immediately, and hoped those suspicious eyes couldn't tell she was lying. Thanks to the TARDIS's arcane sensors and its translation circuit, distress calls could arrive at the console room in a number of ways: not just through the millions of frequencies it could detect, but through telepathic calls, hypercubes or phone calls from Winston Churchill. The Doctor thought she had experienced all the myriad ways the universe could ask for help.

She'd never heard anything like the call that had brought her here.

A word. A curse. A threat.

Paradox.

3

Before

26 June 2010, somewhere in the United Kingdom

'You know you're going about it the long way round.'

Sibling Different was tall, and striking, and her red hair spilled around her golden mask like the heat corona around an eclipsed star.

When the war had ended – when it had *been* ended, Sibling Same reminded himself, crossed out like a wrong answer on a school exam – the line that had been drawn hadn't just gone through places and timelines. It had gone through people. Sibling Same and Sibling Different had ended up on one side of that line, and their past had ended up on the other. He no longer remembered who he had been before the war. He didn't think Sibling Different remembered either.

She spoke like she did, though. She spoke with steely confidence. Every idea she had was the right idea. Every whim, the only course.

'Kill the Doctor,' she said. 'Take what we need. Simple.'

As she spoke, she flickered, her skin flashing to a negative of itself. That had been happening a lot more lately, like the warning light of a battery about to fail. The war had changed them, which in itself wasn't a surprise. War transformed people. That was what it did. Mostly, it transformed them from *alive* to *dead*, but it had made the Siblings something else entirely:

Ghosts, of a timeline that never was. Ghosts, on the verge of fading away.

'It's too risky,' he said, scanning the empty street. 'My way is better. Safer.'

It was almost impossible to explain what it felt like to stand in a dead timeline before it was erased. The closest comparison he could make was that it was like stepping into a display home, or the sample family photos in a picture frame. There was no one thing you could point to. Everything felt real; arranged as it should be. And yet, there was a falseness to it. A hollowness, as if the very atoms in the air were going through the motions until the clock turned back.

Or maybe, he thought, *that's just how Leadworth feels all the time.*

The houses were settled and comfortable, stacked beside each other like seat cushions. It was nearly midnight, and all the lights in all the windows were out. Cars sat on driveways, still warm to the touch from the sun.

Sibling Same let his hand linger on a car bonnet, trying to soak up the heat. Sometimes he worried they *were* ghosts. That they hadn't managed to escape the Time War after all. That this was the afterlife, and they had died. Dead souls wandering dead timelines, wanting . . .

There was a blue box sitting on the end of the street.

'Let's just *take* it,' Sibling Different hissed. 'The Doctor isn't even *here*.'

Paradox energy sizzled around her fingertips. They were still learning about this strange power that infected them – the power that let them glide through dead timelines like spectres through a wall. Maybe it was a by-product of that line that had bisected them. Maybe it was a remnant of the War itself – some contaminant or scar. Everything had been weaponised eventually, Sibling Same remembered. Everything from the stars in the sky to the beats of your heart.

Even that memory felt fragile in his head.

'If we take it, the Doctor will hunt us,' he said finally. It was an old argument. 'The last TARDIS? *Their* TARDIS? They will never stop, and we will never have peace.' Threads of paradox light dribbled from his own fingers.

'I don't want their attention, Sibling. Look what it did to us last time.'

That stung her, and not least because it was a lie. The Doctor had erased the Time War, split the Siblings down the middle and cursed them to this flickering half-existence without even knowing they existed. Sibling Same didn't want to know what might happen if the attention of a Time Lord fell on them for real.

'Besides,' he said, watching a figure step out of one of the houses. 'You're right. The Doctor isn't here. And I am not unsympathetic to who is.'

They had done their research when it came to the TARDIS and the known associates of the Time Lord who called it home. Henrik Chyll had been useful for that, at least, even if it had been clear he hadn't believed the words coming out of his mouth.

'A child touched by the Vortex,' Sibling Same said. 'Made singular and unique, and cast adrift to wander through the universe, never belonging anywhere. Another one of Gallifrey's callous accidents.'

Sibling Different's voice was sombre. 'The closest thing to family we will ever have.'

They watched River Song run to the TARDIS. In minutes, the timeship would explode, taking this entire timeline with it.

'We want to leave the War behind, Different,' he said. That made him think of ghosts too. Ghosts all wanted second chances, didn't they? *Or revenge.* 'Why steal someone else's TARDIS when we can build our own?'

4

Now

Possibly December, definitely the Shadow Proclamation HQ

'I really don't need guards,' the Doctor said, stepping up on to the platform. 'And I'd much prefer to bring my ship.'

'I'm sure you don't, and I'm sure you would,' said the Architect from the teleporter control station. She was wearing a look of uncharacteristic amusement. 'I remember how useful you find that machine when you need to leave us behind. If it remains in our custody, your fate is bound to ours.'

'Doesn't that count as stealing?' the Doctor asked wryly.

A ghost of a ghost of a smile might have crossed the Architect's face. 'Confiscating.'

'Flirt,' the Doctor said, and looked round at the two guards she had been assigned. 'Right. Introductions, then. I'm the Doctor.'

The first guard was a robot the shape of an archaeologist's trowel – wide at the bottom, narrowing to a point at the top, where a single gleaming lens peered out through plates of black armour. It clicked forward on a hundred spindly legs.

'Praetorian X-B1,' the robot buzzed. 'A pleasure to serve.'

'Good,' the Doctor said. 'Thank you.'

'Sincerity Value ten per cent,' it added.

'Oh,' the Doctor said.

'Transparency is important with our officers,' the Architect said. There was that amusement again. 'And this –' she indicated the second guard '– is Praetorian Mae. A human. I know how you like those.'

'Happy to help,' the other guard said, face hidden behind a mirrored helmet. She didn't add a Sincerity Value, which the Doctor supposed was something.

'Prepare for teleportation,' the Architect said, activating the console. 'I expect to be kept abreast of what is happening.'

'Of course!' the Doctor said, popping the commlink Mae offered her in a pocket and immediately forgetting it existed. 'And, just checking, obviously just checking, you'll give me a good heads-up before you open fire on the moon, won't you?'

The Architect was suddenly very engrossed in her screen.

'Typical,' the Doctor said. 'Just typical. Shall we –'

A pillar of blue light lanced upward to connect the platform and the moon like the laser sight on a sniper rifle. Then, with a roar, they were airborne. The Doctor had ample time, in the sparkling transference beam, to observe the moon grow larger and larger, its surface pocked and pale and strangely fragile, like a shed snakeskin. She instinctively flinched as they went *through* that surface, and then the beam faded away, leaving them standing in . . .

'Odd,' Praetorian X-B1 said. 'Sincerity Value ninety-five per cent. We appear to be in a –'

'House,' the Doctor said. 'An Earth house, by the architecture. Maybe early twentieth century?'

The hallway was narrow, its ceiling low, the floor darkly varnished wood. The wallpaper was yellowing flowers, struggling to grow through a layer of dust. *Not a home,* the Doctor decided. If a person lived long enough in one place, they imprinted it with their personality. They made it theirs. But this place was giving the Doctor the same feeling she got in bus stations or airports or hotels. Nobody *lived* in those places; they just visited, and afterwards their presence was meticulously tidied away.

There were many doors leading off the hallway. The Doctor tried each handle as they passed. All of them were locked.

'Where do you think it came from?' Mae asked. The hallway eventually gave way to what might have been a ballroom. White sheets covered the furniture, and dust covered the sheets. Every door they found was locked. The windows were shuttered, their clasps glued shut by dust. The trio moved slowly, poised for any sign they were not alone in this echoing, abandoned place.

'Could be a spaceship,' the Doctor said. 'A spaceship made to look like a moon. Or a moon converted into a spaceship. Or a moon converted into a creepy old house and *then* converted into a spaceship. I've seen spaceships that looked like forests. Spaceships that took the form of people. I mean, my TARDIS alone can . . .'

Something was itching at the Doctor's senses, rasping against them like a file. 'You two been with the Shadow Proclamation long?' she asked. Maybe if she distracted herself, it would click into place.

'Since activation,' the android said. 'It is a pleasure to serve. Sincerity Value eighty-five per cent.'

'That's nice,' the Doctor said. 'Good to like your job. What about you, Mae?'

'I'm new,' Mae said. 'Why are *you* here?' They made their way down another corridor, identical to the one that had gone before. 'Just arrived out of nowhere, same day as the moon? What's that about?'

Accusation, the Doctor noted. *They must teach that tone in basic training.* 'I got a distress call,' she said. 'Or my TARDIS did. A single word, phrased as a cry for help.'

'What word?' Mae asked.

'Paradox.' The cheer had drained from the Doctor's voice. 'So I came, as fast as I could.'

'Feels like it fits,' Mae said. 'Moon appears out of nowhere, all done up like a house –'

'That isn't a paradox,' the Doctor said. 'That's just *weird.* And, don't get me wrong, if the distress call had been "Help, there's a weird abandoned house-moon," I still would have come. Mostly because calls like that are brilliant, but also because that's what I do. Travel around the universe. Try to keep things ticking over. Keep things tidy.'

'Thought you didn't like maintenance,' Mae said. She sounded . . . annoyed.

'You were listening to that, were you?' the Doctor said. 'Well. Some types of maintenance are more important than others. Maintenance was what my people were all about, once upon a time.'

'And what people are those?' Mae asked.

The Doctor hesitated. Gallifrey had a weight to it. The Time Lords were an old race. That came with responsibilities. It also came with guilt. Being around a long time meant you had plenty of time to make mistakes.

The Doctor had once been proud to be a Time Lord. Now, it was something she wanted a break from. *I'll tell Team TARDIS about my past some day. Definitely.*

'Oh, you know,' she said. 'I'm a citizen of the universe.'

She peered at a painting on the wall beside her. It appeared to be a replica of 'Napoleon Crossing the Alps' by Jacques-Louis David. *Not a very accurate one*, she thought. She'd crossed the Alps with Napoleon. She didn't remember any stegosaurs. *What am I missing?*

'Is paradox a dirty word where you're from, then?' said Mae.

'No,' the Doctor said distractedly. 'It's just one we use correctly. Does it bother you when people say "literally" when they actually mean "figuratively"? Or when people say "how ironic" when actually they just mean bad cutlery management?'

The two guards stared blankly at her. The Doctor shrugged.

'Some words mean very specific things. Are you familiar with the grandfather paradox?'

Praetorian X-B1's lens clicked. 'Travel back in time. Kill your grandfather. But then you no longer exist. You did not travel back to kill your grandfather. Which means he is alive, which means you exist, which means you do travel back. So you didn't. So you did.'

'Exactly,' the Doctor said. 'When you travel through time, you have to keep things neat. Hands and other extremities inside the timestream, please. But a paradox is what happens when you don't. A paradox is the unanswerable question. The repeating impossibility. The loose end that could unravel everything. Dangerous. *Untidy*. Also, very hard on grandfathers, which, as a former grandfather, I have to take issue with. Clocks!'

She spun suddenly, causing Mae to step back, torch beam jagging crazily.

'Excuse me?' Mae said.

'That's what this place is reminding me of,' the Doctor said. 'Don't ask me how. It takes a little while for the rest of my thoughts to catch up.' She started to jog, feet echoing on the worn floorboards. 'Clocks. Why am I thinking about clocks?'

The hallways led to two more, stretching away into the gloom. She chose one at random – *Is it random? Why do I feel like I know where I'm going?* – and ran down it, each step prompting an exhale of dust. There were more paintings here – a replica of 'American Gothic' by Grant Wood, showing a morose Silurian couple posed with pitchfork and apron. There was a copy of poor Vincent's 'The Starry Night', except the suns were Angels that wept and burned as they fell.

Not replicas, the Doctor thought. *Alternates.* Glimpses into paintings that never were.

'Makers' marks,' she said suddenly. '*That's* why I was thinking about clocks. Clockmakers often etch little messages inside the casing to aid future repairs. "Mind that ball joint" or "use a size-three screw".'

'Interesting,' the android said. 'Sincerity Value five per cent. Why is this relevant?'

'Because everything *made* has makers' marks,' the Doctor said. They ran down another corridor, and yet another – all with that stained wooden floor, and fading wallpaper, and windows that looked out on nowhere. 'Intended or otherwise. The passage of a chisel. A scar from a misplaced nail. A spot of paint where the painter was careless. It's the artist's signature. Even the most precisely machined component will show some sign of the tools that were used to create it.'

'I don't understand,' Mae said.

'Neither do I,' the Doctor said. The hallway they were in ended in a set of doors far bigger than any they had passed before. She paused in front of them, running her fingers along the panelling as if searching for some hidden clasp or catch. 'The floorboards, the windows . . . they don't have makers' marks at all. Nothing by chisel, or laser-cutter, or hammer, or nail. Look at the paintings! No brushstrokes. No sign of an artist's hand at all.'

She took a step backwards, hands pressed to her temples.

'I don't think this place was made. I think it was grown.'

'Try the handle,' Mae said quietly.

The Doctor turned the handle and stepped through.

Falling through time was not a new sensation for the Doctor. She had tumbled through the Time Vortex in the TARDIS, of course, and knew that thrill as millennia ran like raindrops inches from her skin. She'd free-fallen with a vortex manipulator, which bore the same resemblance to travel in the TARDIS as bungee jumping did to a first-class flight. She'd stowed away in Gallifreyan paintings that were actual timelines frozen in place, and even jumped unprotected into her own timeline, which was one hundred per cent absolutely the stupidest thing she'd done that day, maybe even that week.

This wasn't a literal plunge through time, but that made it more disturbing, not less. The space beyond the door was inky blackness. The Doctor held up her sonic screwdriver for light, but it was like the searchlights of a deep-sea explorer vessel trying to make sense of the ocean's depths. All it did was illuminate just how much darkness there was.

The Doctor ran forward and the light of her sonic began to pick out looming shapes – five great hexagonal structures curving down from the ceiling like the fingers of a colossal hand. Every centimetre of the inverted towers was as busy as a coral reef – exposed machinery sparking and humming, bundles of wiring bulging out between arcane arrangements of circuitry and crystal.

The floor too was cluttered with components; dissected and dismantled or piled in tottering heaps. There was an aprioritron – abandoned and dusty, its gauges and nozzles crusted with rust. There was an ambiguous resolver, and a great holding jar for symbiotic nuclei, and there was a dimensional adjudicator, sitting upright in an old chronon shell like a flower in a pot. The stark contrast between the advanced technology and the rundown architecture outside made her think of clocks again, of humming gears hidden behind antique wood.

Or, the Doctor realised suddenly, like stepping into a police box and finding that it wasn't quite the same size as its dimensions might suggest.

'Makers' marks,' the Time Lord whispered.

'I thought you said the place didn't have any,' Mae said from behind her. The praetorians had advanced warily into the space, panning their torch beams through the junkyard heaps. X-B1 looked as worried as it was possible for a triangular robot to look.

'The outside doesn't,' the Doctor said. 'That's the point. The outside is just what it looks like. The shell around the core. These components . . . This . . . machine is the heart of it. And there are makers' marks everywhere.'

'Can you read them?' Mae asked.

'Of course I can,' the Doctor said. 'They're mine.'

'Good.' Mae raised her rifle and shot X-B1 through the visor. 'Then we can begin.'

5

. . .

The Siblings ghosted through reality, through timelines alive and dead, and everywhere they went they collected.

They visited a timeline where the Doctor had fallen on Agrippina Primus, and a billion Cyber-Mites besieged a grieving TARDIS, desperate to convert the most powerful ship in the universe. The TARDIS had shut down its chameleon circuit in retaliation, swelling to the size of a planet, and starving Cyber-Converters and the TARDIS's own self-repair systems duelled under a blue wooden sky.

Locating gravitic drift compensators took them to a timeline where the Doctor and the TARDIS themselves were at war. An ancient hunger had burrowed into the timeship's heart, and now it hunted across the cosmos, consuming all it could find. A weeping Doctor raised an army in pursuit and, in the light of a dying sun, two old friends laid each other low.

Sibling Different had laughed at that. Sibling Same had not.

We don't have a choice. That's what he told himself, as they plundered. *The Doctor took that from us.* The Time Lord got to rewrite the universe, to edit the course of events so that *they* were the winner, so that they were the heroes, time and time again.

All the Siblings had was the paradox energy that guttered in them like candles, and that was a double-edged sword. It gave them access to dead timelines, true, but every component they stole cost them, used them up just a little more than before.

That scared Sibling Same, on the days when he could remember to be scared. Every day brought a new gap where a memory should be. They *were* ghosts – figuratively and literally. They had been killed when the war had ended. It was just taking longer than usual for their bodies to lie down and accept it. They were, quite literally, running out of time.

Unless we get to undo what was done to us. Unless we rewrite ourselves.

And for that, they needed the machine.

Timelines where Donna Noble never existed. Timelines where Clara never died at all. Timelines where the Bad Wolf and the Daleks fused, and a garden of metal Roses grew across all of time and space. The Siblings ran up and down the Doctor's histories like a bead of water on a string, and bound TARDIS component after component together with the energy that pulsed through them like blood. They sat in the Masque Magestrix and heard about the end of the war, and all Sibling Same could think was that it seemed like something that had happened to someone else.

They hunted, and they collected, and they excavated, and they stole, and, piece by piece, they fed themselves to the paradox moon.

6

Now

Possibly December, in orbit round the Shadow Proclamation HQ

'You know,' Mae said casually, 'my plan was just to kill you.' Smoke wafted from the charred crater of Praetorian X-B1's sensor lens. She lifted a hand to waft it away. 'Simple, effective . . .'

'Yes, but *historically* quite a high failure rate.' The Doctor didn't even really hear herself say the words. People threatened to kill her a lot. She could usually deliver a comeback on autopilot, and there was always the chance it might break the tension and they could all have a nice laugh together instead.

Right now, that didn't seem likely. Not just because there was a gun pointed at the Doctor's head – she was used to that – but because the Time Lord found herself beset by a precise and steely rage.

'These are pieces of my TARDIS,' she said. '*My* TARDIS.'

Mae was angry too. The Doctor could tell. For all her smirking bravado, her fingers were trembling on the butt of the gun. *Anger and . . . fear?*

'But Sibling Same convinced me we were better off flying under your radar until we were properly up and running,' she said, as if the Doctor hadn't spoken. 'Appearing in front of the Proclamation was a test run. Sharpest eyes in the galaxy, and they never saw us coming.' The sardonic mirth in her voice vanished. 'But you did. We picked up your arrival on the scanners. That's why I had to infiltrate them. How did you know we were here?'

'Pieces of *my* TARDIS,' the Doctor said again. She was distantly aware neither one of them was really listening to the other but was far too angry to care. 'Where did you get them?' She pointed. 'Synapse link for a translation matrix. I know I'm not missing that. I was working on it this morning. How is it here?'

'Kill your grandfather.' The voice echoed through the cavern, and the Doctor saw a second figure emerge from behind one of the tottering stacks. It was a boy; barely in his teens, his face hidden behind a mask of bone – a fearful, inhuman thing with long fangs and dark eye sockets. 'Kill your grandfather and vanish from existence. Then reappear because you never killed him at all. So back to work. Lots to do. Grandfathers to kill.'

'What are you –?'

'And you *think* those timelines vanish, but they don't.' Mae turned her face away, replacing her helmet with a mask – the long avian skull of some vicious carrion crow. It could have been the light, but for a moment she appeared *faint*, like a drawing someone had tried to rub out. 'It's like extinction. When a meteor impact kills everything on Earth, those creatures don't *go* anywhere. They fall, and get buried, and passing time crushes them to a line of strata in the ground. Life moves on, ignorant of all the dead under their feet.'

'Sibling Different and I have seen them,' the boy said. 'All the timelines you've ended in your long and illustrious career. You come down like a comet, Doctor, and there are many, many skeletons under your feet.'

'That's where you got these pieces,' the Doctor whispered. 'The moon – it's just a shell. You're building a TARDIS from . . . from pieces of its alternate selves.' It wasn't just her signature she could see on the components littered around them. She could see scars from Cybermen blasters, burns from Dalek guns. Damage, from battlefields she knew she had undone. 'You've stitched it together from the shrapnel of its own destruction. From timelines *my* TARDIS undid.'

Mae – *Sibling Different* – executed a short, mocking bow. 'Well, TARDISes don't have grandfathers. Sibling Same and I had to do the best we could.'

'Why?' The Doctor said. It was a weak word to convey the disbelief and horror in her heart, but it was all she could think to ask. 'Why would you do this?'

'Because you killed us,' Sibling Same said, and now he flickered too, warping like a reflection in a broken mirror. 'You ended the Time War. Changed all of time and space. Did you really think there'd be no loose ends? We're just outlines, Doctor. Shadows burned into a wall. And even that is fading away.'

'Unless we change the timeline,' Different said. 'Our next run will take us through time, all the way back to the War. History is written by the victors, Doctor. You get to do it all the time. Why shouldn't we?'

Her lips twisted in a grin beneath the hooked beak of her mask.

'*Paradox victorious.*'

'I'm genuinely impressed,' the Doctor said, placing each syllable slowly and carefully, like someone defusing a bomb, 'with just how *catastrophically* that is not going to work.' She waved a hand at the great machine surrounding them. 'Your little practice run blinded a world –'

Sibling Different snorted. 'Collateral damage. They got off lucky –'

'Yes,' the Doctor interrupted. 'They *did*. They should be thanking their lucky stars. I'm amazed this thing hasn't exploded already and taken half the universe with it.' She stalked towards them, ignoring the rifle in Different's hands. 'And even if it doesn't pull itself apart, even if you manage to enter the Time Vortex with this . . . ailing, contradictory *mess* of a ship . . . I have no idea what would happen if you tried to go back and undo my decision. I genuinely don't. I don't have room in my brain to figure it out. Do you remember the War? Do you remember what it was like?'

Sibling Different stuck out her jaw like an insolent child. 'Yes. I do.'

Was it the Doctor's imagination? Did she hear . . . uncertainty?

'Then you remember it was hell. Whole civilisations vanishing. Timelines crumpling like paper held to a flame. And all that destruction will be a *picnic* if two meddling idiots decide to go back and start it all over again.'

'Tough,' Different snapped. 'Sibling Same. Activate the machine.'

'Are you sure?' the boy said. He *definitely* sounded uncertain. 'Just travelling in space nearly used me up. We need more time to –'

'Now!'

He ran. It took the Doctor a second to recognise that what she had taken for another pile of detritus was in fact a console – a twisted creation of warped pillars and fused-together instrument arrays, as mangled as a Frankenstein heart.

'Don't do that,' the Doctor warned. 'Don't –'

Sibling Same pulled a rusting lever, and the world went mad.

The towers above them spasmed, expanding and contracting as if trying to make a fist. Metal charred. Sparks spat. A blinding knot of light bloomed above the console, wrenching itself from side to side as thorns and vines of energy spiked outwards, fighting for purchase on a reality that knew this machine could not exist.

It was horrible to watch. The Doctor's TARDIS was a living thing – a graceful creature born to dart and dive through the currents of time. This was like watching a sickly animal try to stagger up a hill, falling and rising and falling again. The whole chamber trembled, and the Siblings collapsed against each other, the light catching on their masks and turning them a blinding, hateful white.

'I told you!' the Doctor shouted. 'This machine *cannot* work. The pieces you've assembled know they're not meant for this timeline –'

Sibling Different flickered out entirely – just a bundle of lines drawn on the air – before resolving again and collapsing. The boy left the console and rushed to her, kneeling by her side.

'You're using yourselves up,' the Doctor said. 'Using your paradox energy to anchor this machine. To *force* it to be real. It's killing you.'

'Not if we make it work,' Sibling Same snapped, but the anger drained from his voice as he stared down at Different. A great arc of eye-achingly bright light lashed out from between the towers, scratching a crazed line of destruction across the walls.

The communicator in the Doctor's pocket buzzed. '*Doctor? Doctor!*' Interference and anger had turned the Architect's voice into a staticky bark. '*We're detecting a massive energy build-up. The gravitational distortion is a hundred times worse. A fleet is inbound. They have orders to open f–*'

'Oh good,' the Doctor said. 'Well. We'll probably have blown up before then.' The towers were vibrating with the strain of trying to contain the force that crackled and spat between them. The moon would tear itself apart trying to do what the Siblings were asking of it. The Doctor had seen what happened when a TARDIS exploded. She never wanted to see it again.

'OK,' the Doctor said. 'Yeah. Disassemble a living TARDIS on the brink of exploding before it gets shot out of the sky. Can definitely do that.' *Sincerity Value ten per cent,* she added in her head. 'Sibling Same!'

The boy flinched from her outstretched hand.

'You could help,' the Time Lord said. 'This TARDIS shouldn't exist. It doesn't *want* to exist. Your energy is what's holding it together. If you let it go, the pieces might snap back to their own timelines. You can undo the machine. *Please.*'

'I . . . I don't . . .'

'Then why call me here?'

Sibling Different jerked up, gasping as if she had just broken the surface of the sea. Her body solidified, and she pushed Same away.

'We didn't call *you*,' she hissed. 'Why would we –'

And then the Doctor understood. 'You didn't call me here,' she said. '*She did.*'

The TARDIS. *Her* TARDIS. Her poor, tortured girl.

The Doctor ran to the console. Sibling Different tried to rise and intercept her, but weakness and the chamber's shaking sent her spilling across the floor, and Sibling Same went after her. The roiling supernova that was building above the console spasmed and spiked, and beneath the guttural roar of tortured space–time the Doctor could hear it – the sound of a TARDIS in agony. The distress call that had brought her here.

'I know I've changed things,' the Doctor said, her fingers racing across the controls, searching for something, *anything* she could do to ease the timeship's pain. 'I've made choices. I've ended wars, and started them, to my shame, and I have made decisions nobody should ever have had to make.' Her voice shook, and the TARDIS shook with it.

'But you've got it wrong. I don't do it for myself. I don't do it to *win*.' Another quake shook plumes of sparks down around them. One of the towers came loose with a groaning shriek, swinging like a guillotine on its cables to smash another tower free.

'I do it because I want there to be another tomorrow, and then another one, and then another one after that. And I know they come with a price. I remember all these battles. All these scars.' She stroked the console beneath her. 'I remember all those cries for help. And so does she. I'm sorry for what happened to you, but if you don't at least *try* to see past it, there will be so much more pain to come.'

'*No!*' Sibling Different snarled, raising her gun. The Doctor flinched as she fired, but the shot went wild, deflecting from some invisible barrier around the Time Lord. No – not invisible. *Materialising.* 'You don't get to win! You don't get to just escape again!'

'There's no escape,' the Doctor said, as her own TARDIS began to shimmer into view around her. She had taken her hands away from the controls now, and was just looking up, bathed in the hideously bright light. 'Not from this. She just wants to be with me. At the end.'

Sibling Different raised her rifle again, but Same grabbed the barrel.

'We have to let it go,' he whispered through translucent lips. 'If we don't, it'll kill us *and* millions of others. Think of the destruction we've seen. Do you want to cause more?'

'If that's what it takes.' Sibling Different's mask had come away, and Same winced as he saw the inky black unswirl of paradox energy beneath. Had they ever had faces? It was becoming harder and harder to remember. 'My timeline. My victory. Or none at all.'

'I understand,' Same said. He could feel the Paradox TARDIS straining against them – every piece they had so laboriously collected trying to pull themselves apart and return to where they were supposed to be.

I'm sorry, he thought, and began to let them go.

'What are you doing?' Different snapped. She could feel it too. The true timeline was starting to reassert itself. With a roaring crack, one of the towers dematerialised, pieces folding into themselves – vanishing as they returned to where they were supposed to be.

Second chances, Same thought. Not everybody got them. Not everybody should.

And you were selfish if you tried to take them for yourself.

'You know, for a while I really believed we could do it,' he said, withdrawing the last of his energy from the Paradox TARDIS and sending it into his sibling in a crackling vein of light. 'But that timeline is dead. I won't see you die with it.'

'NO!' Different screamed, as the detonation of uncoiling paradoxes threw them apart. Sibling Same had just enough time to see her land at the Doctor's feet a heartbeat before the walls of the true TARDIS solidified around them. His last thought, as the towers above faded away, as rubble fell *through* him to smash on the floor, as the chamber's roof collapsed, was that he didn't feel hollow any more.

And then even that was gone.

7

Now

Possibly December, definitely the Shadow Proclamation HQ

When Sibling Different woke, the Doctor was standing over her.

'Tea?' the Doctor said.

Different staggered to her feet, clutching for a rifle that wasn't there.

'I wouldn't bother,' the Doctor said, taking a long sip from her own mug. Sibling Different stiffened as she looked around her. She had spent what seemed like her entire life staring at the outside of the TARDIS, coveting it, pillaging its past. Actually being inside it was . . .

'It's beautiful,' she said. 'Really beautiful.'

'I know,' the Doctor said. 'I'd do anything for her.' She held out a mug and Different took it without thinking. That was when she realised that she was solid. The flickering inconsistency of her form was gone. 'Sibling Same. He gave the last of himself to stabilise me.'

The Doctor nodded. 'And, providing you don't use that energy to delve into dead timelines or build an impossible time machine, it might actually last long enough to give you a normal life.'

They stood in silence for a moment.

'So,' the Doctor said. 'You want the chance to change things. To edit the universe, the way you see fit. So let's do that.'

Different pulled away her mask, revealing a long, freckled face and an explosion of curls. 'What do you mean?'

The Doctor pointed at the door. 'Beyond that door are about fifty praetorians. I don't know what you did with the real Mae, or if there was a real Mae at all, but you could go back and be her. If you want. Or I can drop you on pretty much any world you want in pretty much whatever century you want. Do you remember who you were before the war?'

Different gave an imperceptible shake of her head.

'There was a group, in those wild times,' the Doctor said. 'They chased paradoxes. Wore masks. I thought most of them had left this universe far behind before the first shots of the war were even fired. Maybe you were one of the fraction who remained. We could go looking for them, if you like.'

'Why?' Different snapped. 'Why would you help me?' Her eyes were red.

'Because you're right,' the Doctor said. 'Why should I be the only one who gets to change things? You can choose who you want to be. Take my help or walk through that door. Your choice.'

It took Mae two tries to stand up, scooping the bone mask from the floor. She crossed to the door of the TARDIS in three long strides, ignoring the eyes of the Doctor on her back, and opened the door halfway.

Then she threw the mask away and closed the door behind it.

'OK,' Mae said. 'Where to?'

-1

CANARIES

ONCE UPON A **DARK** TIME . . .

The Doctor declared themself the Time Lord Victorious.
Death spread through the universe.
War raged. Empires fell.

This is not that story.

This is a story of what happened next.

First published on the BBC website as part of the
Time Lord Victorious arc.
(we told you things arrive out of order . . .)

In the small alpine village of Verbier, there is a museum for things that shouldn't exist.

It doesn't look like much; just a little house at the end of a long lane, with low eaves and a green door. You mightn't notice it at all except for the neat little sign in the window. When people think of museums they think of marble floors and pillars and security guards and gift shops, but the world is full of neat little signs in windows, put there by hobbyists with skin wrinkled as walnut shells, to draw you into a room you might wander around for five minutes on holiday and then never think of again.

The Shanghai Museum of Propaganda Posters is cloistered in the basement of an apartment block. The

Darwin Twine Ball Museum is just a community centre with a four-metre ball of twine outside. The Bendery Military Museum is a converted Soviet steam train beside a disused station in a country that officially no longer exists.

Any building can be a museum if someone cares enough about the things inside it.

The Verbier Museum of the Impossible is run by Anke Von Grisel. Arthritis has made Anke's knuckles big as baby turtle shells, and it takes her longer and longer each morning to wrap a tie around itself and fit the knot to her neck. As proprietor and sole employee of the museum, the opening hours are whatever Anke likes, but Anke likes being punctual, and so she unlocks the front door at exactly a quarter to ten each morning, and most days there is at least one curious tourist outside.

This is because of the sign. The sign reads;

VERBIER MUSEUM OF THE IMPOSSIBLE
ESTABLISHED 2044
NO TIME TRAVEL PLEASE

'Yes, yes,' she says, by way of welcome. 'We begin.'

The Museum is a single room at the front of her home. The floor is white pine and the walls are hung with age-faded tapestries in wool and cotton and silk. Twelve exhibits sit on plinths around the room. Anke makes these plinths herself from the native Verbier birch. Word is that Gunther, whose museum two towns over houses a collection of seventeenth-century marionettes, orders his plinths online.

This horrifies Anke. Anke has standards.

'Now,' she says carefully, taking her position at the first plinth. There are small indentations worn into the pine floorboards, and the heels of her hiking boots slip into them with a sigh. 'This is a pipe.'

It is. It's fifteen centimetres long and entirely ordinary. The only thing remarkable about it is that it has been laid out on a square of gleaming white silk. All the exhibits are. Anke's standards are exact.

'Polyvinyl chloride,' Anke explains. 'Nothing exciting. Made in the Eighties. Never fitted or used.'

Anke has a very particular way of speaking. Clipped. Careful. Like everything she says is taken from a cue card, and there are only so many words that will fit.

'Made by a company called Marburg Plastic. See?'

She points at a little stamp.

At this point, she waits. She always waits. Anke is small, and she is thin, and her voice is nothing more than the rasp of wheatgrass, but she is, in her own way, a performer.

'Except that this company does not exist. It never has. Marburg has never had a plastic factory. I went there. I researched. This pipe is machine-made, mass-produced. There should be thousands. But I can find no others like it. No factory. No employees. No records. Nothing but this pipe, sticking out into the world.'

The next plinth has another white silk square, and on it sits a coin.

'I hate this one,' Anke says quietly.

The coin has a double-headed eagle on one side, and the face of Adolf Hitler on the other. The date on it reads 1954.

'Do you begin to see?'

The third plinth holds a metal sphere, covered in a grid of circuitry.

'I don't know what this is,' Anke confesses. 'It was sent to me by a British collector. He found it in his garden.'

The card reads *Toclafane.*

'He could not explain to me how he knew the word,' Anke says. 'It was just in his head. No memory. No context. Just floating, unsupported. Like a nightmare.'

The fourth exhibit is a cameo painting of Napoleon on a stegosaur.

It is at this point that Anke pauses, as if suddenly aware that without explanation these are just confusing little trinkets, and that the relics that are the obsession of her life can so easily come across as nothing more than junk.

'Other museums . . . *normal* museums, hold relics. Pieces of the past. Evidence of lives and cultures lived.'

She indicates the twelve plinths.

'I think these are relics of other pasts. Pasts that never happened. A factory. A regime. An invasion, by creatures not of this Earth. Alternate histories. Now, all that remains of them are these exhibits, poking out into our timeline like a foot from out of a duvet. Glimpses into the might-have-been.'

Anke rubs at her temple, and rushes through the final exhibits quickly, though when she reaches the twelfth exhibit, she says nothing about it at all.

'Look around if you like. I do not have a gift shop.'

Later, the ancient landline on Anke's desk begins to ring. Anke has never married and has no family. Only one person ever calls her.

'Anke! Hello!'

The caller is young, and English, and speaks so quickly that his words trip over each other. Wherever he is, there is something very loud happening. Anke can hear deep booms and roars, the fierce blart and crackle of electricity. There are other voices too – mechanical snarls that sound more like the tread of tanks than anything that could come from a human throat.

++ *EXTERMINATE* ++

'Oh, do shut up! Can't you see I'm on a call!'

The caller does not always sound young. Sometimes, he sounds old, and archly frustrated, or kind and faintly amused. Sometimes he sounds Scottish, growling like an idling engine. Once, when the caller rang, they sounded female, which might have confused Anke, except for the fact that she owns a museum for impossible things. It takes a lot to confuse Anke.

No matter what the caller sounds like, Anke always recognizes their voice.

'I tell you again,' she says. 'You cannot come here. You cannot take my exhibits away.'

There is a roaring crackle down the line, static or fire or snarling beasts, and Anke instinctively jerks her head away.

'Anke,' the caller says. 'Listen – these things you've collected. They're symptoms. Signs that something's wrong. If you'd just let me study them –'

She looks around at the exhibits. Very few are valuable, in any understandable sense. And yet, she would lose none of them, even the coin.

Her gaze lingers on the twelfth plinth the longest.

'Goodbye, Doctor,' Anke says, and hangs up the phone.

The next day, the masks arrive.

It was a bad night for the exhibits. It always is, after the Doctor calls. The shard of impossibly ancient crystal from a place called Mordeela trembled and fizzed on its silk. The black tuxedo bowtie rustled against itself like a frightened snake. The pages of Adelaide Brooke's biography have again gone blank, as if unsure what the famous astronaut's end should be. Anke sat up with them – speaking to them, soothing them – and when she woke up there was a box outside her door.

She places the picture frame back on the twelfth plinth, and brings the box inside.

People often send things to Anke to be assessed. Old photographs. Newspaper articles about alien invasions that the newspapers themselves say they never wrote. Blood tests that prove the British royals are werewolves. Nearly all of them turn out to be worthless.

Inside the box are two masks. The note with them reads: *Worn by a long-forgotten cult who worshipped impossibility and contradiction.*

Anke lifts the masks out carefully. The first is male and made of silver. The second is female, and gold. The faces they depict would be beautiful, if not for a certain subtle quirk to their features. A . . . slyness. A dispassionate cruelty. Like trickster gods from an old myth.

They make Anke uneasy.

Summer turns to winter. The stream of tourists slows. Anke begins work on a plinth from the masks. It is hard work, and she takes many breaks, carving an old log to create the shape she sees in her head. It is foolishness, she knows, but when she places the masks upon it she imagines they are pleased with her work. Spirits, receiving tribute.

In the evenings, she makes minute adjustments to her cue cards, and tries to find any mention of a cult who might have worn such masks, or any clues as to who might have sent them to her. Anke has reached the end of her life's savings. It is likely that the masks will be the last exhibit she ever owns.

One night in November, the Doctor calls again. This time, the sounds of battle are fiercer, and the voice is smooth and rich. There is a touch of the pirate in it, or the poet, and Anke, dry and scowling, cannot help but imagine what the man behind it looks like.

'Anke! Doctor here. I need you to –'

'I have told you,' Anke snaps. 'These exhibits are mine. I protect them.'

'There are fractures in *time*, Anke. Someone is causing time to skip, like a needle on a record. These things you have collected – they're . . . canaries. Canaries in a coal mine. Proof that something is wrong. That dark times are coming.'

'Proof,' Anke says. The word comforts her. She had hoped . . . 'Then I must keep them safe. From everybody. From you.'

'Listen to me. Those relics are like thorns poking into our reality. Keeping all of them together might cause a tear. A fracture. Something could come *through*, Anke, and I don't know what that might be.'

The masks gleam in the corner of the room.

'Good,' Anke snaps, and hangs up the phone.

Christmas Day in Verbier is white and red and stubbornly evergreen. The ringing of bells echoes off the mountain and, as always, Anke eats her modest Christmas dinner at her little kitchen table, trying not to look at the extra place she has set. Twenty years. It has been twenty years.

Next year, I will not set it, she thinks, as she thought the year before. *Next year.*

That night, a storm breaks over the mountain. The first crash of thunder is so loud that Anke is out of her bed before her bones remember they are old. Lightning cracks the sky, bright enough to leave a memory of itself in her eyes, bright enough that it slices through the swirling snow.

It is not the thunder that woke her, Anke realises.

The phone is ringing.

She staggers downstairs, shrugging on her housecoat. Another peal, and Anke has to grab the bannister to keep from falling. The thunder feels like it is shaking the house apart and yet, despite the apocalyptic crash and roar, the artificial chirp of the phone cuts through.

By the light of slashing lightning, Anke picks her way through the darkness. The wind has broken a window, and now snow is piling beneath it. Plinths have toppled in the gale. Flakes of white are everywhere. The tapestries have fallen off the wall.

My exhibits. My treasures.

She runs to the twelfth plinth, and it is only when the battered old photo frame is safe in her hand that she crosses to her desk and answers the phone.

'Anke?'

It is not a voice he has heard before, and yet she knows immediately who it is.

'Doctor?'

'Not anymore,' the voice says. It is an old voice, deep and warm as a mine, rich as Christmas and twice as kind. 'Now,

I'm really more of a curator. Like you, Anke. And you must listen to me now, because we do not have much time.'

Anke looks down at the photo in her hand.

'I have made mistakes, Anke. I have been arrogant. I have thought only I knew the answers. That only I could fix things. A bad time. A dark time. The things you have collected, they're evidence of that. Glimpses into dead timelines. Fragments of the never-was.'

'I don't understand,' Anke says, though she does. She has thought of little else these last twenty years.

The argument. The storm, so much like tonight. The way he ran out the door. The way he ran from her. He vanished, vanished so completely that she began to distrust her own memory, until the photo in her hand was the only evidence that there was a gap in her heart where a person should be.

'I don't understand either,' the Curator says. 'Not all of it. It's always a mess when more than one of me gets involved. I changed things. Anke, I worry that in doing so I opened a door. That I might have let something in.'

'That's why I keep them,' Anke whispers. Snow is melting into the photo in her hand. 'I thought . . . I thought maybe if I collected all these things, then he might come back too.'

There is a noise behind her. Anke turns, and the lightning cracks the darkness in two.

She sees that the masks are not on their plinths any more. They are not on their plinths, but they have not fallen. Instead, they hang in the air, the way another museum might hang its masks from wires.

There are no wires here. The masks hang exactly at head-height. As if being worn by people she cannot see.

It is the most frightening thing Anke has ever seen in her life.

'Anke,' the voice in her ear whispers, as the thunder booms and the lightning howls and the masks slowly begin to turn towards her, their cruel smiles shining wide. 'Do you know what a paradox is?'

ENJOYED

THE WINTERTIME PARADOX?

Explore another incredible collection of *Doctor Who* stories from the masterful Dave Rudden in:

TWELVE ANGELS WEEPING

Turn the page for a preview of
Daleks and destruction . . .

DALEKS

THE THIRD WISE MAN

It was in the first year of the Time War, though we did not call it that at the time. We were not to know what it would become.

Indeed, it was only much later that we realised it would be a war at all. For too long, we believed it a simple series of skirmishes, similar to the clashes along the raw border of the time field separating us from the wretched and primitive races of the universe. It was in those patrols that I gained my captaincy, piloting one of our few Battle TARDISes against the aliens foolish enough to seek our technology, or those who simply blundered into the constellation of Kasterborous and the Seven Systems – our home.

We Time Lords are jealous of our secrets. We must be. We do not seek to preserve our way of life simply for ourselves. We do it because only we are advanced enough to wield the power that we do. Anything else would be catastrophe. I am convinced of it, even now, as the younger races' awe of us has been lost and our enemies hammer at our doors.

In a way, that is what this entire war has been about.

The Daleks came for us in that first year, and we did not see it as war. We saw it as pest control. They amassed in their millions, and rather than face them as equals on the battlefield we simply detonated the nearest star and consumed their entire fleet in fire. Such was our power. Such was our arrogance.

War is poison. We wished to demonstrate this to the Daleks, to sicken them with might, dissuade them from challenging us. There are battlefields on Gallifrey from before the Stellar Age where the fighting was so fierce that the ground ran with blood and the soil was sown with arrowheads like seeds. There are places war has poisoned so completely that nothing will ever grow again.

Shock and awe. Those were our watchwords in that first year, when we were buoyed and comforted by knowing that *we* were the most superior, that *we* were better defended and that, at the end of it all, we simply had more *time* to respond than any other race.

We did not understand our enemy. For all our knowledge, we knew nothing.

The Daleks were indefatigable. They were remorseless. Everything we did, every attempt to scare or reason with or deter them was met with the pathological, twitching hatred with which they draw every breath. We learned this after Spiral Furl, when Harlan Castellos turned the death of his TARDIS into an electromagnetic extinction event and Daleks fell from the sky like hail. We learned it after the first volleys of the Anything Gun crumpled space–time like fire consuming parchment. We learned it as battle overturned the universe like a child raking dirt, and the lesser races squirmed and died like worms exposed in our wake.

You cannot intimidate a Dalek. You cannot frighten them.

I will speak now of the Nightmare Child.

It was supposed to be a small battle. There had been silence along many fronts for weeks now, and there was hope blooming on Gallifrey that perhaps the new generation of Battle TARDISes had proven our superiority. There were those on the High Council who still believed that the attacks were simply Daleks being Daleks, and not steps on the way to all-out war. 'One more battle,' they counselled. One more crushing defeat, and the little monsters would flee.

I was in the Scaveline system, investigating some intercepted Dalek communications. My own TARDIS led a strike-force – even then, the military language felt strange to me – of a hundred recently grown battleships. Scaveline's star was a white dwarf, struggling against its own weight to stay in the heavens. I remember wondering, as we emerged in the system, whether any of the planets had ever been inhabited.

Curiosity was not a trait that the Time Lords ever encouraged. What need had we for it? Everything in the cosmos was there, waiting – every time, every moment – and we could observe it all as completely as we desired.

'All ships are in-system,' my lieutenant, Orlock, murmured at my side. 'Awaiting orders.'

We were not a warrior people. We had never had to be. Belligerence had gone the way of curiosity, because all of time and space was ours. Our tiny contingent of warships (of which I commanded a significant portion) were stretched thin across space, and many were still adolescent and untested.

No TARDIS takes to war with relish. I knew it pained some of those under my command. TARDISes were not ships, were not dumb beasts of burden or mere transports across the heavens; they were our allies and our compatriots, and we did them a disservice.

I mourn them still.

We inched through the Scaveline system, scanners at maximum. General practice during manoeuvres in uncivilised space was to take the form of ships designed by lesser races – a way to hide our own advancement, or a tactic to create confusion in our enemies. A competent commander can make much use of a moment's hesitation. For a Time Lord, a moment is an eternity.

However, such tactics fared abysmally against these new, frenzied Daleks. The simplicity that had once been a flaw in the Daleks became in war a hideous strength: they simply opened fire on every ship, no matter its origin.

My own Type 94 had therefore taken the form of interstellar debris: a slowly spinning chunk of rock made pale and shimmering with ice. Its interior was designed after the manner of an old observatory – a spherical space with seats on gimbals so that my crew could swing from console to console, and myself on a central leather chair. The entire arrangement looked rather like the model of a solar system, with the console our gleaming, silver sun.

'Scouts,' I murmured, knowing my TARDIS would relay my words to every other ship in the fleet. 'Range forward, pattern nocturne.'

Pattern nocturne: caution. The less-armoured Type 90s and 91s peeled off and dematerialised. Some ranged out into the system, rendered invisible by their chameleon circuits, and others darted into the timestream to scan the approaching seconds for peril. It may seem strange, the idea that our foes were not immediately detectable, but a star system is a gigantic place, even to craft such as ours. There are many ways to hide. Much of space warfare is not attacking or defending, but simply finding your enemy before they find you.

'Sir, this is Scout Circle Eight. No sign in the system's western quadrant.'

'Sir, Scout Circle Three reporting. No Dalek presence five minutes from your now.'

Strange. There was a psychotic honesty about the Daleks. They never encrypted their communications, never used stealth, never fled from battle even against terrible odds. There was a desperate, crazed need to them – either something inherited from their mad creator, or a behavioural side effect of being just a few tatters of flesh smeared over the trigger of a gun.

That was why I took the risk I did, my fingers dancing over the communications relay that connected me to my fleet.

'Pattern daylight. Show yourselves so that we may draw them out and end this. Scout Circles Three and Eight, loop back round and cover our retreat.'

'Yes, sir. How far?'

'A day. But be sure to stay hidden.'

'Understood. Should we establish a position in the future as well?'

'Negative,' I responded. *Not until I know what happened here. Not until I can be sure they're not waiting for us.*

Scaveline continued its turgid spin. I stretched in my chair, one eye on the scouts' reports. The fleet hovered awkwardly on the system's edge. I could not help but check and recheck the space–time co-ordinates, though the idea of a TARDIS getting lost was ludicrous. As the long silence stretched, I began to stupidly hope that the High Council had been right. Maybe this war *was* no war. Maybe for once in their pitiful, cyborg lives the Daleks had admitted that they were not the superior beings in the galaxy.

'Sir, we have something. Transmitting co-ordinates now.'

We are not the only race to have discovered time travel. Our battle to keep it so failed; a fact which is now even more painfully clear. But Time Lords were the first, and understanding time will always be as easy to us as breathing.

My screens showed me two star systems – the mundane, physical movement of planets, and the swirling overlay of the timestream beneath. Physical and chronological movement, like a flower blooming in four dimensions at once.

I could see the slow roll of asteroids from one moment to another, and the bacteria-like scurry of life still clinging to a couple of distant worlds.

The other TARDISes were like stars, each one a flare of time energy skating towards us like stones across the top of a lake. They looked omnipotent, perfect, navigating the fabric of our universe so deftly that it was impossible to imagine anything laying them low.

We followed the shining scouts as they led us into the shadow of a broken planet on the system's far edge. Something had dug into the world's crust, scoring a hole the size of a continent – huge by planetary standards, big enough to hide a fleet of Daleks in, but minuscule on a stellar scale. *That* was where they were hiding.

Clever. They were getting cleverer all the time.

'There, sir,' Orlock said.

For all our vaunted foresight, I had not anticipated this.

I do not relish the death of my enemies, and it chilled me at the time to hear some lower crew members whoop across our shared communications. It is unbecoming – and seductive – when dealing with such a terrible enemy to take pleasure in destroying them. My reaction upon seeing the debris was more akin to my TARDIS's. They do not hate the Daleks. I believe, if such a thing is possible, that they weep for the marriage of flesh and metal the Daleks have created, and the potential of such a symbiosis.

No such symbiosis was possible now.

Something had come upon these Daleks like a storm, tearing through them so completely that not a single fragment of their casings was left. Something had eviscerated them, cracked them open like crustaceans, the soft creatures within mercilessly flung to the void. Each rubbery cycloptic tangle floated alone, stiff with interstellar frost.

And floating serenely within that nebula of shredded Dalek was a small blue box.